ASHFALL LEGACY

BY PITTACUS LORE

The Lorien Legacies
Novels
I Am Number Four
The Power of Six
The Rise of Nine
The Fall of Five
The Revenge of Seven
The Fate of Ten
United as One

The Lorien Legacies Reborn
Novels
Generation One
Fugitive Six
Return to Zero

The Legacy Chronicles Novellas
#1: Out of the Ashes
#2: Into the Fire
#3: Up in Smoke
#4: Chasing Ghosts
#5: Raising Monsters
#6: Killing Giants

The Legacy Chronicles Novella Collections
Trial by Fire (Contains #1–#3)
Out of the Shadows (Contains #4–#6)

ASHFALL

LEGACY

PITTACUS LORE

HARPER

An Imprint of HarperCollinsPublishers

Library of Congress Cataloging-in-Publication Data
Names: Lore, Pittacus, author.
Title: Ashfall legacy / Pittacus Lore.
Description: First edition. | New York : Harper, an imprint of
    HarperCollinsPublishers, [2021] | Audience: Ages 13 up. | Audience:
    Grades 10-12.
Identifiers: LCCN 2020032660 | ISBN 978-0-06-284536-8 (hardcover)
Subjects: CYAC: Sixteen-year-old half-alien Sydney Chambers leaves Earth to
    seek his long-missing father, and unearths a devastating, centuries-old
    secret about humanity. | Extraterrestrial beings--Fiction. | Adventure
    and adventurers--Fiction. | Missing persons--Fiction. | Science fiction.
Classification: LCC PZ7.L87855 Ash 2021 | DDC [Fic]—dc23
LC record available at https://lccn.loc.gov/2020032660

Typography by Chris Kwon
21 22 23 24 25 PC/LSCH 10 9 8 7 6 5 4 3 2 1

First Edition

PART ONE

EARTH: THE NOT-SO-DISTANT FUTURE (SPOILER: IT SUCKS)

1

My last day on Earth started out pretty ordinary. My mom shook me awake at eight a.m. and told me she was driving into the city to sell some weed.

"The crop is ready, and I don't want to sit on it with all those hippies hanging around," she said, talking fast. Mom was already two cups of coffee deep. "Hope that farm-to-table dispensary is still open; they overpaid. We might need some bug-out money soon."

I yawned and blinked sleep out of my eyes. "Good morning."

"Oh, good morning, honey," she said, brushing hair off my forehead.

I guess Mom hadn't bothered to fire up the wood-burning stove yet, because my room in our little cabin was cold and damp. Gray light filtered through my curtains, rain pattering against the tin roof. It was late October and cold, that rain just dying to turn into snow. I hiked up my pajama pants and wrapped my comforter around my shoulders, then lurched over to check the bucket in the corner where the leak had sprung last week. It was dry, so I guessed my repair job on our rusty-ass roof had held. My library still smelled like damp paper, though, the damage done. I had like two hundred books stacked over there, so many that I couldn't even see the shelf—mostly sci-fi novels but also some classics and a couple dozen math and science textbooks—all the pages I'd burned through in this cabin, a lot of them now swollen and moldy. Made me sad to see them ruined like that; they'd been good company. But, if we bugged out like Mom was talking about, they'd all get left behind anyway. Free books for whatever squatter came to this place next.

For almost a year we'd been hiding in this cabin in Washington State, just a short drive to the border of British Columbia. It was the longest we'd stayed in one place since we left Australia ten years ago, when we first went on the run. We had an actual home back then. Mom had a real job, and I had a dad.

I barely remembered any of that.

"Two hours to Tacoma, two hours back," my mom recited as I followed her into our cramped kitchen/living room. "An hour for errands. Two hours flex time in case I hit traffic or need to shake a tail." She pulled up the sleeve of her flannel to look at the two watches strapped to her birdlike wrist, faded scars crisscrossing her forearm. "Let's call it sixteen hundred. If I'm not back by then . . ."

I knew this part. We had a version of this conversation every time Mom left me alone. "I grab my go-bag and hike to the campground at Ross Lake. There's a pay phone there. If you don't call in twenty-four hours, I'm on my own, and it's best that you don't know where I go."

Mom nodded. Her brown hair was streaked with gray, the crow's-feet around her eyes pronounced. She was thin like a marathon runner. The muscles on her neck stood out, and so did the veins on the backs of her hands. Sometimes I worried that she wasn't eating enough, but she'd never slowed down in our ten years as fugitives. As I watched, she strapped on her holster under her left arm, carrying her Walther PPK. It seemed like such a small gun now, but I remembered needing both hands on the grip when she taught me how to shoot.

I was eight years old.

There was a Glock in my go-bag and a loaded shotgun next to our front door. Just in case.

My mom pulled on her leather jacket, hiding her weapon. "Current alias?"

I pinched the bridge of my nose, a habit that I picked up from her. She did it whenever I broke a rule or annoyed her. She narrowed her eyes at me, recognizing her own mannerism used against her.

"Current alias, please, Sydney," she said firmly. "I know we do this all the time, but it's the repetition that keeps us safe."

I sighed. "Wyatt Williams."

I hated being Wyatt Williams. It made me sound like the world's most generic country singer.

Our aliases were all the way up to "W" now. Mom kept the fake names alliterative, each new identity following the previous one in alphabetical order. Made them easier to keep track of, she said. I could trace our zigzagging path across North America by my discarded names. When we got off the plane in Los Angeles, I'd been Aaron Abrams. I'd been Darren Drake when we camped in Utah's Red Rocks and Mom taught me how to make a fire and find my own water. I'd been Mike Martinez in Mexico City, where two guys in dark suits and darker sunglasses chased us through a street market. I was Vincent Vargas last year in Peoria, the last time I went to an actual school.

I wasn't sure what we'd do with "X" looming on the horizon.

Xavier Xtreme? I planned to pitch that.

The only time I got to be myself—Sydney Chambers—was with my mom.

I was named after the city where my parents met. I'd spent my first few years on a ranch outside Sydney. My memories of the place were hazy, but I could picture the way the crispy green grass in our backyard hurt my bare feet and how once you left the range of our house's sprinkler system the landscape turned to burned dirt and red rocks. I remembered there was a single road leading away from our house—not so different from our current hideout—and that we lived close to where my mom and dad worked. It was the outback, basically. Our place was cozy, and I don't remember ever feeling afraid out there, although there was the time that a wild dog got loose in our living room. That was how my mom got the scars on her arm, actually. It happened right before we left Australia. I think she interpreted the dingo trying to eat me as a sign we should leave.

Anyway, I barely remembered Australia, and ten years in America had scrubbed any trace of an accent. I definitely wasn't going to blow our cover by saying *G'day, mate.*

My mom motioned to our plastic dinner table, where she'd left me a stack of textbooks and a Pop-Tart still in the wrapper. "Today, I'd like you to complete two chapters in math and finish up your reading on East Asian history."

I yawned into my shoulder. "Come on, Mom, it's Saturday."

"It's Tuesday."

"Oh." I paused. "Are you sure?"

"Did you get enough sleep last night, Syd?"

I had *the dream* last night, the one about my dad, but she didn't need to know that. Talking about him always put my mom into a funk—half-melancholy and half–bloodthirsty guerrilla fighter without a mission.

"If I say no, can I go back to bed?"

My mom snorted and peeked out through our front curtains. In the early light, the smoke from the Green Guard's bonfires was visible through the trees. The ecological direct action group had shown up a few weeks ago to protest the oil pipeline getting built at the edge of the woods. There were like forty of them camped out there, although their members came and went, so even after spying on them for days it was difficult to get a perfect count. They were mostly high school–aged runaways and college kids, with a few middle-aged lifer protestors as leadership. They'd stopped by our cabin to check that it was cool if they camped next to our land. We'd fixed up the abandoned cabin, but we were just squatters, so what were we supposed to say?

"I'd like you to stay inside while I'm gone," my mom said. "We know all we need to about our neighbors. No need for another operation."

An operation. That's what Mom called it whenever she sent me to be around people. Like the other day, when I'd popped by the Green Guard campsite to chat them up. It was important, Mom said, that I learn social skills. I'd been to eight different schools over the years, never for longer than a few months, though. When I made friends, I always knew I'd have to leave them behind.

Fugitives don't get to have friends.

That used to bother me more. One time, in Florida, I flipped out pretty bad. That was when Mom and I had "the talk."

I'd eased into being a friendless fugitive since then. But that didn't mean I wanted to go through life as a hermit.

"I liked them," I said, referring to my latest batch of temporary pals at Green Guard. "They were cool. They actually care about stuff."

"They're young. They have that luxury," my mom replied, rolling her eyes.

"Wow. Did you sprinkle a little extra cynicism in your coffee this morning?" I craned my neck to look over her shoulder at the sleepy campsite. "I thought you'd be down with the cause. Aren't you always saying that the capitalists have doomed this planet?"

She frowned. "Groups like that always have some undercover FBI scum attached to them. I don't want you getting close. We don't need them looking too hard at Wyatt Williams, you know?"

I tossed my blanket across my shoulders like a cape. "Mom,

come on. I know the deal. I was careful."

She dropped the curtain and eyed me. "Don't get cocky, Syd," she said. "This place has been good to us. I don't want to burn it down unless we absolutely have to."

Knowing my mom, she probably meant that literally. I glanced around our cabin—the cramped living room with its threadbare couch and antennae-equipped TV, two bedrooms that fit our lumpy twin mattresses, the bathroom with a curtain for a door, and a toilet that backed up biweekly. I had to be the only sixteen-year-old in a hundred miles who could unclog a septic tank. No internet, no landline, much less a cell phone. The finest in off-the-grid living, basically.

Still, it was home. Or the closest we'd come to one in a while.

"Don't worry, Mom, I'll lie low," I said, waving at the books she'd left out for me. "I'll do my homework."

"Good boy," she said. "See you tonight."

Once my mom rumbled down the dirt path that led away from our cabin in our beater of a pickup truck, I plopped down on the couch with my Pop-Tart and checked out what was on the four stations our TV picked up. Nothing but morning news shows.

Flooding in Venice had completely engulfed the city.

Border guards in Texas were letting loose attack dogs on refugees.

A six-month drought in Pakistan had led to the complete collapse of the government, with petty warlords now fighting over individual neighborhoods. The Indian army was massing on the border.

Not a lot of good news.

"They could fix all this," I muttered.

That was Mom's favorite line whenever she saw some horrific story on TV about our messed-up world.

They.

The same people chasing us.

Chasing *me*.

Thinking about *them* made me want to check myself for signs, so I headed into the bathroom, where I stared at myself in the mirror.

I was a few inches taller than average. Long-limbed and wiry. No pimples. Hair straight and black, longish for now, which I liked, although Mom would insist I cut it if we had to move on. In the dull overhead light, my hair looked so dark that it had an almost purple sheen. My eyes were large, almond-shaped, the irises an icy light blue.

"My dude," I said to my reflection. "You are looking human as hell today."

Most of the time, life as a half-alien fugitive was really freaking boring.

2

I was twelve years old when Mom told me. My alias at the time was Quentin Quill, probably my most ridiculous name of all time, but one that lent me a certain air of mystery in the halls of Dan Marino Middle School in Miami. I had my first girlfriend there. We nervously made out in the music room while some sophomores honked through saxophone practice.

I flipped out when Mom declared the operation was ending. We were moving on, leaving Miami. I think she was worried that if I fell too deep into preteen lust, I might let one of our secrets slip.

I tossed my plastic TV dinner tray against the wall of our apartment, splattering Salisbury steak gravy everywhere.

"You're ruining my life!" I screamed.

My mom drummed her fingers on the table. "Calm down."

"This is all bullshit," I replied, pointing at her. "You're a crazy person. There's no one after us. It's all in your head."

"They almost caught us in Mexico," she said. "Did you forget?"

"Maybe those guys were chasing us because of our fake passports," I said. "Or because of those tourists you pickpocketed. Maybe they were after *you* because you're a *criminal*. There's no conspiracy!"

This was a theory I'd been developing for a while at the time, ever since I'd read this book about a kid whose parents kept him trapped in a bunker, convinced the apocalypse had happened, even though it was totally normal outside. My mom made a lot of wild claims about the government. She said they were after us, but she never elaborated on why. I'd gone along with her for years because, well, I was a kid and didn't know any better. She was my mom, and I believed her. But that night, at the ripe age of twelve, I thought I was wising up. The things I'd witnessed—like those meatheads running after us in Mexico—were they *really* proof of some insidious government plot?

"Do you think I'm insane? Some kind of sadist? That I enjoy dragging my son around the country and making his life miserable?"

She asked these questions coolly, her voice flat.

I swallowed. "I don't know. Maybe. *Yes.*"

My mom got up from the table, and I flinched when her chair squeaked across the floor. She came over to my side of the table and put her hands gently on my shoulders.

"It's okay. I raised you to be skeptical. To be paranoid. I'm glad you're suspicious. Even if it's of me." She looked into my eyes. "I wish you could have a normal life, Sydney. I really do. But that's never going to be possible for you."

"Why not?"

"They've taken so much from me already," she grumbled, her lips curling, a private thought making her suddenly angry. "I won't let them take you, too."

"They," I repeated, remembering my righteous anger from a moment ago. "You always talk about 'them,' but you don't actually tell me anything. You don't—"

"Your father came from a planet called Denza in a solar system millions of light-years away," she said. "He was an extraterrestrial. You are half-alien."

I blinked. Then I gently slid her hands off my shoulders.

"Holy shit," I whispered. "It's true. You *are* nuts."

My mom shook her head. "Go put your bathing suit on."

"What?"

"Put your bathing suit on and fill up the bathtub," she said, straightening up. "I'll prove it to you."

That night, my mom drowned me.

Most of the time, I followed my mom's orders. But, after an hour reading about the Opium Wars, which weren't nearly as cool as they sounded, I needed to stretch my legs. Our backyard was out of sight of the Green Guard campsite. I figured that would work as a compromise. Mom wouldn't want me to stay inside all day if it meant suffocation or muscle atrophy, right?

Out back, I crouched over our garden, which was pretty sparse now that my mom had harvested all the weed. I peered under the plastic tarps to see if there were any carrots or zucchini in need of picking.

Footfalls crunched in the woods behind me. I jumped up and spun around. Thanks to my mom's lifelong paranoia, I was trained to think anyone approaching me could be a potential danger.

"Hey," Rebecca said, stopping in her tracks. "Didn't mean to scare you."

"I thought you could be a bear," I said quickly.

She made her fingers into claws. "Growl."

I pretended to shriek.

Okay, so maybe I'd gone outside hoping that she would pop by.

Rebecca was with the Green Guard. We'd met the other day. In fact, I'd spent most of my time at the Green Guard's campsite chatting with her. She claimed that she was eighteen, but I didn't believe her. She seemed only a few months older than me. She'd dropped out of high school, she told me, because it all seemed pointless when the world was dying. She had wavy blond hair that looked like it'd been gone over with a pink highlighter. She wore ratty Converse sneakers and one of those puffy life preserver vests. She was cute. And I'm not just saying that because I'd been cooped up in the woods with my mom for a year.

"Wanted to let you know, some of us are going to sneak onto the despoilers' work site tonight and siphon gas from their trucks," Rebecca said, joining me by the garden. "Maybe slash some tires.

If you want to come along."

"Oh, uh, I probably can't. My mom wouldn't go for it."

Rebecca raised an eyebrow. I cringed inwardly. *Cool excuse, bro.*

"Your mom's not into ethical vandalism?" Rebecca asked with a smirk.

"No, actually, I think she is, but . . ." I shrugged. "It's really hard to sneak out of our house."

"I get it," she said, shuffling her feet. "Maybe next time. I've been looking for a new protest buddy."

Rebecca rubbed her arms in the damp air, leaning closer to me, her breath misting. My eyebrows popped as I realized this hot budding ecoterrorist might be a little bit into me. Inviting me along for some property destruction could be what passed for a first date with the Green Guard kids.

"My mom's out for the day," I said, shooting my shot. "You want to chill inside?"

"God, yes, I haven't been under an actual roof in like weeks," Rebecca replied. Then she took a moment to look me over. "You and your mom aren't cannibals or something, are you?"

I shot a look at our sparse little garden. "My mom's more into cannabis."

"Nice," Rebecca replied. "Pretty sure I could overpower you, anyway, if you try something. You're pretty skinny. Has anyone ever told you that you look like an anime character? I wish I had big eyes like that. I could've been a model, gotten tight with Leo, and saved the rain forest."

"That's always been my fallback plan, too," I said.

Slender. Long-limbed. Larger-than-normal eyes. These were some of my half-alien tells. Of course, no one I met on the street or in the woods would ever look at me and jump to a crazy conclusion about extraterrestrial life. I was just a little unusual-looking.

I showed Rebecca into our cabin. My mom wouldn't be happy about this if she found out, but it's not like we left any evidence of our situation lying around. All our fake IDs and bundles of cash were hidden under a floorboard in Mom's closet.

Rebecca warmed her hands by the woodstove while her eyes roamed the interior. After a few seconds, she nodded to herself. "Okay. Everything looks normal."

"Wait," I said. "Did you really think we were backwoods cannibals?"

"I mean, no, not exactly," she replied. "But the two of you living out here in the woods by yourselves . . . I was wondering if you were like a kidnap victim. Or if we were dealing with one of those syndromes, you know? Munchausen? Stockholm? Things look pretty wholesome around here, though."

I smiled. My mom would've liked Rebecca. She appreciated anyone who was suspicious by nature.

"Usually I'm chained up in my room," I said. "You caught me on a good day."

Rebecca thumbed her lip. "I was all set to help you escape captivity if you wanted. Was kinda excited about a jailbreak."

My heart would've swelled to hear that like ten identities ago. Now the thought of running away with this strange girl—well, it still seemed pretty exciting, but it wasn't something I'd seriously consider. She didn't want my kind of trouble.

"I guess our life does look kind of strange from the outside," I said noncommittally.

"Nah, I've met weirdo homeschooled kids before," Rebecca said, thumbing through the textbooks stacked on the table. "Whoa. Except you're a really *smart* homeschooled kid. You actually do this stuff?"

She held up my Advanced Multivariable Calculus textbook. I'd always been a prodigy when it came to math. Back in Miami, they'd talked about bumping me up to AP Trigonometry as a seventh grader and finding me an apprenticeship with a local engineer. That attention was another reason Mom had moved us out.

I'd inherited my instincts with numbers from my dad. Math was like a language I could read without trying.

With Rebecca I played it cool. "Oh, that—yeah, I'm trying it out. It's hard."

It wasn't.

"I get it now," she said. "You're gifted, and your mom's got you hidden out here so your big-ass brain doesn't get corrupted by regular society." She finally finished snooping through our cabin and flopped down on the couch next to me. "Maybe you can help me with something."

She reached into her vest and took out a Nintendo Switch. The handheld system was in rough shape—a corner of the screen was cracked, and one of the joysticks was secured with electrical tape—but the thing turned on okay. I'd had a few portables float in and out of my life, like a thrift-store Game Boy from the

'80s and a Neo Geo I'd found at a yard sale. Nothing modern. Nothing that could connect to the internet. That wasn't allowed. Rebecca's Switch was pulling a weak signal from a mobile hot spot at the Green Guard campsite. I definitely wouldn't be telling Mom about any of this.

"Do you ever play Dungeon?" she asked me.

"I don't even know what that is."

"Oh, a nerd like you is going to love it," Rebecca said. I was very aware of our shoulders touching as we leaned together to look at her screen.

"I don't know how you can infer I'm a nerd after hanging out with me twice, by the way."

"Well," she replied, "you just said 'infer,' for starters."

Dungeon was a cross between an MMORPG and a level creator, Rebecca explained. The graphics were sixteen-bit pixels like old-school Japanese RPGs. Rebecca guided her avatar—a walking pine tree dressed in a leather miniskirt and wielding a chain saw— around a landscape littered with ominous caverns and castles.

"See, those are all dungeons," Rebecca said, pointing at the different locations. "Other players create them, and you get experience points for beating them, or the creators get XP if you lose."

"Experience points," I repeated. "And I'm the nerd?"

She elbowed me. "There's some monster fighting involved, but the best dungeons are the ones with crazy puzzles. Hold on, let me find it . . ."

Her avatar approached the entrance to a gleaming silver tower. The details of the dungeon appeared on-screen.

THE INTERSTELLAR CONUNDRUM
DIFFICULTY: MAXIMUM
RAID ATTEMPTS: 1.2 million
SUCCESSES: 0

"This one appeared like three weeks ago and no one's been able to beat it," Rebecca said. "The hard-core Dungeon delvers usually beat *everything* in like twenty-four hours. People on the forums think some theoretical physicists at MIT made it. There's also a rumor that if you beat it, you'll win a million dollars and a trip to space."

I stifled a shiver. *A trip to space.* My grandfather had made one of those, then returned to Earth and died. My dad had also gone to space—where he was from—and never come back. Since then, my mom had devoted her whole life to making sure I *never* went up there.

"You okay?" Rebecca asked. I'd fallen suddenly quiet.

"Just thinking about what I'd do with the money," I said.

"I'd buy a new tent and then overthrow the government," she replied.

"Not sure you could pull that off with just half a mil."

"It's a whole million," Rebecca said.

"Not when we beat this thing together and split the prize," I replied.

She grinned. "Big confidence from the shut-in. I like it."

Rebecca marched her avatar into the tower.

In the first part of the dungeon, three bodyguards stood before a wrought-iron gate. A text box that appeared above their heads declared, *We are the guardians. One of us always speaks truth, one of us always speaks false, and one of us speaks at random. You must figure out who is who . . .*

I was sucked in.

First came the logic problem of identifying the bouncers by typing in yes-or-no questions.

Once we got by them, the next room was tiled like a sudoku. Rebecca filled in the grid with her avatar, using only diagonal jumps.

"I've done this level a bunch of times," she said. "It's the next floor that always kills me."

The following puzzle was an electrical grid of over a hundred nodes that needed to be seamlessly connected in less than three minutes. Rebecca raced her avatar across the board, but couldn't make all the connections in time. I squinted. Her movement inefficiencies were pretty obvious to me.

"Can I try?" I asked once she ran out of time.

She handed me the Switch, and I breezed by the bodyguards, skipped around the sudoku, then blitzed across the electrical grid. I'd never handled the system before, but my thumbs seemed to know exactly what to do.

"Whoa," Rebecca said. "Keep going."

A floor of pattern recognition . . .

After that, a room that was basically Minesweeper . . .

A backgammon board . . .

My hands were slick with sweat. At some point, Rebecca and I pretty much stopped talking. She knelt on the couch next to me so that she could peer directly over my shoulder, sometimes whispering some hint for using the controls or explaining when to whip out her avatar's chain saw. Mostly, though, she let me slip into the zone.

I was locked in.

The puzzle . . . It was almost like it spoke to me.

"Damn, how many levels does this thing have?" Rebecca asked. I didn't answer. Her voice sounded faraway. "You okay?"

"Just focused," I managed to respond.

"More like hypnotized," she said.

She got herself a glass of water. I barely noticed.

I entered a room of total darkness. No walls, no floor, no graphics to speak of. A void. I sucked my teeth in frustration, thinking the game had glitched, feeling strangely sad that I was cut off from the puzzle.

But no, I could still move my avatar around, could still see my full health bar and inventory icons.

"This has to be the end," Rebecca whispered.

The Switch's battery felt hot beneath my fingers. I think maybe an hour had gone by. Maybe more.

I stared into the vast darkness, trying to figure out what I was supposed to do.

Something moved in the black. A pinprick of light, almost as if a pixel had blown. My eyes went in and out of focus. I lost sight of my avatar. It felt like the screen of the console had swallowed me up, until the darkness wasn't just in front of me but all around me.

There were dozens of *layers* to the darkness. I could see them. No—*sense* them. Each layer was like a piece of silky black fabric with a tiny hole in it. None of the iotas of light lined up. But I could move the layers of shadow themselves, tugging and pushing until the tears sat on top of one another.

I could make a path through the dark.

I was vaguely aware of my thumbs moving the controls in complicated swivels and sudden jerks. My fingers were just following orders, though. It was my mind doing the real work here.

No wonder no one had solved this puzzle. I doubted most people could even *see* it.

That should've been a red flag. I should've known this wasn't right. But I was too invested. The final puzzle called to me. With every layer I lined up, the pinprick of light got brighter and brighter.

Until it exploded.

The dot of light became the fire at the base of a rocket that blasted through the dark room, illuminating the whole space. I was being carried up . . . up . . .

CONGRATULATIONS! YOU HAVE SOLVED THE INTER-STELLAR CONUNDRUM! I blinked.

Reality came rushing back. The Switch was white-hot and drained to like 2 percent battery. The dim light of my cabin hurt my eyes, even though I wasn't even fully aware of it. A part of me was still stuck out there—in that strange in-between place that the video game had shown me.

"Oh my god," Rebecca said. "Oh my god! You really did it! I don't even know what just happened!"

She danced around in front of me, but I couldn't focus on her.

Rebecca shook me by the shoulders. "Wyatt, you did it!" she yelled. "We're going to be rich!"

My head hurt. I felt dizzy. The Switch felt like it weighed a thousand pounds, but my fingers were clenched tight around it. They were cramped; I couldn't let go. My knees bucked up and down, out of control, vibrating.

Rebecca kissed my cheek—her lips red-hot against my clammy skin. She pulled back and stared at me.

"Hey—," she said, shaking me again, not in a playful way. "Hey, what's wrong? You're freaking me out."

That's when I started having the seizure.

A message appeared on the Switch's screen. It flickered there for only a few seconds before the system winked out for good, but I noticed it. The words were the last thing I saw before my own battery went dead.

HELLO, SYDNEY. DON'T BE AFRAID. I WILL SEE YOU SOON.

3

In the dream, I was back in Australia. Young. Three or four years old, my legs short and stumpy, splayed out on the hood of a parked car, the metal still warm from the engine.

The car was parked on the side of a dirt road that cut between a sprawling field of overgrown grass and a looming chain-link fence. Beyond the fence were a half-dozen satellite dishes, all pointed at the sky, like metal flowers reaching for the sun. The sky was pink and blue, early morning.

My dad sat next to me.

His hair was dark, like mine, with a faint purple shine. He wore aviator sunglasses to hide his eyes, jeans, and a T-shirt. His limbs were long and lean.

I had this dream on a weekly basis since we'd gone on the run. When I told her about it, my mom said it was nice that I could remember my father. But this was *all* I could remember. The same scene, over and over again. The only bit about him that stuck around.

Before the night that my mom revealed I was half-alien, my dad looked completely normal to me. Like my mind had rationalized his appearance, protected me from details that didn't make sense. I'd read that could happen with stuff beyond human understanding—our minds would warp reality to process the incomprehensible.

Once my mom told me my dad was a Denzan, though, the details snapped into place.

His big sunglasses hid huge dark eyes. His hair moved on its own, even though it wasn't windy, almost as if each strand was a super-thin tentacle. His skin was gray like a shark's belly. His hands each had six fingers.

I wasn't afraid of my dad, even once his appearance crystalized in my memory. I was always happy to see him.

"You're a very special young man," he told me. "Our little rebellion."

Young me looked up at him. "What's that mean?"

"We weren't supposed to have you, Syd, but we did anyway," my dad said. "Because we love each other. And we love you."

There was a box of donuts on the hood between my dad and me. We'd gotten up early to snag them from the bakery as soon as they came out of the oven. My dumb-ass younger self was more interested in sugary treats than my dad's heartfelt words.

I plucked a donut out of the box. "Thanks!"

"You're welcome," he said with a chuckle.

He reached into his pocket and pulled out a small wooden box, offering it to me. I wiped my little hands on my pants and took it.

"I want you to have this, Syd."

It was a ring. Polished gold with a gemstone at its center that was like nothing I'd ever seen. The stone sparkled and swirled like it contained a solar system inside of it—because it did. A vision of the Milky Way rippled beneath the facets of the gem.

My dad slipped the ring out of the box because I was afraid to touch it.

"I have to go on one of my trips for a little while, buddy," my dad said.

I frowned. "Aw, Dad. You just got back."

"I know. Trust me, I wouldn't leave you and Mom unless it was really, really important."

"You're going to help people," I said.

"That's right," my dad replied. "People like your grandpa."

If my dad was a ghost confined to my dreams, then my grandpa was like a half-remembered figment. I'd only ever met him once or twice, always in a hospital room, where I was afraid of all the wires sticking out of him. He was thin like a skeleton, and his skin felt like paper.

"Grandpa died," I said.

"I want to keep other humans from dying, too. It's something I have to do. But I'm sad to leave you." He held the ring up so that it caught the light of the sun—that same sun reflected inside the jewel. "With this ring, you'll always be able to see where I am."

"Really?"

"Really. It'll keep us tied together, even when we're far apart," he said. "And if I ever get lost, you can come find me."

A distant rumble shook the ground and rattled the car beneath us. A flock of birds erupted from the tall grass, taking flight in response to the sudden din. On the horizon, a billowing plume of white smoke expanded and expanded.

And there, thrusting forth from the smoke, its tail a burning dot of bright orange, was a rocket. My mouth was a tiny O of awe. Even in the dream, the feeling of wonderment was so vivid.

I always woke up as the rocket got swallowed up by the blue.

"Gone," my mom told me when I asked her about my dad's ring. "Just one more thing that they took from us."

"We were just playing video games, I swear! We weren't doing drugs or anything! He collapsed, and I didn't know what to do!"

"Did you tell anyone? Call anyone?"

"No! I, uh, I didn't think you guys were 911 types."

"How long?"

"Like an hour? Two? I don't know! It's hard to think when— when you're—"

I opened my eyes, feeling like I was coming up from a really replenishing nap. I was stretched across the couch, a pillow shoved under my head, a warm washcloth draped across my forehead. My mom stood over me, holding my wrist to check my pulse.

She was pointing her gun at Rebecca, who was backed up against the wall with her hands up, looking terrified.

So much for that relationship.

It was almost dark outside. Late afternoon. I'd lost some time there.

"We . . . we won *a lot* of money," Rebecca said shakily.

"You didn't win shit," my mom replied.

Dungeon. The message. Someone knew I was here. I'd given away my location.

We needed to get gone.

"Mom," I said, my voice scratchy. "Chill. I'm okay."

Rebecca breathed a sigh of relief as I pushed up onto my elbows. My mom dropped my arm and looked down at me, not taking her gun off Rebecca. Her face was stony.

"What happened, Syd?"

Using my real name in front of an outsider. Yeah. She was freaked.

"We have to go," I said, sitting all the way up. "I did . . . I did something bad."

She nodded once. There wasn't any discussion necessary between us. If I said we needed to go, then we needed to go. She looked me over and must've been able to tell that I still felt a little woozy.

"I'll get the bags," my mom said, taking long strides to her bedroom.

Before she left the room, my mom handed me the gun. I pointed it at the floor instead of at Rebecca—that would've been too messed up—but that didn't seem to make her any less scared.

"Really wish we'd done something else instead of video games,"

I said, frowning. "Anything else."

"Dude," she whispered so my mom wouldn't overhear. "What the *fuck*?"

"I know." I shook my head. "Look, don't worry. We aren't going to kill you or any—"

Rebecca bolted out the front door. I didn't blame her, and I obviously didn't make any move to stop her. We'd be gone in a few seconds, anyway. A bizarre story for her to tell her friends around the campfire.

"It was fun," I said, as the door slammed shut behind her.

I'd ghosted on every friend I'd ever had—disappeared in the middle of the night, identity erased, never to be heard from again. Rebecca was the first person I'd known who actually saw a bit of my real life.

Except for the holding-her-at-gunpoint stuff, it was kind of nice to be seen.

Mom came back with our go-bags—two duffels stuffed with essentials that we kept packed at all times.

"Your girlfriend ran away," she observed.

"You didn't have to threaten her," I replied. "It wasn't her fault."

I stood up to take one of the bags, but still felt wobbly.

My mom touched my cheek. "Honey? Are you okay?"

"Something weird happened to me."

"Tell me on the road."

We didn't bother locking the cabin behind us. We'd never be coming back.

It was sunset. The roads were empty leaving the woods. It was always dead out here—that's why we picked it. But now the lack of traffic worked against us.

"We're conspicuous," my mom said, banking around a curve at a speed that made our truck groan. "We need to get around people. Switch cars. Blend in."

"They've got hours on us," I replied, trying to piece together exactly how long it'd been since I fell into Dungeon's trap. "There's been enough time for them to get checkpoints on the highway."

"Only if they've involved local law enforcement," my mom replied. "Maybe the Consulate won't bother."

The Consulate. A facility in Australia outside of Sydney (not me, the place) co-run by NASA and Earth's other big space programs. It was the place I'd seen in my dream, sitting outside its fence with my dad, watching a launch. The Consulate's public mission was to monitor deep space for signs of life, but that was all bull. In reality, they were the Denzan embassy on Earth. The aliens monitored us from there, made sure we didn't steal any of their technology, and selected candidates worthy of leaving Earth for Denza. They liked humans up there and wanted to keep them around, but as far as saving Earth went, we'd need to find our own way. Basically, the place was the heart of a worldwide conspiracy with moles in all the major intelligence agencies.

I knew all that because my mom told me. She used to work there.

It's where she met my dad.

My mom turned on our police scanner. We listened in silence as we shot down the back roads. If the Consulate had gotten to the local cops, we'd probably hear talk about a kidnapping—that's the story they would use to get local cops hunting a mom and her son without raising any red flags. The radio was quiet, though. Maybe we'd get lucky.

"Tell me what happened," my mom finally said.

Buckled into the passenger seat, I took a deep breath and went over the details. That I'd broken a number of her rules didn't matter now. I started with inviting Rebecca inside. Told Mom about the game. The mysterious puzzle. The message.

As I thought back to the Dungeon's final puzzle, a shiver went through me. The truth was, I'd kind of liked it. I was scared, but also curious. Something in me had awakened.

"It was like a jigsaw puzzle made out of space, and I had to align the stars," I told my mom. "It felt like it was put there for me to find."

"Because it was," my mom said. "It sounds like a rudimentary version of a Wayscope."

"A *what?*"

"A tool that Denzans use to navigate the universe," she said. "Beyond any technology that we have on Earth. Not something that they could fit into a common video game system, but . . ." She thought for a moment. "Maybe a training module of some kind? Something that would interact with your half-Denzan side while being impossible for a human mind to comprehend."

Of course it was my malnourished Denzan half that had gotten the warm fuzzies. "It was . . . interesting."

"You liked it," my mom said, her voice neutral.

I got the feeling that I was supposed to say no. But I rarely got to exercise the part of me that was half-alien. That head trip in Dungeon was one of the first chances I'd ever had to satisfy a hunger that I couldn't ever really explain.

"Yeah," I said quietly. "Sorry."

She shook her head. "It's okay. I knew college-level trigonometry wouldn't do the trick forever."

We sped out of the woods and drove parallel to a railyard. There were a bunch of rusty warehouses and old timber sheds from when there used to be more logging up here. I noticed a couple of train cars stamped with the logo of the corporation Green Guard was protesting, probably transporting in heavy equipment for their pipeline. I rubbed my temples, feeling bad that I wouldn't be there to see that through.

"I blew it," I said.

"Not yet," she replied, reassuring herself more than me. "We have time. As long as they don't send . . ."

She leaned forward, her chest against the steering wheel, and peered up at the sky. Night had fallen while we drove, the sky purple and cloudy.

"As long as they don't send *what?*" I asked.

Before she could respond, the moon fell out of the sky.

At least, that's what I thought happened at first.

A white disc of light swooped down from the heavens and hovered over our truck, flooding the interior with cold illumination. This wasn't like a spotlight shot down from a helicopter—for starters, there was no sound at all. On top of that, the light seemed . . .

purer, somehow. Cleaner. I was frozen beneath the beam, shocked into stillness.

Not my mom. She slammed her foot down on the gas. Her teeth were gritted, and she started weaving across the lanes, our old truck groaning in response. Her evasive maneuvers didn't seem to have any effect on whatever was shining down on us. She couldn't shake the spotlight.

And then, as quickly as it appeared, the light was gone. My eyes stung from the sudden return to darkness. Mom swerved back into our lane and started slowing down.

"Shit, shit, shit," she said.

"Was that them?" I yelled, embarrassed by the way my voice cracked. "The Denzans?"

Mom wasn't slowing down on purpose. There was something wrong with the truck. The lights on the console were all dark, the electrical system fried.

We coasted to a gentle stop in the middle of the road.

"Come on," my mom barked, lunging out of the truck. "We need to run."

I followed her out of the truck and looked at the sky, spinning around. It was empty now. No strange lights, no pursuers. I could only remember my dad from that dream; I'd never actually seen another Denzan or their alien technology. All these years on the run from them and—well, it's not like I *wanted* to get caught. But I did want to know. I wanted to understand where I'd come from. *Who* I'd come from.

"They have flying saucers?" I asked.

"Not exactly," she replied, surprisingly blasé as she grabbed my shoulders and pointed me toward the railyard. "We can lose them in there if we're quick enough. Find a new car. Get back on the road. It's possible. If we can get around people, find a crowd, they won't want to make a move. Won't want to expose themselves." She took a breath. "And we still have one advantage."

"We do?"

She had her gun out.

"Denzans don't believe in violence," my mom said. "But I do."

4

When you're a kid, you'll believe anything your parents tell you.

Dead teeth that fall out of your face are worth money? Cool!

Fat bearded guy commits annual reverse burglary? Sure!

The government is after us and we can never have normal lives? Secret identities are neat!

But then you—well, me, I'm talking about me here—get a little older and start to question things. Like maybe all that shit is made up and your mom is just a crazy person. But even when that skepticism started to take root, I couldn't fully shake my mom's authority. Years on the run, packing up whenever she said, lying whenever she said—it was hard for me not to listen and obey.

That's why, that night when she first claimed I was half-alien, I did what she told me. I put on my bathing suit and sat in a warm bath, feeling like this was all completely ridiculous but that I had to let it play out.

"You're going to hate this at first," my mom said, standing over the tub. "You're going to be scared. But I promise you're going to be fine. Do you trust me?"

"At this moment?" I asked. "Not really, no."

She nodded. "In a few minutes, you will."

Then my mom rammed her knee into my chest, pushed down on both my shoulders, and held me under the water.

At first, I was too shocked to do anything. I let her dunk me like we were playing a game. But then, from the way her fingers dug into my shoulders, it became clear that she wasn't going to let me up. I started to thrash. My heels couldn't get any purchase against the smooth bottom of the tub. I shoved at my mom's forearms, but she was stronger than me, and I couldn't shake her grip. The air in my lungs burned as I tried to hold my breath—not easy with my mom's knee dug into my sternum. I couldn't see her face through the choppy surface of the water, but I could tell my mom had her head turned away like she couldn't bear to watch. Stupidly, I opened my mouth to shout at her—the words bubbling out.

And then something clicked.

I realized that I didn't need to breathe.

It's not like I'd started gulping down lungfuls of water or spontaneously developed gills. I was just *fine*. Normal. The panic I'd been feeling subsided; my brain relaxed. Breathing was suddenly optional. My body had found another way to sustain me. My mom must have felt me stop struggling, because she loosened her grip. I could get up if I wanted to.

Underwater, I laughed like an insane person. Like a person who'd just learned that they weren't fully human.

I sat up. As soon as I burst from the water, my lungs started working again. Good old breathing was still my main way of getting oxygen. My mom sat on the edge of the tub, wiping the back of her hand across her eyes.

"I'm sorry," she said quietly. "Are you okay?"

"Holy shit," I said. "*Holy shit.* What—?"

"Spontaneous nutrient absorption," she replied. "Denzan biology can adapt to almost any atmosphere. One of the side effects, though, which you'll have to be careful about here on Earth, is the luminescing."

"Lumi-what-now?"

"Your skin pulled oxygen from the water to keep you alive. Meanwhile, nonessential elements were excreted through your . . ." She gestured to the bathroom mirror. "Well, see for yourself."

I stood up, feeling profoundly energized, and looked at my reflection. The roots of my hair had turned light blue in color. So had the fuzz on my arms and legs.

I'm not sure how long I stared at my reflection. A long-ass time, I think. Long enough that my mom tiptoed back to our kitchen, leaving me alone to come to terms with my new reality. I ran my fingers through my hair and watched as the color spread a little farther, each strand feeling a little slippery and squirmy, even when I'd dried off.

I was half-alien.

A Denzan.

Just what the fuck was a Denzan?

When I finally emerged from the bathroom, my mom had a bunch of pictures and documents spread out on our kitchen table. I'd never seen this file before; she must have kept it hidden away in her go-bag. An hour before, I'd thought she was a crazy person and been super pissed at her dragging me around the world, screwing up any chance I had at a normal life. Now I understood her—that I couldn't be normal because I wasn't normal. But the stuff that I still didn't know, it was dizzying and frustrating. She'd dunked me underwater, but there was still a little ember of anger burning alongside my curiosity.

"Mom," I said, "you have so much explaining to do right now."

She nodded. "I know."

"Half-Denzan," I said, trying out the name of my new species. I waved back at the bathroom. "How did you know that would work? That I would luminesce like that? I've never done that before. You could've killed me."

"You were born a month early," my mom replied. "Your little lungs weren't quite ready. The first time I held you, you were glowing. That's how I knew."

I swallowed and sat down across from her, eyeing the documents. "Tell me everything."

"First contact happened in the seventies," she said matter-of-factly. "We aren't sure how long the Denzans were watching Earth before they made themselves known. The way they work, probably a long time. They have a strict policy of noninterference when it comes to primitive societies."

I scratched the back of my neck. "We're a primitive society now?"

"To the Denzans, any species that hasn't achieved interstellar travel is primitive."

"Kind of a high bar," I said.

"You'd be surprised."

My eyes combed across the documents. A star chart that mapped systems beyond the Milky Way. A bunch of partly redacted medical reports from some organization called the Consulate—my mom would tell me more about her old coworkers later. Blurry satellite images of what could be UFOs or flocks of geese. Basically, the kind of stuff you might find taped to the walls and connected by strings in a conspiracy theorist's basement.

"The Denzans recruited twelve astronauts from around the world. Turns out, they needed humanity's help."

"With what?"

"Fighting a war."

"Hold up," I said. "If we're a bunch of dumb cavemen, what could we do for some highly advanced ETs?"

My mom hesitated. "I guess our aptitude for violence is unique in the universe."

That seemed a bit like a dodge, but before I could follow up, she pushed an old photograph toward me. Three people—two men and a woman—posed together in their flight suits. The woman was pretty, with a mane of curly blond hair, the sleeves of her suit rolled up to show off her biceps. The man next to her was short and hairy with a devilish grin. And, next to him, a generic handsome dude with a flask poking out of his pocket. They stood in front of a ship like nothing I'd ever seen on Earth—sleek, circular, floating without any visible propulsion. The photo could've been a still shot from some old science fiction movie.

I blinked and took a closer look at the All-American on the end. "Whoa. Is that Grandpa?"

My mom nodded. "One of the First Twelve."

The man in the picture was so much healthier than the withered skeleton I barely remembered from dimly lit hospital rooms. For years, my mom had claimed the government killed him, that some experiment had made him deathly ill. Apparently, that experiment was traveling to an alien planet.

"What happened to him?" I asked. "What *really* happened?"

"He went to Denza when I was little. For the longest time, I thought he was just some deadbeat. That was until the Denzans recruited me, too. My dad was a hero to them, so I guess they figured I'd be a safe bet." She snorted. "I went to work for them—here, on Earth—after your grandpa returned. He'd helped win their war, and his reward was illness. They call it the Wasting. A disease that affected all of the astronauts that tried to come home. A gradual breakdown at the cellular level that they can't find a cure for. And yet the Denzans are still recruiting humans, just in case we ever need to fight for them again. They'll want to send you, if they ever find us."

"The war made him sick?" I asked.

"Coming back to Earth triggered the Wasting. No one's sure

exactly why. Maybe something from the war. Maybe the change in atmosphere. Maybe space travel. Their very DNA breaks down. The body can't support itself, a slow disintegration over years . . ." Her eyes were dark as she spoke, staring down at the picture of her dad. She cleared her throat. "To their credit, I guess, the Denzans didn't completely abandon your grandfather and the others. They sent some of their best minds to Earth to try to cure them. They failed, but . . ."

"But?"

My mom looked up at me with a sad smile. "But that's how I met your father."

We grabbed our bug-out bags and sprinted into the cover of the railyard. I tripped over a wooden slat that had come loose on one of the train tracks, and Mom caught me firmly under the armpit, pushing me onward. She had her gun out, cocked and ready.

We reached a metal fence, not realizing until it was too late that it was topped with coils of barbed wire.

"Which way?" I asked, peeking again at the sky.

My mom pointed farther down the tracks, where dozens of rusty boxcars sat idle.

"There!"

Our sneakers crunched over gravel. Maybe we'd get lucky and one of these trains would start moving. They all looked broken down, but I wasn't ready to give up on a hobo-style escape. I was about to suggest as much to my mom when I spotted him.

A thin man in a trench coat watched us from atop the nearest train car. We were running right toward him. I skidded to a stop.

"What are you doing?" my mom snapped, overtaking me.

I pointed. "We've got company."

In an instant, my mom leveled her gun at the shadowy figure.

"Get away from us or I'll shoot," my mom called out, her voice hard. There was no doubt in my mind that she meant it.

The man cocked his head in response. Finding himself down-barrel didn't seem to be an immediate cause for alarm.

"I didn't mean to scare you, Beth," the figure replied, using my mom's first name. "Well, maybe a little bit. It's been a frustrating ten years."

The gun trembled in my mom's hand. "Tycius? Is that you?"

"Long time, no see."

Tycius leaped down from atop the train. That was a fifteen-foot drop, and it barely registered for the guy; he hardly even bent his knees when he landed. Weird, because he didn't look like the athletic type. He was a middle-aged man with slicked-back black hair and a five-o'clock shadow that spread down his throat. He wore a trench coat with the collar flipped up, his hands shoved in the pockets. He looked like one of those hard-boiled detectives from a black-and-white movie.

"You look like an idiot," my mom said.

"Really? I thought this worked for me," he replied, sounding sincerely wounded.

It was more than just the inappropriate grace of Tycius's movements that seemed off. The more I looked at him, the harder it got to bring him into focus. He was a ghostly shimmer in the moonlit railyard. My mind went back to Dungeon's final level, where secrets lurked beneath the surface. It was like there was another layer to Tycius that I couldn't quite see.

"I can't believe the Consulate would send you," my mom said. "I can't believe you would accept."

Tycius snorted. "Who else but me?"

"Some of your FBI goons."

"It's been years since we used them," Tycius replied. "They asked too many questions. Fact is, the Consulate likes to pretend you and the boy don't exist. They figure if you were going to go public, you would've done it already. They're satisfied they've penetrated enough of the media to bury any publicity. At worst, the kid's autopsy gets passed around the dark web by the usual yahoos. In other words, who cares?"

Who cares? I didn't expect to hear that from someone who'd been doggedly pursuing us for the last decade. I glanced at my mom who seemed equally taken aback.

"Bullshit," my mom said.

"No bullshit. The Consulate was happy that you disappeared," Tycius replied, bitterness in his voice. "I'm the only one still looking, Beth. You've been my shame to carry for the last ten years."

I edged forward, squinting at this out-of-place detective, still trying to figure out what exactly seemed so off about him. "Who are you?" I asked, finally able to get a word in. "Mom, who is he?"

"You don't remember me?" Tycius asked, then shook his head. "No, of course you wouldn't. You were in diapers the last time I saw you. And I didn't look like this." He grimaced—no, actually, that was what a smile looked like on his hangdog face. "I'm your uncle, Sydney."

"My . . ." I turned to my mom. "You told me all our family was dead."

"Dead? That's pretty rude, Beth." Tycius rubbed his stubbly cheek, shaking his head in wonderment. "Meeting you, Syd, finding out what you look like, getting to talk to you—it's what's kept me going. Do you know how many video games I implanted puzzles in for you to find? I never gave up on you. Never stopped searching."

"Um." I glanced at my mom, not sure what to say. "Well, here I am."

"Chasing," my mom corrected Tycius, stepping in front of me. "You never stopped *chasing* us."

"How could I?" Tycius asked. "With Marcius still lost out there?"

"He's dead," my mom snapped. "Accept that and move on with your life. Leave us alone."

"He's alive," Tycius countered, his voice hardening with conviction. "He's alive, and Sydney can find him."

My dad. They were talking about my dad.

"Mom, come on," I said. I put my hand on her forearm, trying to ease the weapon down. "I want to hear what he has to say."

"No," she whispered, and there was suddenly something wild in her eyes, like a cornered animal. She shook loose from me and sneered at Tycius. "I *do* know he's dead. Because if he were alive, Marcius would've come back to us, you bastard."

She pulled the trigger.

I flinched at the *bang*. It was thunderous in the empty railyard.

As soon as the gun went off, a silver mass appeared at chest level in front of Tycius. It looked almost like Tycius had opened a silk umbrella, a rippling octagon of quicksilver floating before him. It soundlessly absorbed the bullet.

"Mom, don't—!" I yelled as she prepared to take another shot.

The mass zipped through the air toward my mom. It looked like some cheap Halloween decoration, like a paper ghost on an invisible wire. The silver blob enveloped my mom's hand before she could fire, covering her from barrel to wrist, sticking to her like glue.

"Damn it," she said, deflated.

My first reaction was to lunge forward and pry at the thing on my mom's hand. I didn't really appreciate her hair-trigger temper or how she'd tried to gun down an uncle I'd only just met, but I wasn't about to let some magic goo eat her arm. The stuff was cool to the touch and completely smooth, hugging tight enough to her skin that I couldn't work my fingernails into the seam.

"Are you okay?" I yelled. "Is it dissolving your flesh?"

"No, I'm fine, it's—ow, Syd, you're scratching me."

Relieved that she wasn't dying, I took a step back and glared at her.

"Jesus, Mom, you tried to kill him!"

"Not really," Tycius interrupted, coming closer. "She knew she couldn't. Your mom, I think, was just expressing her emotions in a way very common to her people. Right, Beth?"

Her nostrils flared, but the wildness had gone out of my mom's eyes, leaving behind a deep sadness and resignation. Her shoulders sagged. "Piss off, Ty."

I couldn't resist once again poking the wrap on my mom's hand. "What the hell is that thing?"

"Portable bodyguard," Tycius replied offhandedly. He said something in a language I couldn't understand, and the quicksilver unfurled from around my mom. Her hand was perfectly fine. In fact, her skin glowed like it'd been freshly moisturized. But the gun was bent back on itself, crumpled like it was made of tinfoil. She tossed it aside. The portable bodyguard shrank down to a tennis-ball-size orb and floated back to Tycius, disappearing into his trench coat.

I stared at him. The closer he got, the more I could sense something wrong with his appearance. It was like a mirage, blurring at the edges.

I blinked. "Wait a second," I said. "My uncle on *whose* side?"

Okay, I'll admit it. I was a little slow on the uptake there.

He pressed a trigger hidden inside his coat and the hologram—that's what it was, I realized, a really advanced projection—flickered off.

I had never seen a Denzan in person before. Only my father in my recurring dream, and the finer details there always escaped me.

Tycius was tall, his limbs long and thin, his torso narrow and tapered. His true face was a rounded triangle—a broad forehead, high cheekbones, and a pointed chin. His hair looked like mine after Mom's attempted drowning; the dark emerald tendrils started far back on his scalp and writhed in every direction, like tall grass blown by a breeze. Ty's eyes were almond-shaped and huge, colorless, shadowy pits. He didn't have a nose so much as a bump with two slits, his granite-colored skin smooth and flat above his small, thin-lipped mouth.

Tycius smiled at me. "Whose side do you think?"

5

When I was twelve, after Miami, where my mom told me everything—or, well, it turned out, *almost* everything—I went through a phase where I stared up at the sky a lot. Gazing into space. Trying to imagine what was out there.

There was part of me—a half of me, really—that was from a place beyond. I'd always had this feeling like I was searching for something, but I'd chalked that up to us being on the road so much, never settling down, never getting a normal life. Now I realized there was more to it. I was addicted to sci-fi novels. Ship battles and alien warriors and laser swords—that was cool shit. But maybe I liked that stuff so much because, without even realizing it, I was drawn toward the unknown.

I couldn't tell any of that to my mom. She painted a picture of the Denzans as cold and dispassionate, looking down on humanity as we destroyed our own planet, unwilling to help. They'd used my grandfather until the day he died. My dad had disappeared while searching for a way to cure the Wasting, and, according to my mom, the rest of his people didn't even care. *Our little rebellion*, my parents called me. Just by existing—a cross-species person—I violated the Denzan policy against noninterference with so-called primitive races. If they found us, Mom was convinced the Denzans would want to take me back to their planet and we'd never see each other again. I didn't want to leave her all alone.

And yet a part of me was still so, so curious.

We drove north from Florida. The plan was Kansas. I'd become Robert Ritter there. I remember the sky was blue and cloudless and I hung my arm out the window. It was one of those days when you could already see the moon in the afternoon.

"Can you tell me about him?" I asked out of the blue. "About my dad?"

"What do you want to know?"

"Anything."

My mom thought for a moment, then chuckled at some private memory. "Marcius was so stubborn. He worked so hard. I was the same way, I suppose. We butted heads over the silliest things. When we met, he was just discovering Earth culture and had the worst taste in books—dime-store Westerns and novels about the Mafia. He hated the term 'Martians' as a catchall for extraterrestial life, so I started calling him Mars for short. I was always trying to prove that I was as smart as them—the Denzans—that humanity wasn't all primitives. He never thought that, though. Not your father."

"He could still be out there, couldn't he?" I asked, gazing up at the sky. "We're so good at hiding. Maybe he came back and couldn't find us."

My mom's hands tightened on the steering wheel. "He'd find us," she said. "That's what your dad was best at."

We drove through what used to be a town but was now reduced to scattered piles of brick, only the foundations of homes left standing. There were pictures of missing people stapled to telephone poles that had been sheared in half, not a soul around to look at them. Tornados had ripped through this part of the Midwest last summer. The weather was getting worse and worse every year.

"Why didn't you guys just go back to his planet?" I asked.

"We talked about it, especially once we had you," my mom replied. "I didn't want to abandon Earth, though, and neither did your father. He'd made a vow to help the astronauts who returned home, to cure the Wasting. The Denzans take their vows seriously. Your grandpa had died years before, but a couple of the others were still hanging on. Your dad had some far-out ideas. He'd located an unexplored planet that he thought might have answers. Something about a lost species that had evolved to thrive in different conditions . . ." My mom shook her head, like the whole thing was a fairy tale. "God, we were both so naïve. Thinking we could change things."

An unexplored planet. The words sent a tingle down my spine. I wondered if that was how my dad felt before he left. I peered up at the sky again, imagining how much bigger my existence could be than just our crappy car and these small-town hideouts.

"Maybe he found what he was looking for," I suggested. "Maybe . . ."

"No," my mom said firmly. "I'm sorry, Sydney, but no. Hope is a distraction. What your father was looking for—a way to help humanity—the Denzans didn't *want* it to be found. They made sure he'd never come back." She rubbed her forearm where her scars were. "They made sure we'd never be able to find him."

"I love places like this," Tycius declared as we walked into a twenty-four-hour diner attached to a highway rest stop. "The gigantic menus, so full of possibilities. And yet most of those options are barely edible, the cooks only capable of a few flashes of competence. It's so human."

I gave Tycius a look. He'd reactivated his holographic projector and appeared human again. There were dark circles around his eyes, but the pupils shone happily as he eyed the pies in the spinning dessert case.

"Do you program your face to look like that? Or does your tech, like, sync your Denzan expressions to human mode?" I asked, wondering if he was really that haggard or if it was all for show.

"Both," he replied, winking at me. "The face is based on Bogart."

"Who?"

"Humphrey Bogart?" When I gave him a blank look, he turned to my mom. "I thought you'd at least be eductating the boy."

My mom responded with an icy look. She'd barely said two words since we left the railyard, all of us packed into the front seat of our truck, which Tycius was able to get working again thanks to a quick battery jump from a device he kept in his pocket. My mom drove with her hands strangling the steering wheel. Even now, I could see her assessing the diner's windows and exits, maybe considering one last-ditch escape effort.

The diner had been my idea. I wanted to hear what my uncle had to say. We'd all sit down together, eat some breakfast for dinner, and hash out the family secrets.

A gumdrop-shaped waitress approached us. "You folks can take that booth by the window."

"Here's looking at you, kid," Tycius said and tipped an imaginary hat. The waitress giggled, mostly out of bewilderment.

She'd never know that was an extraterrestrial badly flirting with her.

The little diner was populated by a couple burly long-haul truckers, hunched over the coffees that would get them through the night. They had no clue there was basically an interplanetary summit happening right under their noses. I almost wished that Ty would turn his cloak off, not to freak everybody out, but so I could keep staring at him like I had back at the railyard.

My first Denzan, live and in person. It was mind-blowing and frightening and awesome. It's one thing to *know* about aliens, to have a fuzzy vision of one of them in your dreams. It's entirely different to actually see one. It's like—I know about whales, I've seen them in nature documentaries, but I've never been on a boat and had one of those behemoths surface alongside me. Tycius was person-size, but he still made me feel like my universe had just gotten bigger.

I slid into the booth next to my mom, Tycius on the other side. I couldn't keep my eyes off him.

"I understand your excitement," Tycius said, eyeing me back. "But can you maybe stop staring quite so much? It's making me uncomfortable."

"Okay, dude," I said, leaning back. "I'm sure you were totally chill when you met your first alien."

"No, actually. I asked a Vulpin diplomat if I could touch her mane. She allowed this indiscretion." Ty closed one of his eyes. "Later, I learned that she'd laced her fur with a hallucinogen just in case she encountered such ignorance. For a week, I thought I was a tree."

"Cool story," I said. "What the hell is a Vulpin? Are those the guys you're at war with?"

"We aren't at war with anyone." Ty glanced at my mom. "How much have you told him?"

Everything. That's what I hoped she'd say. I really wanted her to have been honest with me, at least after Miami and the bathtub incident.

My mom sighed, looking away from me. "He knows enough."

A bitter lump of disappointment formed in my throat. Of course there were still secrets. Hell, I was sitting across the table from one of them.

Tycius patiently laced his fingers in front of him. "Tell me, Syd, what do you know about the universe and your family's place in it?"

I took a deep breath. This was like a quiz and I wanted to impress him. "You're from Denza, a planet way more advanced than ours. But you guys aren't fighters, so you needed beefy humans to back you up in some war. You recruited my grandpa and a bunch of others. You won the war thanks to us. Then the humans tried to come home, but they got sick when they did. My dad, a Denzan, came here to try to cure the Wasting. He met my mom. Romance ensued, fast-forward through that part, thanks. I was born. My dad got a lead on a cure, but he disappeared. The other Denzans were happy about that because they don't actually want to help humanity. They just want to use us, keeping humans around in case they need to win another fight." I inhaled. "That's what I know."

While I blitzed through my recap of the universe, Tycius slowly turned his gaze from me to my mom. She wouldn't look at him, instead staring out the window at the parking lot.

"First of all, it wasn't simply *some war*," Tycius said when I'd finished. "It was an unprovoked invasion of our planet."

"But not by those Vulpin guys who made you trip balls."

"No. The Vulpin are our allies."

My mom chuckled derisively at that, but I pressed on with my questions.

"Goddamn, how many aliens are there?"

"Including Denzans, there are six known species capable of

interstellar travel," Tycius replied. "And there are fourteen other life-forms that have achieved a level of sentience that we project will one day allow them to reach the stars. Including humanity."

"That . . ." I scratched the back of my neck. "That's a lot of aliens."

"The species who attacked us are called the Etherazi," Ty continued. "They are monsters whose very appearance is toxic to my people. In a war, each side wants something—there can be dialogue and peace. Not with the Etherazi. They wanted nothing but destruction and chaos. Our entire civilization would've been wiped away if we hadn't made contact with humanity. Your grandfather and the others were great heroes, Syd. They're worshipped on Denza. Legends. After all they did for us, to learn about the Wasting—it broke our peoples' hearts. Your father and I, along with many others, came here to do whatever we could to help."

I could sense the reverence in his voice when he talked about my grandfather. It was still hard for me to imagine the disintegrating old man I'd glimpsed as a child was some kind of intergalactic bad-ass.

I thought back to the brief scuffle in the railyard. Tycius possessed technology that could swallow up bullets and fry cars. It didn't make any sense that his people would need humans to fight for them.

"Not to dog grandpa or anything, but I never understood this part," I said. "What could a bunch of humans do for aliens that have like lightsabers? Those are real, right?"

Ty's eyes narrowed in confusion. "Light *what*?"

I waved a hand back and forth through the air and made a *womp-womp* noise.

Tycius glanced at my mom. "He doesn't know . . . ?"

She shook her head, massaging her forehead so she didn't have to look at me.

"Sydney, humans are the most dangerous species in the galaxy," Tycius said with a completely straight face. "Away from Earth, they are nearly invulnerable to harm and possess unrivaled physical strength. Just twelve of them fought off the Etherazi and saved countless lives."

I blinked. "Oh."

At that exact moment, our waitress trundled over. "Sorry for the wait, folks. Ready to order?"

I caught myself staring at our waitress. This lady was the apex predator of the galaxy, apparently. If given the chance, she could toss off that dirty apron and go battle space monsters. I looked down at my own narrow bicep and surreptitiously flexed. There were multiple times I'd eaten plain peanut butter sandwiches because I couldn't get a new jelly jar open.

My mom ordered a black coffee. A Greek salad for Ty.

"The lumberjack breakfast, please," I said. "I need to bulk up."

As soon as the waitress was gone, I braced both my hands on the table. "So you're telling me that on Earth I'm Clark Kent, but up there I could be . . . ?"

"This is why I didn't tell you," my mom said sharply, finally looking at me. "These promises of unlimited power. What teenage boy wouldn't want to run off to be a hero? But there are sacrifices.

The strength changes you, alters your DNA. Coming back to Earth causes those changes to unravel. The strength leaves, and your body can't handle it. That's the Wasting. This planet is our home, Sydney. It's where we belong. Your grandfather wanted to come back to be with his family, his people—and it killed him."

"I'm only half-human, though," I said quietly. "Maybe I'd only get half, uh, wasted?"

"Our projections do show that the effects would be slower to progress on a hybrid," Tycius offered. "But, ultimately, still terminal."

One of the truckers at the counter coughed raggedly into his shoulder. I glanced over at him, then at our waitress, who was currently leaned against the register, stretching out her sore calves.

"I don't know," I said. "I feel like anyone in here would choose superstrength and invulnerability over . . . over this."

My mom shook her head. I could tell she was disappointed in me, although I couldn't understand why she would be so pro-Earth. As we traveled North America, all she ever did was complain about how screwed up our planet had gotten.

"It doesn't matter," she said with a narrowed-eyed glance at Tycius. "It's not like the Denzans are offering to build us an ark."

"But you're still bringing humans to your planet, right?" I asked Tycius, trying to keep the hope out of my voice considering how it would probably offend my mom. "Even though your war—er, invasion—is over?"

"Yes, of course. And they know, going in, that returning to Earth will be deadly," Tycius replied. "There are now more than a thousand humans living on Denza or on ships in service of the Serpo Institute."

"What's that?" I asked. "Space college?"

"Essentially," Tycius replied. "The Serpo Institute was founded on Denza. Its goal is to foster understanding and cooperation among all species throughout the galaxy, to protect those beings who cannot yet protect themselves, and to explore and map the endless Vastness of space. The institute accepts only the best and brightest from Denza and our allies. Interspecies crews train together and eventually graduate to serve on exploratory vessels in the institute's fleet. Humans are an important part of that."

I crossed my arms and leaned back in the booth, trying to think this all through. On Denza, I'd be stronger than what was humanly possible on Earth. I could be part of some real-world Starfleet shit, scanning fuzzy little aliens for fungal infections and getting into ray-gun fights. My mom had kept all that from me, preferring instead to teach me college math from secondhand text-books and sending me off on the occasional monthslong stretch in a public school whenever I started getting too mopey. There was a whole life—a brand-new identity, with no need for alliteration—out there waiting for me. All those years on the run. I suddenly felt like I'd been cheated.

Even considering all that, when I looked at her, I couldn't feel any anger toward my mom. The way she slouched in the booth, staring at her own reflection in the window instead of making eye contact—I'd never seen her so defeated. For her, this was the end she'd spent all those years running from. It hadn't come in some explosive confrontation but had crept up on her in a sad little diner.

"Why did you quit working with the Denzans?" I asked my mom, wanting to understand her side. "Is this all because of Dad?"

"No," my mom said, then went quiet as the waitress dropped off her coffee. "I worked for the Consulate first to save your grandfather and the others like him, and then because I thought the Denzans would eventually get off their asses and help us. They have the technology to save our planet. All they have to do is give it to us."

Ty's eyes narrowed. "That's an oversimplification."

I turned to Tycius, feeling like the moderator at an interstellar presidential debate. "You *have* noticed that our planet is kind of a mess, though, right?"

"I've been here for more than a decade, Sydney. Of course I've noticed humanity's slow murder of their home."

"You've got a zero-emissions spaceship that can shut down cars with beams of light," I replied. "You've got to have the technology to help with, like, climate change."

Tycius unflinchingly met my eyes. "I'll be the first to admit that the Denzan Senate moves slowly, but they haven't ignored humanity's plight. The electric car, for instance. The Denzans leaked that technology to your people some forty years ago, and what happened? Your corporations buried it."

"Is that true?" I asked my mom.

My mom sighed and squeezed the bridge of her nose, ignoring me—which meant that Tycius was telling the truth. "Is this really why you've stalked us for the last decade, Ty? To rehash these same old arguments?"

"No. Of course not."

"Then cut to the chase, would you? Get to your offer. Tell my son he's got a bright future at the Serpo Institute. Tell him he can leave this dying planet behind . . ."

"Beth . . . ," Tycius said with a sad smile. "It's so much more than that."

He reached into his trench coat and produced a small wooden box, sliding it across the table to me. Of course, I recognized the case right away; I'd seen it a hundred times in my dreams. It was the one that contained my dad's ring, which my mom had told me we'd lost long ago. She obviously recognized the box too, because I heard her breath catch in her throat. She sat up a bit, more alert now, more coiled. Her hand gripped her fork like she might try to stab Ty.

"Where did you get that?" she asked through her teeth.

"You know where," Tycius responded frankly. "Off the dead body of a Vulpin in Australia."

"So I did kill her," my mom said. "I've always wondered."

"Hold up," I interrupted. "You killed an *alien*? In Australia?"

My mom pointed her fork at Ty. "A Vulpin mercenary that *his* people sent."

"No," Tycius said. "Not true."

"The Vulpin stole that from me," my mom said, looking down at the ring box. "From *us*."

"Open it," Ty told me. "But be careful. Don't let anyone see."

I nodded and cracked the box just enough to catch a glimpse of the blue glow of the cosmos, suspended there in the ring's gemstone. Exactly the way I'd dreamed it. My mom's shoulder pressed against mine as she, too, peeked into the box. She clapped a hand over her mouth to suppress a noise—something between a scream and a sob—like nothing I'd ever heard from her.

"The light," she said, her voice brittle, shaky with disbelief and something else. "The light hasn't gone out."

That was hope in her voice.

"Because he's alive," Tycius said, focusing on me now. "That ring is what we call a cosmological tether. It's tied to a beacon implanted in your father's brain. If Marcius were dead, this ring would go dark," he said. "But it hasn't. All these years and he's still out there. Waiting for us. Waiting for *you*."

6

What did I remember about the night we left Australia? The incident with the dingo, when my mom got those scars on her arm. I was only five years old then. I'd buried that memory, choosing to accept my mom's version.

My mind protecting me from stuff I wasn't ready to deal with.

I remembered waking up to the sound of growling. It came through the wall that I shared with my parents' room. The snarling almost seemed to form words.

"I want the boy . . . I'm here for the boy . . ."

That had to be my imagination.

Broken glass crunched. Bodies slammed against the wall, vibrating my bed frame.

I don't know where I found the courage to get out of bed. It felt almost like I was on rails. I heard a sharp cry of pain from my mom and couldn't help but press forward.

Then a muffled *pop*. A gunshot.

I peeked in from the hallway. My mom wrestled on the floor with a furry shape, the creature clawing and snapping at her. The beast's claws tore up our carpet where they missed my mom.

Pop. Another gunshot.

The monster pinning down my mom recoiled and rolled away from her. My mom's pistol gleamed in the moonlight. She'd fired a round point-blank into the beast's belly.

The creature lurched toward the window and dove out. My mom sprang to her feet after it, firing two more shots into the night.

"Give it back!" she yelled out the window. Her knees bent like she might hurdle out the window herself. "Give—!"

"M-mom?" I stammered.

She spun around and saw me there. Hiding her gun in the back of her jeans, she knelt down in front of me. Dark blood dripped down from her forearm onto the carpet.

"It's okay, Syd," she said. "It's okay. A bad dream."

I rubbed tears out of my eyes. "What was that thing?"

"A wild dog," my mom said quickly. "A dingo."

Strange. I could've sworn that the thing attacking my mom had run off into the night on two legs.

Like I said, the mind has a way of rationalizing the impossible.

"We can't stay here tonight," my mom said, standing up. She put a hand on my shoulder, guiding me out of her bedroom. "Come on. Let's pack some things."

When we left that night, with the first-ever version of my go-bag slung over my shoulder, I thought eventually we'd come back to our little house in the outback. It all seemed like we were just on a grand adventure. Eventually, we'd go home and Dad would be there waiting for us. It wasn't until later—when we'd already escaped to America—that Mom told me we couldn't go back. My dad was gone. There were people after us.

A few years later, she'd reveal to me that I wasn't entirely human.

Against all of that—the running and the ever-changing identities and the constant threat of enemies lurking in the shadows—the monster in the outback seemed to me like something I'd partially dreamed up. Sure, my mom had scars on her arm that proved it happened, but that rampaging dingo was ultimately just a scary Australia story.

Until it wasn't.

My mom rubbed the faded scars that crisscrossed her forearm. "It was a Vulpin. She broke into our home and found . . ." She looked at my dad's ring box. I'd closed it up so our waitress didn't spot the glow when she brought our food, but I kept my hand resting atop it. "She would've taken you, too, if I hadn't—"

"Shot her," I said.

My mom nodded.

I tapped the box. "She stole this."

"I couldn't go chasing after her, not with you. I couldn't risk that," my mom replied. "Your father was supposed to return months before. No one from the Consulate would tell me anything, but I knew something must have gone wrong. I spent every night staring at that ring, Sydney. Waiting for the light to go out."

"It never did," I said quietly.

My mom opened her mouth, but no sound came out. She pressed the heels of her hands against her eyes and sat there like that, her shoulders shaking. She'd given up on my dad to keep me safe. At some point in the last ten years, she'd decided that he was dead. He had to be, she always told me. If he were alive, my dad would've come back.

She was wrong. And now she knew it.

"You shouldn't have run," Tycius said coolly.

"A Vulpin broke into my house, stole my husband's cosmological tether, and tried to kidnap my son," my mom replied, her voice hoarse. "What was I supposed to do?"

"The Consulate would've protected you."

"Or maybe the Consulate sent her," my mom replied. "I know how you Denzans hate getting your hands dirty."

"They would never—"

"*Please*, Ty," my mom interrupted. "Tell me what happened to Mars."

"Tell *us*," I put in, tired of being left out of all the family secrets.

"Your father believed that he'd found a cure for the Wasting," Tycius began. "He commissioned an exploratory mission on the ISV—interstellar space vessel—*Clarity*. Your father served on the *Clarity* before coming to Earth. He was friends with the crew. They filed a mission plan with the Serpo Institute. But, at some point, they veered off course. This wasn't necessarily unusual for an exploration; travel between uncharted systems can be a tricky business, but . . ."

I found myself leaning forward. My mom was too, I realized.

She didn't know these details either.

"Two weeks after they were supposed to have reached their destination, the ISV *Clarity* sent a message back to Serpo command. But it wasn't a message, it was an attack. A pulse of concentrated data that scrambled our archives and erased their flight path, essentially rendering us unable to track them. Someone on the crew wanted the *Clarity* to stay lost."

"Sabotage," my mom whispered.

"Most of the *Clarity*'s crew was equipped with cosmological tethers," Tycius continued, nodding at the ring box. "All of them went dark. The crew was presumed dead except for . . ."

"Except for my dad," I said.

"Australian park rangers found the body of that Vulpin and recovered the cosmological tether," Tycius said gently. "The Consulate covered it up, yes, but you have to know, Beth, that we would never send someone to hurt you and Syd. I'd never stand for it."

My mom couldn't speak, so I asked the question I knew she'd want answered.

"Then who did?"

"We don't know," Tycius responded. "Nonhumans aren't allowed to visit Earth without approval from the Consulate. That Vulpin managed to get here without our knowledge. There was an investigation afterward, but we hit a dead end. We don't know who she was working for or what her plan was if she got you and the cosmological tether." He paused. "But when we go looking for your father, I bet we'll find out."

When we go looking. Not *if*.

"Why haven't you *already* gone looking for him?" I asked, tapping the ring box. "You've had this for like ten years . . ."

"Before he left, Marcius locked his tether. He granted access to only one person. That's you, Sydney."

I blinked, then turned to my mom. "Why would he do that? I was just a kid when he left."

My mom shook her head. "I don't know. He didn't tell me that." She sighed. "Marcius could be paranoid. Maybe he thought a five-year-old was the only person he could trust."

"I have a standing arrangement with a captain at the institute," Tycius continued. "You and I will join her crew. You'll be enrolled at the Serpo Institute to study and learn, but, when the time is right, we will use her ship to go searching for your father."

I leaned back, hugging myself. I felt a bit like I couldn't breathe.

"Who is this captain you've got in your pocket?" my mom asked, hitting Tycius with the practical questions that I couldn't or didn't know to ask.

"Marie Reno."

The name didn't ring any bells for me, but my mom wrinkled her nose like she'd smelled something rotten. "And the institute authorized this mission of yours? The Denzan Senate?"

Tycius hesitated. "No," he said finally. "It's off the record."

My mom's eyes widened. "Wow, Tycius, a decade goes by and suddenly you're a rule breaker."

"I want to find him, Beth. I need to know what happened," he said. "Don't you?"

While they talked, I stared down at my untouched plate, the two sunny-side up eggs, the yolks bright orange and gelatinous, flanked by greasy hash browns, pancakes, and two slabs of sausage. I suddenly felt queasy. My entire world had been turned upside down in the last twenty-four hours. Breakfast for dinner now seemed like an awful idea.

I was being offered a chance to go to space, experience the wonders of the galaxy as only a handful of human beings had, and enjoy godlike power while I was there. I could see where my father was from. I could find him.

But I could never return to Earth.

I had butterflies because I already knew what I was going to do. I'd known from the second Ty mentioned the Serpo Institute.

My mom and Ty were both looking at me now. I might have been silent for a minute there, thinking things through.

I turned to my mom. "I—"

She cut me off. "It's in your blood to want to be up there. It's in your blood to go searching. I know . . . I know it was selfish, but I wanted to keep you here. On Earth. With me."

"Mom, I—"

She squeezed my hand. "I watched my father waste away. I lost my partner to the Vastness. I didn't want to lose you, too. But now there's a reason, there's a chance . . ." She paused for a moment to take in a shuddering breath and her eyes hardened. "You know what you have to do, Syd."

I nodded and turned back to Tycius.

"When do we leave?"

7

Tycius drove us north on the highway until the other cars thinned out and it was just us and the pine trees. Eventually, we got off the main artery and started navigating switchbacks up a summit. There were signs along the road advertising a ski resort at the top of the mountain, *CLOSED* splashed in bright red paint across all of them. The road was lit only by our headlights; the night was cloudy, the stars hidden.

I'd be getting a closer look at them soon enough.

I sat between my mom and Tycius, my palms sweating. My mom had her arm draped across my shoulders and every so often would squeeze me against her, then realize she was doing it and release me, only to gradually start clinging to me again a few minutes later.

I didn't mind.

We'd skipped our last town together.

"There's still a job waiting for you at the Consulate," Tycius told my mom. "You'll be able to monitor Sydney's progress from there. Keep in touch."

"Great," my mom replied flatly. There was a note of resignation in her voice, but I thought I also sensed some relief coming off her. We'd been caught. The worst had happened. And it wasn't that bad.

In fact, there was hope. My dad was alive.

Now all I had to do was find him.

"We'll be able to visit, won't we?" I asked. "Couldn't my mom just move to Denza?"

Tycius hesitated. "The Serpo Institute prefers to recruit younger humans. Their minds have an easier time adjusting to species outside their own."

"But my mom's already seen all the aliens," I replied. "That doesn't make any—"

"They don't want me, Syd," my mom said gently. "I'm not allowed off Earth. The Denzans rated me as a risk. Unstable."

"Unstable?" I opened my mouth to say how ridiculous that was, but then I remembered how just a few hours ago my mom had been waving a gun at Rebecca. And then there was that time she proved my alien heritage by trying to drown me. "I mean, I guess you've got a temper sometimes, but . . ."

My mom touched my cheek. "It's okay. You'll find Marcius out there in the Vastness. Our family will be whole again." She gazed out the window, looking up at the blank night sky like I'd done so many times before. "It'll work out."

I peered out the window with her. Everything had happened so fast, I'd barely had time to really digest it. I was leaving Earth. And, like a good fugitive who never went back to the same location twice, I could never come back. Not unless my dad's mysterious research paid off and he found a cure out there that would stop the Wasting.

I was going to live among aliens.

My DNA was going to mutate. I was going to let that happen.

I was going to be strong. Invulnerable. An interstellar representative of what was apparently the most dangerous species in the universe.

My knee bounced up and down. I steadied it after a look from my mom. I was abandoning her. Leaving her behind. Of course there was sadness and a big glob of nerves in my belly.

But mostly what I felt was *a pull*. The unknown tugging me forward.

I could feel it out there now. I finally had a name for it.

The Vastness.

It called to me.

We reached the mountain's summit, the ground flattening out and the skeletal remains of a burned-down ski lodge looming before us. The truck's high beams illuminated whorls of ash blown by the wind. The slopes were muddy and snowless. The rails of the ski lift sagged where they'd come unmoored. Maybe this had been a vacation spot once, a place for happy memories.

"This would've made a good hideout," I said to my mom.

She smiled. "I was thinking the same thing."

"Tonight, it's a good place to bring down a spacecraft," Ty said.

Ty's tone was light. He was excited, a man at the end of a long mission. He swung open his door and hopped out of the truck, practically whistling. It didn't seem to me like he was going to miss Earth very much.

Was I going to miss it here?

Earth. What had it ever done for me? I'd seen more of this place than most people my age, and yet I felt like I'd never really gotten to experience it. Never connected. There were dangers around every corner, and not just the ones my mom and I thought were pursuing us. The planet was dying, humans one water shortage away from killing one another. Maybe I was lucky to be getting out.

But there was also kindness here. Those protestors fighting a losing battle against the gas company. Every math and science teacher who had recognized potential in me and tried to nurture it. The friends I'd made and bailed on, who never even got to know my real name.

Earth was a mess, but it was *ours*. I guess that's what my mom had been trying to impress on me back at the diner, when she got defensive over the Denzans not doing enough.

It was only half *my* home, though. There was a whole other piece of me that I'd never understood, that I'd never gotten an opportunity to know.

Denza.

As I made to get out of the truck, my mom put her hand on my arm to stop me.

"I need a moment with my son, Tycius," she said.

Tycius glanced across me to my mom, and he made a visible effort to erase any trace of his good mood. He cleared his throat uncomfortably.

"Of course," he said, pausing a moment, like he couldn't decide exactly what to say. "Beth, I know we've had our differences, but it was good to see you again after all these years. I'll take care of Sydney, I—"

Mom reached across me to slam the truck's door. Outside, Tycius looked crestfallen. He stared at us through the window for a moment, then trudged toward the burned building. He got some device out of his pocket and began punching information into it, presumably to call down his ship.

"He doesn't seem so bad," I said.

"No, he's not," my mom agreed. "I'm glad it's him that's taking you away."

"So, I mean, you could be nicer to him."

She smirked. "That's not how my relationship with Tycius works. He's a decent man, but there's a lot we don't agree on. He wasn't supportive of the work your father and I were doing."

My eyebrows knitted together. Even now, I still didn't have the whole story. "What work? You mean curing the Wasting? He seemed pretty supportive of that."

"Oh no, not that. Tycius worshipped the First Twelve and your grandfather like they were superheroes," my mom replied. She started rifling through the contents of her go-bag. "It's what we intended to do *after* we cured them."

"What do you mean 'after'?"

"You heard Tycius back at the diner. He and the Denzans don't want to help humanity, even though our planet is dying. They claim that our culture is so fractured and unenlightened that to upgrade our technology would only result in more war and death."

The idea that humanity was a primitive society seemed pretty insulting to me, but then I thought back to the ugliness I'd seen on the news that morning, the same as every morning. I tried to imagine Denzans coming down to Earth and creating a utopia using their technological advancement. Some wackjob with a machine gun would probably shoot them up for fun.

"Maybe they aren't wrong about us," I said quietly.

"They aren't," my mom replied bluntly. "We're a shitty species that has chosen to live in a system that eats the weak and destroys the environment. Some extraterrestrial savior isn't going to fix what's wrong with humanity."

I raised an eyebrow. "So you agree with him."

"Don't tell him that," she replied. "In fact, don't tell him any of what I'm about to tell you."

"Wait, so I can't trust him?"

"No, you can trust him. He's your uncle. Plus, Ty's too noble not to trust," my mom said. "Here. Look at this."

She popped up from her bag with a document in hand. It was a photograph, one that I'd seen before. My grandfather in his flight suit alongside a muscular bombshell and a little hairy guy.

"Your father wasn't just trying to cure the Wasting," my mom said. "Humans get stronger after prolonged exposure to the

Vastness. They get weaker upon returning to Earth, waste away, and die. He wanted to stop that. He wanted to find a way for the humans who'd been to space to maintain their power once they got back here." She glanced out the windshield at Ty, then lowered her voice a bit more. "The Denzans don't want to help us because we aren't united as a people. But if the evolved humans from Denza could come home . . . with their strength and invulnerability, just a couple hundred of them could get this whole planet in line."

I blinked. "Get it in line? You mean . . ."

"We were planning an invasion of Earth," my mom said simply. "Your dad liked to call it an intervention, but I don't want to dress it up."

I started to laugh, but by the stony look on my mom's face, I could tell she wasn't joking. She never really joked, actually. Hearing your parent tell you she's planning to take over a planet is just too ridiculous not to chuckle at, though.

"You're serious?" I asked, then dropped the question mark. "You're serious."

She nodded. "When the Consulate started stonewalling me about your dad's mission, I knew something was wrong. And then that Vulpin showed up. I figured that was either the Consulate's way of tying up loose ends or someone else got wind of our plans and sabotaged your father's mission."

"Tycius said the Consulate wasn't involved."

"Right." My mom hesitated. "And I guess I believe him. Which means someone out there wanted your father gone and all ways of finding him erased. Marcius once told me there are radical antihuman factions on Denza . . ."

I massaged my forehead. "Shit, Mom. This is too much."

"You have to find him, Syd. Not just for me. Not just to complete our family. But possibly to save the entire human race."

I leaned back and took a deep breath. The ring box containing my dad's cosmological tether was shoved into the front pocket of my jeans. Unconsciously, I'd been rubbing my fingers against its edges. The key to finding my father, which only I could use.

"Okay," I said. "So, no pressure."

My mom tapped the hairy guy posing next to my grandfather. "This man's name is Rafe Butler. He was organizing the humans on Denza. Once you're up there, you should find him. He might know something about what happened. And this woman . . ." She tapped the lady. "That's who your captain will be. Marie Reno. She was also working with us."

I took in the names and faces—members of the First Twelve who hadn't come back to Earth to waste away like my grandfather. They'd be like forty years older now.

I looked up at my mom. "Is that everything? Do I know all our secrets?"

She nodded. "I'm sorry to have kept so much from you all these years. When your dad didn't come back, I lost my hope. I focused all my energy on keeping you safe. But now . . ." My mom glanced out the windshield at Ty. "You can bring Marcius home, Syd. And then, if he found what he thought he would, we can bring *all* of them home. We can fix this place."

I tried to picture it. An army of astronauts-turned-Supermen returning to Earth to unify the planet. I got the same feeling that I first had when my mom told me I was half-alien—that she was totally nuts. My dad was alive and I was going to space, where I'd develop superhuman abilities. Damn, wasn't that crazy enough?

My eyes must have gone big and distant, the look I got whenever my brain swelled beyond capacity, because my mom touched my cheek.

"It's okay," she said. "I know it's a lot to put on you, but I wanted you to have the whole story finally. I've had years to adjust to the idea of intergalactic life and to consider our problems here on Earth. You've had like ten minutes. Take some time. Think things through."

I laughed a bit incredulously. "I mean, gosh, Mom, it's not like I don't *want* to help you and Dad take over the planet—"

She snorted and shook her head. "I know you've ached to go up there ever since you found out about your heritage," she said. "So go. See what you think of the Serpo Institute. Find Marcius. Find what you're looking for. I love you, Syd. I'm proud of you. I know you'll do what's right."

And, with that, my mom pulled me into a hug. It was a tight one, her arms digging into my ribs, but I didn't mind. I squeezed her back just as hard.

"I love you, too," I replied. "I promise I'll find Dad. Everything will work out."

Outside, Tycius waved to get my attention. He pointed up into the night.

A silver object was slowly descending.

My first spaceship.

"I can't watch you go," my mom said, her eyes suddenly welling up. "I can't do it."

I hopped out of the truck, and we hugged again once through the window. My mom seemed so small and fragile, particularly for an intergalactic revolutionary. My head was still spinning. I slung my backpack over my shoulder, my dad's ring pulsing in my pocket.

The truck kicked up dirt as it sped away from me. I missed Ty's spaceship touch down. Instead, I watched my mom disappear into the forest. I jumped when Ty patted me on the shoulder.

"I don't mean to rush you," he said, "but we've got a small window where the Consulate can guarantee we won't be visible to any human air traffic."

I turned to him, nodded, and walked toward the unknown.

PART TWO

SPECIES OF ALIENS RANKED FROM LEAST TO MOST HORRIFIC

8

To be honest, Ty's spaceship sucked ass.

I expected something at least on the level of a flying saucer. What I got was a titanium-plated pyramid about the size of a tent. The thing sat there in front of the collapsed ski lodge looking more like some abstract artist's misplaced sculpture than a means for interstellar travel.

"Is that what you were chasing us around in?" I asked.

"Yes," Tycius replied.

"I'm surprised you caught us."

"She's faster than she looks."

The wall nearest to us peeled back, revealing an unlit interior. The inside of the ship was completely empty except for two cushioned swivel chairs bolted to the floor. Looking closer, there weren't any controls—no levers to kick on the hyper-speed, no giant red buttons to mash for photon torpedoes.

Tycius needed to duck his head to enter. He sat down in the chair on the left, and a seat belt slithered across his lap, the thing made of the same quicksilver material as his portable bodyguard. As soon as he was strapped in, Ty brushed open his coat, his fingers hovering over the button that controlled his holographic projector.

"I'm going to turn this off now, if it's okay with you," he said.

"Sure," I replied. "Be yourself."

My uncle nodded, but his fingers hesitated for a moment. "Good-bye, Bogie," he murmured. I wondered if he was feeling a bit sentimental about the identity he'd been hiding behind for the last decade.

Tycius hit the button, and the rumpled detective disappeared, replaced by the thin-limbed Denzan. Smooth gray skin, wide black eyes, tangle of dark green hair, an extra finger on each hand. I reminded myself not to stare too much.

It sank in that I was alone with my alien uncle.

I hesitated getting onto the ship. I mean, this situation was truly, truly insane. I was going into space. With an alien relative that I'd known for all of four hours. I glanced over my shoulder, down the road where my mom's truck had disappeared into darkness—my only link to the familiar gone.

Ty didn't have eyebrows, but his prominent eyes were very expressive. One narrowed to a slit while the other widened, his head tilting.

"Coming?" he asked.

I took a deep breath. "Yeah," I replied. "Just thinking about

Neil Armstrong all of a sudden."

"'One small step for a man, one giant leap for mankind,'" Tycius quoted with a smile. "Pretty appropriate."

"He went to space and didn't come back to Earth with super-powers," I said, thinking out loud.

"No offense to the brave astronauts of Earth, but popping into orbit is hardly the same as going into the Vastness." He looked into my eyes. "You're about to travel far beyond the imagining of most humans, Sydney. It's okay to take a moment to appreciate that."

I didn't bother to hide the chill that sent through me. Then I shuffled inside, set my backpack in one of the ship's four corners, and sat down. Even though I'd seen it happen with Tycius, I still jumped when the seat belt curled around me. Another tentacle of liquid metal emerged from the floor, securing my backpack.

"What is that stuff?" I asked.

"Ultonate," Ty replied. "It's an alloy mined from volcanic deposits on Denza, then imbued with nanobots. Very versatile. We use it for almost everything."

I looked around at the featureless interior. "Where's the bath-room?"

"You won't need a bathroom," he replied. "The ship will see to that need."

"I know we're supposed to be family and all, but I'm not ready to pee in front of you."

He sighed. "This is just an interplanetary skiff. We'll only be in here for a short ride to Jupiter, then the ISV *Eastwood* will scoop us up."

"Oh, well, if it's *only* until Jupiter."

Ty touched the wall in front of him, and it lit up, a digital control array fanning out beneath his fingertips. The entrance sealed up behind us without a sound. I swiveled around in my chair, bumping knees with Tycius. It was tight in there.

The space tent was only dark for a split second before all three walls went completely transparent. I had a 360-degree view of the ruined ski lodge and the woods. The only things that remained solid were the floor and our chairs.

"I think you're going to dig this part," Ty said.

"How were you passing as human, saying stuff like 'dig this'?"

Ty gave me a look. "This liftoff is going to be lit, my dude."

"Please stop."

Smiling, he hit a button, and up we went.

The skiff soundlessly shot into the sky. I rocked back in my chair as we floated into the night, first above the trees, then to the point where I could make out headlights on the highways and the patchwork of buildings beyond. I wondered if my mom was in one of those cars down there.

Strapped into that little chair with nothing but dark sky on every side of me, I felt like I'd been flung out of a plane in an ejector seat, and what little I'd eaten at the diner squirmed up my esophagus. I felt like if I tipped the wrong way, I'd go tumbling right off what now felt like little more than a platform. I squeezed Ty's shoulder.

"Maybe, uh, some smaller windows?"

He took one look at me, saw that I was turning green, and hit the outline of a button on the transparent wall. The ship regained its solidity, keeping a porthole in each side so that we could see out, as well as the point of the ship above us for some literal moonroof action.

"Better?"

I exhaled as the nausea subsided. "I've only been in an airplane the one time, and I was really little," I told him. "Space travel is a new frontier. This is *all* pretty new, actually."

Ty paused for a moment, considering me. "I'm sorry. I thought it would be exciting for you, but I can understand how this would be overwhelming. You're going to miss Earth, your mother . . ." He sighed and smoothed back his hair. "And here I'm trying to be the fun uncle."

I looked out one of the portholes. Higher and higher we went, passing through gray wisps of clouds. I could see the ocean now, the Pacific like a sheet of black silk rippling on the horizon, an embroidery of lights stitched along its edge.

"Hey, it's a pretty amazing view," I said. Glancing over at my uncle, I saw the slits on his nose area flare happily, his eyes slackening. Even though his features were unfamiliar, I read relief in that expression. "Are you happy to be leaving?"

"Yes," he answered quickly.

"Wow. Earth is that bad, huh?"

"No offense intended," Ty replied. "But I was never supposed to stay for as long as I did. I could never bring myself to take even a short return trip home and risk missing a clue to your whereabouts. I can't remember a time when I wasn't homesick."

Homesick. That wasn't so far from the feeling I'd had all those years on the run, especially once my mom told me I was half-Denzan. Except I wasn't homesick for any place in particular. It was just a general emptiness, like Earth wasn't enough.

"I'm not sure I'm going to miss it either," I said quietly.

Ty looked at me but didn't respond.

The clouds thinned out around us. Washington was long gone now, and so were all the other places that Mom and I had hid out. All of North America was just a blob beneath us, a tiny blemish on an otherwise navy-blue marble. As we glided farther and farther away, the planet began to seem so small, half of it swallowed up by the shadow of space. The moon floated to my right, pale and solitary. And beyond that flared the sun, a furnace, tongues of flame leaping out from the darkness. I knew you weren't supposed to look right at it, but I looked right at it. Through the windows of our skiff, the brightness didn't hurt my eyes.

"Wow," I breathed. "Wow."

"Welcome to the Vastness," Ty said.

My mom always said how easy it was for us to get lost in the US, how the two of us could just disappear. If I'd felt small then, like a needle in a haystack, now I felt infinitesimally tinier, like a dust mote on a mountain. Earth itself was so small and fragile, surrounded by so much *nothing*. Hard to believe there were billions of people back there, all of them with stories and problems, none of them realizing how they were just tiny specks with only gravity keeping them from spiraling off into an endless cold expanse.

"You okay?" Tycius asked.

I shook my head. "Having some deep-ass thoughts over here."

"There's an entire genre of Denzan poetry dedicated to the feelings inspired by floating free in the Vastness," Tycius told me. Then he recited something in his own language, the words rhythmic and singsong.

"What's that mean?" I asked.

"Loosely translated, it says I hunger for your touch with the increasing velocity of a magnesium fragment caught in orbital decay."

"So your poets are thirsty dorks."

"You'd be surprised how many young women appreciate a well-timed zero-gravity haiku."

"Yes, cool uncle," I replied. "I would be surprised by that."

He smirked at me, then tapped some buttons on his display. "It's about thirty-six hours to Jupiter."

"I thought you said this was a short ride."

"In terms of interplanetary travel, that's *incredibly* short."

A sharp vibration rattled our skiff's smooth ride.

"What was that?" I asked, trying not to sound panicked.

"Nothing to worry about," Ty replied. "The sails extended."

I leaned against the window to get a better look. Two protrusions had unfurled from the seams of the skiff. I guess you could call them sails, but they looked more like bat wings to me.

"The panels harness the solar winds," Ty explained. "We'll be picking up speed soon. Lean back. You're going to feel a pinch."

"What do you mean, a pin—ow!"

A needle of liquid metal extended from my headrest and jabbed me in the back of the neck. The same thing happened to Tycius.

"It's an organic serum that will make the speed we're traveling at bearable," Ty said. "It will safely suppress your excretory system, thin your blood to prevent clotting, and relax your muscles."

I gingerly touched the back of my neck. The needle still connected me to my seat. When I leaned forward, it moved with me, like an IV bag. "Too weird."

"The ship will continue monitoring your health throughout our voyage," Tycius said. "You'll probably experience some drowsiness. Some lost time. We both will."

I could already feel it, a stoned sort of melty-ness to my whole body. There was an extraterrestrial ice pick jabbing into my neck, and I couldn't remember if I'd ever gotten a tetanus shot, but that didn't seem to matter. I was chill.

There was a sudden pressure on my chest. We'd picked up speed. The weight gradually eased as the drugs kicked in. The stars ahead of us blurred, some of them flashing blue or red as our velocity wreaked havoc on the light spectrum. I waved a hand back and forth in front of my face, watching light from the blurring stars split between my fingers.

"Rad," I murmured.

I'm not sure how long I played with the light, but at some point I started clenching my fingers to make a fist. I studied my knuckles, the fine lines there, the little hairs. I'd thrown a few punches over the years—we'd moved around a lot, and bullies always sought out the new kid. But soon, that fist of mine was going to be one of the most dangerous weapons in the universe.

"I don't feel stronger yet," I said drowsily.

"No, you wouldn't," Ty replied. "It'll take some time for the DNA changes to begin."

"My dad . . ." I wasn't sure where I was going with that statement. The hyper-speed drugs had me feeling loopy.

"Yes?" Tycius said.

"Does he—I mean, do you—I mean, do *we* have other family on Denza?"

"No. After the Etherazi invasion, it was just me and your father."

"Oh," I said.

So my dad and I were the only family that Ty had left. It made more sense to me now that he'd spend ten years on Earth looking for me, especially since I could potentially lead him to his brother.

"Are you older than my dad or . . . ?"

"Younger," Tycius answered.

I felt sleep settling over me, and I grooved back in the chair, getting comfortable, hugging myself.

"Can you tell me about him?" I asked. "I hardly remember anything."

There was a long pause, and for a moment I thought Tycius might have lost consciousness. When he did finally speak, he kept his eyes closed.

"Marcius, your father, he . . ." Ty trailed off. "I looked up to him. I followed him into service at the Serpo Institute."

"You guys were doctors, right?" I asked. "You came to Earth to try healing my grandfather."

Ty shook his head. "Neither of us were doctors, actually. Your father's primary role in Denzan society was as a theoretician. He's a bit eccentric. Outside-the-box. Such traits are respected on Denza. He was expected to formulate hypotheses, no matter how absurd, and chase them down. Even his failures brought us illumination."

"Sounds like a cool gig," I said. "Are you a bad idea tester, too?"

"No. I was on Earth to observe the progress of humanity and report back to my people."

"A spy."

"Basically," Ty agreed. "Marcius was obsessed with the Lost People. All the theoreticians are, to some extent."

"The Lost People?"

"A species that predates ours. The Serpo Institute has found relics of their civilization scattered throughout the galaxy, but nothing useful, nothing that tells us anything about who they were or where they've gone."

"Oh cool, there are precursors," I said, stifling a yawn against the back of my hand. "That's like my favorite sci-fi trope."

"Yes, your Earth writers truly thought of everything," Ty said with a snort. "The planets where we've found their artifacts share nothing in common. Your father theorized that this might mean the Lost People were capable of surviving in a wide variety of climates and atmospheres. From there, he reasoned that perhaps studying how they evolved such traits might shed light on why humans flourish away from Earth but waste away upon their return. He believed he'd found the home world of the Lost People when he . . ."

I tried to picture my dad—the hazy memory I had of him, anyway—exploring the ruins of an ancient alien civilization. Did he find what he was after out there? Why would someone want to stop him? How was he the only member of his crew to survive?

I wanted to follow him. In the drugged haze, I realized that's what I'd been feeling all that time.

Like my dad, I wanted to dive into the unknown.

I couldn't tell if I'd dozed off or if Tycius had, but it seemed like we hadn't spoken in a while.

My fingers felt clumsy and heavy, but I managed to maneuver them into my pocket and retrieve the box containing my dad's cosmological tether. I took out the ring, turning it over in my fingers, examining the swirling cosmos contained in its jewel.

I glanced over at my uncle. His eyes were closed. "Ty? You awake?"

"Hmm?" he replied, in a drugged haze of his own.

"How does this thing even work?" I asked.

"What thing?" he asked, opening one eye, then the other. "Be careful with that—"

My leaden fingers slipped off the ring's delicate gold band. It floated in the air in front of me for a moment, then zipped at my face with the speed of a bullet.

"Whoa—!"

A tentacle of ultonate from my seat belt lanced out and speared the ring just centimeters from my cheek. Gently, the ultonate secured both the ring and its box against my hip. My heart pounded, but that only lasted a second as the ship corrected my dosage to calm me down.

"We're moving at a very high speed," Tycius said calmly. "Holding loose objects in front of your face is not recommended."

"Noted," I replied. I'd been in space for only a few hours and had already nearly killed myself. Great.

"To answer your question," Ty continued, "you'll need to use a Wayscope to access the information on the cosmological tether."

I thought back to the conversation I'd had with my mom when we were fleeing the cabin. "A Wayscope . . . that's like what you put into Dungeon to track me down?"

"A very rudimentary version, yes. Your mind unraveled that puzzle simply because it could. Because it came naturally to you. I assume you've always been good at math, yes?"

"Yeah," I replied. "Not to brag, but like multiple high school teachers said I could be a national champion mathlete."

"Ah, listen to my *cool nephew*," Tycius said with a smile.

"Ouch."

"You see, we Denzans have evolved in such a way that we are capable of seeing spectrums beyond what other species can process. We can sense values like chemical composition, light wavelengths, and units of measure with the same ease that a human nose identifies which variety of butchered livestock is cooking on their stove. A Wayscope is a device used to magnify our vision into the Vastness."

"I'm only half-Denzan, though," I said. "You're sure I'll be able to do it?"

"Yes, after you receive the proper training," Tycius replied. "Hybrids like you are exceedingly rare, but you aren't the only one in existence."

My eyes widened. "There's other people like me?"

"A few," Tycius replied. "In fact, there will be a hybrid your age on the *Eastwood*'s crew with us. A young woman."

"Our little rebellion." I said the words as they popped into my head, thinking back to the day when my dad told me he was leaving.

Ty's smile was tight and melancholy. "Your dad used to call you that," he said. "There's no law against humans and Denzans getting together, but some people on our planet look at it as meddling with a primitive species. Marcius thought that was idiotic."

I turned to look out the window. We were alongside Mars. I wondered how many times my dad had made this same voyage, how many times he'd had this same impossible view.

I wondered if he would even recognize me when we found him.

I zoned out and must have slipped into unconsciousness. When I blinked awake, Mars was well behind us. We'd gone more than halfway—at least twenty hours I'd been literally pinned to this seat—but it felt like I was just coming up from a very peaceful catnap.

Next to me, Tycius had taken off his trench coat and peeled up the sleeve of his shirt. There were three bands of obsidian metal stretched around his bicep, tight enough that they must have dug into his muscle anytime he lifted something. Tycius murmured what sounded like a prayer in his own language. As he did, he ran his finger around the edge of the band closest to his elbow.

When he finished his whispered incantation, the band gave off a hiss like water on a hot pan and dissolved into Ty's skin. Although Ty didn't react like it hurt, I still winced on his behalf— the band left a dark gray scar on his slate-colored skin. My uncle rubbed the new marking with a look of relief.

"Dude," I said. "What was that?"

I waited for a response. And waited. Either Ty was pretending not to hear me, or he'd passed out immediately after doing his weird ritual.

I blinked, and time slipped away again. When I came to, Ty's coat was back on.

"Are you awake?" he asked me.

"Yeah," I said, smacking my lips. "I think so."

"We're almost there."

Jupiter loomed before us, a titanic orb of swirling crimson and silver bands. On the surface—or whatever you called the upper-most layer of ever-shifting ammonia and sulfur—was a dark red cyclone that moved counter to the planet's rotation. It looked like a violent lipstick kiss, turning across Jupiter's atmosphere. Our skiff was heading right for its center—right into a chemical storm that was bigger than Earth itself.

My fingers gripped the armrests. "We're safe in here, right?"

"Yes, of course," Tycius replied dismissively. "Listen. There are some things we should discuss before you meet the others."

"Okay," I said, wary of the edge in Ty's voice.

"The captain of the *Eastwood* is Marie Reno. One of the First Twelve. I've been in contact with her and believe we can trust her."

My mom had said pretty much the same thing. They meant different things, though. Tycius was strictly thinking of the off-the-books mission to find my father, which we'd be keeping secret in case the people who wanted to disappear him and kidnap me were still paying attention after a decade. My mom, on the other hand, wanted me to know that Reno was down with my parents' plan to bring enhanced humans back to Earth.

"I'll be the first mate once we're aboard," Tycius continued. "There will also be a ship's proctor and a chief engineer. I don't know who they'll be, but I imagine Reno will have chosen people we can trust."

I nodded. "Sounds cool so far."

"The variable that we can't account for is your crewmates," Ty said. "Reno already had a crew assigned to her when I notified her that you'd been found. They aren't aware of your real purpose here. The Serpo Institute recruits the best and brightest from across the universe. You'll have to be careful around them. You should keep the cosmological tether hidden at all times."

"Don't worry," I replied. "I've got a lot of experience being sneaky."

"Good," Ty replied. "Also, you should know that the institute makes sure each crew in the training fleet is diverse with at least one representative from all the member species."

An image popped into my head. A ferocious doglike creature crouched over my mom, snapping and biting at her.

"You're warning me there's going to be a Vulpin on board," I said.

"Yes," Tycius said. "And, to be frank, you may find some of the other species a bit . . . disturbing."

9

Our skiff rocked back and forth as it entered Jupiter's Great Red Spot, the hellish chemical storm that raged across the gas giant's surface. My heart pounded, and a cold sweat broke out across the back of my neck.

"Should we really fly into this mess?" I asked Ty, my voice cracking.

"Relax," he replied. "I've done this a few times."

The ship must have sensed my distress, because I felt something fresh and frosty inject into the back of my neck. A full-body spearmint iciness lowered my heart rate and mellowed me out.

"Oh yeah, this is fine," I said.

And it was. Because just when the pressure in Jupiter's atmosphere should've turned us inside out, the maelstrom parted and we entered an unnatural pocket of calm.

At the center of Jupiter's never-ending storm—maybe even its cause—was an *absence*. A gap. A tear. A blot of nothingness that I couldn't quite get my brain around. I mean, space is a lot of nothing to begin with, but it's still pretty noticeable when the fabric of the universe has a rip in it. There was no *distance* in here, no context for anything.

"Is this a black hole?" I asked, knowing even as I said it that my guess was wrong. The gravity in a black hole is so strong that nothing can escape it, not even light. My half-Denzan eyes told me that if I somehow entered this anomaly, I would come out the other side. Somewhere else. The space chasm was safe, relatively speaking. In fact, I was drawn toward it.

"Picture a map of the universe," Tycius said. "All the star systems in existence, millions of them, mostly unexplored. At one end is your Milky Way and Earth. All the way at the other end is my home galaxy and Denza."

I nodded. "Okay."

"What are you picturing?"

"A map of the galaxy, dude."

Tycius sighed. "What does it look like? How is it printed?"

I closed my eyes, trying to play along with Ty's random exercise. "I don't know. It's on a big, old-ass parchment and was drawn by Michelangelo or something."

"Good," Tycius said. "Now, a journey between our two planets in a straight line across your map would take eons. But if you were to crumple up your parchment into a ball, that would be a more accurate depiction of the universe. Perhaps now our two galaxies are separated only by a bit of air, the fold of a paper. And if we were to rip through that paper and gain access to the *in-between* . . ."

I opened my eyes. "A wormhole. That's how you travel between galaxies."

"Correct."

"You could've just said 'wormhole,'" I replied. "I've read a lot of science fiction. I know my stuff."

"I'm sure you do."

"What are those things?" I asked.

I hadn't noticed them at first—I was too focused on the wormhole itself—but around the edges of the cosmic emptiness were sections of ultonate scaffolding. While they looked small against the size of the wormhole, each of the rectangular structures was probably a few miles long.

"Girders," Ty explained. "The universe wants to heal itself after we tear holes in it. Those keep the wormholes open. We also use them to monitor what kind of traffic is coming through."

"So, my dad . . ."

"Whatever door he opened, he closed it behind him," Ty said. "That doesn't mean we can't find it again."

Our skiff slowed down considerably, and the needle that had been impaling the back of my neck for the last day and a half finally withdrew, taking its cocktail of space-travel drugs with it. I immediately got a groan-inducing pins-and-needles feeling in my legs, which I hadn't really stretched in the last thirty-six hours. With our skiff no longer racing forward, there was no force holding me down. I began to float, restrained only by my seat belt.

"What now?" I asked, shaking some feeling back into my limbs.

As if in response, a woman's voice crackled over our speakers. She spoke English, her voice deep and authoritative.

"This is Captain Reno. Reeling you into the *Eastwood* now, Tycius."

"Good to hear your voice, Reno," Ty said with a smile.

I'd been so focused on the wormhole, I hadn't even noticed the alien ship floating nearby. I whistled.

The ISV *Eastwood* was a hell of a lot bigger than Ty's crummy skiff. The bulk of the ship was a massive ring, constantly spinning to create artificial gravity. A network of spokes connected the ring to a tubular rocket at its center. The whole thing looked very much like a donut with an arrow through its middle.

"I've been meaning to ask, what does 'Eastwood' mean in your language?"

Tycius shook his head. "Captain Reno chose the name. She wanted to honor her favorite Earth actor."

I sort of remembered an old man who made movies about yelling at young people, but I'd never seen any of them.

I noticed a long barrel on the underside of the *Eastwood*'s rocket. It looked very much like a massive cannon.

"Pretty big gun," I said, pointing that out. "My mom made it sound like you guys are a bunch of pacifists."

"Denzans do abhor violence like any species should," Ty replied. "And that is not a gun. It's the Subspace Piercer. That's how our ships create wormholes. Though I suppose in the wrong hands, it could be used as a weapon."

A beam of white light similar to what Ty had used on my mom's truck shot out from the *Eastwood*. The spotlight enveloped our skiff and guided us toward a small opening in the *Eastwood*'s rapidly spinning ring.

We floated into a domed docking bay shaped like the chamber of a revolver, the bullets in this case being skiffs just like ours. My stomach swooned as I adjusted to the *Eastwood*'s artificial gravity, my seat belt digging into my abdomen. Our skiff tilted as it parked top-first in an open slot, my feet now dangling toward the ceiling. Outside, I heard seals pressurizing, the vacuum of space shut out beyond the docking bay, fresh oxygen rushing in around us. What was once the ceiling of our skiff peeled open, our seat belts snaked away, and Tycius and I both lightly dropped to the sloped wall leading out.

I'd told Tycius that I'd read a lot of sci-fi, and that was true, but none of my books had prepared me for the interior of the *Eastwood*. I'd been expecting futuristic flashing lights and sleek metallic hallways. Instead, beyond the cold functionality of the docking bay, the *Eastwood* looked like a yoga retreat. The floors and walls were all paneled with a soft wood that reminded me of bamboo. The lights were warm, like a summer sunset. There were plants everywhere, shelves in every wall dedicated to the greenery. Some of the plants I recognized—a patch of violets, a spiky green fern—but most were completely alien. Dark vines that pulsed with a neon-colored ink, swaying palm trees the size of my pinkie finger, a flower with delicate petals that looked like flickering flames. After the cramped and drugged journey aboard the skiff, I felt a rush of fresh oxygen in my lungs, the whole scene somehow both invigorating and homey.

"Welcome aboard," boomed Captain Reno as she emerged through a sliding door flanked by three other . . . people? Humanoids? I wasn't entirely clear on the nomenclature. Two of them were Denzans, and the other some kind of robotic stick figure.

Anyway, at that moment, Reno demanded my full attention, swaggering ahead of the aliens. If she was supposed to be
around the same age as my grandfather, she sure didn't look it.
The *Eastwood*'s captain was a powerfully built woman with curly
blond hair streaked through with silver. Some wrinkles around
the eyes and mouth, but mostly her skin was tan and smooth.
She reminded me a bit of one of those rich housewives from reality TV who could afford a ton of really good plastic surgery. She
wore an unzipped flight suit that showed off an amount of freck-
led cleavage that made me immediately self-conscious of where I
was looking, especially when she stopped right in front of me and
pinched my cheek.

"My lord, you look just like him," Reno told me. "A bit under-
fed and missing a flask of scotch, but otherwise you're a dead
ringer. Your gramps—let me tell you, there was a man who knew
how to keep a lady entertained on a long voyage between systems."

"Uh . . ." I only managed a single syllable in response. It didn't
matter. Reno had already moved on from me.

"And you, you're a sight for sore eyes," she said to Tycius, pushing
some of his wiggly hair out of his face. "Took you long enough."

"They didn't want to be found, Captain," Ty replied.

"The good ones always play hard to get," Reno said.

While Reno and Tycius got reacquainted, one of the Denzans
shuffled toward me. His thin frame was bent into the shape of a
question mark. Besides his posture, I could tell he was older than
Tycius by his hair—it wasn't gray but translucent, the color completely sapped from it. Despite his advancing age, the Denzan's

hair was wrestled into a swooping pompadour. Coming from Earth, I didn't know anything about Denzan style, but I still got the sense he was wearing his hair like someone much younger. Unlike Reno and the other crew members, this Denzan wore a flowy tunic thing, splotched with food stains, that reminded me of an old-timey nightshirt. He looked like a retired wizard with an interest in ska.

The Denzan smiled at me, then said something in his language. I shook my head.

"I don't understand," I replied.

He smiled wider, like we were now playing the fun game of shouting foreign words at each other. He tapped his chest. "Vanceval." Then he tapped my chest. "Sydney shush."

"You're Vanceval," I responded. "And I . . . should be quiet?"

The Denzan chuckled and shook his head. "Sydneycius," he enunciated, and I realized that he was attaching "-cius" to my name, like Tycius and Marcius. That must have been how Denzan names worked.

"Oh no, I mean, yeah, but . . ." I stammered my way through first contact. "Just Sydney is fine."

Watching from behind Vanceval, the other Denzan let loose a sigh, like this was all a waste of his time. He looked about the same age as my uncle, his dark purple hair patchy and receding. One side of his face was badly scarred and droopy, like he'd been splashed by acid. Perhaps what stood out most about this Denzan was the sleeve of obsidian metal that covered his entire right arm. Like the bands I'd seen squeezing Ty's bicep, this Denzan's metal sleeve seemed to be uncomfortably tight, pinching him at the shoulder and wrist.

The second Denzan brushed aside the smaller Vanceval and held up a sliver of ultonate, a writhing bit of quicksilver that looked like a slug.

I took a step back since this guy felt the need to be right in my face. "Okay? What—?"

At "okay," the Denzan grabbed me roughly by the chin. I yelped and tried to brush his hand away, but his long fingers were surprisingly strong. He pressed the sliver of ultonate into my ear canal. I felt a brief slurping sensation, like my ear was filling up with water, and then a cool numbness.

The Denzan let me go and took a step back. Vanceval clucked his tongue in disapproval. Now Tycius and Reno were paying attention. My uncle glared at his fellow Denzan while Reno simply chuckled.

"Do you understand me now, mutt?" the rough Denzan asked.

At that moment, I was too bewildered to even take exception to this rude-ass alien calling me a mutt. I *could* understand him. I still heard him speaking Denzan, but a split second after he spoke, an echo of his words translated to English played in my ear. The little device he'd shoved in there even did a decent job of matching his tone and timbre—in this case caustic and gruff.

"Wow, yes," I said. Still feeling a bit like my ear was full of water, I instinctively jammed my pinkie in there.

He slapped my hand down. "Don't touch until it's finished calibrating."

I held up my hands. "Okay, man. Not big on personal space on your planet, I take it."

"There's no need to be so rough, Arkell," Vanceval said, gently scolding his fellow Denzan. "Sydneycius and I were just beginning to understand each other." We were not, but okay. "And besides, we prefer to *explain* the personal translator before jamming it into a cadet's head."

Arkell only sniffed in response, turned on his heel, and shuffled out of the corridor.

"He seems nice," I observed.

"You're working with him now?" Tycius asked Reno, his voice low. "Really?"

"The Senate assigned him to me," Reno replied, throwing up her hands. "He's been the *Eastwood*'s engineer for five years, and we haven't had any problems. He's either a changed man or a neutered burnout. Don't much matter to me which. He's given me no cause to transfer him, I'll tell you that. And no, a little rough handling of a cadet isn't going to do the trick."

By the way my uncle's eyes narrowed, I could tell he hadn't planned on this Arkell guy's presence. Him calling me a mutt told me all I needed to know about his opinion of half-Denzans. Before I could eavesdrop on any more of Ty's tense conversation with Reno, Vanceval gently patted my shoulder.

"Young Sydneycius, I am pleased to welcome you aboard the ISV *Eastwood*, a Serpo Institute training vessel," he said. "I am Vanceval, this ship's proctor. My teaching assistant, Aela, will be supervising your orientation as we travel back to Denza." He glanced at the mechanical figure still lingering by the doorway. "Come forward, Aela."

"Cool robot," I said to Vanceval.

"Not a robot," the robot said, their voice a pleasingly generic alto, like a car's GPS.

They came forward, slender as a skeleton, and definitely modeled on Denzan anatomy. The not-a-robot's body was made of a sturdy chrome-colored material. Where their face should have been instead was a glass plate behind which I saw a swirling cloud of magenta gas. Streaks of electricity occasionally flared through the gas, like little bolts of lightning in a storm cloud.

"Glad to meet you, Syd," Aela said, firmly shaking my hand. "I've never been friends with an Earther who shared my place in the life cycle before. New experiences sustain us."

The mechanized voice was endearingly upbeat, so I smiled dumbly, seeing my teeth reflected back in Aela's faceplate. Just because I had a universal translator jammed in my ear didn't mean I had any idea how to talk to new life-forms. I already hadn't hit it off with Arkell, although that didn't seem like my fault. I didn't want to offend anyone else.

"So, if you aren't a robot, you're a . . ."

"I'm a wisp of the Ossho Collective, contained by a mechanized exo-suit." Aela tapped their faceplate, and the cloud inside wiggled in response. "That's me you see in the tank."

"Oh, hello," I said. I was talking to an alien cloud now. Dope.

"I'm very excited to teach you all about my culture," Aela said enthusiastically. "By necessity, that'll be the first part of your orientation."

"Let's not overwhelm the Earther," Vanceval said, then laughed merrily. "I'm kidding. Of *course* let's overwhelm him. Your first voyage into the Vastness! We are going to explode your brain, young Sydneycius."

I didn't necessarily want my brain exploded, but the ancient Denzan seemed so hyped about knowledge that I had a hard time not smiling in response. Before Vanceval and Aela could get any further into my crash course, Reno broke away from Tycius and clapped a hand on my shoulder.

"Do you feel it yet, young buck?" she asked me, grinning.

"Feel what?"

Without warning, her hand slipped off my shoulder and under my armpit. Effortlessly, the old lady lifted me off my feet, dangling me in the air like a doll. So far, I was getting manhandled a lot on the *Eastwood*.

"The strength," she said. "Want to see if you can throw me?"

"Not really," I replied.

Tycius shook his head. "Put him down, Captain. He's only thirty-six hours out. You're going to traumatize the kid."

Reno did set me back down, then ruffled my hair. As she did, I got the sense that she could've squeezed my skull like a ripe orange.

"Welcome to the Vastness, my dear, where you'll discover great power and endless possibility," she said. "You're going to love it."

10

My fingers brushed the leaves of a ghostly pale plant in one of the shelves that lined every hallway on the *Eastwood*. The entire branch curled in my direction and let out a low keening noise, like it wanted me to pet it.

"The *Eastwood*'s onboard AI is capable of producing artificial life support in case of an emergency," Aela explained, the wisp's voice tinny and chipper. "But, under normal conditions, the atmosphere is entirely sustained by the flora you see around the ship."

"Oh," I said, drawing my hand back. I didn't want to mess up the air I was breathing. "Should I not touch them?"

"They're all perfectly safe to touch, or pet, or rub your whole face in," Aela replied happily. "Some are even meant for eating."

Aela paused the tour to pluck a round fruit from a branch that emerged from the wall, tossing it to me. The thing looked like an oversize grape or a small, purplish peach.

"What is it?" I asked.

"A plum," Aela replied, pausing. "I thought they were native to Earth."

"Oh, oh yeah," I replied sheepishly. "I guess I expected everything on here to be extraterrestrial. Didn't expect there to be a random-ass plum tree."

"Random-ass," Aela repeated, testing out the phrase. "Interesting!"

My stomach growled. I hadn't eaten any solid foods since the diner. The drugs I'd taken on the flight here were wearing off, my body's systems waking up. I turned the fruit over in my hand, shaking my head. "You know, I don't think I've ever actually eaten one of these before. I came all the way to Jupiter to eat my first plum."

Aela rounded on me immediately, drawing uncomfortably close. "Your first? Yes! May I watch you eat it?"

I blinked. "Um, sure."

We stood in the hallway between the docking bay and the lavatories, and Aela watched me eat the plum, wiping the juices on my sleeve as I did. The wisp didn't say anything, but the magenta cloud behind their faceplate let off a lot of static shocks, so I think they enjoyed the show.

"Thoughts?"

"I liked it." I felt like I should elaborate. "Sweet. Good, uh . . . good mouthfeel?"

"Excellent!"

Aela moved on, leading me through a sliding wooden door and along a gently curving hallway. A large room opened up on my right. The centerpiece was a circular table definitely meant for family-style dinners. One wall was covered in glowing compartments that looked like microwaves, each filled with ready-made foodstuffs. The only thing I recognized on the meal wall was a dehydrated plate of spaghetti and meatballs.

"The canteen," Aela announced. "The captain likes us to eat our main meal together as a crew, but you can snack whenever you want . . ."

I nodded distractedly at Aela, more interested in the two Denzans seated at the table. They were both my age, with stouter builds than the Denzans I'd encountered so far, shorter and broader of shoulder. They both had bright white hair streaked through with pale blue that had grown long, although the boy kept his tied back in a strict ponytail while the girl let hers squirm about loose. They wore matching outfits, too—dark blue shirts that seemed light and comfortable and gray slacks. Their shirts bore an insignia stitched into the shoulder—a cursive English "E" embossed over an Old West six-shooter. That must have been the symbol for the *Eastwood*.

The girl waved when she saw me and Aela peeking in. She lounged in her seat with a steaming bowl of a pinkish goop that resembled oatmeal. The guy was too engrossed in some work on his paper-thin tablet computer to even notice me.

"Hey there, I'm Melian," she introduced herself warmly. "This is my twin brother, Batzian." She nudged him with her foot when he still didn't look up. "Batzian, it's our new crewmate. You know, the one we came all this way for?"

Sighing, Batzian gave me a once-over. "Where's your uniform?"

"Um, I just got here," I replied.

He gave me a look like that wasn't a good enough excuse. "Yes, well, like my sister said, I'm Batzian. Never Batz. *Batzian.*"

"Got it," I said, knowing that I would almost definitely slip and call him "Batz" within the next day.

"We're actually nice, I swear," Melian said, wagging her spoon at her brother. "Batzian is just stressed because he's in Chief Engineer Arkell's Advanced Thermodynamics class—did you meet Arkell?—anyway, he decided this mission would be a good time to spring a massive lab report on his pupils."

"We aren't supposed to have coursework during missions," Aela said.

"Tell that to Arkell," muttered Batzian.

"He called me a mutt as soon as I got on board," I added. "Don't think I'll be telling him anything."

Melian winced on my behalf, and Batzian looked up at me with renewed interest. The initial reception from him might have been frosty, but I could tell the difference between a genuine dick and a stressed-out overachiever. I didn't take it personally.

"He's always threatening to send us back to the mushroom farm where we grew up," Batzian told me.

"Seems like a great dude," I replied.

"The Earthling is being sarcastic," Aela informed the twins.

"Really?" Batizan replied.

"Oh wow, Aela, we couldn't tell," Melian added with a crooked grin.

Aela turned to me. "Now they're messing with me." The wisp tugged my arm. "Come on. Let's continue the tour."

We said good-bye to the twins and continued down the hall. I'd just met my fifth and sixth Denzans and joked around with them like it wasn't a big deal at all that we were floating inside Jupiter while preparing to return to their home galaxy. I shook my head in disbelief at how quickly I was adjusting to this new reality.

"You seemed comfortable back there," Aela said, as if reading my mind. "Some cadets have trouble with the transition to being around different species."

"I moved around a lot on Earth, so I'm used to being the new kid," I replied. "Dogging an unpopular teacher is a solid way to make friends."

"An interesting sociological observation," Aela said.

We passed through the engineering section. From here, an airlock led off the ring and to the rocket that propelled the *Eastwood*. There was an array of workbenches and tools, spare parts and replacement panels for around the ship. A narrow staircase led up to a second-level office, where, through a window, I spotted Arkell hunched before a network of monitors.

"Seriously, though, what's up with that dude?" I asked, lowering my voice.

Aela shrugged. "He doesn't make the best first impression. Or second. Or third. He did a good job fixing my exo-suit when I got a puncture during a space walk, though."

I rubbed my upper arm. "What's with that thing he wears?"

"His shame?" Aela glanced over their shoulder at me. "You're half-Denzan. Are you not faithful?"

I raised an eyebrow. "Faithful to what?"

"I thought your uncle Tycius would've explained," Aela replied, with a tone like they were happy to be the one delivering this information. "The primary religion on Denza is the Great Shame. According to their lore, eons ago the Denzans did something really, really horrible. It was so bad that it led to planet-wide strife and a dark age. So much time has passed that there aren't even records of what they did, but the shame left an indelible mark on Denzan culture. They practice nonviolence and are extremely conscientious about any harm they cause, whether it be physical or mental. When they do something that they view as negative to society—such as a violent altercation with a stranger or lying to a spouse—they bind a part of themselves until they've repaid their shame."

I thought about the three narrow bands that Tycius wore around his bicep—only two now, actually; he'd removed one on the ride here. My uncle had mentioned his shame back at the diner—maybe that band he'd freed himself of represented how he'd lost track of me. Anyway, Ty's shame seemed like nothing compared to Arkell keeping his whole arm locked up.

"Arkell must have done something really messed up," I said.

"It's not really polite to gossip about, especially not with Denzans," Aela warned me. "It's probably good you didn't mention it around Batzian and Melian. Such a misstep could've hurt your attempts to bond with them."

"Thanks for the heads-up," I said.

The next section of the ship was broken up by a dozen rooms, most of the doors closed, accessible only by handprint scanners.

"These are the crew quarters," Aela said. They stopped in front of a door and gestured for me to press my palm to the scanner. "This one is yours."

After recording my biometric data, the door slid open, revealing a space that was comfortably larger than any of my old bedrooms on Earth. A queen-size bed decorated with shiny, soft-looking sheets jutted out from one wall. I also had a simple metal desk, a couple of lounge chairs, and a whole bunch of leafy green plants. Off to one side was a sliding glass door that led into a private bathroom. The far wall was dominated by a window—more likely a touch screen, like the walls I'd seen on Ty's skiff—currently displaying a view of the wormhole pocket inside Jupiter. There was also a closet full of uniforms, so next time I could look spiffy enough to meet Batzian's approval.

"The *Eastwood* currently does twenty hours of light followed by ten hours of artificial night," Aela said. "Right now, it's what you would think of on Earth as the afternoon. Midshift, we call it. It'll take some getting used to, so don't feel guilty if you need to nap."

Now that Aela mentioned it, I was feeling a bit wrung out—probably a comedown from all the drugs that were pumped into me during our high-speed voyage here. I was far from ready to nap, though. I was in space, chilling with an alien entity contained in a high-tech exo-suit. I wanted to learn *everything*.

"I'm right across the hall here," Aela said, opening the door to their room.

Aela's room was completely empty. No furniture or plants. Nothing. Just the touch screen on the far wall and a bunch of extra vents on the floor and ceiling. I raised an eyebrow.

"I like what you've done with the place," I said.

"Thanks!"

"You don't sleep?"

Aela shook their head. "No. My consciousness doesn't need a reset like you organic creatures. Thank goodness. I don't know how you stand it."

"Sleep is pretty good, actually," I replied. "Definitely one of my top five favorite activities."

"It's a good thing you came to the Vastness," Aela said, "because it sounds like you need to do more stuff."

It was hard to tell with Aela's super-positive voice, but I was pretty sure they were making a joke at my expense, so I laughed. Anyway, they were right—I hadn't gotten to experience much on Earth. Up here, I was going to jump in with both feet. "You said before that we share the same point in the life cycle," I said, the two of us continuing down the corridor. "Does that mean we're the same age?"

"Not exactly. How long have you been alive?"

"I'm sixteen," I said.

"I've only been in this exo-suit as a solitary entity for three years," Aela replied. "But I've amassed the experience of a human roughly your age."

"So you're a toddler."

Aela put their arms out, locked their knees, and waddled. "There actually was a period where I couldn't operate the limbs of my suit." They jumped up and clicked their heels. "Only took me a few weeks to master, though. I'd like to see one of your human toddlers match my moves."

I chuckled. "Me too."

Before we could leave the crew quarters, a clamor erupted from within the cabin at the end of the hall. I noticed that the door to that room had been specially modified to be wider and taller than any of the others. But what was more bewildering were the high-volume shouts emanating from within, each punctuated by punching and crunching sounds.

Someone in there was watching Japanese professional wrestling.

"Whose room is that?" I asked.

Aela hesitated. "Once you've had a chance to settle in, we have a day planned for integration training where you'll get to spend some closely monitored time with the species that are typically difficult for Earthlings to accept. Until then, Captain Reno has asked our Panalax and Vulpin crewmates to remain in their quarters. It's a standard cultural quarantine."

Tycius hadn't mentioned these Panalax guys, but I breezed right by that anyway. I knew what a Vulpin was. I'd seen one attack my mom. Now I found myself staring at that oversize door.

"There's a Vulpin in there? Watching wrestling?"

"No, Zara is down the hall," Aela replied. "That's H'Jossu's room. Our resident Panalax." The wisp tugged at my arm. "We shouldn't linger. He's eager to meet you and . . ."

I heard the wrestling's volume click down, and then something large shuffled toward the door.

"Eager to meet me?" I asked, confused. "Why—?"

"He's a scholar of Earth culture," Aela said. "Now, we should—"

Before the wisp could urge me along, the overlarge doors zipped open.

The Panalax was enormous. It had to be nine feet tall and about four hundred pounds. The thing was like a giant sloth, fur shaggy and matted, long clawed fingers, an ample backside. Its face was more bovine than marsupial, though, with a thick snout like a cow that featured three prominent horns.

All of that I could've handled, I think. But the creature was also very obviously dead and decaying.

H'Jossu was covered in snowy mold, like hummus that had been left in the fridge too long. The growth was focused around his eyes and mouth—filled them, in fact, so that his orifices were just fungal mounds. The mold spread across his massive body and seemed to be holding him together in places. At first, I thought he wore a floral-print shirt like some kind of beach bum cadaver, but those pink flowers were actually sprouting right from his skin. The Panalax looked like he should stink, but I had to admit that he smelled kind of good, like a pine forest air freshener.

He stared at me. I stared at him. I felt hot bile rising in the back of my throat. I wanted to scream and run away, but my feet were frozen to the floor.

"Yes," H'Jossu said, his voice like rustling leaves, emanating from the mold itself. "*Yes*, you are finally here."

"He's not ready for you yet," Aela warned H'Jossu.

The Panalax ignored them and advanced toward me, one of his hooked claws extended in my direction.

"I have so many questions," he rumbled. "First . . ."

Before H'Jossu could finish, I swatted at his claw. Punched at it, really. All I knew, in that moment, was that I needed to keep this monster out of my personal space. Humans have evolved to fear large animals and be repulsed by dead things, so that was my natural reaction when confronted by both. I couldn't stop myself.

My fist struck H'Jossu's outstretched finger with enough force that the entire digit ripped off and flew down the hallway. Aela made a sound like a gasp and put their hands atop their helmet. H'Jossu barked in pain.

I stared down at my fist.

I was getting stronger.

I was getting stronger, and I'd just maimed one of my new crewmates.

11

I braced myself for this undead Chewbacca to retaliate, but H'Jossu only turned to watch his finger fly down the corridor. The severed claw bounced to a stop a few doors away.

I'd wanted to come to the Vastness with an open mind. I'd hoped that my mom's training would have prepared me for anything. But I'd barely been aboard the *Eastwood* for an hour, and I definitely wasn't doing any favors for the reputation of "primitive Earth." I immediately felt bad for letting my instincts take over, and I wanted to say so, but my heart was still pounding and there was cold sweat dripping down my back. He'd really scared the shit out of me.

"Damn, dude," H'Jossu said in his raspy voice. "That was badass. True Earther mind-set. Strike first, ask questions later."

H'Jossu trundled down the hallway. He shoved his finger back onto his paw, a coil of foamy mold securing it. My stomach turned over.

"You scared him," Aela said, scolding H'Jossu. "You were supposed to stay in your quarters. I haven't even had a chance to brief Sydney on your species."

H'Jossu's shoulders sagged. "My bad."

I cleared my throat and finally managed to speak, my voice nearly as scratchy as the Panalax's. "No, I mean, I'm sorry—I, uh, didn't mean to punch your finger off."

H'Jossu flexed his paw. "It's cool. Things fall off me sometimes."

My face felt flushed. I looked down at my hands, clenching the fingers, which vibrated like I'd just smashed a fastball in a baseball game. All my muscles felt like that, actually. Like they were just waking up.

Aela touched my arm. "Are you okay, Syd?"

"I'm not contagious," H'Jossu offered. "Don't worry."

"I'm fine," I replied, pinching the bridge of my nose as I fought off a sudden feeling of vertigo. "Just a lot happening right now."

"I think you broke the Earthling's brain, H," said a silky voice.

In the ruckus with H'Jossu, I hadn't even heard the door behind me hiss open. I glanced over my shoulder and found a Vulpin girl eyeing me. I recoiled immediately and took a stumbling step into the middle of the hallway, trying to keep my distance from this latest extraterrestrial.

"Yep," the Vulpin confirmed. "Definitely broken."

Ever since the memory of my mom's attack resurfaced, I'd

been dwelling on the nightmarish werewolf creature that I'd seen mauling her in the shadows. Honestly, though, this Vulpin wasn't all that scary, especially not compared to H'Jossu. Her skin was bronze where it wasn't covered in patches of rust-colored fur. The fur across her shoulders was styled in a puffed-out shelf that made it look like she was wearing a regal mantle. The Vulpin had a dog-like snout and pinned-back, pointy ears. A bushy tail protruded from her uniform, swishing around behind her. She was about a foot shorter than me and barefoot—barepaw?—her claws clicking idly on the floor.

Basically, she looked like a talking fox straight out of some video game or puppet show. If I hadn't seen how savagely these creatures could behave, I probably would've found her cute, like a cat wearing a sweater.

"You guys are really bad at following orders," Aela said.

"I heard a commotion," the Vulpin said, her hard eyes still fixed upon me. "I thought we might have been boarded by pirates."

"There are no pirates out here, Zara," Aela replied. "You know there aren't pirates."

Zara shrugged. "A girl can hope." She sniffed the air in my direction. "You smell scared, human. You should go wash that off. It's rank."

With that, Zara slid back into her room and closed the door. I begrudgingly sniffed one of my armpits.

"That was Zara," Aela said. "You weren't supposed to meet her yet either. She's—"

"A Vulpin," I said, then quickly added, "My uncle told me about them."

For a moment there, I actually forgot all about H'Jossu. When he rustled a step closer, though, I shot a look in his direction, immediately feeling that revulsion once again. The Panalax stopped trying to come closer.

"Sorry I scared you," he said, clasping his mammoth paws behind his back. "I just—well, I'm a huge fan of Earth."

"You're—?" I rubbed the back of my neck, forcing myself to look at him, completely baffled by his statement. "A fan of *what* exactly?"

"Oh man, where to begin?" H'Jossu sounded relieved and excited that I was talking to him instead of hitting him. "Like, everything?"

"H'Jossu, this really isn't the time," Aela interrupted, the mechanical voice infinitely patient. "We're going to be jumping soon, and I'm supposed to bring Sydney to the bridge. You should secure yourself in your room."

H'Jossu nodded obediently, but then flashed me a grin that looked absolutely hideous on his mold-filled snout. "Total C-3PO vibes from this one, right?"

I forced a laugh and was relieved when Aela took my arm and led me into the next section of the ship. The corridor we entered was empty, and I let loose a long breath, happy to be done with extraterrestrial encounters for now.

"Sorry about that," Aela said, sensing my discomfort. "The captain wanted to work up to you meeting them, but . . ." The wisp opened their hands and shrugged.

"A mold monster and a homicidal fox," I muttered to myself. "These are your new friends."

The audio sensors on Aela's exo-suit must've been pretty strong. "Those are some harmful stereotypes I'd be careful about, Syd." The wisp paused. "Although Zara *is* a touch homicidal. How did you know that?"

"Wild guess," I replied.

One section later, we reached the *Eastwood*'s bridge. The nerve center of the ship was a circular room with a ring of chairs and consoles, all of them arranged around two central projections. The first was a holographic diagnostic of the *Eastwood*; I didn't know what any of the floating symbols and readings meant, but the fact that there weren't any flashing red lights or sirens seemed to indicate everything on board was in working order. The second projection was a complicated map of the cosmos and its interlocking systems. A blue line indicated our flight path. Over the next fourteen days, we'd be popping through three different galaxies before finally reaching Denza.

Reno and Ty were already on the bridge, seated at consoles next to each other. Ty's eyes were heavy-lidded, his arms crossed and legs stretched out, looking like he might nod off at any moment. Probably suffering from the same rocket lag that was beginning to wear on me. Reno was parked in front of a monitor displaying a high-resolution live feed of Earth. There were two teenage humans, a guy and a girl, peering over her shoulder.

"That's where I was born," Reno was saying when I walked in. "A place called Florida."

"Looks like a dick," the guy said.

"Language, Cadet."

"Looks like a penis."

"Do you miss it, Captain?" the girl asked quietly.

"Hell no, I do not," Reno replied brusquely. "You know how much shit I had to eat on a day-to-day basis back there, first in the air force and then at NASA? My goodness. Even if I *could* go back, it wouldn't be until they put all the women in charge." She spun in her chair, noticing that I'd entered. "They do that yet, Cadet? Put the women in charge?"

"Uh, no, Captain, I don't think so," I replied.

"Then I'll stick to the Vastness, honey," Reno said. She waved a hand across her console, wiping away the image of Earth.

The human guy with Reno strode toward me with his hand thrust out. I don't think I've ever used this word before, but the dude was a total beefcake. He was my age, yet already more than six feet tall, blond-haired and broad-shouldered, his skin tanned golden. He looked like a Ken doll, basically. On Earth, he'd already have college football coaches chasing after him, promising a bright future as a keg-standing tight end.

"Hiram Butler." He introduced himself and immediately yanked me into a bro-hug with a back pat that was hard enough to make me hiccup. "Welcome to the crew, new guy."

It took me a second to realize he wasn't speaking English but fluent Denzan. Thinking back on how he'd been studying the image of Earth with Reno, I quickly put two and two together. This guy hadn't been born on Earth; he'd been born on Denza. I couldn't help but wonder if I'd look like Hiram if I'd grown up never knowing anything but supernatural strength. His last name was familiar, too. Rafe Butler was the hairy guy in the photograph with my grandfather. They must be related.

"Syd Chambers," I introduced myself. After Zara and H'Jossu, I was relieved to meet another human, even if his grip crushed my hand. "Excited to be here."

"Can't wait to learn all about our ancestral homeland," Hiram said. I thought I saw him rolling his eyes as he turned away from me.

The girl who had been standing with Hiram hung back with Reno. She wore a baggy sweatshirt with the hood pulled up over her uniform. There was something about her that I recognized. Maybe it was because, back on Earth, antisocial had been one of my default modes.

"Darcy Ward," she finally introduced herself after a nudge from the captain. "Hey."

"How'd the tour go?" Reno asked Aela, who was still standing at my side.

"I believe Sydney can now navigate the ship on his own," Aela announced proudly. "He also encountered Zara and H'Jossu earlier than planned, but at least that means he's now met the whole crew. We are ahead of schedule!"

I appreciated that Aela left out the bit where I punched off part of H'Jossu's paw. "Wait. That's the whole crew? This giant ship runs with only a dozen people?"

"A captain, a first officer, a chief engineer, a proctor, and eight cadets." Aela ticked them off on their fingers. "More than enough, actually."

"The ship's AI handles the real difficult stuff," Reno told me, then hit a button on her console. "Arkell? How we looking?"

Arkell's voice crackled over the microphone, gloomy and curt. "All systems go, Captain."

"Did you scan for Etherazi activity?" Reno asked into the comm.

"Of course I did," Arkell snapped back.

"Whoa, there, don't get snitty with me," Reno responded, turning off her comm. "Wish we could replace *him* with an AI."

Tycius stirred at the mention of Etherazi. "Have there been any sightings?" he asked.

"Nope," Reno replied. "Been at least a year, and the institute's cracked open eight new galaxies in that time. Maybe we finally eradicated the suckers."

"Of course the Etherazi would disappear when I finally get into the Vastness," Hiram complained, cracking his knuckles. "I never get to do anything cool."

"Cool," my uncle repeated dryly. "Battling interdimensional horrors that threatened to execute an entire species is cool. Beasts that would've driven our entire planet mad. Creatures that feed on misery."

"Technically, we don't know what the Etherazi feed on, or even what they call themselves," Aela said in my ear. "They're named for a Denzan myth about sea serpents that swallowed up the first explorers."

"Fun fact," I whispered back, focused on the exchange between Hiram and my uncle.

"I misspoke, sir," Hiram said, acting chastened. But as soon as Tycius turned his attention elsewhere, he muttered to Darcy, "The new first mate is a real douche."

I chose to ignore Hiram's comment, but the guy was definitely in the running with Arkell for biggest dickhead I'd met in space.

Reno punched some instructions into her console, then began an announcement that echoed over all the ship's comms. "All hands, prepare for intergalactic travel." She turned in my direction. "First time through a wormhole can be a little trippy. You might want to grab a seat."

I looked around at the unoccupied spots on the bridge and noticed that one of them was very unlike the others. The chair sat beneath a complicated mechanism that hung down from the ceiling—it was like a chandelier with a pair of goggles at the end. The thing reminded me of the multilens binoculars they used on you at the eye doctor, except these had the complexity of a nuclear reactor. Fanned out from the goggles were dozens of screens, all currently displaying empty expanses of space.

As I edged closer to the high-tech device, Darcy brushed past me. "Can't sit there," she said quietly. "That's the Wayscope."

Aha. So that was the machine I'd be using to locate my father. Without thinking, I touched the ring case in my front pocket. "Oh cool," I said to Darcy when I realized she was still looking at me.

"Sure, it's cool," she muttered. "If they let you use it."

I didn't know what Darcy meant, but the bitterness in her words made me take a closer look at her as she sat down next to

Hiram. Her eyes were wider than normal, her fingers long, and the dark hair she tried to keep hidden beneath her hood glowed with a fluorescent sheen.

She was half-Denzan, too. Duh. My uncle had mentioned there'd be someone like me aboard.

Apparently, I was just standing there like a goofball, first staring at the Wayscope and then at Darcy. "Syd," my uncle called. "Come on."

I grabbed a seat between him and Aela.

"You okay?" he asked.

"Just . . ." I nodded my chin toward Darcy. "She's . . ."

"A hybrid," Tycius said. "Born on Denza to a human father and Denzan mother."

Before I could ask any follow-up questions, I felt a pressure on my sternum as the *Eastwood* subtly picked up speed.

"Say good-bye to the Milky Way, Cadet," Captain Reno shouted to me.

A vid-screen that encompassed the far wall activated, displaying a live feed from the front of the *Eastwood*'s rocket. We were surging right into that rip in space, a place that both *was* and *wasn't*, an invisible bridge between moments. For the moment, I forgot all about Darcy, the Wayscope, and all the other weirdos I'd met on board. I couldn't look away.

We sailed into the wormhole. The lights on the bridge suddenly seemed solid, lances of illumination bouncing off my body. Some of the plants on the wall curved in on themselves while others expanded, leaves floating outward, bleeding into the wooden panels of the walls. I looked at my uncle—his eyes were impossibly wide, an almost euphoric expression on his face. I felt like I blinked out of existence, like *everything* blinked out of existence. I had the sensation of falling upward, of swimming into a gaping chasm, of time itself coming apart. All in the space of a breath.

And then it was over.

"Whoa," I said.

"Jump complete, all systems normal," Arkell reported over the comm. "Four mission days until our next jump."

I stared at the screen. The raging storm of Jupiter, the pocket of calm around its hidden wormhole—it was all gone. What replaced it now was the Vastness. Space. Stars. The constellations were different, rearranged in a way that would've driven an astronomer nuts, although the space on this side of the wormhole, to me, looked pretty much the same as what we'd left behind. But I knew.

I knew I was in another galaxy.

"This system is called Hindra," Aela offered helpfully from my side. "The sun's a white dwarf. Three planets, all of them iced over. All fully surveyed by the Serpo Institute."

"It's a backwater," Hiram said with a sigh. "Nothing to see for half a week."

"You should get some rest," Tycius said to me. "You look beat."

"Yeah, sure," I replied. "In a second."

The others gradually filtered out, but I hung around on the bridge for a while, first waiting for the dying sun of this new galaxy to become visible, then staring into the bluish-silver star until my eyes got heavy. It was really sinking in. I was far away from home.

Or maybe the *Eastwood* was home now. Or maybe the Serpo Institute would be.

Or maybe the stars themselves.

Eventually, I drifted back to my room, this time without getting jumped by H'Jossu. The air in my cabin was cool and crisp, the lights already set at a warm dimness perfect for napping. I played around with the touch screen on my wall until I figured out how to bring a vid-feed of Hindra's white dwarf on-screen. The new sun would be my night-light.

I took my father's ring out of my pocket. The cosmological tether. I held the gold band between my fingers and peered into the gemstone, studying the blinking stars and swirling cosmos captured within.

"When I'm away, you'll be able to look in here and find me . . ." That's what my dad had told me. The promise that I dreamed of for so many years. Destiny.

It didn't even have to be that big of a thing. I didn't need a whole destiny.

I'd settle for an identity.

I'd been so many different people on Earth, lived in so many different places. But none of that was ever permanent. Sixteen years old, and I was still getting used to the idea of being Syd Chambers.

"I'll find you, Dad," I said aloud. "I'll find us both."

12

After the Jupiter wormhole, I slept for what felt like an eternity. When I finally staggered zombielike out of my bed, the vid-screen on my wall lit up with an incoming call from the bridge.

"Do you accept?" a mechanical voice asked.

"Uh, sure," I replied.

My uncle Tycius appeared on-screen, looking more than a little refreshed himself, his hair smoothed back in a neat ponytail.

"You're awake," he observed.

"Barely," I replied. "How did you know?"

"The ship's been monitoring your vitals for the last twenty-four hours. The comedown from the high-speed travel drugs can be intense."

"Twenty-four—?" I stretched and, as I did, felt a steadily building pressure in my bladder. "Damn. Was I in a coma?"

"Get yourself together," Tycius said. "Aela will be by soon to continue your orientation. I don't mean to rush you, but it's required."

After a pee that lasted longer than most sitcoms, I attempted to take my first shower since Earth. Operating the touch screen proved difficult, though, mainly because I forgot about my developing superstrength and jabbed my index finger right through the glass and into the wall. Sparks belched through the crack in the screen, but at least the hot water came on.

"Damage detected," declared the ship's AI. "A report has been made to engineering."

"Uh-oh," I said to myself cheerfully as I let the hot water pound the top of my head. It felt great to get cleaned up. I wasn't sure if the water on the *Eastwood* was crisper and more refreshing than the polluted stuff on Earth, or if it was the newfound vitality coursing through me.

Either way, I felt amazing.

The door to my room chimed just as I finished getting my uniform on. I'd been expecting Aela, but instead got Arkell. The ship's engineer glowered at me, a replacement panel for the one I'd broken tucked under his arm.

"Morning—er . . . afternoon?" My good vibes barely faltered under the glare from the scarred Denzan. "Sorry about the wall. I literally don't know my own strength."

"An untrained animal making a mess in the house," Arkell muttered as he brushed by me.

"Okay, well, I'll leave you to your work and casual racism,"

I replied, popping into the hallway when I saw Aela's door open across the way.

"Yes! I know that look!" Aela declared when they saw me. "It's the look of a young hybrid male ready to begin learning about our universe's many interesting species."

I smiled at the swirling cloud behind the faceplate. "Wow. You really are great at reading organic facial expressions."

"I know!" Aela replied. "Are you ready?"

"Sure. Which way to the lecture hall?"

Aela cocked their head. "Who said anything about a lecture? I'll be putting you into a dreamlike state and guiding you through a tour of the galaxy's major species."

"A dreamlike state," I repeated.

"A bit like an out-of-body experience," Aela replied.

I shook out my limbs. "I think I just had one of those."

"Excellent! Then you're adequately prepared."

Aela led me into their empty room, closing the door behind us. The wisp called up a touch screen on the wall and inputted some instructions. The walls and door shivered with a hydraulic hiss, like we were being sealed within a plastic bag.

"To do this, I have to leave my exo-suit. My chemistry is a very fragile thing," Aela explained. "Any contaminants in the air could damage my structure and cause me to lose experiences." They paused. "Do you want to take your clothes off?"

"Do I—?" I squinted at the wisp. "Why would I want to do that?"

"The room is going to sterilize you," Aela said. "You're going to get wet."

"I just took a shower."

"That was a waste of time." Aela made an excited *hurry up* gesture. "Naked or not?"

I glanced up at the vents in the ceiling. "Clothes on, if that's okay."

"Suit yourself," Aela said. "Ready?"

"Rea—"

With a whoosh, vents above and below let loose bursts of steam. The room was suddenly humid, filled with a smell like fresh aloe. Puffs of air burst toward me from every direction. My eyes stung, so I squeezed them shut until the process was over. For about ten seconds, it felt like I was standing in the middle of a car wash. At the end, my clothes were heavy with moisture, and my skin felt completely scoured.

"Whew," I said. "I don't think I've ever been this clean in my life."

"Interesting!"

Aela checked the touch screen, verifying that the room was free of contaminants. I pushed a hand through my dripping hair.

"Perfect," Aela said. "Now, just relax and breathe me in."

"Breathe you in?"

"Did I not mention?" Aela brought their palm up to where their forehead would be. "Simply put, what I'm going to do is enter your body and then fire your brain's synapses to share my experiences with you."

I laughed. "Get out."

"I will not," Aela replied. "Ready?"

Maybe most people would've asked for more clarification here, before huffing a sentient gaseous entity of extraterrestrial origin. But I'd woken up on the right side of the damn bed. There wasn't anything I couldn't handle.

I shrugged. "What the hell? Let's do it."

Aela's faceplate popped open. The exo-suit went limp as the cloud rolled slowly free of their metallic limbs. Aela wasn't much bigger than a basketball. The magenta puff infused with little lightning strikes floated slowly in my direction.

"Weirdest thing I've seen yet," I remarked. "Congratulations."

The cloud didn't reply. I took a breath, and, as I did, Aela zipped forward, their body shaping itself into two tendrils that shot directly up my nose. For the briefest of moments, my ears popped, and I smelled burned toast.

And then I was floating in space without a space suit.

Even though I knew on some level that this was all in my head—a lucid dream directed by Aela—I still started to panic a bit, holding my breath and ineffectually flailing my limbs. There wasn't anything for me to swim toward, emptiness all around me, but I guessed swinging my arms like helicopter propellers was my go-to reaction when finding myself in the vacuum of space.

"Easy, now, you're okay"—that was Aela's voice in my ear, similar to the generic robot voice of their exo-suit, but far more melodious and lively.

Satisfied that I wasn't going to immediately suffocate, I flipped head over heels. Below me—well, above me, now in front of me—was a gargantuan version of Aela. The enormous, planet-size gas cloud blotted out the stars. The streaks of lightning that ripped through its roiling shape looked big enough to level mountains.

"Oh damn," I said, realizing that I could talk normally in this simulated space. "Aela? Is that you?"

"This is the Ossho Collective," the cloud responded. "As Aela, I am a wisp, a mere fragment separated from the greater collective. You are looking at the whole—*the us*—as we are currently progressing through the Lambda-6 star system."

I squinted. "Your people just float out here all the time?"

"The Ossho Collective aren't people; we are one," Aela corrected me. "Ever since we first achieved sentience three millennia ago, our primary drive has been to explore the stars and observe. To experience and remember."

"So you drift around looking for cool shit?"

"Pretty much," Aela replied. "Twenty years ago, we tentatively approached the planet Denza. We're always wary of getting close to societies that might view our appearance as apocalyptic, even though we mean them no harm."

"I could see how a giant purple cloud filled with lightning might freak some people out," I mused.

"Lucky for us, the Denzans were more curious than hostile. They learned how to communicate with us and constructed the first exo-suits so that we might walk among them. Thanks to the Denzans, we can now place portions of ourselves into suits, exploring farther and faster than before. Individuality is still a new concept to us, but we like it."

I swam a little closer to the Ossho cloud, using my willpower more than my arms or legs. "So you used to be part of this big thing, but you split off."

"I became a wisp," Aela replied. "Eventually, when I feel that

I have seen enough, I'll return to the Ossho and share my experiences with the collective. You'll be stored there too, Syd. Or my memories of you will be."

My brow furrowed at that. "Doesn't that mean you'll stop existing?"

"As I am now, yes, but I'll also be whole again," Aela replied. "I'm only a fraction of myself right now."

I tried to wrap my head around that. Aela basically got to live forever as a spacefaring fog composed of millennia's worth of memories. That seemed like a better deal than getting eaten by worms or cremated and stuffed in an urn. But it still oddly bummed me out to think of Aela getting absorbed back into the collective.

"You're making a strange face," Aela observed. "Do you have questions?"

I shook my head. "No, no. Just coming to grips with the pointlessness of existence, I guess."

"Neat," the massive cloud replied. "I'm going to move us on to an overview of the Denzans."

A dark blue planet zoomed into view. Denza. The home world of my father and Tycius. Denza was roughly the same distance from its sun as Earth was to Sol, but it was significantly smaller than my home planet. Also, I noted, it was orbited by five small moons, the satellites crisscrossing one another in an endless looping helix. There weren't any significant landmasses on Denza. Instead, the planet was composed of one massive archipelago.

"This is the view the Ossho Collective had when they first

approached Denza," Aela said. "I'm going to transition us between memories now. It might be disorienting."

I felt like I was in a movie that had just cut from one scene to the next. My feet plunked down into soft sand. Suddenly, we weren't floating in space but were standing on a moonlit beach. Purplish water lapped at the shore, the air tangy with salt. Boats glowed as they traversed the reefs. On the horizon, a bullet-shaped capsule streaked soundlessly across a high-speed rail line that connected two far-out islands. Behind me, inland, were buildings constructed right into the cliff face, the stone hollowed out, doorways connected by ultonate bridges. There were gleaming towers nestled in the shadow of the cliff, and then, closer to the beach, blocks of quaint cottages. The place was part futuristic metropolis and part seaside resort.

One of Denza's nickel-colored moons loomed overhead, a ring of fire lapping at its edges. It took me a moment to realize that we were in the midst of an eclipse.

"I love this spot," Aela said.

I glanced to my right and found Aela transformed yet again. They weren't a cloud or an exo-suit now, but something else. Humanoid in shape, Aela stood a few inches taller than me, with broad shoulders and curving hips. Their skin was the color of lightning, and their flowing mane of hair was swirling magenta, trailing off behind them like the tail of a comet.

"Whoa," I said. "You changed."

Aela smiled at me. "Is this okay? The Ossho have found that it's easier for humans to absorb information when it's delivered by something more representative of organic life."

I rubbed my eyes. Aela's new form was simultaneously striking and elegant, like a sculpture that changed shape depending on what angle you looked at it from. Maybe it was because we were in mind-space, so my body's natural fight-or-flight instinct didn't take over like it had with H'Jossu and Zara, but Aela's form put me at ease.

"It's cool," I said. "How'd you choose that form?"

"Good question!" Aela replied, brushing their hands down their simple cotton T-shirt like they were flattered I'd asked. "It's hard to explain, but this is—well, I suppose this is a manifestation of how I feel as an individual. If I could design an exo-suit, it would look like this body."

Aela waded into the water, and I noticed for the first time that we were both barefoot. I followed them, the ocean warm and frothy, filled with speedy neon starfish that flitted about our feet like we weren't even there. Because, well, we weren't really there.

"So, this is someone's memory?" I asked.

"It's a memory that a Denzan shared with the Ossho Collective and that was loaned to me when I became a wisp," Aela replied.

I kicked at the water, amazed to see foam splash up from my toes. "How come we can move around like it's virtual reality? Shouldn't we be stuck in the point of view of whoever really experienced this?"

"We could go into first-person mode if we wanted," Aela replied. "Some memories have more complete sensory information than others, and that lets me reconstruct them with room for us to mess around."

I glanced farther down the beach. There were some Denzans spread out on the sand, others waist-deep in the water, dragging nets through the waves to collect creatures.

"Are the Denzans nocturnal?" I asked.

"No, this is actually daytime," Aela explained. "Because of the orbiting moons, most areas on Denza only receive about six hours of direct sunlight per day. There's an eclipse every few hours here."

I put my hands on my hips and took in a lungful of warm air. "I could get used to this."

"You'll be here in the flesh soon enough," Aela replied. Then their voice turned grim. "I'm afraid what I have to show you next isn't so pleasant. It's a requirement for all Earthlings recruited into the institute, though."

I raised my eyebrows. In the short time I'd known Aela, I'd never heard their voice go any lower than chipper. "What is it?"

"You have to see why the First Twelve were brought here," Aela replied. "You have to see the Etherazi."

The scene changed again.

We stood on a tower rooftop looking down at the same seaside Denzan city. The time of day had changed—the sun fully out from behind the moons, Denzans frolicking in the sand and surf. The place still struck me as serene, which made the gnawing feeling of dread in my belly all the worse. Because I knew Aela was going to show me something bad.

"The mere sight of an Etherazi is often enough to drive a Denzan mad," Aela told me. "Because you're a hybrid and because this is just a memory, you should be fine. But if it gets to be too much for you—"

"I'll be okay," I replied, squaring my shoulders. "I want to see."

"The Denzans developed a warning system for Etherazi attacks," Aela continued. "The creatures have a highly unique energy signature, and Denzans could detect them by changes in the local atmosphere. But even that system only gave them about a five-minute head start."

Sirens blared throughout the city, shattering the peace. People on the beach began to flee for shelter. A fleet of pyramid-shaped skiffs took off from one of the towers in the town center, the ships zipping down to pick up as many Denzans as possible.

"Their only option was evacuation," Aela continued. They pointed. "See it?"

Of course I did.

The Etherazi came from out of the ocean. It was under the water, but the scales on its back were visible. Maybe "scales" wasn't the most accurate way of describing it. The monster's carapace resembled spiky, overlapping plates, but they weren't exactly solid. Instead, they had a consistency that reminded me of the flickering blue flame on a gas stove. I squinted and pinched the bridge of my nose; even only seeing its back, it hurt my head to try making sense of the Etherazi.

"There have been no successful studies of Etherazi anatomy," Aela said. "When they're killed, they combust in on themselves and leave no remains. As best as we can tell, they exist in a state of flux, between universes, outside of time, composed at least partially of psychic energy."

There were still boats stuck out on the water. When the Etharazi passed beneath them—passed through them—they completely unraveled. Their planks and fittings broke apart and separated. Power sources exploded.

"How does it . . . ?" I shook my head, trying to focus. "Why does it hurt to look at?"

"The Etharazi defy all laws of physics and accepted mathematical principles. Your half-Denzan brain has trouble processing that. Meanwhile, a full Denzan . . ."

Down on the beach, many of the Denzans who weren't quick enough to evacuate collapsed onto their knees at the sight of the approaching Etherazi. They grasped at their temples and clawed at their eyes. Others reacted even worse, turning on one another, pummeling their friends with wild blows.

"Fuck," I whispered. "They're losing their minds."

"Survivors would say that their very notion of the world was stripped away," Aela confirmed grimly. "They become ruled by their most primal instincts—fear and rage."

The Etherazi made land, rising out of the ocean with a gleeful shriek. Despite the fact that this was all a shared memory, I stumbled back a step in fear.

The thing was huge. Bigger than any of the buildings in the Denzan city, although its energy-based form seemed to expand and contract at will, so it wasn't clear exactly how huge it could get. Regardless, it was some real kaiju shit.

My brain was freaking out, trying to come to terms with the Etherazi's form, to put it into some kind of context.

"It looks like a dragon," I said aloud.

Aela nodded. "Yeah, that's how some people interpret their shapes. Dragons, dinosaurs, mythological serpents. Very angry whales."

Even though it was composed of some kind of incomprehensible energy, the Etherazi still had a distinctly reptilian vibe about it. All jutting angles and sharp edges, overlapping scales, a long neck, six legs, massive wings, and a horned, snakelike head. All those details came and went, though. Sometimes the Etherazi was nothing more than a roiling energy ball, with no more defined shape than a cloud in the sky.

The marauder swiped one of its spiked appendages down on some Denzans who had been too slow evacuating the beach. They weren't smashed or crushed—instead, the Etherazi passed right through them. Some of the Denzans disintegrated, reduced to nothing but bleached skeletons, those bones crumbling into the sand. Others, though, were changed.

Where a man had stood, seconds ago, there was now a baby, crying and screaming. A woman nearby—she couldn't have been more than a teenager, I swear—was now suddenly old, her frail legs buckling beneath her as the Etherazi passed her by.

"What the hell just happened?" I asked.

"Temporal anomaly," Aela said. "The Etherazi's touch transplants a victim to another point in their life cycle. For the ones who survive, the effect wears off eventually, although I've heard the experience is cripplingly traumatic."

I ran a hand through my hair, staring at the writhing baby that used to be a man. "No shit."

The Etharazi trampled on from the beach, reaching the nearest block of cottages. When it touched them, the buildings simply unmade themselves, the lumber transforming back into trees, the windows reduced to grains of sand and blown away.

"It returns civilization to a state . . . a state *before*," Aela said. "That seems to be their purpose. Some theoreticians believe they feed off the energy expelled from temporal chaos."

Curiously, when the Etherazi reached the downtown area, its touch had no effect on one of the skyscrapers reinforced with ultonate. This only seemed to piss off the beast. It tipped its head back and let loose a piercing shriek. Its body seemed to solidify.

"The ultonate's nanoparticles were programmed with the Etherazi in mind," Aela explained. "They provide a temporal anchor."

"Why didn't they put that stuff on all the buildings?" I asked.

The Etherazi tilted its head to the side and lunged forward, taking a massive bite out of the skyscraper, ripping girders free. The building collapsed in seconds.

"Because it didn't stop them," Aela said.

Insane. The Etherazi first wreaked havoc from outside our reality but could, when it felt like it, become corporeal enough that it could straight-up thunder-stomp buildings like a more traditional monster. I shook my head.

"How *do* you stop them?" I asked, thinking of my grandfather, the war hero. "How did a bunch of random humans . . . ?"

Aela pointed toward the edge of the town. "Here they come."

While hundreds of skiffs fled the wrath of the Etherazi, a

single intergalactic cruiser flew in the opposite direction, coming in hot. The ship pulled up short before it got too close to the Etherazi, slowing just enough that four boxy shapes could drop from its belly.

"Are those . . . ?"

"Humans," Aela said. "Some of the First Twelve."

The humans all wore intimidating mechanized suits. In their armored shells, they stood about ten feet tall. As soon as they hit the ground, two of them opened fire on the Etherazi using forearm-mounted laser cannons. The energy beams seemed to hurt the creature—or at least annoy it—enough so that it turned in their direction and advanced. When it did, the two humans not laying down cover fire took to the skies, the height of their jumps augmented by propulsion systems in their boots.

"Their armor—Battle-Anchors—are lined with ultonate to prevent temporal disruptions," Aela explained.

"Why didn't the Denzans just make an army of armored dudes?" I asked. "I mean, I get that they've advanced beyond violence or whatever, but if anything would make me want to fight, it'd be a giant monster turning my friends into dust."

"The suits weigh nearly half a ton," Aela said. "The Denzans needed a species with humanity's strength to successfully wield them. Not to mention, the bluntness of a human mind can handle direct contact with an Etherazi's form. There's even evidence that humans are resistant to the temporal disruptions. An army of armored Denzans would all go nuts."

I rubbed the back of my head. "Never thought my 'blunt' brain would be an advantage."

"Victory still wasn't guaranteed . . ."

As I watched, the Etherazi raised one of its clawed limbs and swatted down an approaching Battle-Anchor, spiking the human into the street below. Was that my grandfather down there? Captain Reno?

"How do they actually kill one of those things?" I asked.

"I told you that the Etherazi exist partly out of sync with time and space. But there's always a piece of them that is here, tangible, in our reality. It's the core. The heart, I guess. One just has to reach it and . . . well, blow it up. Stab it to death. Kick it a bunch. All of the above."

One of the charging astronauts reached the Etherazi. A lance of pure energy erupted from the Battle-Anchor's forearm and spiked into the creature's side. Then the human pushed farther, following its lance into the Etherazi's body until it disappeared. This seemed to infuriate the Etherazi—the creature curled in on itself, trying to shake loose the human that had burrowed under its "skin."

"Damn," I said. "Intense."

"After the humans thinned their numbers, the Etherazi retreated from Denza," Aela said. "Luckily, we don't see much of them anymore. There hasn't been a battle like this in years."

I breathed a sigh of relief, but I couldn't take my eyes off the scene below. Two of the humans were still blasting the Etherazi with concentrated fire, while the third one was just now picking himself up from the ground.

Aela turned away from the fray to look directly at me. "I'm

supposed to impress this upon you. The Serpo Institute welcomes humanity to intergalactic society to learn and flourish, but you must never forget that you may be called to an even greater purpose. Do you accept that?"

It was a total nerd fantasy to get stuffed into a mech-suit and fight a rampaging monster. But seeing the destruction done by the Etherazi—dead Denzans littered the beach and streets—the prospect didn't seem fun or thrilling. Godzilla would've sucked if you had to focus on all the poor Japanese people he smooshed. I remembered the eager bravado in Hiram's voice on the bridge when the Etherazi came up. I couldn't understand how someone could see a battle like this and wish they were there.

"I hope I never see one of these bastards," I said quietly. "But yeah. If they show up again, I'll fight."

13

"I got a report from Arkell that you punched a hole in the wall of my ship," Captain Reno said.

I'd been summoned to the captain's quarters shortly after my orientation with Aela. Reno's room wasn't any bigger than mine, but it definitely looked more lived-in. There was a bearskin carpet (or, well, I thought it was a bear, but it could've been some alien beast) and wall hangings that depicted scenes out of Greek mythology. Stuff like Icarus flying too close to the sun and Zeus taking on the shape of a bull to creep on girls. Reno also had an extremely well-stocked liquor cart.

I clasped my hands behind my back. Spending the last few hours with Aela in mind-space or whatever it was, I hadn't had to think about the changes to my body. But now, I once again felt coiled and antsy.

"It wasn't a punch," I said softly. "More like I poked a hole in the screen. A *small* hole. By accident."

Reno seemed more amused than anything. "We all went through that, coming off Earth for the first time. None of us were used to the power. You're lucky that I'm here to guide you. I'd just gotten a new puppy when NASA picked me for the Serpo Project. They let me bring him into the Vastness. A week in, I stroked poor Mittens so hard that one of his eyeballs popped clean out."

I stared at her. "What."

"Your face, my goodness. I'm yanking your chain, Cadet," Reno said, shaking her head. "Come with me. I'll sort you out."

The captain brought me over to the *Eastwood*'s gym. Mostly, the equipment was pretty standard—weights, resistance, cardio—albeit built for various-size creatures. I did note some standing chunks of wood that had been shredded with claw marks. Probably how Zara the Vulpin filed her nails.

"See, you got used to life as an Earthbound weakling," Reno explained. "You punch a wall there, you maybe put a hole in the drywall and bust up your hand. Here? In the Vastness? You punch a wall, you could bring down a building."

I thought about how I'd lopped off one of H'Jossu's fingers during my tour of the *Eastwood*. I swallowed, feeling a bit like a loaded gun.

"It's okay," Reno continued. "You'll get used to it. You just have to relearn how to be gentle. And that means, first and foremost, knowing your limits."

To start, she made me lift weights, ticking new pressure plates onto the bar with every set, until I was benching a little more than half a ton. Reno kept forcing me to do more reps until the lifting became almost hypnotic—I was coated in sweat, and my muscles ached, but they didn't feel close to breaking down.

Then she got out a case of racquetballs.

"Brought these just for you," Reno said, tying her silvering curls back in a ponytail. "Well, actually, I kinda enjoy this game, too. Your grandfather always said I had a bit of a sadistic streak."

"What are you—?"

At that point, she started whipping the racquetballs at me, forcing me to catch them. If I brought my hands up too fast or squeezed too tight, the balls would explode in my bare hands. Reno really gunned those things too—it was like standing in front of a pitching machine. My palms stung, and the balls I misjudged left red welts on my arms and chest. At first, I destroyed more balls than I saved, but by the end my touch was lighter and I was able to lob the intact balls back to Reno.

After about an hour of that, Reno wrung out her shoulder.

"I'm almost eighty years old, Cadet, give me a break," she said, sitting down on the edge of a bench. The woman sure didn't look eighty, or act like it. Being out in the Vastness was like the fountain of youth. "I meant to ask, how's your mom doing?"

The question caught me off guard. It'd been almost a week since I'd left my mom on Earth. I'd been so busy, I hadn't had much time to think about what she might be doing back there.

"You know, it was hard on her when I left," I said, shrugging, not sure how deep I wanted to get into it with Reno. "We'd been on the run for so long, I bet she doesn't know what to do with herself now."

"She's a tough one. I'm sure she'll figure it out," Reno said.

"Not that I ever got to meet the woman. Just what I heard. She tell you anything about me?"

I puzzled over that question for a second. My mom had mentioned Reno as one of the humans who was helping her and my dad with their far-out plan to basically invade Earth. But what really stuck out to me was how my mom reacted when Tycius told her Reno would be my captain. She'd pulled a face like she wanted to barf.

Reno detected my hesitation. "Your grandpa and I got close on Denza," she said. "Not saying it was some grand love affair or anything. But when you fight a war together, you know, feelings get heightened. After the war, we shacked up for a few years until he heard your grandma got sick. Then he went running back to Earth." She shook her head. "Noble idiot decided he'd go ahead and die there."

I never knew my grandma. She'd died of cancer before I was born. But now my mom's distaste for Reno made sense.

"Yeah," I said, looking around awkwardly. "She didn't tell me any of that."

Reno chuckled. "Ah, well. Listen to me getting sentimental in my old age." She massaged her shoulder. "She must've told you about our hopes for Earth. About why finding your father is so important. I'd have plugged you into that Wayscope as soon as you got on board, but Tycius says you need training first."

I thought of the cosmological tether that contained my dad's coordinates. I was supposed to keep it a secret, so I'd hidden the box in one of the planters in my room. I'd already taken it out of the dirt twice, brushed it off, and checked to make sure the light hadn't gone out. They wanted to locate my dad in the hopes that he'd discovered those mythical Lost People and a cure for the Wasting. I just wanted to find him.

"Imagine if everyone on Earth could feel the way you're feeling now," Reno continued, eyeing me. "Imagine if the old biddies my age down there, dragging oxygen tanks on the backs of their scooters, could live like I do."

"There'd be a lot of holes getting punched in a lot of walls," I replied. I'd meant it as a joke, but the words came out flat. Just like when my mom first told me about her plan, the whole thing gave me a strange feeling—like I was part of something secret and dangerous. It didn't feel quite right. "Anyway, you guys aren't talking about making people on Earth stronger and healthier. You're talking about sending enhanced humans back to rule the rest."

Reno smiled at me. "That's the half-Denzan in you, honey. Worried about making waves. Our entire species would be uplifted, in time."

"You're assuming my dad even found anything," I replied.

Reno nodded. "It's a long shot. I know."

"I just want to know why he left us. I want answers."

"Same here, Cadet. Same here." Reno patted her thighs and stood up. "Hot shower time for me. You, on the other hand, need to keep working out. Until you've adjusted to the power, exhaustion is the best way to keep you from accidentally maiming one of your crewmates."

I winced. "You heard about that."

"Sure," Reno replied. "H'Jossu thought it was *dope*, apparently.

Whatever that means."

Before the Captain left, she inputted some commands into a touch screen, and what looked like a heavy bag for boxing lowered from the ceiling. While it looked like sand and leather, the bag was actually reinforced with adaptable ultonate. Basically, I could hit it as hard as I wanted.

So I did.

It felt good to simply unleash. To release all the new power boiling inside me and pummel that heavy bag until my mind turned off. I'm not sure how long I went at it, but by the end my uniform was soaked through with sweat and I was panting.

My knuckles weren't even red, though. I wasn't sore.

"You see that, Darcy? That's a killer Earthling right there."

I'm not sure how long Hiram and Darcy were watching me. Long enough that Hiram had taken a seat, Darcy hovering behind him. From what little I'd seen of these two around the *Eastwood*, Darcy was never far from Hiram. She was like his shadow.

"Hey, guys," I said. "Just, uh, creepily watching me work out, huh?"

Hiram tossed me a towel. "Man, you were in the zone. Didn't want to mess you up."

I caught the towel out of the air and draped it around my neck, looking past Hiram to Darcy. She eyed me back, hands thrust into the front pocket of her hoodie. There was an awkward moment where we were both kind of sizing each other up, not sure what to say. Hiram crossed his arms, seeming to enjoy the awkwardness.

"Too much eye contact," Darcy finally muttered, tugging at her hood.

"Sorry," I said. "I've just—I've never met anyone like me before." Hiram grinned at that, pumping his eyebrows at Darcy. She didn't seem at all amused.

"Like you," she repeated. "Like you *how?*"

"You know . . ." I felt suddenly nervous, like I was falling into a trip. "A hybrid."

"I'm a human," Darcy said sharply. "I identify as human."

"Oh," I replied. I took another look at her and was sure that my eyes didn't deceive me—she had all the quirks that identified a half-Denzan. The long fingers, the big eyes, the faintly glowing hair. I knew the look; I'd seen it in my own mirror often enough. "But . . . are you really?"

Finally, Hiram groaned, like he was tired of this conversation. "Come on, Darcy, quit screwing with him. You can't blame the Earther for not knowing what's up."

"I'm a human," Darcy reiterated to me.

"She's a hybrid," Hiram confirmed to me with a sigh. "Darcy's bitter because her mom turned out to be one of those Merciful Rampart freaks."

Darcy scowled. "You don't have to immediately tell that to every new person we meet."

"We're getting to know each other!" Hiram responded. "No secrets allowed on the *Eastwood*'s crew."

"Merciful Rampart?" I asked. "I don't know what that is."

"They're a political organization on Denza that thinks humans should be quarantined to Earth because we're dangerous for the universe," Hiram replied, making a jerk-off motion. "They never actually do anything except give us dirty looks. Occasionally, they get a couple of their people on the Senate and lobby for restrictions on immigrating humans or try to get us all sent back to Earth, but that trash never goes anywhere."

"Sometimes they do worse than that," Darcy said darkly.

Back on Earth, I wouldn't have pried into her business, but I couldn't resist. "Your mom was an antihuman Denzan, and she . . . ?"

"Hooked up with my dad?" Darcy made a face. "Yeah. She was spying on him. He's first officer on the ISV *Searchlight*. I think her plan was to frame him for smuggling Denzan technology back to Earth—which he *wasn't*—and make all us humans look bad."

"How did she get caught?"

"She confessed!" Hiram answered for her, laughing incredulously. "The Denzans are always apologizing about something or confessing they stepped on somebody's toe or whatever. Huge consciences, little biceps."

"She exiled herself to an ultonate processing plant after that," Darcy said. "I haven't seen her since I was five."

"Things are kind of weird with my mom, too," I said to Darcy, feeling like I should give her something after Hiram forced her to spill her family secrets. "She spent ten years making me hide all over Earth because someone was after us. Turned out it was just my uncle Tycius trying to bring me here."

Darcy perked up a bit. "Wow, you—"

"Seriously, though," Hiram spoke over her. "How screwed up is Earth? I mean, part of me wants to visit there someday, it being the birthplace of humanity and all, even though the Denzans still haven't figured out why we get so sick when we go back."

"They don't want to figure that out," Darcy muttered. "They don't care."

I knew that wasn't true. My dad and uncle were both searching for a cure for humanity's strange affliction. I decided against bringing that up, though. I still couldn't quite get a read on whether I should trust these two.

"All our people, like, living in their own shit basically, sick all the time." Hiram shook his head. "It's unreal to me. I don't think I could stand it."

"I didn't know," I said, looking down at my hands, flexing my fingers. "I didn't know what else was possible. Didn't know I could feel this good."

"Ignorance is bliss," Darcy said.

"Man, H'Jossu made me watch this ridiculous Earth show. Shit wasn't even 3-D. It was about this sad, sick old man who forces his slave boy to start making poison with him. Poison that Earth humans smoke. On purpose. You ever see anything like that?"

Before I could answer, we all turned to the sound of shuffling footsteps in the hall outside. Arkell stalked by the doorway, pausing for a moment to look in at us with his nose upturned. His gaze focused on me, the scars around his eye and mouth pinching as he spoke.

"Break anything else today, Cadet?"

"No," I said. "Again, sorry about—"

He didn't let me finish. The Denzan simply grunted and resumed his path down the hall.

"He's one of them," Darcy said quietly, once Arkell was gone. "He used to be in the Merciful Rampart."

"Rumor is he once tried to blow up the wormhole to Earth," Hiram added. "It's how he got his scars and why he keeps his whole arm bound. Shit, I can at least respect that."

Unlike Aela, Hiram didn't have the tact to avoid talking about a Denzan's shame. I was glad to get the scoop on Arkell, though, even if it came from Hiram. Of course the guy who'd welcomed me to the ship by calling me "mutt" would be part of some racist antihuman organization. I shook my head.

"Why would they let him serve on a Serpo Institute ship?" I asked.

"Probably punishment," Hiram said. "Force him to work with humans so he'll understand us better."

"We're his rehabilitation," Darcy added. "Denzans actually think that kind of crap works."

I rubbed the back of my neck. Someone had sabotaged my dad's mission and caused him to get lost in space. And someone had sent a Vulpin assassin to Earth to clean up the trail. Considering what my mom and dad were up to, it seemed like these Merciful Rampart guys would be the sort of Denzans who might want my dad disappeared.

I had my first suspect.

14

"The purpose of today's orientation seminar will be cross-species acceptance," Aela said, the tinny voice of their exo-suit echoing in their furnitureless room. "I will be pulling the two of you into a memory that H'Jossu has kindly chosen to share with us."

Even though I told myself not to, I pressed my back into the wall behind me. I couldn't help myself. The whole purpose of this exercise was to get me more comfortable around extraterrestrials like the Panalax, and I was already off to a bad start.

H'Jossu stood across the room from me—huge, shaggy, rotting. He happily shook out his furry limbs, and white mold spores, like dandruff, floated through the air. They were promptly sucked into one of Aela's ceiling air vents.

"I've been a little homesick, so I'm totally amped for this," the Panalax told me. "You excited?"

My mouth felt dry. "Sure."

Aela stood in the space between us. This time, they didn't ask me if I wanted to get naked. "Ready?"

"Yup," H'Jossu said happily.

I nodded grimly.

We went through the same procedure as in my last class with Aela. H'Jossu and I were both sprayed down by the showers in the room's floor and ceiling. The mold that filled H'Jossu's eyes and mouth wiggled happily in the moisture. Then, with the two of us thoroughly decontaminated—but one of us feeling like he might puke—Aela's gaseous form poured out of their exo-suit and up our noses.

I entered the mind-space, my revulsion level cratering now that I was out of my own body.

The jungle was hot as balls. No better way to put it.

Actually, I'm sure there are a million better ways to put it. But I'm sticking with "hot as balls."

I stood under a dense canopy of greenery, like the Amazon rain forest on steroids. The trees were massive, with bark that looked like turtle shells, the bulbous roots creating waist-high hills in the soft black soil. Bat-shaped creatures flitted through the branches, drilling their pointy hummingbird beaks into the juicy melons that hung from the boughs. Sticky nectar spilled down like rain.

"Welcome to the Ghost Garden," H'Jossu said. "My home world."

He was right next to me, swaying happily in the humidity. Aela was with us too, once again in the striking humanoid shape that reminded me of a living lightning storm.

In a small clearing ahead of us, surrounded by a circle of ornamental rocks, an animal was dying.

The creature was about the size of a golden retriever, with reddish, leathery skin and a long floppy trunk. It lay on its side, its eyes glazed over, each slow breath rattling around in its rib cage. Dude didn't have long to go.

Outside the circle of stones, a whole alien zoo's worth of creatures stood somberly by, watching as the old elephant-dog slowly expired.

"This is fucked," I blurted.

Aela elbowed me. "Syd."

"Actually," H'Jossu said, not seeming to take offense, "this is my little brother's birth ritual."

The creatures standing on death watch were a menagerie—there were some shaggy teddy bear things, a couple of literal spider monkeys with chimp torsos that ended in six skittering legs, a few other elephant-dogs, and more. These beasts all shared some common traits, though. For one, they stood upright like people. For two, they were all dead-looking, frozen in a state of decomposition. And finally, they were all covered in a bright white fungus.

"Personally, I find the sacred rituals of the Panalaxan Growth Mandate to be beautiful," Aela said, giving me a disapproving look. "Please try harder, Syd."

I forced myself to look at the creatures. Some of them had only small growths of fungus around their eyes and mouths, with sparse tufts popping up along their limbs. They were the younger

Panalaxan. The elders were absolutely covered in the stuff, thick mounds of mold making their animal bodies nearly unrecognizable. One big dude in particular, who I took to be the leader because he carried a gnarled bow staff in one clawed paw, had grown what appeared to be a functioning third arm made entirely of fungus.

H'Jossu patted my shoulder. "I get it, dude. I've seen enough Earth art to know how freaked out you guys are by death. Plus, my people have the word 'mandate' in their name. I mean, that's totally a villain thing, right?"

I actually cracked a smile at that. "'Panalaxan Growth Optional' doesn't have the same ring, I guess."

H'Jossu let loose a raspy chuckle, then pointed into the crowd. "Look. There's me."

Of course I could see him there among the other mold-covered beasts. He was a big boy. This version of H'Jossu, from his memory, wasn't quite so thickly covered in spores.

He was also singing.

They all were. The animals let out a dry, croaking sound, like wind rustling dead leaves. That was the fungus, operating the lungs of its deceased hosts.

"What are they saying?"

"It's a chant to ease the dying mohunk's passage," H'Jossu replied.

The elephant-dog—a mohunk—must have gotten tired of listening to the creepy Panalaxan singing, because it let loose one last, heavy sigh, and then was completely still, its glassy eyes staring into space. Dead.

The ring of Panalaxan went silent.

After a few moments, the leader thumped his staff—once, twice, three times—into the dirt. At that signal, two other Panalaxan extended their fuzzy limbs toward the newly dead. Bright spores like snowflakes broke off from them, intermingled, and floated into the nostrils and eyes of the corpse.

It only took a few seconds for the mohunk to begin convulsing. Blossoms of mold pushed out from its eyes and nostrils. The recently dead creature flopped around, then let loose a shrill, raspy cry that seemed to silence the entire jungle. Finally, the mohunk—or was it a Panalax now?—stumbled to its feet like a newly born foal, uncertain of its own limbs. The thing took a few floundering steps out of the stone circle, then collapsed again and let out a whine. The rest of the Panalaxan onlookers came forward, crouching down and soothing the newly reanimated creature. The H'Jossu in the memory was first among them, reaching down to cradle his little brother.

Meanwhile, the H'Jossu next to me blotted at his eyeholes like he was crying. "Oh, Muf'Tong, he was such a sweet little growthling." He paused. "Now he's annoying as shit."

"You've just witnessed your first Panalaxan birth," Aela said cheerily to me. "Pretty cool, huh?"

"They're zombies," I said. "Plant-based zombies."

"I find your revulsion quite interesting," Aela said. "As I understand it, Earthers kill one hundred fifty million animals per day for food. A Panalax can live for a hundred years, sustaining itself on a single host body, water, and sunlight. Which do you think is the superior use of organic matter?"

I mean, the answer to that was obvious, and rationally I understood it, but I was still having a hard time accepting a society of friendly undead mildew. I crossed my arms and stood there silently.

"Speaking of zombies," H'Jossu said, "what's the superior version of *The Walking Dead*? TV or comic book?"

I gave him a mystified look. "The comic, obviously," I replied. "How are you so into Earth stuff, anyway?"

"I took an elective on it during my first semester at Serpo and fell in love," H'Jossu replied, clasping his paws over his chest. "So much action and suffering, so much hope, constantly grappling with your short life spans. It really speaks to me."

Despite finding him kind of gross, I *was* starting to feel comfortable talking to H'Jossu. He spoke my language—not literally, of course, but still. Even the humans on the *Eastwood* hadn't given me such a warm reception.

"H'Jossu," Aela prodded gently. "Maybe now would be a good time to explain to Syd all the ways your people aren't like made-up Earth monsters."

"Well, we aren't played out as all hell, for starters," H'Jossu said. He thoughtfully scratched at his furry snout. "I guess Panalaxan are like zombies in that you have to eradicate our host brains to kill us. But we aren't contagious, and we don't kill our hosts—we wait for them to pass on naturally. And we're really nice."

"The Ghost Garden is the most biodiverse planet in all the systems," Aela added, "largely thanks to the Panalaxan maintaining it."

"We also supply a bunch of medicines to the Serpo Institute worlds," H'Jossu said proudly. "All the quick-heal salve on the *Eastwood* was grown in the Ghost Garden."

I gave the group of Panalaxan a second look. Most of them were still gathered around the newborn dead thing, playing with the little guy like you would a baby, picking him up and tossing him in the air. Others had formed a small ring around the two Panalaxan that had shed spores into the baby and were performing some kind of swaying dance. It was a celebration.

"Okay," I said. "I'm not going to lie, the whole thing still makes me feel a little squeamish. But I'm going to try to get past it. And I'm really sorry I punched you the other day."

"A breakthrough!" Aela cried.

Almost immediately, the jungle faded away. We were returned to Aela's room—the Ossho wisp went out of our brains and back in their exo-suit. H'Jossu hopped excitedly across the room toward me. I still flinched a little, but mostly because he was nine feet tall.

"We are going to be best friends," he declared.

I cautiously patted his wooly arm, surprised that his fur felt so soft. "Let's not rush it, buddy."

"Thank you for your assistance, H'Jossu," Aela said. "Can you please send Zara in?"

Once the Panalax had shambled out, Aela turned to me.

"I apologize if I was harsh in there, criticizing your Earther eating habits."

I waved my hand. "You made a good point for someone who's never eaten a cheeseburger."

"Oh, but I have *experienced* eating a cheeseburger," Aela said. "As an Ossho, I try to collect as many memories as possible, whether firsthand or through others. It's why I'm so passionate about interspecies understanding. One foolish bias could stand in the way of thousands of interesting encounters. And that's why you've come to the Vastness, isn't it?"

I'd come to the Vastness to find my missing father, but Aela's version—where I traveled through space in search of the exciting and the mind-blowing—sounded pretty good, too. "Yeah," I replied. "Of course."

"Anyway, it will be easier with Zara," Aela said. "Humans typically respond well to Vulpin."

I wasn't so sure that would be the case with me, but I stayed silent. At that moment, Zara swept into the room, her rust-colored tail swishing behind her.

"Let's get this over with," she said, flashing me her fangs. She smoothed down the spiky shelf of fur across her shoulders. "Your damn chemical shower is hell on my coat."

The door to Aela's room sealed us in and the routine began again. The vents in Aela's floor and ceiling doused us, then, with the air clean, Aela came spilling out of their exo-suit and flowed toward Zara and me.

Yet again, the scene changed.

The three of us stood on a cliff of red stone that reminded me of the sunburned peaks I'd once seen while driving through Arizona. The air here was dry and dusty, a huge crimson sun burning overhead. In the distance, beneath the crags, a city gleamed like a jewel in the middle of the desert. The buildings there were mostly domed and castle-like, small spacecraft zipping between sandstone obelisks. A Denzan interstellar vessel—the same model as the *Eastwood*—hovered over a tall building that gleamed with importance.

"Welcome to Stonlea," Aela said. "Home world of the Vulpin One Pack."

A happy shriek drew my attention away from the distant city. The first Vulpin I laid eyes on was a child, naked except for its patches of burned-orange fur, splashing around in a pool of crystalline water. My first thought was that it looked like a baby fox in a viral video.

"Aw," I said, before I could stop myself. "Cute."

"Cute," Zara spat. "Any one of these cublets would eviscerate you, Earthling."

I blinked, not sure how to respond to that. Zara sounded serious, but the idea was so ridiculous that I kind of felt like she was trolling me. She walked ahead of Aela and me, snout up, breathing in the dry air of her memory.

Next to me, Aela chuckled and shrugged. "The Vulpin are really sensitive about their resemblance to unevolved Earth mammals. Do not coo at them. Do not try to take their picture. Do not—I repeat—*do not* pet them."

I smirked, thinking of my uncle Tycius. "Already knew that one."

The rocks ahead parted to form a natural waterslide—a shallow crevice of smoothed stone covered by a twisting and turning stream that ended in a swimming hole. There were Vulpin everywhere, mostly younger ones. They took turns racing down the stony slide or else sunbathed by its edges, while small groups observed the action from the rocks above or floated idly in the pool below.

On average, the Vulpin were about a foot shorter than humans. Their skin was varying shades of bronze, where it wasn't covered in patches of fur. Their pelt colors varied from deep mahogany to almost pink, as did the styles and cuts that they wore—some combed ornamental spikes along their shoulders and down their arms, others wore fancy manes, and some kept full heads of braids. Even the so-called cublets had sharp teeth and hands tipped with claws. They all had bushy tails that seemed like they would constantly get in the way, but judging by how they ran and swam—agile and carefree—tail awareness wasn't a problem for these people.

"They must have to vacuum so much on this planet," I said.

"Coat-sculpting is a big part of clan identity for the Vulpin," Aela said. "Zara, would you like to explain?"

"Nope," Zara replied, standing at the edge of the water. She stared down at a pack of buff Mohawk-sporting dudes glowering at the edge of the watering hole. They reminded me of a dozen hot-shit varsity sports teams I'd encountered back home.

Aela frowned but pressed on. "They call themselves the Vulpin One Pack during interplanetary relations because they want to present a unified front when dealing with other species, but politics on Stonlea are almost always in flux. You can tell who supports which faction—or *den*, as they call them—by how they groom themselves . . ."

While Aela explained the intricacies of Vulpin hairdos, I tried to picture the Vulpin who had attacked my mom. If I could remember how her coat was styled, maybe I could learn what den she was from and, from there, track down who sent her. I wondered if Ty had that kind of information from when he and the Consulate people found the Vulpin's body in the outback.

"There's never been a single war on Stonlea," Aela was saying, having moved on from grooming. "Not a war like you'd think of one, anyway, with armies and widespread battles."

"We humans do like blowing one another up," I said.

"The Vulpin dens are involved in constant power struggles. It's basically a planet-wide pastime," Aela continued. "Instead of outright war, they engage in subterfuge and assassination. It's a point of pride for them. Any loss of life seems totally wasteful to me, but at least the Vulpin are circumspect when it comes to killing each other."

"Look," Zara said, pointing up the cliff. "Here I come."

The Zara-of-memory picked her way down from higher up. She must've been observing this scene from above, but now she cut a determined path toward the preening Mohawk boys at the watering hole.

The magenta streaks that made up Aela's hair stood up. "Wait, what is this memory, Zara?"

Zara's tail wagged. "I told you. It's my proudest day, the day I left for the Serpo Institute." She flashed Aela a feral grin. "Can you put me in first person, Aela? I want to really relive it. The Earthling can come, too. Get a true taste of Vulpin life."

"I think I'm good," I said.

"This isn't exactly the formative experience I hoped you'd share," Aela said, annoyed. The wisp squinted for a moment, and then Zara simply blinked out of existence.

"Where'd she go?" I asked.

Aela pointed toward the Zara sauntering closer to the swimming hole. "She's experiencing the memory firsthand, like she asked. I have to warn you, Syd, this gets a little gruesome. We can stop now . . ."

"No," I said. "No. I'm supposed to understand the Vulpin, right? I'd like to see."

Aela nodded, and we both turned to watch.

"Oh, Kungo, where are you, Kungo?" Zara called out in a singsong voice.

The biggest Vulpin of the clique—or maybe he just had the tallest Mohawk—stepped forward. He grinned and waved at Zara, showing off a front fang that was cracked and broken, his snout laced with pink scars.

"Here I am," Kungo declared. "You come to kiss me goodbye?"

Zara smiled back at him. I got the sense that the Vulpin showed teeth a lot, even when they weren't necessarily happy. Sure-footed, Zara hopped across the slippery rocks, putting her on the same side of the stream as Kungo as she neared the pool.

"I hear you been talking mess, like you some big alpha," Zara said. "Here I am, to hear it in the flesh."

"And I hear you talking about how going off-world means you special or something. But we all know why you're jetting. It's because you come from a den of ass-sniffers and your daddy wants to whore you out like he did your momma. That what you came to hear?" Kungo waved a dismissive hand in the direction of the city. "Lucky your ride is here, Zara, you better run along. You keep looking at me with those heat eyes, I might not be able to control myself, get you tail-up right here on the rocks."

All the action around the waterslide and on the rocks had completely stopped, every Vulpin tuned in to the confrontation. Even the little ones had given up on swimming to watch. No one seemed remotely interested in deescalating the situation.

A glint of metal caught my eye. Zara had a small, flat knife tucked against her palm. "You're right. I got a ship to catch," she said. "So hurry up and get your spanking, sister fucker."

Kungo looked around at his friends, mocking disbelief on his face. "Can you believe this bitch?" He ran a hand through his Mohawk, and, when it emerged, he'd slipped on a spiked knuckle-duster.

The talking was done. Both Vulpins' fur bristled as they hunkered low, teeth bared in snarls. Scattered shouts and yips sounded from around the rocks, the onlookers encouraging this duel.

When Zara and Kungo went for each other, it happened fast. Kungo bull-rushed ahead, and Zara came to meet him, lighter on her feet. He snapped off three heavy punches, pretty much trying to knock Zara's head off. She ducked one, absorbed the second on her shoulder, luckily from the fist not wrapped in spiked metal, and then swayed backward under the third, using her tail to prop her up.

Still balanced on her tail, Zara's foot shot up, catching Kungo right between the legs. He doubled over, wheezing and clutching at himself.

Without hesitation, Zara spun her little knife around in her hand and plunged it dead into Kungo's eye.

I clapped a hand over my mouth. "Holy shit."

"Yeah," Aela agreed. "She really goes for it."

Kungo fell forward, whimpering and holding his face. Zara flicked her hand, spraying droplets of Kungo's blood onto the rocks. Her knife was gone. At some point, she'd hidden it somewhere in her fur, so smooth I missed it. She reached down and patted Kungo's back.

"See you never," Zara said. She bowed deeply to the onlookers, turned on her heel, and sauntered back the way she'd come.

As Kungo's friends dragged him away, playtime resumed on the rocks, young Vulpin sliding down into the pool, mere feet from where someone had just lost an eye. It was crazy. I thought I was going to watch the equivalent of a schoolyard brawl, not a maiming. Now, it wasn't so hard to imagine one of the Vulpin attacking my mom. It was a little harder to imagine how she'd survived.

"I'm sorry, Syd," Aela said. "This wasn't the most helpful memory for an orientation. Zara's impossible sometimes."

I shook my head. I actually felt better now that I'd seen the two sides of Vulpin life—cute furballs frolicking in water and brutal knife fights. The creatures were no longer boogeydogs from a childhood nightmare. Now I knew what they were like—and I understood how nasty someone would have to be to send one to Earth after a mother and her child.

"Actually," I told Aela, "I learned a lot."

15

"So? What do you think so far?"

My uncle Tycius and I sat next to each other at the round table in the *Eastwood*'s galley, the first to arrive for dinner. In the ten days that I'd been aboard the *Eastwood*, Tycius and I hadn't really had much time to catch up. When I wasn't crashing hard from adjusting to space travel, I was working out to master my new strength or getting a rundown of alien cultures from Aela or training to operate the various environmental and navigation systems aboard the *Eastwood*. My uncle, meanwhile, was usually stuck at a terminal or in private meetings with Reno and Vanceval, catching up on all the Denzan current events he'd missed while stuck on Earth.

I puffed out my cheeks. "That's a big question."

Tycius leaned back in his seat. "First impressions. Whatever comes to mind."

I tried to sort through all the reality-warping information I'd been bombarded with since my last night on Earth—the Wasting, the Etherazi, the Lost People, the Merciful Rampart, my missing father.

"The Vulpin that attacked my mom," I finally settled on. "Do you know what kind of haircut she had?"

My uncle chuckled. "That's what's on your mind?"

"If we could figure out what den she was from, we could—"

Tycius cut me off. "I get it. The Consulate looked into the incident at the time and determined the Vulpin was an exile. She didn't belong to any pack. When the Vulpin are disowned like that, they sometimes turn to mercenary work."

I frowned, crossing out a lead in my mental notebook. Ty reached over and patted my forearm.

"Listen, Syd, finding Marcius is our top priority, but you should know it isn't our *only* priority," he said. "The Serpo Institute is an opportunity for you. I know it might feel wrong with your father missing, but you should make the most of it. He would want that."

I thought that over. Basically, my uncle was telling me to chill. On Earth, I'd always had a purpose—run, keep my identity a secret, watch out for the evil government. With all my fake identities and the constant moving, I'd never really learned what it was like to just be Syd Chambers. Kind of nuts that I'd come all the way to the Vastness to do it, but the more I thought about it, the more I wanted to take advantage of this situation, just like my uncle said.

I wanted to find my dad. But I also wanted to be a good cadet.

I wanted to be like an Ossho wisp—floating through space, seeing dope shit.

And one day, maybe I could even be like Reno, bopping around the universe on my own interstellar vessel.

Assuming that I wasn't back on Earth, beating up regular humans for not recycling. Like my mom wanted.

Pretty soon, the rest of the crew filed in. Melian sat next to me, with Batzian on her other side—once again, Batzian was poring over some assignment on his tablet. The elderly Vanceval creakily lowered himself into a seat next to my uncle. Darcy and Hiram, together as usual, sat next to him. Captain Reno, Zara, and Aela finished the circle. Even though Aela didn't eat, they still liked to take part in the "group feeding experience." H'Jossu also didn't eat and couldn't fit in at the table, so he rested in a hammock-like contraption at the back of the room, shining a UV light on his mold growths. Arkell was the only crew member who didn't show up. He never did, preferring to eat his meals alone in his workshop. Reno let this go—nobody missed the chief engineer's bad energy.

Dinner that night was a spicy mushroom stew that was considered comfort food on Denza. Since joining the *Eastwood*, I'd pretty much become vegetarian. The Denzans, as a culture, didn't eat meat, and the food selections on the ship reflected that. The Vulpin were actual carnivores, so Zara was given special meals—skewers of juicy pink flesh that she smugly savored. In truth, though, I didn't miss Earth food. I felt better than I ever had in my life, although that might have had more to do with my super-strength than with my diet.

Toward the end of the meal, Melian held out her tablet. "Hey,

Syd, I made something for you . . ."

"Really?" I asked, grabbing my own tablet and holding it out so that she could beam the information my way. I'd never been allowed a cell phone on Earth, so I was already pretty attached to the paper-thin handheld I was issued upon boarding the *Eastwood*. I could use it to communicate with my crew and, once classes started for me on Denza, it's how I would do my homework and research.

"It's a map of cool spots on Denza for you to check out," Melian explained as an aerial view of the sprawling Denzan archipelago filled my screen.

I smiled, touching various islands that Melian had highlighted and annotated, little blurbs about diamond rock formations and sensory museums popping up beneath my fingers. "That's awesome, Mel," I said. "Thanks."

"Hey, Batz . . . ian," Hiram said exaggeratedly. "Are you working on a map for the tourist, too? Maybe of all the best places on Denza to have a nervous breakdown?"

Batzian had spent most of dinner on his tablet, barely touching his meal. He flicked a glance at Hiram. "No. I'm working on a proposal to improve the *Eastwood*'s efficiency, gaining us speed without compromising gravity."

Hiram blinked. "Is that extra credit or something? I didn't think we were supposed to do classwork on board." He turned to Reno, clearly eager for the captain's approval. "Got to stay prepared and alert, even on a milk run like this."

"It's not classwork," Batzian replied curtly. "It's my own project."

Hiram groaned. "You make the rest of us look bad."

"You make *yourself* look bad," Zara remarked to Hiram. "With your ugly face."

Hiram stroked his jawline. "Perfect symmetry, furball."

Reno sighed. "Hiram, clear the dishes, please."

I'd thought the elderly Vanceval had been napping through the end of dinner, his chin pressed to his chest, but he suddenly leaned forward to look at me. His swooping pouf of hair bobbed back and forth. "Young Sydneycius, have you given any thought to which classes you'll enroll in once we reach the institute?"

I shook my head. "Figured I would just do whatever the required stuff is to start."

"Yes, yes, you'll be entered into math and science courses for your skill level, but that isn't the fun stuff," Vanceval replied. "You must also choose a selection of electives. And teach one as well."

"I have to teach a class?" I asked, raising my eyebrows.

"Of course! All cadets must teach something related to their home culture," Vanceval explained. "Overall, there are hundreds of classes available at the Serpo Institute, taught by a mixture of expert faculty like myself and your fellow cadets. You are in charge of creating a curriculum that will shape you into a well-rounded explorer of the Vastness, so that one day you might join the crew of an interstellar vessel."

I looked around. I thought I was *already* on the crew of an interstellar vessel . . .

"A *real* ship," Hiram said, catching my look as he snatched my empty tray. "This is just a training ship. Which is why we don't do anything cool."

"I do hope you'll sign up for my seminar on the Lost People,"

Vanceval said. "Your father found it very inspiring."

That got some looks from some of my crewmates—like Darcy and Melian—who hadn't really been paying attention. Everyone on board knew that I was a hybrid and that Tycius was my uncle, but I hadn't been very forthcoming with other details about my backstory. Telling anyone about my missing dad would mean lying to them about the fact that I was out in the Vastness to look for him.

Before anyone could ask any questions, Hiram blundered into the conversation again. For once, I was grateful.

"No offense, proctor, but the Lost People are pretty much a fairy tale for old people," he said. "You're going to want to sign up for my judo class, Syd. Darcy and I will whip you into shape."

"Hmm," Vanceval murmured. "Some offense taken."

"I asked you to clean up so you'd stop talking so much, Cadet," Captain Reno said to Hiram. "Was that not clear?"

"Um, no, ma'am, it was not."

My uncle tapped my arm. "If you're feeling overwhelmed, I can help you choose some classes later."

"Hey, Zara," H'Jossu said. "Are you going to teach the same class again this semester?"

The Vulpin looked up from dragging her claw across her napkin. "Of course. Why wouldn't I?"

"Because no one ever signs up for it?" Melian asked timidly.

"And that is my fault how?" Zara responded.

"The institute does pay attention to one's success as an instructor," Vanceval said diplomatically. "It's a good way to demonstrate leadership and communication skills."

I was about to ask what mysterious class Zara was teaching—

maybe it would give me some inspiration for my own, which I was already drawing an absolute blank on—when Arkell barged into the room, holding some shining object aloft.

"The ship registered an obstruction in one of the biomes," Arkell announced, his voice scratchy and harsh. "Why do you have this hidden in your room?"

It took me a moment to realize Arkell was talking to me.

And he was holding up an open ring box. My dad's cosmological tether.

I sensed everyone's eyes on me. When I hid the box in one of my cabin's planters, I'd had no idea the ship's AI would snitch on me. Especially not to the one guy on the *Eastwood* who I definitely didn't want knowing about my father. Arkell had ties to an antihuman organization and an arm fully bound in metal because of all the bad shit he'd done. And now he was holding my dad's ring. My mom had trained me for situations like these where I'd been found out, my cover blown—I was supposed to act quickly and decisively. I wasn't supposed to think.

Maybe that wasn't such a good thing.

"That's mine," I said, shooting to my feet.

"Syd—," Ty said warningly, but I wasn't listening.

"Yours?" Arkell snorted. "Impossible. This is—"

I snatched at the ring. Arkell took a sharp step backward and then, with an embarrassing shriek, completely toppled over. As he did, I was able to snatch the ring from between his fingers. To most of the people watching, I'm sure it looked like I pushed him over.

But what really happened—what I noticed as it went down—was Darcy stuck her leg out and tripped him.

"Oh my," Aela remarked. I heard Zara let out a snort and noticed Batzian shielding his tablet out of the corner of my eye.

"Assault!" Arkell bellowed from his back. "You've just assaulted a senior member of the crew, you beast!"

Apparently, Arkell didn't realize that it was Darcy who'd tripped him—his anger was focused entirely on me. I clutched the ring to my chest.

"I'm . . . I'm sorry," I stammered. "I—"

"Cadets!" Reno shouted, pounding her fist on the table so hard that I thought it might shatter. "Clear the room!" She snapped her fingers at me. "Not you, Chambers."

At that moment, Hiram returned from the recycler. "Whoa. What did I miss?"

I'm sure the others would tell him as they quickly fled the scene. Melian flashed me a sympathetic look, and I swear Darcy winked, but the others mostly seemed curious about what they were missing and why the heck the new Earthling was in possession of some important Denzan tech. As they filed out, Arkell remained on his back, sprawled out like a turtle.

"May I stay?" Aela asked in the doorway. "I feel this is an experience worth cataloging for—"

"Out," Reno said through her teeth.

"For shame, Arkell," my uncle said coolly, standing at my side. "Get yourself up already."

Reno moved swiftly around the table and slapped the button that sealed the door to the canteen. Arkell, his dark eyes narrowed, picked himself up with what I felt was exaggerated care—he'd only fallen over; it's not like I'd decked him or something.

Vanceval was completely unruffled by the whole altercation, his eyes half-lidded, hands folded before him.

I was surprised when the first thing Reno did was round on Arkell. "That was an unnecessary brouhaha, Officer."

"You're reprimanding *me*?" Arkell's lips pressed into a flat line. "A physical assault occurred. My personal space was violated."

"Oh, get over yourself," Tycius said.

"Sounds to me like you violated Syd's space, too," Reno added, sitting back down. "Going through his room without permission. We don't do that on my ship."

Arkell's hair flattened back across his skull, his teeth grinding. "The boy is in possession of a cosmological tether. I'd like to know where it leads and why he's seen the need to hide it from us."

"What makes you think it was hidden from us?" Reno asked. "I'm the captain of this ship, Arkell. You think anything goes on without my knowing?"

"The tether is his inheritance," Tycius added. "I gave it to him and told him to keep it secret, primarily because of *you*, Arkell, and your backward beliefs."

Arkell rubbed the cold metal that encased his one arm. He was taken aback. "My beliefs—my beliefs are not in question here," he said. "That was a long time ago."

"Once a specist, always a specist. Don't you have any shame, Arkell?"

The elderly engineer stiffened, staring coldly at my uncle. Suddenly, I was an afterthought, the two of them totally forgetting about me as what seemed like an old grudge reignited. Aela had mentioned how it wasn't polite to talk about a Denzan's shame;

my uncle didn't seem to have any problems stepping over that line when it came to Arkell.

"I carry my shame, Tycius," Arkell said, tapping his shoulder. "Every day, I try to make amends for what I did."

"And yet, since he got here, you've called Sydney a mutt, a beast, and that's just what you've said loud enough to hear," Tycius replied. "You're the same old bomb maker with no respect for what humanity did for us. You're too demented to be rehabilitated. The Senate should've sent you to a mushroom farm in the dark hemisphere."

Damn, my uncle didn't pull any punches. I was glad he had my back out here. Ty had also just confirmed the rumor I heard from Darcy and Hiram: that Arkell had basically been a terrorist back in the day. He didn't look like much now, though. I could tell my uncle's words had stung him by the way Arkell's shoulders hunched.

"The arrogance of you to judge me," Arkell said quietly. "For the last ten years, I've been serving at the institute. Training the next generation. Unlocking new worlds and keeping our galaxy safe. And where have you been, Tycius? Vacationing on a backwater on a wild-goose chase?"

"It's not a wild-goose chase if we find him," I muttered.

"Gentlemen, I think that's enough bickering," Reno announced, turning to me. "Cadet, you need to be careful with your hands. Get me?"

I nodded once, not about to sell out Darcy. "Yes, Captain."

"The soil in the biomes needs to be turned over every ten days, correct, Arkell?"

"Correct, Captain," Arkell responded.

"So the cadet will take care of that. A little manual labor as penance for manhandling you. Sound good?"

Arkell didn't look at me. "I could've been gravely injured," he said flatly.

"But you weren't," Reno responded. "I've made my decision. Do you want to drag out this humiliating incident further?"

I could tell Arkell was fuming. He stood still for a moment, looking from Reno to Tycius, his hands clenched into fists. Then he turned on his heel and left.

I'd almost forgotten Vanceval was in the room until he tugged on my sleeve.

"The tether," he said. "Is that . . . is that Marcius?"

I nodded. "Yeah."

The old Denzan's mouth quivered. "He's alive?"

I held out the ring so that Vanceval could look at the glowing cosmos. My dad was still sending a signal, still waiting for someone to find him. Vanceval's eyes glistened.

"You've had this . . . ," Vanceval said. He turned to Reno. "And you knew?"

"Yes, Vance," the captain said, her cheeks still red from lecturing Arkell.

"Then, with all due respect, Captain . . . ," Vanceval said. "What the hell are we waiting for?"

16

I held the cosmological tether between my fingers. Ever since Tycius told me the significance of the glowing cosmos inside the jewel, I'd been waiting for it to suddenly wink out. At least now that the ring wasn't hidden, I could check on my dad whenever I wanted.

"There's some danger to doing this before you're ready," Tycius told me.

"Continuing to delay is its own danger, I would think," Vanceval added gently.

We'd relocated from the canteen to the *Eastwood*'s bridge. On the way, I'd noticed H'Jossu and Aela hanging around in the passageway, eager to find out what was going on with me. I flashed them a reassuring smile as Captain Reno and Tycius ushered me forward. I wasn't in trouble. Arkell, at that point, was basically an afterthought.

I'd come to the Vastness to find my father, and I was going to do that. Right now.

I sat in the Wayscope—well, on the edge of the seat—the complicated goggles and their rigging dormant above me. Vanceval shuffled around the machine, flicking switches and peering at readings. I felt the processors hum beneath me. The old Denzan had been animated and excited since the moment he saw my dad's cosmological tether. My uncle was a bit more circumspect about this sudden plan. Reno, too, was surprisingly quiet, watching Vanceval prepare the Wayscope for use.

I hadn't said much of anything, instead letting the momentum sweep me along.

"Syd?" Tycius asked. "What are you thinking?"

I looked up from the tether and met my uncle's eyes. "We don't know what's happened to him. He's already been stranded out there so long. Any day, he could . . ."

I didn't need to finish that sentence. I thought about my mom— how she'd spent so long missing my dad, how she'd assumed he was dead. And now we could find him if we wanted, just by hooking me up to this big Denzan machine that I didn't entirely understand. We were so close. I'd never forgive myself if the light in the tether blinked out before I got the chance to find him.

Reading the resolve in my face, Tycius turned to Reno. "Thoughts, Captain?"

"Not ideal timing," she replied. "But I guess that depends on where the tether leads us. We have a few days before we're due back on Denza. If we took the *Eastwood* off course, the Senate wouldn't notice we were missing right away."

Vanceval paused in his preparations. "Ah. So finding Marcius has not been officially approved?"

Reno and Tycius exchanged another look. "Not exactly," Ty said.

Vanceval considered this. "Then, all the more reason to proceed," he said. "Now that Arkell is aware that the boy has a cosmological tether, it's unlikely to stay a secret for long."

My uncle crossed his arms, still not sold. He stood protectively close to me. "Some basic training, at least . . ."

"Doesn't that thing you slipped into Dungeon count as training?" I asked, conveniently leaving out how that experience had put me into a coma for a couple hours.

"That was a game," Ty replied. "It's like comparing a kiddie pool to deep-sea diving. Actually navigating the Vastness is infinitely more complex."

"Please, Uncle," I said, realizing for the first time just how badly I wanted to do this. I wasn't just caught up in the momentum. I wanted—needed—to find my father. I needed answers to those whys that I'd been chasing my entire life. "Let me at least try. What's the worst that could happen?"

"Brain hemorrhage," Ty responded.

"Oh." I swallowed.

"I want to find him too, but . . . ," Tycius said, hesitating.

"Now, I'm not an expert on these things," Reno said, leaning against her console, "but won't the tether guide him to where he's supposed to go? Isn't that the whole point?"

"He'll still need to open his mind to the Vastness," Ty replied. "He's untrained."

Vanceval stepped back, his preparations complete. I sensed energy pulsing through the goggle mechanism that hung over my head.

"His exposure will be minimal," Vanceval said. "Besides, most Wayscope training begins with the assistance of a cosmological tether to reel a cadet's consciousness back in. Accidents are exceedingly rare."

"See?" I said to Tycius. "Brain damage odds are low." My uncle frowned, so I pressed. "I have to start my training at some point, right? What better time than now? You're here to keep an eye on me."

I could tell Ty's eagerness to find my dad was gradually outweighing his reservations. He finally cracked and nodded to Vanceval.

"Please sit back," the older Denzan said. "Beneath the mechanism."

I pushed myself back in the seat, which cradled me like a lounger. Vanceval tapped on the console, and, with a whir of gears, the Wayscope descended until the lenses were directly in front of my face. The massive goggles inched forward, gently sealing at my temples. Through them, I saw the space just outside our ship. Peaceful and endless. A cozy recliner with a view of the stars—this would've been a pretty chill place to catch a nap.

"Be aware of the warning signs," Tycius told me. "Don't take in more information than your mind can handle. If your head starts to hurt or you begin to feel completely disembodied—"

"I'll let you know if my brain starts to melt," I said. "Don't worry."

"Cadet, I order you not to let your head catch on fire," Reno said gruffly. She'd taken a backseat in the discussion between Tycius and Vanceval. I realized the captain wasn't exactly well equipped to deal with matters of Denzan technology. Her voice was sincere, though. "Good luck out there."

"Sydneycius, you should put the ring on now," Vanceval said.

I did as I was told, not fumbling at all even though I could no longer see my fingers. I'd slipped my dad's ring on a few dozen times since I'd gotten it back, so I had practice.

I stifled a gasp as a cool coil of ultonate flowed from the armrest and enveloped my hand. The view through the goggles changed. The Vastness flickered and stretched, the stars throbbing, the Wayscope magnifying the galaxy, trying to connect to the coordinates stored within the tether. A message popped up in my face.

LOCATION ENCRYPTED. DNA MATCH REQUIRED. PROCEED?

"Um, yes?" I said aloud. "Proceed?"

"You may feel a pinch," Vanceval warned.

I barely noticed when the Wayscope pricked my finger. I was locked in on the space beyond the words. The Vastness beckoned to me.

DNA VERIFIED. ACCESSING.

Using the Wayscope was a bit like looking through a really intense telescope—or more like becoming a human telescope, with my mind functioning as the lenses. The Vastness spread out before me, the stars pulsing and calling me forward. My mind expanded. I could see the local planets of this system, the wormhole we'd passed through hours before, and the places where this galaxy butted up against others in the overlapping structure of the universe. I could drink it all in if I wanted, pull the entire universe into my mind and . . .

"Easy, now . . ." Ty's voice, in my ear, like an anchor. "Focus. Don't let it pull you out too far."

I dragged my consciousness back. It was like squinting your eyes to not let the light in.

"Do you see the tether?" Ty asked. "Try to hold on to that."

There. A glowing blue line leading into the distance, cutting through layers of the universe. The real-life version of the star system in my father's ring was out there, at the end of the lifeline. I reached toward it—or, more accurately, I urged my mind forward. Once I'd focused on the tether, I sensed it tugging me. I could see the layers of the galaxies, like an onion, star systems on top of star systems, a zigzagging map that I would need to follow, through the buffer dimensions that connected the galaxies. I opened my mind a little more, trying to absorb the winding path that would lead me to my dad.

I could see it. The place where he was stuck.

A distant planet. Ash gray. Dead-looking. I urged my mind closer. I sensed the way. We could jump through three existing wormholes, but then we'd need to open a new one to reach the system where this barren little rock was hiding.

I tried to speak and found using my mouth to be like groping around in the dark for a light switch, my sensations all confused.

I tried to focus, but there was something wrong. There was static at the edges of my vision. More information seeping into my mind—unnecessary paths through the subspace, distant wormholes stacked on top of one another, bizarre swirls of asteroids.

Useless babble, burying the glowing path that led to my father. It was like the faucet had been turned on inside my mind.

And the water was boiling.

"Syd?" my uncle asked, raising his voice. "What do you see?"

I tried to say something, but I tasted blood. I'd bitten my tongue.

"What's wrong with him?" I heard Reno shout.

"He's off course," Vanceval answered. I was vaguely aware of him clicking buttons on the Wayscope. "He's taking in too much data."

"Pull him back," Tycius commanded.

"I'm trying," Vanceval responded.

My body seized, and I felt my shoulders smack against the back of the chair. The goggles felt like hot lava against my face, but I was powerless to pull them off. It felt like my eyelids had been forced open, peeled back, and then the rest of my skin too—like I was an exposed skull. Hundreds of suns burned through my brain, the entirety of the universe trying to force itself into me. My mind skipped across the molten surface of a small magma planet six galaxies away. At the same time, I was hyperaware of meteoroids whipping through the rings of a gas giant in another galaxy entirely.

It was too much, and it was tearing me apart.

And then, suddenly, there was *something else*. Something clear and bright and easy to focus on. Not the lifeline of my father's tether. A ripple of energy. A golden spike. The energy coalesced from the Vastness, summoned from the in-between. Huge and bright, with skin that bubbled like cosmic fire.

An Etherazi.

The thing was enormous, much bigger than the one I'd seen attacking Denza, its jagged gold body five times the size of our ship. Through the Wayscope, I could see how it stretched between dimensions, parts of it still tied to the spaces in between, a bit of its tail coiled in the past, one of its claws poking tenderly at the future.

I could anchor myself to that. All of the garbled data that I'd accidentally accessed via the Wayscope—this singular shape cut through all that. The searing pain in my forehead subsided. My muscles relaxed. I couldn't take my eyes off the golden aura. It was like a scab on reality that my mind couldn't help picking at.

It saved me.

And it looked back at me.

It was coming toward me.

Coming toward us. It swam between universes with ease. It didn't need a ship. It was fast. Faster in space than in atmosphere.

A voice roared to life in my mind. It was like ice water splashed directly across my brain.

HELLO, LITTLE ONE. BE THERE SOON.

"Disconnect!" Tycius shouted. "Pull back!"

Too late.

The Etherazi knew where we were.

17

I pitched forward from the Wayscope and landed on my hands and knees, scraping the top of my head on the goggle apparatus on the way down. My eyes were filled with stinging tears, like they'd been pinned open for hours. My nostrils were filled with a burned smell that I'm pretty sure was coming from somewhere inside me.

I'd almost just died from data overload. TMI. I was never going to use that stupid acronym again.

I'd survived, though. When the Wayscope had overwhelmed me, when I'd opened myself to more of the Vastness than a normal mind could handle—that Etherazi had arrived. A creature of psychic energy. A monster.

Its presence had pushed my consciousness back into my own body.

"It . . . talked to me," I murmured, my mouth feeling stuffed full of cotton.

I don't think my uncle heard, even though he knelt on the floor next to me, his hand on my back. The sirens blaring throughout the *Eastwood* were too loud.

"Etherazi sighted! Closing fast!" Captain Reno shouted over the comms. "This is not a drill! I repeat, this is not a drill!"

A golden dragon. That's what I'd seen, basically. That's what had saved me from the overwhelming Vastness.

"Sydney, are you all right?" Ty's voice in my ear—gentle, but with an edge of panic. "Can you stand up?"

I grunted and got shakily to my feet, leaning on Tycius. I wiped my sleeve across my eyes, but that didn't clear the huge black spots that were floating through my vision. My ears were ringing, and not just from the warning siren. My knees felt wobbly, like I was on the deck of a boat in a squall.

Some of the others had rushed onto the bridge when the alarm sounded. Aela stood next to Reno, typing quickly on a console. Hiram and Darcy watched from the doorway. For all his bluster about this being a boring trip, Hiram was now pale and obviously spooked. Darcy looked from me to the Wayscope and raised her eyebrows. I shrugged in response, sensing that I must look insane—blood dripping from my nose, eyes swollen, singe marks on my temples.

"Aela," Reno said. "Can you confirm these readings?"

"Ten minutes," Aela said without the usual metallic chipperness. "It'll be on top of us in ten minutes. Even at maximum burn, we can't outpace it."

"Shit," Reno said. "Not enough time." Then she started

barking orders. "Hiram and Darcy, you're with me. I need help prepping my Battle-Anchor. Haven't worn the thing in going on fifteen years, but sure, now seems like a good time to take the old girl for a spin."

The Battle-Anchor. The mechanized suit that Denzans built for humans to fight off the Etherazi. Reno's was on board, so we'd at least have a chance if the Etherazi attacked. But something nagged at me . . .

"I think . . . I think it just wants to talk to me," I mumbled.

Captain Reno sized me up. "So much for a fourth set of hands to get my armor on; the kid's delirious," she said, turning to my uncle. "Get him to the escape pod with the other Denzans." Reno turned to Aela. "You're in charge of making sure that escape pod launches, Aela. Don't pull the trigger until the Etherazi engages with me or the *Eastwood*. We want him distracted so the survivors can get away."

With that, Reno, along with Hiram and Darcy, sprinted from the bridge toward the docking bay. I wanted to help them, but there was no way I could keep up with them in my condition. Tycius tossed my arm over his shoulders and helped me toward the exit. Vanceval was on my other side, his hand on my elbow—it wasn't much help, but the old man was doing what he could.

I glanced over my shoulder, surprised we were leaving Aela behind on the bridge. "Wait, Aela—"

The exo-suit's head turned in my direction, the magenta-streaked cloud swirling within. "Don't worry about me, Syd. If the ship is destroyed, I can survive in the vacuum of space." Aela's head cocked. "I'm rooting for your survival. The death of my entire crew is not an experience I'm eager to encounter."

"Good luck to you, too," I said.

As we stumbled into the passageway, my uncle turned to look at me. "What were you saying before? About the Etherazi?"

I shook my head. "I . . . I don't know. In the Wayscope it felt like . . . like it saved me?"

"Impossible," Tycius said.

"Sydneycius, I am truly sorry," Vanceval said.

I could still feel my dad's cosmological tether on my finger, the metal band warm. "No biggie, Vance. Just a beginner's aneurysm. We'll try again."

"Optimism," Vanceval said. "Yes. Good."

We rounded a bend and encountered the others, also heading for the escape pod. Arkell stood gripping both Melian and Batzian by their shoulders, steering them forward. Melian looked absolutely terrified, tears in her eyes, lips shaking. Batzian was doing a better job of keeping it together, but I could tell he was shaken. They were too young to have lived through the invasion, so this must have been like a nightmare come to life.

"The escape pod is lined with ultonate," Batzian reassured his sister. "We'll be fine."

"He could still destoy us," Melian said.

"For what it's worth," Arkell added morosely, "I've heard it's better to die in a fiery explosion than to let the temporal madness take you."

"That's not worth a damn, Arkell," Tycius said.

"Damn, dude, you look wrecked," H'Jossu told me as he shambled up behind the others. Without asking, he brushed the Denzans aside and hoisted me up in one of his huge arms. I actually didn't mind. After having your mind shredded by the contents of the universe, it was comforting to be hugged by a giant sloth creature. Even a moldy one.

Zara popped up behind H'Jossu. The Vulpin had her dagger at the ready—the same one I'd seen her use to carve out Kungo's eye in her cherished memory. I didn't think a knife would do a whole lot of good against a creature like the Etherazi, but I admired her spirit.

The nearest escape pod was situated in a spoke around the corner from the gym. Our group had just reached it when Aela's voice came over the comms.

"I'm sorry for the troubling update," Aela said, "but the Etherazi has picked up speed. It's closing rapidly."

Melian let out a squeak, and Batzian hugged her close. Tycius slapped the panel on the wall that opened the doors to the escape pod. The thing was basically the size of a minivan. It was going to be a tight squeeze.

"Get in, get in," Ty said.

Meanwhile, Captain Reno shouted back at Aela over the comms, as if the wisp could somehow slow the Etherazi's approach. "Not yet!" I heard the clatter of metal and Hiram cursing in the background. Apparently, the Battle-Anchor wasn't ready to deploy. "Damn it, Aela, we need more time—!"

"You do not have it," Aela said. "I'm sorry. It's upon us."

As the others piled into the escape pod, I broke loose from H'Jossu. The Panalax said something to me, but I wasn't listening. I *couldn't* listen. The voice in my head was too loud.

DO NOT RUN. I HAVE COME ONLY FOR YOU.

"Did you hear that?" I asked as I stood rooted in place, staring at the blank wall of the passage.

H'Jossu's floppy ears twitched. "Hear *what*?"

"Sydney!" my uncle shouted. "Get in the pod!"

"What's he doing?" I heard Melian ask.

"He wishes to die facing his enemy," Zara replied. "I approve, but I will not be joining him."

The entire *Eastwood* lurched. Something huge had just brushed up against us. I could sense the Etherazi out there. In fact, I could *see* it. Ripples of its golden energy filtered through the wall before me, defying logic and physics. The way the Etherazi's aura moved through the solid wall of the ship reminded me of bubbles floating to the surface of boiling water—*and that made no sense.* My sense of textures and space was thrown out of whack being so close to the thing. Behind me, I heard Arkell cry out in pain. I remembered the vision Aela had shown me, how gazing upon the Etherazi could drive a Denzan mad.

I turned around and shoved H'Jossu into the escape pod. He was a big boy, so I had to use some force—he almost took out Batzian on the way down. My uncle, shielding his eyes from the Etherazi's glow, lurched toward me.

"Sydney! Wait—!"

I slapped the panel on the wall, sealing up the escape pod. I was alone in the passageway.

GOOD.

The screech of rending metal stung my ears. The Etherazi ripped a hole in the wall in front of me. A new batch of sirens went off as this section of the *Eastwood* lost atmosphere. Emergency airlocks crashed into place at both ends of the passage, maintaining the rest of the ship. I was sucked toward the opening—no amount of strength would've stopped me from flying toward that jagged gap and the airless vacuum beyond.

Gold energy lapped me up, like a giant tongue. The Etherazi swallowed me.

And then it receded from the ship. Receded from the universe. Dragged me into the space in between.

I was a boy. Five years old. Riding on an airplane for the first time. I looked up at my mom, sitting next to me, as she gulped down some ice water, her hand shaking.

And then I was a man. In my forties. My beard scratchy. My arm ached all the time because of the metal sleeve I'd donned—my shame. I stood on the bridge of a spaceship with strangers all around me and stared at a screen, gazing out at a planet wreathed in fire. A hand patted me on the shoulder. I turned and came face-to-face with what was most definitely an older version of Zara, one of her ears missing, scars covering her snout.

"You did what had to be done," she said. "You—"

DON'T GET LOST NOW.

I'd been unstuck in time. Adrift in my past and future. The Etherazi shoved me back into the now, just as it had when I'd been overwhelmed by the Wayscope.

I floated through an emptiness, a stillness. The Etherazi was coiled around me. I could see into the beating core of the thing. A writing mass the size of a car, the thing was shaped like a heart—not a cutout Valentine's heart, but a gory and twisty science-class-dissection-day heart—ventricles and arteries and all that good stuff, tangled around one another, pumping out the incomprehensible energy that gave the Etherazi its dragon-like form.

"Yikes," I said, surprised my voice worked in this place. Surprised, also, that I wasn't dead. Unsurprised, at least, that the first thing I said was dumb as hell.

Two leathery flaps on the Etherazi's core peeled back, revealing an enormous eye—reptilian, jaundiced, and ancient. The sight of a massive floating eye was way grosser in person than those boring hobbit novels suggested. I tried to recoil, but the Etherazi held me in place.

THE BOY OF MANY NAMES. I HAVE WAITED GENER-ATIONS FOR YOU.

The Etherazi's voice was in my head with all the subtlety of an anvil. I tried to keep my cool.

"My ship, my friends, what did you—?"

THEY ARE WELL. I HAVE SPARED THEM TO CONSE-CRATE OUR ALLIANCE.

"Um, what?"

THE PLACE YOU SEEK. DEATH AWAITS YOU THERE.

I slid into another spot on my timeline, a place I didn't yet belong.

I stood on a planet where ash fell like snow. The clouds were dark overhead. Huge buildings cluttered the horizon, their windows shadowy gaps, many of them crumbling in on themselves. I got some real post–nuclear holocaust vibes. I held out my hands and let some of the foamy ash collect in my palms. My father's ring glowed brightly on my finger.

I was there. The planet where my dad was stranded. How far into my future was this?

Turning around, I caught sight of a massive structure at the end of the debris-covered road. A black pyramid, its walls a dull metallic black. There was a crashed spaceship—an ISV, like the *Eastwood*—broken against the side of the temple. It looked like someone had plowed the ship right into the building kamikaze-style, but the pyramid wasn't damaged in the least. In fact, considering how desolate everything else was around here, the temple was in remarkably good shape.

Whump!

Something struck me between the shoulder blades. I staggered forward two steps and fell to my knees. My chest was hot and sticky. I looked down—there was a dark hole in my sternum. I'd been shot clean through the heart.

I was supposed to be invulnerable. But something with enough force had lanced straight through me. I tasted and smelled fumes from my own insides, like motor oil. In those last moments, the worst part was not understanding. I didn't know how or why or—

COME BACK. THAT FUTURE IS NOT FOR YOU. ONLY IF YOU GO UNPREPARED. ONLY IF YOU DO NOT LISTEN.

I snapped back into my present, still floating through the Etherazi's energy field. I groped at my chest and gasped for breath.

"Did I just—?" I swallowed. My tears were cold on my cheeks. "Did I just die?"

The eye stared at me, completely unfeeling.

ONLY ONE END. OF MANY POSSIBLE. YOU ALWAYS DIE. ALL YOUR KIND MUST. BUT YOU MUST NOT DIE SO SOON.

"This is fucked," I said. "Why would you show me that? Why are we even talking?"

It occurred to me only after I said it that the alternative to talking with the Etherazi was getting eaten or turned to dust or whatever. Luckily, the monstrosity enveloping me didn't seem to mind my tone.

YOU WILL GO TO WHERE THE ASH FALLS. FIND WHAT IS LEFT OF YOUR FATHER.

"I was trying to do that when you showed up," I said. "I was trying to find—"

YOU WOULD FAIL. THERE ARE ENEMIES WITH YOU. IT IS NOT SAFE TO GO YET, BUT THE TIME WILL COME SOON. AFTER WE MEET AGAIN.

Enemies with you, said the colossal creature made from psychic energy whose species perpetuated planet-wide massacres for no apparent reason.

"This—this—!"

I shouted incoherently. Trapped in this in-between space with a cryptic-ass time-traveling intelligence, I was getting more than a little freaked out. I pinched the bridge of my nose and tried to regain some composure. This Etherazi had saved me from getting lost in the Vastness. It knew about my father. It knew a frightening amount about *me*. I needed to ask the right questions.

"Who are you?" I asked. "Why are you helping me?"

I AM THE GOLDEN PROPHET WHO LIGHTS THE WAY, THE KINSLAYER, HE WHO WALKS AMONG THE ENEMY, ARCHITECT OF LIBERATION.

"Oh," I replied, blinking. "That's your name?"

YES.

"It's long."

YOU ARE SYDNEY CHAMBERS, HUMAN, DENZAN, WORLD KILLER.

World killer?

"Um, no, just Syd is fine," I said.

SOON, THE MASTERS WILL RETURN.

"What masters?"

OUR OLD MASTERS FROM THE TIME FORGOTTEN. YOU CALL THEM THE LOST.

I blinked. "You mean the Lost People? My dad's research—"

THEY SEEK TO RECLAIM THEIR UNIVERSE.

"Uh, which universe is that, exactly?"

ALL.

"Oh."

YOU WILL KILL THEM IN THEIR CRADLE. I HAVE SEEN THIS.

The brief vision I'd had of myself—it wasn't exactly a vision; it was like jumping ahead to another part of my life. I'd stared down at a planet on fire. I knew, somehow, that I was the one who'd given the order. I'd torched that planet. And Zara was with me.

"Look, I don't know what you're talking about, but I don't really see myself becoming, like, a world killer, okay?"

INEVITABLE.

"Agree to disagree."

WE WILL MEET AGAIN WHEN IT IS TIME.

"When? What happened to my dad? What did he find out there? *Who—?*"

Even as I asked these questions, the giant eye flapped closed. I could sense the Etherazi beginning to recede from me, so I started shouting.

"Hey! Wait! You can't just—!"

It was gone.

I floated in the vacuum of space. Something like a daze came over me, an empty feeling in my mind due to the absence of the Etherazi's booming voice. And into that absence shot the knifelike pains of a major migraine.

Also, I couldn't breathe. The oxygen in my lungs was frozen. My skin crackled.

Exposed. In space. It left me out there.

And I was too messed up to care.

I remembered only fragments of Reno coming to get me, the captain buckled into her Battle-Anchor, the mech-suit even more intimidating up close. The bulky arms were surprisingly gentle as she wrapped me up and tugged me back toward the ship.

"Hang in there, Cadet," she told me, her voice shaky. "Hang in there."

I didn't know it then, but the Denzan part of me was working overtime, converting light rays from this galaxy's sun into nutrients, keeping me alive. Surviving in the vacuum of space was a lot like getting drowned by your mom.

Also, it wasn't just light rays my body was absorbing. There was a warmer, more powerful energy that I'd been exposed to. The Etherazi. It had fed me just enough to keep me going.

By the time Reno got me back on the *Eastwood*, my hair had turned a glowing shade of gold.

18

I tiptoed my way back to consciousness, coaxed awake by whispers. My nerve endings were slow to fire, but once they did, hoo boy, did I hurt. My headache was at spike-through-the-forehead level. My skin had a frostbitten sting; even the smooth-as-silk extraterrestrial sheets felt like they were covered with coarse bristles. Every inch of me screamed like tenderized meat.

It took some effort to stifle a moan, but I wanted to hear what they were saying about me. This was one of Mom's oldest lessons. Play possum until you know what's up.

"I need something that approaches an explanation, Tycius," Captain Reno said. "Because I don't know what in the blue blazes just happened."

Reno and my uncle were watching over me, whispering just a few feet from my bed. I could tell by the smell—like aloe and lemon—that we weren't in my room but in the *Eastwood*'s medical bay. I sensed a monitoring device squeezing my upper arm.

"I'm as baffled as you are," my uncle replied. "I've never seen anything like it. I'm not sure *anyone's* ever seen anything like it."

"Arkell and Aela were able to patch the breach in the ship," Reno said. "Arkell called the damage 'surgical.' Have you ever known one of those monsters to be surgical, Tycius?"

"Of course not."

"Our guard was down, and that son of a bitch should've torn right through us," Reno continued, with a mixture of relief and mystification. "The kid was *enveloped*, Tycius. The Etherazi had him out in the Vastness for some three minutes before I got to him. The monster kept him alive out there and then lit off like it'd just popped by to say hi."

If either of them were paying attention to the monitoring equipment, they would've noticed my pulse going up. It was really sinking in now. An extraterrestrial destroyer that even the Denzans didn't fully understand had sought me out.

World killer.

"The Etherazi incursion pinged on the institute's sensors," Reno continued. "They want to know what happened, and I've got no idea what to tell them."

"Tell the institute that we had a close call, but the hostile didn't seem interested in us."

Reno scoffed. "Close call? That was more than a—"

"Ten years ago, my brother disappeared, destroying his own trail and years of research in the process, and both the institute and the Senate were ambivalent about it," Tycius hurriedly whispered. "Now we have his son, the key to finding Marcius, and not two weeks after we leave Earth the kid turns into an Etherazi magnet. How do you think they'll respond to that news?"

Reno paused to consider this. I held my breath.

"I don't know," she admitted. "Your people love to talk. They'll talk the whole thing to death. The cadet will be my age before they so much as assemble a panel to debate the issue."

"Exactly," Ty said. "They'll take control away from us. I can't let that happen. Don't you want to find Marcius? Don't you want to know what he found?"

"Of course."

"Then we keep this quiet," Ty concluded. "The other cadets think Sydney tried—stupidly or bravely, depending on who you ask—to distract the Etherazi while you finished prepping your Battle-Anchor and that you saved him just in time. Vanceval wants to find Marcius as badly as we do; he'll play along. All we have to worry about is Arkell."

"I can keep Arkell in line," Reno responded. "I'm one of the First Twelve, and he's an ex-Rampart wannabe terrorist who couldn't blow up a balloon. For all his attitude, he loves the Vastness, and he knows one bad report from me will keep him planetside for the rest of his life."

"Good," Tycius replied. "We'll still want to keep an eye on him."

Reno's comm beeped, and I heard her suck her teeth. "The institute is hailing me again." She sighed. "I'll be back. I want to be here when he wakes up."

"I'll let you know," Tycius said.

Once Reno left, Tycius sighed deeply and sat down in a chair next to my bed. He brushed some hair out of my face, and I didn't feel at all weirded out by his long extraterrestrial fingers. It was comforting.

"I know you're awake," he said. "How much did you hear?"

I popped one eye open. "Most of it."

"How do you feel?"

"Like shit."

Tycius nodded. "Your hair is gold now."

"Seriously?"

I reached for the tablet on the table next to my bed and turned it to mirror mode. Tycius wasn't kidding. My hair was the color of coins in a video game, of bars in a bank vault. I matched the Etherazi who'd taken me.

"I kind of like it," I said.

"It'll fade once the Etherazi's energy leaves your body," Ty said. "I think. I'm not sure. I don't understand what happened at all, Sydney. I'm sorry."

"Don't worry about it," I replied. "I don't understand half the stuff I see up here either."

Ty shook his head like that wasn't much comfort. "I should've never let you use the Wayscope. I should've never rushed you."

He produced the cosmological tether and held it out to me. I took the ring, examining the faraway cosmos contained in the gemstone. A golden streak flashed across the surface—or maybe that was just my imagination.

"We've long known that it was possible to spot an Etherazi

through the Wayscope," Tycius continued. "But we never imagined that they could see us, too. That's what happened, right? It came for you."

I swallowed, setting the ring down, suddenly afraid of my only link to my father.

"I think it was waiting for me there," I said. "It knew we'd come looking."

"The way to Marcius . . . Did you see it? Could you find him?"

I shook my head. "I saw too much. It's all jumbled. I don't know where I was."

"Jumbled" was an understatement. Words got jumbled. My memory of the Vastness was like a broken window. Nothing fit together.

"We'll work up to it," Tycius said. "With training—"

"He said I wasn't ready yet, but when the time was right, I would know."

My uncle's mouth hung open. He gave me a look like I'd just said something insane.

"*Who* said that?"

The Golden Prophet? Kinslayer? The Architect of Liberation? The psychic space dragon had a ton of really dramatic names.

"The gold one," I settled on. "The Etherazi."

"You . . . you spoke to it?"

"Mostly he shouted words into my brain, but . . ." I hesitated because of the wide-eyed way my uncle was looking at me. "Yeah?"

Ty sat back. "Amazing," he said, stroking his chin. "There were attempts to communicate during the invasion of Denza. Some survivors of their temporal violence reported voices. None of it made sense. It all sounded like madness driven by contact with the Etherazi. But you're saying that the two of you . . ."

"Chatted," I said. "Yup."

My uncle leaned forward again. He was having trouble sitting still.

"You shouldn't tell anyone about that. Not even Captain Reno."

After listening in on his conversation with the captain, I didn't need to ask why. It would freak people out. "Okay."

"What did it say?" he asked.

What did the Etherazi say? Oh, well, it called me a world killer. Showed me my death. Showed me another future where I was watching a planet burn. Pretty good talk we had.

I decided right then it was probably smart to keep a few prophecies to myself. It's what my mom would've done.

"He told me that the masters were coming back," I said. "He seemed shook."

"What masters?"

"He said we call them the Lost. Like the . . ."

"The Lost People," Tycius finished, his eyes widening. "Why did he tell you this?"

Because I'm supposed to kill them in their cradle. Whatever the hell that means. Couldn't tell my uncle that.

"I think he was warning me," I replied. "He said these masters wanted to reclaim their universe."

"Mind games," Tycius said with a dismissive wave, then squinted, pondering the matter further. "But what would be the point of that?"

"I don't think he was screwing with me. I think he feels

threatened by . . . by whatever's out there. He said we should form an alliance."

"Diplomacy," Tycius said. "With marauders. This is unprecedented."

"I know you made fun of my Earth sci-fi, but in those books, like nine times out of ten it's the precursor aliens that come back from a cryogenic stasis or some shit and wage war against the younger species."

Ty's hair sprang up, then eased back down across his head. "Marcius's research focused on the Lost People. Their artifacts are so widespread, he thought they might have evolved traits or created tech that could help humans beat the Wasting. He thought he'd found their home world . . ." My uncle stroked his chin. "I've considered dozens of scenarios for why he was stranded out there. An accident. Sabotage. But what if Marcius found something that frightened him badly enough to cut himself off? What if he was trying to protect the rest of us . . . ?"

I nodded along. "And now, just when we come close to finding him, there's a big bad waiting out there to warn us off."

"I checked the Wayscope. An energy spike caused by the Etherazi erased the data it collected. We're still at square zero." Ty's mouth formed a tight line as he glanced down at the cosmological tether. "Knowing all this, I'd understand if you didn't want to try again."

"Whoa, I never said that," I replied. "The Etherazi didn't give me the impression that this is something we can just ignore. Not to mention, based on the Vulpin who attacked us on Earth, we aren't the only ones looking for my dad. We need to find him. I *want* to find him. I just think—I don't know—that we should be better prepared next time?"

Ty rubbed his arm, probably feeling like it was his fault that we'd jumped blind into this mess. Maybe he'd be attaching another metal band to his bicep later. I hoped not. I'd wanted to try locating my dad just as badly as he had.

"Next time, you have my word, we'll be ready. I'll get you ready. And we'll face whatever is out there together."

I clasped his hand. "Can't wait."

But that was a lie.

I'd seen my future, staring down at a burning planet.

What could bring me to that?

PART THREE

DENZA (I HALF BELONG HERE)

19

I stood with my hands pressed against the wall that I'd flipped to transparent mode, staring down at the approaching planet. The *Eastwood* coasted between two low-hanging moons, the satellites glowing orange from the rising sun. The ocean came into view—rippling and wide, dotted everywhere with islands. Those little havens were all connected by a spider's web of high-speed rail lines. As we got closer, I could see trains zipping between islands, the swaying tops of trees, people paddling boats down the coastline. I felt a drop in my stomach like an elevator going down too fast as the *Eastwood* slowed its descent. That was real gravity grabbing hold of me for the first time in weeks.

This was Denza. Not one of Aela's tutorial memories either. The real thing.

My first sunrise on another world.

"Pretty dope," I said to myself. I was alone on the *Eastwood*'s viewing deck. I'd gotten out of my cabin early, my trusty Earther backpack slung over my shoulder, hyped to explore a new planet.

I heard a small laugh behind me and turned to find Melian watching me with her hands clasped behind her back. "You're going to leave nose smudges on the wall, getting that close," she said.

I didn't step back, but I did buff the sleeve of my uniform against the wall-screen. "First alien planet," I said. "I'm kind of geeking out."

She came to stand next to me. "It's nice to come home."

After the incident with the Etherazi, I'd spent a few days recovering in the sick bay and then in my cabin. My advanced half-human metabolism stomped all over a little vacuum-caused frostbite, and I was back on my feet in a few days. The official narrative, which had come down from Captain Reno, was that in an act of foolish bravery I'd distracted the Etherazi long enough for her to scare it away in her Battle-Anchor. The rest of my crewmates weren't stupid—well, maybe Hiram was—and surely knew there was more to the story, but with all the senior members of the crew behind it, they had no choice but to accept it.

Melian, I thought, accepted it more readily than some of the others. She'd been looking at me with starry eyes for the rest of our trip to Denza. I didn't mind. It was nice to be the hero for once, instead of the lurking new kid with a dangerous secret. I mean, I still had dangerous secrets, but the heroism was fresh.

"That's Primclef down there," Melian said, "the world capital."

She pointed at the huge island we were gliding toward. Primclef was essentially a giant crater, mountainous on all sides except for what the locals called Keyhole Cove at the north end. Most of the important government buildings were housed directly in hollowed-out portions of the mountain ring; these included the Serpo Institute, the Denzan Senate, and the state-owned mining company that regulated the production of ultonate. These mountainside locales were connected by walkways, systems of elevators, and of course ample docking for skiffs ready to ferry passengers from one side of the island to the other. Down below, crater-side, as they called it, were the tightly packed Denzan neighborhoods. In all my travels on Earth, I'd never actually been to New York City, but that's what crater-side reminded me of with its regimented grid of city blocks and crowded streets, minus all the pollution, honking horns, and general chaos. The city was crisscrossed by a light rail system, some of the tracks disappearing into the mountains to zip passengers to other islands. There was precision to every bit of Primclef's design that satisfied something in me, a mathematical logic that scratched a mental itch.

"The mountain is a source of ultonate, so all the important buildings are housed in its caverns, since the metal repels Etherazi temporal attacks," Melian explained, an eager tour guide. "That little gap to the north—"

"Keyhole Cove," I said. "I know all this."

"You do?"

"Sure. It was all covered in that guide you made for me."

Melian's eyelids fluttered. "You actually read all that?"

"Like three times," I told her.

"Oh." Melian hugged herself, trying not to look too happy. I really had pored over her guide while I was bedridden, eager to know everything I could about Denza. "Well, then I guess I'll just say welcome to your new home, Syd."

I didn't expect it, but her words gave me a chill, made me feel at once hopeful and overwhelmed. Finally, I was in a place that I didn't need to run from.

Ten minutes later, the *Eastwood* docked in a mountainside shipyard, and the entire crew piled toward the exit ramp. After a few weeks in space, everyone was eager to stretch their legs and breathe some fresh air. As the exit ramp lowered, I found myself standing next to Darcy. She already had her hood pulled up to hide her face.

"Here," she said, shoving a wad of fabric into my chest.

It was a black winter hat. I raised an eyebrow. "What's this for?"

"Your head," she said. "Hide your hair. Unless you like getting stared at."

Contrary to what my uncle told me, the golden glow hadn't faded from my hair. I still looked like my head had been dipped in liquid metal, although some of my old color was coming back at the roots. My mom would've hated this look. Impossible to fly under the radar. I knew Darcy liked to hide her hybrid nature and thought the Denzans looked down on her, but I wanted to give them the benefit of the doubt. I stuck the hat in my back pocket.

"Thanks," I said. "But I'm going to see how it goes."

Darcy rolled her eyes. "Suit yourself."

The ramp lowered, and the entire crew exited onto the busy spaceport. The building was like a honeycomb carved into the side of the mountain, ships buzzing in and out from all angles. Most of the vessels were the little skiffs like my uncle had flown back on Earth. I did catch sight of some other massive Serpo starships like the *Eastwood*, with teams of cadets making repairs or running drills. I glimpsed what must have been a Panalaxan freighter wobble into a berth, the ship looking more like an uprooted oak tree than something capable of spaceflight.

As we disembarked, Zara immediately disappeared into the crowd. H'Jossu, meanwhile, bounded ahead, his snout tipped back to breathe in the salt-sweet air. I found myself doing the same, filling my lungs with my first big breath of Denza. I was really here.

Tycius put a hand on my shoulder. "Come on. Let's get you settled."

"Good call," I said. "I have no idea where I'm going."

My uncle led me along the crowded walkway, Denzans all around us. Most of them were too busy with their own lives to give me a second glance, but I definitely caught a few looks. We hadn't gone far when I noticed a group of Denzans that were definitely staring at us. One of them held a blown-up picture of Earth surrounded by the darkness of space, like a satellite photo. My home planet looked lonely floating out in the Vastness.

Before I could ask my uncle what their deal was, the Denzans came toward us.

"Check it out, Darcy." I heard Hiram cackle behind me. "It's your mom's best friends."

Oh, so these were the Merciful Rampart. The group of Denzans that thought humanity should stick to Earth, the ones who Arkell used to roll with. They didn't look like much. I'd been expecting scarred terrorists with missing fingers and eye patches, but this group looked like a bunch of middle-aged academics.

The leader stopped in Reno's way, and she let him, sighing deeply.

"Marie Reno, we appreciate all humanity has done for Denza," the guy said, in what sounded like a pretty well-trod bit. "But it is unnatural for your kind to stay. You have not yet earned your place in the stars. You should return to Earth, where you belong."

"Thank you for your opinion, sir," Captain Reno replied patiently. "I'll take it under consideration."

"And eat shit, buddy," Hiram added, which earned him a dirty look from the captain.

The handful of protestors seemed to take all this like it was part of a routine, and I wondered how many confrontations they'd had just like this one with humans entering the spaceport. I'd built the Merciful Rampart up in my head since I first heard about them, but they didn't seem all that threatening.

Except then the lead one glanced at me and I saw the way his mouth curled back and his nostrils flared, an unmistakable look of cold disgust. I almost reached for that hat in my back pocket.

"Arkell!" one of the protestors shouted. "How do you live with yourself?"

Our chief engineer brought up the back of our crew, dragging behind him a tote full of tools and spare parts. He hadn't said a word to me since our confrontation in the canteen. In fact, he hadn't really spoken to anyone except maybe Batzian, and then only to harangue the Denzan on how behind he was on his assignments (which Batzian actually wasn't, but he never stood up for himself). Just as she'd promised, Captain Reno had kept Arkell in line.

Arkell grimaced in response to the protestor. "With great difficulty," he muttered, then veered away from our group.

Everyone had places to go and people to see, so our crew gradually broke up as we made our way first through the spaceport and then along a series of mountainside walkways. Eventually, it was just my uncle and Aela walking with me. I didn't pay much attention to the route through the mazelike paths and stairwells—I could learn that later—I was more interested in the view. Whenever we were on an outdoor walkway, I couldn't help but stare at the partial eclipse, the choppy purple ocean, the thousands of Denzans going about their daily lives on similar paths on the other side of the crater. I was like a tourist, gawping at everything.

"Wonderful," Aela remarked. "To see you experience this for the first time, Syd, is the highlight of my day. So far, at least. It's early. Still, very good."

I smiled at the wisp, and the magenta cloud behind the faceplate formed a curlicue in response.

"Here we are," Tycius said. "The institute."

I knew we were getting close by the number of cadets I'd seen walking around with uniforms identical to mine except for the different ship insignias stitched into the shoulders. Most of the other ISVs had symbols involving stars, or flowers, or geometric designs. Reno was the only captain to have chosen a weapon.

The institute itself was built into the rock face: six stories of classrooms and dorms, with a cavernous entrance flanked by benches and gardens. The whole thing gave off very Greek vibes to me—open and welcoming, with Denzans and a smattering of other extraterrestrials hanging around engaged in deep discussions.

We passed through the arched entrance, the air inside cool and welcoming. Back on Earth, in my days as a town-hopping fugitive, I'd slouched drowsily into a bunch of different schools. I knew the routine, and it wasn't any different at the Serpo Institute. As soon as you walked through the doors, it felt like everyone in the hallway was staring at the new kid. The thing was, that was mostly in your head. Maybe you caught some looks, but most kids had too much of their own shit on their minds to care about some rando.

The big difference at the Serpo Institute was that the dozens of faces all belonged to aliens.

Oh, and I was pretty sure they *were* actually staring at me. Half-humans were a pretty rare thing. Especially ones with heads of glowing golden hair.

Tycius led us down a hallway of classrooms. They were spacious and furnished with high-backed chairs that looked like seats from the fancy movie theaters back home, the ones with recliners. In front of each chair was a pedestal-mounted touch screen. The stations were arranged in a semicircle around a central lectern.

"Is it very different from your Earth classrooms?" Aela asked.

"Uh, yeah, a little different," I said. "A lot of places I went to school, we had to share desks because some rich dickhead didn't want to pay taxes."

Aela shrugged. "Sharing is nice, though."

We rode a glass-walled elevator up to the dorms. The view was, of course, amazing. It was the time of day the Denzans called Playful Dawn, when the early morning sun rose, then hid behind one of Denza's moons, and then peeked back out again. The sky was rippling orange and purple, and I couldn't take my eyes off it.

The elevator let us out in a curved hallway with dozens of doors on either side. My uncle checked his tablet.

"Forty-two," he said, pointing. "Your room's over here."

The lock on my dorm was biometric, so I had to stand there for a few seconds scanning my palm before it would let me in.

"I'm right down the hall," Aela said. "Our whole crew is on this floor, actually. Except for Hiram and Darcy. They're from Primclef, so they live off campus. Stop by if you want to hang out later."

"I will," I replied. "Your room is the one without any furniture, right?"

"Or windows!" Aela replied cheerily, then paced down the hallway to do whatever wisps do in their spare time.

My room's door finally clicked open, revealing a space not so different from the one on the *Eastwood*. A double bed, desk, bookshelf (empty), closet (stocked with spare uniforms), vid-screen (blank), and private bathroom. My window looked out on the ocean, the frothy waves and glowing reefs, three moons currently visible like pearls in the sky.

Tycius glanced at his tablet again, which was lit up with notifications. "It seems like I've got ten years' worth of meetings today." He sighed. "Are you okay if I leave you?"

"I'm good, Uncle," I replied. "If I need help, I'll track down Aela or one of the others."

Ty nodded and patted me on the shoulder. "Welcome to Denza, Syd."

Once I was alone in my room, I think I spent a good hour just staring out at the ocean and watching the moons slowly inch across the sky. Eventually, I decided I should double-check my schedule of classes. Like a true dork, I was planning to look for the rooms today so I wouldn't be late tomorrow.

In addition to the required math and science courses that were tailored to an Earthling of my experience (remedial, it turned out), I'd signed up for some electives:

INTRODUCTION TO WAYSCOPES (Instructor Coreyunus). RESTRICTION: DENZANS ONLY. If I was going to take another crack at using my dad's cosmological tether, I needed to make sure I could properly use a Wayscope without frying my brain. I figured since I was half-Denzan, I didn't have to worry about the restriction.

DENZAN HISTORY: THE ETHERAZI INCURSION (Instructor Rafe Butler). My mom had told me to track down Rafe Butler, another one of the First Twelve, so I'd made sure to sign up for his lecture. I was sure he was related to Hiram, but I'd never bothered to ask. Personal conversations with Hiram were nonstarters.

ARTIFACTS OF THE LOST PEOPLE (Instructor Theoretician Vanceval). My dad had been one of Vanceval's students, and old Vanceval had personally requested I take his class. Of course, if the Lost People my dad had gone searching for were really some universe-conquering masters like the gold Etherazi (aka Goldy, as I was now calling him in my brain to make him less terrifying) said, then I wanted to know as much about them as possible. Before I fulfilled my destiny of blowing up their world. But I was trying pretty hard not to think about that.

And, finally, I decided to take a chance with my last elective.

I STALK YOU (Instructor Zara den Jetten). It was no wonder Zara's class didn't have any sign-ups. The course description was the same as the title, and there was no set time or location. Something brought Zara and me together in a distant future where I could grow a beard and we blew up a planet. Taking her bizarre class seemed like the only way to get to know her.

I'd also entered my own class into the registry of hundreds of seminars taught by Serpo staff and students. I had titled it Kick-Ass Earth Sci-Fi, but some smug Denzan in the institute's registration office had edited into this:

INTERGALACTIC POSSIBILITIES THROUGH THE LENS OF PRIMITIVE FICTION (Instructor Sydney Chambers). *In this course, you will read fiction created by humans and attempt to discover meaning and value in the words of an unevolved species.*

They didn't make it sound very good, but that didn't stop H'Jossu from signing up.

I figured once I'd prepared for tomorrow, I could spend the rest of my day exploring. I called up the list of hot spots Melian had made for me, which also included helpful instructions on how to get to each one from the dorms. Maybe I'd go check out Keyhole Cove, the neighborhood around the beach.

I soon found myself on one of the institute's open-air walkways overlooking the city. I kept glancing down at my tablet and still got turned around trying to navigate all the different paths. I also just kept staring out at the city, letting all that sprawling alien architecture fizz across my mind.

From behind, a pair of strong hands clasped my shoulders, squeezing hard.

"Don't jump!" Hiram bellowed in my ear. "The institute isn't that bad!"

Hiram and Darcy stood behind me. The big doofus belly-laughed at his own stupid joke while Darcy rolled her eyes and tugged at the strings of her hood.

"Uh, hey, guys," I said, rubbing my shoulders where Hiram had dug his fingers in.

"What're you doing?" Darcy asked me.

I shrugged. "Just getting a handle on things, I guess. Taking in the sights."

"His Earther mind is probably blown," Hiram said. "He's been—what, living in a house made of mud, feeling sick every day, riding a big orange tank to his prison-school. And now he's free!"

"We call them buses."

"Buses!" Hiram laughed. "Fucking Earth. They crack me up back there."

"We've been waiting for you," Darcy said.

"Yeah, man," Hiram said. "We're going to *Little* Earth, and you've gotta come."

"Little Earth?" I asked.

"Where most of the humans choose to live," Hiram said. "It's an island that the Denzans gave to us after we saved their scrawny asses back in the big one."

"I was actually thinking of checking out Keyhole Cove."

Hiram groaned. "What're you trying to catch fleas from some Vulpin? Hell no. Little Earth is mandatory."

With that, he hopped up on the railing of the walkway. He balanced there easily. It was a forty-foot drop to the walkway beneath ours and probably a good mile down to the crater.

"It's tradition with new Earthers that we race to the rail station," Hiram declared.

"You told me you'd never had an Earth cadet before," I replied.

"Well, tradition has to start somewhere, right?"

And with that, Hiram jumped. I raced to the edge of the walkway just in time to see him stick the landing. For a moment, I'd forgotten about our strength here. A drop like that was basically like hopping off a step stool. Hiram glanced back up at Darcy and me, let out a ridiculous *whoop whoop*, and started to sprint to the next railing.

Hiram was an asshole, which made me all the more inclined

to chase after him and win this pointless race. Plus, I hadn't gotten a chance to use my enhanced strength except in the confined environments of the *Eastwood*'s gym. I was eager to discover what I could do.

Darcy grabbed my elbow before I could start. "Hiram should've told you, but try not to hurt any bystanders when we race. That'll get us in deep shit if it happens again."

"I won't," I said. "Wait—*again?*"

In response, Darcy pulled the hat she'd given me out of my back pocket and yanked it down over my eyes.

"You're already in last," she said, then swept my legs out from under me and kicked me in the chest so that my body slid back to the wall. It didn't hurt—I mean, not like it should've—but it definitely took me by surprise. By the time I got my bearings, Darcy was already two walkways below me.

"Cheaters," I muttered and gave chase.

20

One of our most basic instincts as humans is to avoid falling off tall things. Each time I hurdled over a railing and took on the forty-foot drop to the landing below—arms waving, legs bicycling—my stomach curled up in a knot, and my brain screamed *don't do this, don't do this, don't do this.*

And each time I landed—my legs feeling springy and loose, the impact barely noticeable, already gathering steam for the next jump—my body screamed *go, go, go.*

On Earth, I'd been a fragile creature whose ankles would've exploded from a drop half that size.

Not on Denza.

I was rewiring my brain, overwriting my instinct. Learning to function as a superhuman.

From the outset, it was clear that Hiram was letting us back in the race. Despite his head start, I could still see him as he finished leaping down the last few landings. He punctuated each jump with a flourish—a backflip, a midair twist, a ridiculous split where he touched his toes. He was more interested in showing off than in winning. Denzan bystanders leaped back when Hiram landed among them. Some clapped for his gymnastics, but others shot him dirty looks. Mostly, though, the locals seemed used to this kind of behavior.

Unlike Hiram, Darcy wasn't a showboat. She didn't waste movement, and she definitely didn't go for style points. She skipped the landings entirely, instead leaping straight from railing to railing, sometimes landing in a handstand and slinging herself downward with power.

I couldn't throw myself into the descent with the same reckless abandon as the other two. I jumped from each landing with a hitch of hesitation and made sure to bend my knees dramatically upon impact. When I landed near passing Denzans, they didn't look pissed or amused—they looked worried for me.

I was only halfway down when Hiram reached the bottom, Darcy just a couple levels behind him.

Hiram landed in the midst of a circle of Denzan scholars sharing poetry. They recoiled at the disruption, but Hiram barely noticed them. He looked back at the cliff-side walkways, checking to see if I was following. Spotting me midjump, he hooted and waved. Then he saw Darcy bearing down on him and took off at a sprint.

I might have been new to Primclef, but it wasn't difficult to find the train station. Just needed to follow the tracks to the central building twenty blocks east of the institute. There weren't really roads here, because the Denzans didn't have cars. They mostly walked or used electric-powered scooters or piloted airborne skiffs like the one my uncle chased us with on Earth. Even without cars and with a good amount of air traffic, the pathways to the station were pretty busy. There were multiple outdoor tea shops and restaurants, a farmers' market, and a small park's worth of tables where older Denzans huddled over holographic game boards. Too many obstacles down there, I figured.

Hiram seemed to relish the challenge. He bulled through pedestrians or leaped over them, shouting greetings and apologies in the same breath.

Darcy soon overtook him. She kicked Hiram's back leg into his front leg and sent him spilling into a cart of mushrooms, the Denzan merchant's hair flaring up in anger. She held the lead for only a few seconds before Hiram—more focused on the race now that he'd been shown up—tackled her from behind. It went on like that, the two of them pausing to wrestle every few blocks, Darcy's dirty tricks often overcoming Hiram's superior strength.

I wasn't going to mess with all that.

The quickest route didn't involve charging down a crowded street making an asshole of myself.

On the second-to-last landing, with Hiram and Darcy already brawling halfway to the train station, I waited. My shortcut was on its way.

A low-flying skiff passed overhead. I leaped up and grabbed

ahold of the pyramid-shaped ship's edge. At first, my hands slipped right off the smooth metal. My adrenaline was running high, though, and my fingertips dug in, creating little dents to hold on to.

I was sure those would buff right out.

I sailed over the streets below. The skiff was on a direct course for the busy rail station. I'd float right in, way ahead of Hiram and Darcy.

A panel on the side of the skiff buzzed down, and a Denzan woman in a high-necked dress poked her head out. One of her eyes narrowed when she spotted me.

"Human," she said, then took a closer look at me and corrected herself. "Youngling, that behavior is quite dangerous. You're compromising the integrity of our transport, and we're already late for an appointment."

A trio of Denzan children poked their heads out the window, climbing over one another to get a look. They clapped and whistled, grinning like I was some kind of superhero. I crossed my eyes at them.

"Sorry, ma'am," I said. "I'll drop off here."

I hung by one arm and clicked my heels—I guess I had a little bit of the Hiram showboat in me too, at least when it came to clowning for some kids—then dropped lightly to the roof below.

My attempt at hitchhiking hadn't been for nothing. While I was in the air, I'd made note of a route across the rooftops that would get me to the station quickly. It zigzagged a bit across the main thoroughfare, but if I stuck to the map in my head, I'd be leaping across buildings that were uniform in height, no climbing to slow me down.

Easy, right?

Leaping across rooftops. I did that now.

I bounded forward, taking the gaps between buildings easily. I wasn't sure where Hiram and Darcy were until I felt the wall beneath me vibrate just as I was about to jump. The two of them had crashed flush into the front wall of this apartment building. The wood and stone creaked a bit, dust shaking loose.

"Oof," Hiram grunted as Darcy pressed her forearm into his neck. "Where's Syd?"

"You probably scared him off with all your shit talk," Darcy replied.

"If he scares off that easy, then we don't want him around," Hiram said, shoving Darcy away from him.

I glanced back the way the two of them had come. They'd left a bit of a mess in their wake—overturned tables and carts, some Denzans brushing themselves off after getting knocked over.

I wasn't sure this was the best example for human-Denzan relations, but then I wasn't from here. Hiram and Darcy were. If they treated Primclef like a playground, who was I to argue?

On my next jump, my shadow must have been caught in one of the streetlamps, because I heard Darcy shriek from below, "He's above us!"

"Damn!" Hiram bellowed. "That's the kind of cheap shit you would pull, Darcy."

Now that they were onto me, I needed to haul ass. The two of them scrabbled up a wall, and soon their footfalls were pounding behind me. I could tell Hiram was gaining because he insisted on screaming bloody murder every time he made a simple jump from one rooftop to the next. I tried to push myself into another gear, but they were both faster than me.

Hiram pulled even beside me. "Hiya," he said, grinning.

I sucked in a breath and tried to surge forward.

He face-palmed me with enough force to send me flying off the roof.

Not going to lie—I wailed like a banshee going down. I hit the ground on the back of my head, bounced, and skidded about ten feet on my shoulder.

It hurt. I can't say it didn't hurt. But falling off a building and landing on my head shouldn't have *hurt*—it should've *killed* me. I was lightly stunned, at worst. I reached around to touch the back of my head. There was no blood, not even any swelling. Maybe what stung the most were my cheekbones where Hiram had shoved my face.

We were only a block away from the train station at that point. Darcy finished at a sprint across the rooftops, but Hiram bounded down to street level to help me up.

"Didn't hurt you, did I?" he asked, gruffly brushing me off. "I'm never sure how far is too far with you halfies."

"Yeah, chucking me off a roof was maybe too far," I said. I should've been pissed off, but that didn't come through in my tone. I was laughing. Giddy. Hiram grabbed my shoulders and shook me.

"I love that look in your eye. It's really sinking in now that we're off the ship, isn't it?" he asked. "Fucking invincible, pal. It rules."

Darcy was waiting for us aboard the train. The interior was designed a lot like the *Eastwood*—soft lighting, wood paneling, plush private seating compartments. I followed them down the aisle until they picked out an empty booth and piled in on one side.

I glanced over my shoulder. "Don't we need to pay for a ticket?"

Hiram snorted. "I always forget, they charge for everything on Earth, don't they? You sound like my grandpa. He grew up in someplace called Detroit. He's always worrying about how much things cost even though everything on Denza is free."

"Don't listen to him. Everything is not free," Darcy said.

"I'll let you in on a little secret," Hiram said, leaning into my space as soon as I sat down across from him. "They love us here. Forget those fish-dicks at the spaceport this morning. They're like a tiny minority. Most Denzans worship the ground we walk on."

Darcy crossed her arms and slouched in her seat, frowning but not contradicting Hiram.

"That lady whose mushroom cart you wrecked didn't seem happy to see you," I said.

Hiram snorted. "Man, she'll go home and tell her husband about how lucky she got. I'm telling you, I can walk into any food hall in this city and they'll be lining up to serve me. Our species saved this whole planet. It's a debt they can't repay."

Our train started to move, zooming forward like a bullet, yet the ride was completely smooth and soundless, the tracks curving across a series of columns that rose up out of the ocean. The water was tinted purple right now, one of the moons blotting out the sun, but we were riding right into a panel of shimmering light, speeding straight out of the eclipse.

A uniformed Denzan woman appeared at our compartment. Darcy refused to look up at her. "Greetings. May I offer any of you a complimentary beverage or a hot towel?"

"Fuck yes, hot towel, please," Hiram said. He draped the towel around his neck. "Is the snack car open?"

"Yes, sir," the attendant replied, proceeding on her route.

"Watch," Hiram said to me, standing up. "I'm going to come back with so many free salty-doughs, you're going to shit."

I doubted that I would shit, no matter how much free food Hiram scavenged from charitable Denzans, but I flashed him an encouraging smile. It'd be a relief to be without Hiram for a few minutes.

Once he was gone, Darcy and I were quiet. She thumbed her lip, blatantly staring at me. I could tell there was something she wanted to ask me.

"Your dad was Denzan," she finally said.

"*Is* Denzan," I corrected. "Yeah."

"He's the one whose cosmological tether you're carrying around."

I touched the chest pocket of my uniform. Everyone on the crew had seen my confrontation with Arkell. There was no point in lying.

"Yeah."

Darcy nodded thoughtfully. I expected her to ask something about my accident with the Wayscope or the run-in with the Etherazi. She was sharp and observant; I thought maybe she'd push back on the story Captain Reno and the others were feeding her.

"Do you think he loved you and your mom?" she asked instead.

I blinked. *"What?"*

She looked away. "Nothing. It's stupid. Never mind."

"No, it's not—you just caught me off guard," I replied. "I mean, I didn't really get to know him. I was young when he left. But from everything I remember and the stuff my mom told me . . . yeah. He's my dad, right?"

"My mom was in the Merciful Rampart," Darcy replied quietly. "I was her *assignment.*"

I squinted. "What does that mean?"

"They aren't all geeks like those ones being all polite at the spaceport," Darcy said sharply. "They think humans are brutes and savages. That we'll try to take over someday. They think hybrids like you and me are Denza's only hope. *Human in body, but Denzan in mind.* They want to breed ones like us to fight off the other humans if they ever get out of line."

I took a deep breath. That was the most I'd ever heard Darcy speak at once, and it was *a lot.* Heavy shit. No wonder she stalked around like a living storm cloud all the time. I couldn't help but see a parallel between the Merciful Rampart using hybrids to protect their planet and my mom wanting to bring enhanced humans back to Earth to save ours.

I struggled to find the right words. "That's fucked up, Darcy. But, uh, just because her politics are weird doesn't mean your mom doesn't—"

"I don't need your reassurance," she snapped. "I just wanted you to know. In case your dad's the same way. He could be, you know."

I swallowed. Knowing what I did about my dad—how hard he'd researched a cure for the Wasting, how he was down with my mom's plan for world domination—I kind of doubted he was a double agent for the Merciful Rampart. But I couldn't tell Darcy all that.

Hiram came back a few seconds later. Empty-handed.

"The snacks sucked," he pouted.

I sighed and looked out the window.

It was a forty-five-minute ride to Little Earth, our train stopping at five other island hubs on the way north to the equatorial island. Hiram spent most of the time complaining about the classes he was taking, then started grilling me about the ones I'd signed up for.

"You're never going to get in shape if you don't spar with other humans," Hiram said, shaking his head. "Come on. Join my judo class."

"I did sign up for a class on the Etherazi war with a guy named Rafe Butler," I said, trying to change the subject. "Do you know him?"

"That's my grandpa," Hiram said. "He was one of the First

Twelve, like yours. You knew that, right?"

I played dumb and shook my head.

"Damn," Hiram said. "I thought everybody knew Grandpa. Even backwater Earthlings."

Darcy smirked at me. "You signed up for Propaganda 101? Without the Chef even asking?"

"The Chef?"

Hiram slouched in his seat; it was the first time I'd seen him look embarrassed. "Grandpa teaches that same class every semester. Tells the same old war stories. Says it's good to remind the Denzans what we did for them. He expects every human who comes to the institute to take it."

"*You* didn't have to take it," Darcy said to Hiram.

"Please, do you know how many times I've heard about the time he killed an Etherazi with the legs of his Battle-Anchor malfunctioning? It's like every weekend for me." Hiram slapped my knee. "He's going to love that you signed up, though. He would definitely have tried to twist your arm."

Darcy elbowed him. "We didn't tell him he's supposed to meet the Chef."

Hiram snapped his fingers. "Oh, right. So, this isn't totally a spontaneous hangout. We were asked to bring you to Little Earth so that Grandpa could get a look at you. Size you up."

I leaned back in my seat. The island was coming into view now, our train zipping around a curling reef of neon coral, silver-beaked birds taking flight as we scared them off their roost. From our upraised perspective, I had a good look at Little Earth. The buildings on the island lacked the precision of Denzan city planning, that mathematical strictness that was like a balm to my half-Denzan brain. Instead, the island looked like the suburban sprawl of Earth, as if the first buildings had gone up without any foresight, then bigger ones followed with no thought to the skyline, then others randomly set farther away, all this connected by circuitous roads. It was a bit like being home again.

"What does he want with me?" I asked, turning back to Hiram and Darcy.

Hiram shrugged. "Grandpa is friends with everybody. It's a little ridiculous."

"He runs things here," Darcy added. "For humans, at least. He's like a mayor. If you've got a problem, you visit the Chef."

We pulled into the station. The three of us were the only ones getting off, the only humans on the train. The sun was out now, this little enclave of humanity bathed in a golden light.

"Oh," Hiram said, glancing over his shoulder at me. "That's right. I guess Grandpa knew your dad. I think he's got some questions. Like, when are we invading Earth? That sort of thing."

21

I stared at Hiram. "You know about that?"

He rolled his eyes. "Sure. Your dad was supposed to cure the Wasting, and then my grandpa and some of the other old-timers were planning to go back to Earth and set it straight." He puffed out his chest. "Our greatest responsibility is to save humanity from itself." Hiram made a jerk-off motion.

I didn't know what to say. The night I left Earth, my mom had made it seem like their plan was a hush-hush conspiracy of the utmost importance. Hiram talked about it flippantly, like his grandpa had dementia.

He read my expression and continued. "Look, dude, no one wants to go back to Earth. Denza is fucking great. Half of us were *born* here. You think I want to waste years policing a bunch of dirty savages on a polluted wastewater? No thank you. There's a whole galaxy out there to explore."

I glanced at Darcy, and she shrugged noncommittally. I wasn't even fully invested in my mom's bonkers plan. At first, my goal out here was to simply find my dad and, you know, actually get to know the guy. Setting up an invasion of Earth was a distant second, and now it'd been bumped down the priority list even further by Goldy and his creepy prophecies. Even so, the way Hiram talked about my mom's plan goaded me into defending it.

"There's billions of us back on Earth, though. If we don't help them—"

Hiram waved me off. "They'll figure it out," he said. "Just humor my grandpa, okay? He's still in charge here for now. Come on. We'll show you around."

The Denzans made a gift of Little Earth to the astronauts who'd fought off the Etherazi invaders, and, when the Senate decided to allow more humans to immigrate to Denza via the Serpo Institute, it became home to most of them. The island was chosen in particular because of its position on the equator, where it would receive more direct sunlight and fewer eclipses than other spots in the vast archipelago, and so better support human life. It was also chosen because it was completely empty. Previously a recreation island for the Denzans, its entire population and all of its buildings had been destroyed by the Etherazi. After learning all that from Hiram and Darcy, I'd expected Little Earth to have a haunted feeling, the human settlement having been built on top of a mass grave.

Instead, Little Earth was like the quaint town square of a 1950s sitcom. I kept expecting to see a kid with a slingshot following his trusy dog to where someone was trapped in a well. The place was clean, and folksy, and hella dorky.

The cobblestone streets were lined with flagpoles—the US, Australia, Canada, Egypt, Russia, France, and more—all countries, presumably, that the Serpo Institute had recruited from at some point. This apple-pie-ass main street had a barbershop with the red-and-white-striped pole, an old-fashioned two-screen movie theater currently playing a couple of blockbusters that I'm sure came out like ten years ago, and something called a "malt shop." There was also a grocery store with a big sign in the window that advertised imported (from Earth) sugar cereals. And, at the center of it all, a pizzeria.

Part of the reason Little Earth felt like a painted backdrop was because it was so empty. I spotted a few humans wandering around the grocery store, but that was it.

"Where is everybody?" I asked Hiram.

"There's only like five hundred humans that belong to the Serpo Institute," he said. "A lot of them are deployed on ships or working in Primclef or—"

"Or doing literally anything to avoid hanging out in this corny Earth museum," I said.

Darcy tilted her head. "The Chef always says this is an ideal version of Earth. You don't like it?"

I scratched the back of my neck. "I don't know. It feels kind of . . . phony?"

"Don't say any of that to my grandpa," Hiram said.

The two of them walked me toward the pizzeria. I sniffed baked dough and spices in the air as we got closer. At least they'd gotten the smells right.

Just as we were nearing the door, Captain Reno emerged from the restaurant. Off duty, she wore a checkered shirt, some mom jeans, and a visor like she was about to do her taxes. It was the first time she'd actually looked like she was in her seventies.

"Aha," Reno said by way of greeting, putting her fists on her hips. "You know, I just now got complaints about a trio of humans making asses of themselves outside the institute. Any idea who that was?"

We all straightened a bit at the sight of the captain. "Wasn't us, ma'am," Hiram said, unable to keep the smirk off his face.

"Convincing," Reno replied. She pointed at me. "Chambers, you go on inside and introduce yourself to Rafe. I'm going to have a word about manners with these other two."

The interior of the pizzeria looked pretty much identical to one on Earth. Black-and-white-checkered tiles, booths, a glass counter that housed a handful of different pizzas, and a brick oven for reheating slices. I edged over to the counter to scope out the pies. They looked mostly normal to me, if you considered deep dish normal—red sauce, congealed cheese, mostly mushrooms for toppings, except for one that featured some pink circles that looked too spongy to be pepperoni.

"You're not going to eat any of that," a merry voice said. "I won't allow it."

Rafe Butler came through the swinging doors that led back to the kitchen, wiping his hands on his flour-coated apron. Except for his square-shaped head and broad shoulders, Rafe looked nothing at all like his grandson. He was shorter than me and sturdily built with a full head of ink-black hair and a matching goatee, both of which were obviously dyed. He had puffy cheeks and a round belly that had ballooned since the old picture my mom had shown me. He circled around the counter and thrust a hairy hand at me, shaking vigorously as he introduced himself.

"Seriously, you can't have any pizza," he said again. "Don't even ask me."

I hadn't actually planned to eat any pizza, but now that I was standing there, my stomach was a little rumbly. "Why not?"

"It's terrible," Rafe said. He rested his hands on the case, gazing down at his work. "You've just come from Earth. You still remember what pizza actually tastes like. This here is a Denzan knockoff. The cheese is salty and a little chewy because the milk comes from these reef-dwelling amphibians. Those pepperonis aren't the real thing—they're basically shrimp, because the Denzans don't allow us any real meat. And I haven't even gotten to the worst part yet."

I could tell by the twinkle in his eye that this was going to be a well-worn punch line. I went along with it. "What's the worst part?"

"I'm not even Italian!" He chuckled. "I'm from Montreal originally, moved to Detroit when I was a kid. A French-Canadian making pizza. Can you believe it?"

"I mean, we're having this conversation a few million light-years from Earth, so yeah, your pizza isn't the weirdest thing I've encountered lately," I said.

"Touché," Rafe replied. He talked quickly and easily, moving his hands a lot. I could tell he was the kind of guy with an arsenal of anecdotes always at the ready. "After the war, I couldn't get pizza out of my head. I thought about going back to Earth, just to get a slice. Sure, I'd die from the Wasting, but it'd be worth it. Instead, I opened this place." He circled around the counter, looking at me. "Give it a year. Maybe two. Then come back, and my pies will be the best you've ever had."

I tilted my head. "Why? You going to take a class or something?"

"No," he replied. "Because you'll have forgotten what the real thing tastes like. Once that happens, mine won't seem so bad."

The thought gave me pause. I'd just gotten to Denza, and everything here and out in the Vastness was still so fresh and new. As I dived into the experience, I'd never considered the possibility that I could forget things about Earth. Yet, already, my home planet had started to seem a bit like a distant memory.

"You look just like him," Rafe said, shaking his head as if in awe.

I glanced out the front window, but Reno and my crewmates were gone. "Reno said the same thing."

"She was probably talking about your grandpa. Me? I see your dad in there. His mind used to wander off places, same way yours just did." He gave my shoulder a squeeze. "Marcius was one of the good guys. He genuinely wanted to help humanity."

I resisted the urge to correct the past tense. If he'd been talking to Reno, I assumed Rafe already knew about the cosmological tether and maybe even the encounter with the Etherazi. I got the sense that he was feeling me out.

"I didn't really get a chance to know him," I said.

"There's still time, kid." He winked, then untied his apron and set it on the counter. "No customers, as usual. Let's take a walk."

We strolled onto the empty streets of Little Earth. A middle-aged human couple held hands on their way to the train station. They were the only other people in sight. Rafe steered us in the opposite direction, toward a small park with curving Denzan trees that looked like dark green weeping willows.

"You should import some tumbleweeds from Earth," I suggested. "Place has a real ghost-town vibe."

Rafe walked slowly with his hands clasped behind his back. "Funny," he replied with a thoughtful smile. "You know, you're the first human recruit the Consulate has sent us in—oh, probably three years? And you're a special case."

I raised an eyebrow. I'd gotten the sense that the Denzan Consulate back on Earth had a sweeping global operation. I figured they'd been sending candidates to the Serpo Institute all the time. But, now that Rafe mentioned it, the only humans or part-humans I'd met so far had been born here.

"Why so few?" I asked him.

"The Senate would tell you that every candidate has to be properly vetted and that they don't want the Serpo Institute to be flooded with students." Rafe gave me a deadpan look. "Truth is, they don't want too many of us up here. They worship us, but we also scare them."

I nodded. "We had a welcoming committee from the Merciful Rampart waiting for us at the spaceport."

Rafe snorted. "Of course you did. Those guys are dedicated, I'll give them that. They're afraid we'll try to take over. Your average Denzan probably thinks that a little bit too, but at least they feel shame about not trusting us. Generally, they're more afraid of the Etherazi than they are of us. So they keep us around in case those monsters come back but limit our numbers. It's a balancing act. There're exactly 521 humans living in the stars. Some are second- or third-generation, like my idiot grandson. The Denzans prefer that, too. They like humans who were born on Denza because they don't have any messy ties to Earth. That's why we see so few Earth-born cadets."

I thought all that over. The relationship between Denza and humanity was complicated, and I wasn't ready to jump to any conclusions after only having been on the planet for a day.

"My mom said the Denzans should be doing more to help Earth," I said after a moment.

"Hmm," Rafe replied noncommittally. "How much did she tell you?"

I lowered my voice, even though there wasn't anyone around. "She said you wanted to bring some enhanced humans back to Earth and take over the planet."

"No offense, kid, but your mom has a cynical way of looking at things," Rafe replied. "We'd go back as saviors, not invaders.

We'd show the rest of our species what's possible if they got their shit together. And, if it weren't for the Wasting, we'd go back with the confidence that we wouldn't need to worry about getting gunned down because some authoritarian president or exploitative megacorp didn't like what we had to say."

"Sure," I said. "Go all Clark Kent. Topple a few governments, make recycling mandatory . . ."

Rafe grinned. "If that's what it takes."

We'd come to the entrance of the park, an oval area with benches set up around a bubbling fountain. Suspended above the water on an antigravity platform was a gold-plated sculpture of twelve humans. The First Twelve that had come to Denza.

"Gosh, I was skinny then," Rafe said, patting his belly.

Rafe's likeness stood on one end, standing with his arms crossed, posed back-to-back with another astronaut. All of them wore flight suits, some casually unzipped with the sleeves rolled up, others looking tightly wound and militaristic. I recognized a younger version of Reno up there, her head tipped back, either shouting or laughing. And then the handsome man with his arm slung around her shoulders, giving a cheesy thumbs-up for all of eternity—well, that was my grandfather.

"This beauty always gets me sentimental," Rafe said, knuckling the corner of his eye. "How is it back home these days?"

"It's . . . uh . . ." I was a little distracted with the image of my grandfather in full health, looking like me if I lifted weights for the next ten years and had one of those dimpled chins. "Not great, Rafe."

"I hear the ice caps are all but gone. Sea levels swelling. Droughts and hurricanes and unbreathable air. I get estimates that there're about thirty years to go before full societal collapse. Millions dead, slowly, from a lack of clean water or else from wars over the remaining resources." Rafe sighed deeply. "The billionaires with their toy rockets. The politicians with their little armies. All that staring them in the face, and still they don't change a damn thing. No, I wouldn't ask the Denzans to wade into that mess. We haven't proven ourselves to be worth saving."

"And you said my mom was cynical," I replied.

"We have to help ourselves. We could do that, if returning to Earth didn't kill us." He squeezed my shoulder. "We could do that if your dad cured the Wasting."

I stared ahead at the statue. My grandpa up there, grinning and goofing. He'd died on Earth so that he could be with his family and be a guinea pig to figure out what's wrong with humanity. I wondered what he'd thought about Rafe and his big ideas.

"And you know what?"

"What?"

"I think he did it," Rafe said. "I think he found the answer to humanity's illness out there and someone on his crew didn't want it getting out. I think someone sabotaged his way back."

Tycius and I had talked about that theory a little bit. It made sense, at least it had until my encounter with Goldy. But if the Lost People were some cosmic threat lost to history, that complicated things.

"What if he found something else?" I asked, looking over at

Rafe. I wasn't sure how much I should tell him, so I kept it vague. "Something bigger than a cure for the Wasting? Something dangerous?"

Rafe's eyes glistened as he gazed at the statue of his old friends. He pointed out a handful of the more formal-looking astronauts. "He died in the war, and her, him too, and him from his injuries right after. They gave their lives to Denza because they were honorable and brave. The best humanity had to offer." He turned to me. "Sydney, I don't mean to put this pressure on you, but you're our only hope to recover your father's research and hopefully him, which makes you the only hope for Earth. You lived there. You must've seen that there's some good left in our species, even if we've lost our way. At the very least, you remember what real pizza tastes like."

I rolled my eyes, but that didn't stop Rafe from talking. His grip tightened on my shoulder.

"You're half-Denzan, Syd. I know you'll need time to explore that side of yourself. You're going to love it here. Most do." Rafe took a deep breath of the fresh air. "But when the time comes, I hope you'll be with me. I hope you'll remember where you come from and those people who are counting on you. Because, for me, and for your mom and dad, there is nothing—*nothing*—bigger than the fate of humanity."

22

I'd gotten used to the silence of space, the gentle humming of the *Eastwood*, the stillness. The institute was noisy, cadets moving around the halls at all hours. I shared a wall with H'Jossu, and that first night, I'm pretty sure he watched six straight hours of Bruce Lee movies. I thought about going over to chill with him—the unsleeping Panalax would've loved the company—but I had an early class in the morning, my first at the institute, and it was on Wayscopes. After what had happened on the *Eastwood*, I wanted to be sharp for that.

So of course, I tossed and turned all night.

I thought about Rafe Butler and my dad's disappearance, how so many people wanted him found and others wanted him to stay lost. I thought about how everyone had an angle, everyone wanted something—even an Etherazi. If I listened to the Chef, the fate of humanity was pretty much on me. And if I listened to my pal Goldy, maybe the fate of the whole universe, too.

Oh, and I was also going to become an adult capable of destroying a planet.

You try to sleep knowing all that.

When I did manage to doze off, I had *the dream*. My dad and I, eating donuts on the hood of a parked car. The greenery of Australia had been replaced by a gray wasteland. Ash fell all around us, sticking to the pastries. Instead of watching rockets go up, we were watching them come down—Earth under bombardment.

My dad turned to me. "I'm going to be dead by the time you find me, Syd."

I woke up with a start, feeling like a weight was pressing down on my chest. Two glowing yellow eyes peered at me in the darkness.

"Bad dream, human?"

It wasn't just anxiety that woke me. Zara was literally perched on my chest, crouched, her fanged snout just inches from my nose. The Vulpin's fur was delicately perfumed and smelled like a fancy kind of tea that my mom used to drink.

Oh, and she had her little knife—the same one I'd seen her use to take out Kungo's eye—pressed right up against the side of my neck.

"Holy shit," I croaked.

A flicker of amusement in her glowing eyes. "Class is in session."

I was half-awake, so it took me a moment to acclimate to my

situation. Zara had her whole weight on me, but I wasn't having any trouble breathing—she was light, and I was strong. Sharp as it was, I didn't think her knife could pierce my impenetrable skin.

I went to shove her, but as soon as I shifted my weight she leaped backward, a neat little flip landing her at the foot of my bed. Her tail flicked back and forth.

"You're slow," she said.

"People keep saying that," I replied, thinking of Hiram and Darcy. "Get out of my room."

"No. You signed up. This is class."

"Your class is you sneaking into my room and scaring the shit out of me?"

She nodded enthusiastically, tossing her dagger back and forth between her hands. "I get necessary practice. You better your chances of one day surviving a Vulpin assassination attempt."

"I don't think I need training for that," I said. "Your little knife wouldn't hurt me."

"Oh, I could hurt you, human," Zara said, oozing confidence. Her hand flicked in my direction, and, in spite of myself, I flinched, thinking she might toss her dagger at me. Instead, the blade disappeared somewhere into her fur. "Tell me. Why did you sign up? No one ever signs up. Two semesters ago, this Denzan girl tried me. She quit and left the institute. Do you think you're brave? Are you stupid?"

It was a bombardment of questions. "I don't think I'm particularly brave," I replied. "And yeah, I'm definitely stupid."

Zara hopped up so she was crouching on the foot of my bed.

She cocked her head, studying me. "Obfuscating."

"What?"

"You don't want to tell me why."

What was I supposed to tell her? A Vulpin had tried to kidnap me ten years ago and almost killed my mom? I thought some of her species had something to do with my dad's disappearance? Or maybe—*Hey, I saw a vision of the future and you and I were tight, blowing up planets like besties sometimes do*? Should I lead with that one?

I decided to appeal to her ego. "I liked how you stabbed that guy's eye out," I said. "When I saw that, I was like, *Wow, I want to know more about the Vulpin*."

"It made a wonderful sound," she agreed, then cocked her head suddenly. "Now, will you tell me the truth about why you signed up for my class, or must I slowly torture you until you submit?"

Maybe a little bit of the truth was in order. After all, if the two of us were one day going to be planet-killing pals, I could probably trust her.

"When I was little, I was almost kidnapped—"

"Ah, and now that is your fetish and you are excited by the thought of me lurking around," Zara said. "I am both disgusted and intrigued, human."

I sighed. "No. I was almost kidnapped by a Vulpin."

Zara's spine straightened. That had gotten her attention. "My people aren't allowed on Earth. The Denzans have forbidden it."

"And yet it still happened."

She leaned forward. "What happened to this kidnapper?"

255

"My mom killed her."

"Respect." Zara tapped her front fang with a claw. "I see now. You're taking my class so you can know your enemy."

"I mean, I don't think of *you* as an enemy—"

"There is something more, though," Zara said, her green eyes narrowing in the dark. "You've told me a bit of the truth, but not all of the truth. You're a very mediocre liar. We can work on that."

I finally sat up in bed. "Look, Zara—"

"Zarrrra," she corrected, rolling the "R."

"Zar-errrr-ahhh." I went for the over-the-top enunciation. "I—"

"Better," she interrupted again.

"I don't care if you think I'm lying or not," I finally managed to get out. "This is idiotic. I just want to go back to sleep. So far, your class *sucks*."

"Hmm." She picked at her teeth with the dagger, which had reappeared in her hand. "You interest me, Sydney Chambers from Earth. I think knowing you might be entertaining. I'll allow you into class."

"Great," I replied. "Are we done?"

"For now," Zara said. Her fangs glinted in the darkness, my door hissed open, and she was gone.

"Jesus Christ," I said aloud, flopping back into my pillows. I might have bitten off more than I could chew with that one. It wasn't clear if I could learn anything useful about the Vulpin from Zara, but it was definitely clear that she'd be studying me in the meantime.

I sniffed the air. Odd. I could still smell her perfume.

Not going to lie: I screamed when Zara's clawed paw
out from beneath my bed and slapped me in the face.

"Twice in one night!" she yelled. "We have a lot of work

She'd never actually left my room, but had instead sl
across the floor and hidden like a monster under my bed.

"Get out!" I shouted.

That time, Zara listened. She bounded across my roon
leaped out the window. I could hear her claws scratching
the rock face.

Twice I thought she was back in my room and lunged aw
ready to defend myself. It was only the shadows.

I was exhausted for my first class.

Introduction to Wayscopes was held in a lecture hall at
institute that really wasn't all that different from the classroo
I'd been in on Earth, with the obvious exception of the seats bei
arranged in a semicircle around a technological marvel instead o
dry-erase board. The Wayscope apparatus hung from the ceilin
the chair beneath the goggles unoccupied to start, its screens di
playing a view of Denza's local solar system. The room was fille
with Denzan students, most of them a little older than me, all o
them looking very serious and businesslike. They were all assigned
to different crews, so I figured that was why they didn't make any
effort to introduce themselves. I couldn't help but feel like I was
getting a lot of unnecessary side-eye from them as I settled into
an empty seat.

Just before class started, Darcy slipped into the seat next to mine. As usual, she had her hood pulled up, as if she was already prepared for the icy looks we were getting from the Denzans. She slouched low and crossed her arms, looking like she might just nap through the two-hour seminar.

"Hey," I said. "Didn't know you were in this class."

"I'm not," she said cryptically. "And neither are you."

Before I could ask Darcy what she meant, Instructor Coreyunus began her lecture. She was an older Denzan woman, rail thin, with her dark purple hair tied into a severe bun. One of her eyes was sealed shut by an immense scar, like someone had taken a hot iron to her face. I soon learned that she kept that ruined eye on display as a reminder to her students about what could happen if we misused a Wayscope—she'd burned it out during an exploratory session when she'd expanded her consciousness too far too fast.

I swallowed hard. I'd gotten lucky with my mishap back on the *Eastwood*. If it hadn't been for the intervention of the Etherazi, I might've ended up with an even worse disfigurement than some shiny hair.

"We begin, as always, with meditation techniques," Coreyunus intoned. "These may seem rudimentary or even silly to some of you, but learning how to compartmentalize your mind may one day save your life."

It was basically forty-five minutes of Zen-like deep breathing and focused thinking. We were supposed to concentrate on one thought and one thought only, something to anchor us, something that we could retreat back to if our control of the Wayscope ever got away from us.

I thought of the hood of my dad's car. Donuts and rockets. Finally put the dream that had been haunting me to good use.

It was a little difficult to focus, with Darcy gently snoring next to me.

"For today's practical, I ask that you access the Hydari system, located three jumps away from Denza," Coreyunus said, once trance time was over. "Reaching this system via the Wayscope should be relatively easy, but what I would like to see from you students is a *clean* path. Precision, clarity, and safety. Let no excess data enter your consciousness. Volunteers?"

I raised my hand along with the rest of the room. Coreyunus swept the class with her good eye before selecting a Denzan guy in the first row. He buckled himself into the Wayscope, the goggles lowered onto his face, and he was off. We watched on the screens as his consciousness expanded out into the Vastness. It was interesting to see what he was seeing—or rather, *how* he was seeing. He probed the galaxy with pinpoint accuracy, delicately seeking out the places where space intersected, and slipping through to the areas in between. Seeing him operate the Wayscope made me realize what blunt force I'd used in my solitary attempt, even guided by the cosmological tether.

Of course, this Denzan didn't have an Etherazi randomly flaring up in his vision. I'd like to see him handle that shit.

The first student took about seven minutes to navigate to the proper system. The next Denzan up went a little faster, trying to beat the first one's time, and spasmed in the chair when she accidentally veered into a red giant. That got her a stern rebuke from Coreyunus.

Each time a demonstration was over, I raised my hand, hoping to go next. And each time, Coreyunus passed me over for a Denzan.

At some point, Darcy had woken up. She shot me a sardonic look when she caught me waving my hand in the air.

"I think that's enough for today," Coreyunus declared. "For next week, please study your star charts and see if you can devise a more direct route to any of our known systems. Farewell."

I frowned. There were still five minutes left in class. Every Denzan had gotten a chance to use the Wayscope, but Coreyunus never even looked in my direction.

Darcy stood up, sneering at the instructor's back as she paced out of the room. "At least you got an arm workout," she said to me.

"What the hell?" I said, keeping my complaint low as the Denzan students walked by us. "Is this like a hazing-the-new-kid thing?"

Darcy snorted. "It's an *every*-class thing. The Denzan Senate says that us halflings have the right to use the Wayscope. But that doesn't mean they have to teach us."

"That's bullshit," I said.

"Next time, bring a pillow." As we walked out of the classroom, Darcy leaned close to me, lowering her voice. "How did it go yesterday? With the Chef?"

"It was cool, I guess," I said nonchalantly. "He wouldn't let me eat any pizza."

Darcy scowled. "You know that's not what I'm asking about."

"What *are* you asking about?"

"Earth," Darcy said sharply. "I know the Chef wants to go back, and I think you're here to help him. I want in."

I raised an eyebrow. "Hiram said—"

"Hiram doesn't speak for me," Darcy snapped. "If you're going back, I want to come. *I hate it here.*"

Darcy blurted that last part way louder than necessary. A couple nearby cadets—both Denzans with violin insignias to symbolize whatever ship they were assigned to—gave her a look. Darcy wilted under their attention, pulled her hood tighter around her head, and stormed away before I could say anything more.

That afternoon, I met up with Tycius for lunch in the beachside atrium on the institute's bottom floor. I was still fuming after my Wayscope class, but I was also starving. I still hadn't gotten a grip on Denzan cuisine—it was a lot of mushrooms and mutant root vegetables, and tons of seaweed and kelp. I put my hands on my hips and surveyed the dozens of food kiosks along the atrium's inside wall.

"What's most like a burger?" I asked my uncle.

Tycius shook his head. "Still can't shake those carnivore instincts, I see."

He led me over to a stand and bought us two of these big mushroom patties that dripped red juice like raw steak and were sandwiched between two buns made of something similar to pressed corn. It wasn't the most appetizing thing to my Earther senses, but as long as I avoided eye contact with the patty, it tasted smoky and savory, like a freshly grilled burger. With just a little bit of dirt thrown on top.

In between bites, I told him about Coreyunus's class. "How am I supposed to learn anything if she won't even allow me to practice?" I asked. "Darcy says she's never gotten a chance to use the machine."

A dark look passed across my uncle's face, the same look he'd gotten when he flipped out on Arkell back on the *Eastwood*. "That's unacceptable. I'll talk to some people at the institute. Get to the bottom of this."

I looked around the atrium—it was mostly Denzans passing through, with a smattering of humans and Vulpins here and there, none of them paying any attention to us. But I couldn't shake the way the other students had looked at me back in Coreyunus's class. Like I didn't belong.

"Carnivores," I mumbled.

"What?" Tycius asked.

"Just been getting some weird vibes since I got here," I said. "I mean, most of the Denzans are polite as hell. Like annoyingly polite. But sometimes I catch some looks and it's like—it's like they're afraid I'm going to eat them or something."

Tycius nodded, looking around. "I hear what you're saying. I suppose the further away the war with the Etherazi gets, the more my people forget what humanity did for Denza. But most of them *do* remember. It'll get better here. I promise."

My uncle had been away from his home world for a long time. I wondered if he still knew his own people as well as he thought.

"I met with Rafe Butler yesterday," I said. My mom had told me to watch what I said around my uncle, but, so far, he seemed like the only adult I could trust. Unlike the others, he didn't have some political agenda. He just wanted to find my dad.

"Ah," Ty said with a smirk. "Of course. The Chef works quickly."

"What do you think of him?"

Ty dunked a bit of baked seaweed into a pinkish sauce. "I like him, but he's a pain in the ass. Why do you ask?"

I remembered my uncle's penchant for gangster movies. "It felt a little bit like getting brought downtown to see the Mafia don."

"What did he want?"

"To feel me out, I think. See if I thought of myself as more human than Denzan." I shrugged. "He was nice enough. I guess he knew about my dad's work?"

"Doesn't surprise me. Rafe has ears everywhere. I'm sure he was following what Marcius was working on." Ty paused for a moment, as if unsure how much to tell me. "Back on Earth, before I spent ten years chasing you around, my job was to make sure the expatriated humans on Denza didn't smuggle any technological secrets back home. Rafe was always trying to sneak something back. Coded letters, programs hidden in transmissions—he even baked a bit of ultonate into a cake once. We caught him every time, and every time he got off with a warning. Nobody on Denza wants to see a war hero punished, so Rafe's troublemaking gets swept under the rug."

I thought about what Rafe had said yesterday about the

impending extinction of the human race. "Would it be so bad if Earth did get some Denzan technology? It would save a lot of lives."

"Agreed. I think my people should be doing more for your planet," Ty said. "But with so many warring nations and competing corporate interests, the question we always get stuck on is who we trust on Earth to handle such a gift."

"You're worried that humans would go to war over Denzan tech, or try to sell it, or keep it for themselves," I said.

"That sums it up," Ty replied.

"What if humans like Rafe went back themselves?" I asked. "To . . . lead."

"The Wasting would kill them. Unless . . ." Tycius put the pieces together quickly. "Ah."

"What would the Denzan Senate think of that?"

"Meddling with a primitive species is against our ways," Tycius said thoughtfully. "However, if the meddling was done by the *same* species, I suppose that would be something of a gray area."

"We don't even know what my dad found out there," I said. "All Rafe's big ideas might be for nothing."

"Speaking of which . . ." Ty pulled out his tablet and slid it across the table to me. A list of names was displayed there. My father's at the top.

"What is this?" I asked as I read down the list.

"The manifest of your dad's ship," Ty replied. "His crew."

Including my dad, there were six other Denzans on board the missing ship. There were two names that stuck out: Alexander Abe and Ool'Vinn.

"They had a human on board," I said. "And a . . . ?"

"A Panalax," my uncle said.

As I scanned down this list, I noticed that every name had a number beside it. A time stamp, it looked like. All except for my dad.

"What are these?" I asked.

"Those are records of when their tethers went dark," Tycius said.

"You mean when they died," I replied.

"We can't assume anything," Tycius said. "But, unless they were performing brain surgery on one another to remove their beacons—yes."

I took a closer look at the numbers. The Denzans—except for my father—all died first. Each death came minutes apart. I couldn't tell anything from that. That could've been anything—an accident where some died more quickly than others, or something could've been hunting each of them down.

Alexander Abe went next. He lasted hours longer than the Denzans, but he still died.

And, finally, Ool'Vinn. The Panalax survived a whole day after Abe.

My dad had been alone since then.

As I thought all that through, I took another bite of my sandwich. Something popped between my teeth, and my mouth flooded with a sour liquid that tasted like pickled fish. I gagged and spit the stuff onto my plate—a dark blue, viscous solution mixed in with my half-chewed bits of mushroom. Coughing, I

265

gave my uncle a wild look—were these sandwiches supposed to have some awful surprise in the middle?—but he looked as shocked as me.

"Sydney?" he asked, patting my back. "What is that?"

"Gah," I replied. "It's terrible!"

I wiped my forearm across my mouth, smearing blue on my skin. It was like ink.

At that moment, Zara appeared from the crowd. I'm not sure how I hadn't noticed her.

"Now, imagine if that had been poison," she said, her eyes sparkling like she could barely contain her laughter. "Today's lesson: always check your food."

I groaned. I'd just been assassinated for the third time in twenty-four hours. I picked up what was left of my sandwich and tried to chuck it at her, but Zara darted away from our table before I could take aim.

Looking at me—my blue mouth, my frustrated expression—my uncle was trying not to laugh now, too.

"I warned you not to pet the Vulpin," he said.

23

My next few days were packed with the math and science classes required by the institute, plus my seminar on conversational Denzan so that I wouldn't be so reliant on the translator wedged in my ear. Back on Earth, I'd rarely felt challenged in my sporadic high school appearances. The intense concepts I was getting on Denza were a totally different story—complex formulas that tied into fundamental principles of space travel. You know, basic shit. I went to bed with what felt like low-grade brain freeze every night and was too exhausted to even wake up for a Zara ambush.

So it was a relief when Rafe Butler's The Etherazi Incursion class showed up on my schedule. Or Propaganda 101, as Darcy had called it.

The Chef's lecture was held in one of the biggest rooms at the institute, and every seat was packed, not just with cadets but also with ordinary Denzans from off the street. The class was open to the public. For all the antihuman static I'd observed during my first few days, there were still plenty of Denzans who worshipped the First Twelve.

Rafe shed his pizza-maker persona for the occasion. Instead of a flour-covered apron, he wore a light blue suit, expertly tailored to emphasize his bowling ball shoulders. He sat on a stool at the front of the lecture hall, sipping from a silver flask and every so often blazing up a sweet-smelling hand-rolled cigarette.

Basically, he was the picture of an aging war hero. Equal parts polished and damaged.

"That day on Mossisle, it was me, Marie Reno, and Sal Rogers," Rafe's lecture went. "I remember the way the cleats of our Battle-Anchors crunched across the sand-glass . . . like each bit of debris was a memory . . . screaming at us. A little girl approached us—she couldn't have been more than five or six. Told us . . . 'I saw my father transformed . . . to bones. You're stepping . . . on his bones.'"

The dramatic pauses. The distant looks. The gritty details that seemed so perfectly rehearsed. I wondered how many times Rafe had gone through this story. The class wasn't The Etherazi Incursion so much as it was Rafe Remembers.

I understood Rafe's angle—to remind the people of Denza that humans were their protectors. He just took to the whole thing with too much gusto. Chef, mayor, smuggler, war hero—Rafe Butler had too many identities to count. I'd had a lot of identities back on Earth, and I knew from experience, the more characters you played, the harder the truth was to find.

I'd wanted to learn more about the Etherazi. The gold one in particular. I wasn't going to get that from this class, though. The Etherazi in Rafe's stories weren't there to be studied, they were there to be shot at.

Looking around, no one else in the classroom seemed even a little disillusioned. The Denzans hung on his every word.

"We were on the trail of the Emerald Stalker that day," Rafe continued. "She had an affinity for the jungle. Where there'd once been a thriving village, the Emerald Stalker had upended reality . . . turned the entire island back into its primordial state. We all felt like there were a thousand eyes upon us. She haunted the treetops . . . I always call the sneaky ones 'she,' the more brutish ones 'he' . . . We don't know that they have any gender, that's just a random observation from an old warrior . . ."

That was also the closest thing I got to insight from Rafe's yarn. I mean, look, it was interesting to hear a firsthand account of the war my grandfather had fought in—and the sci-fi lover in me was definitely a little roped in when Rafe started talking about blasting a diving Emerald Stalker with his suit's laser array—but I hadn't come to Denza to hear old war stories. I needed information, and so far, all of the electives I'd signed up for were withholding it. Hell, I'd probably learned more from Zara than both Rafe and Coreyunus put together.

I was sitting next to Batzian and Melian. As Rafe's performance droned on, I found myself watching their reactions. Batzian was practically on the edge of his seat, his hands clasped between his knees, vibrating every time Rafe described some burst of violence. His sister, on the other hand, seemed a little more distracted, her eyes wandering the room like mine. She caught me looking and smiled.

I leaned behind her brother to whisper, "Are his classes always like this?"

Mel tilted her head and whispered back, "Like what?"

I struggled to put it into words. "Like . . . a one-man show?"

"*Shh!*" Batzian cut me off, his rebuke way louder than any of my whispering. Multiple heads turned in our direction, and I sank down in my seat, feeling like I'd gotten caught farting in church. Rafe's eyes flicked up at me, and I thought I caught a glimmer of amusement there.

After class, I walked onto the concourse with the twins. Batzian was practically grinding his teeth the whole way, and his sister seemed a bit cowed by his judgmental silence. He stopped on the walkway and pulled at his ponytail, making sure his squirmy hair was cinched extra tight. He gave me a look like he wanted to say something, so I opened my hands.

"What's up, man?" I said. "I can tell you're pissed."

"It's disrespectful to interrupt Mr. Butler's lecture," he said. "The man is a hero."

"I met Rafe the other day," I said casually. Batzian widened his eyes slightly, jealous of my being on a first-name basis with one of his heroes. "He's a chill dude. I don't think he minded."

"A chill dude," Batzian repeated sourly.

"Yeah, he's not like that grizzled war vet in there," I continued.

"He makes crappy pizza. You should go see him on Little Earth. I'm sure he'd hook you up with an autograph."

Batzian tossed his head. "Absurd. I would never bother him."

"We've never been to Little Earth," Mel said, trying to change the subject. "Maybe we should go."

Batzian didn't take the hint, still staring at me. "You have a lot to learn here, Sydney."

"Okay, man," I said, whistling. "I just think some of his material was a little over-the-top." I slipped into an imitation of Rafe's gravelly voice. "The jungle was eerily quiet . . . like two ghosts . . . making love . . . in a graveyard."

Mel had to stifle a giggle after a sharp look from Batzian.

"The man is allowed to be"—he slung air quotes at me—"'over-the-top.' He saved our entire planet. By the tides, I know you've only been here for a few days, but I would think as a half-Denzan and the descendent of one of the First Twelve, you could appreciate what Rafe Butler means to us."

Son of a missing Denzan theoretician. Grandson of a dead war hero. Dirty looks for being too human. Guilt trips for not being Denzan enough. It seemed like everyone on this planet had thoughts on how I was supposed to act.

And I still didn't have a clue.

I was taken aback by Batzian's passion, though. Maybe I was being too cynical about Rafe. "Look, I didn't mean anything by it—"

"It's fine," he concluded curtly. "I have to get to my next class." With one last icy look, Batzian briskly walked away.

"Sorry about him," Mel said with a gentle smile. "My brother doesn't have the most developed sense of humor."

"Nah, it's my fault," I replied. "I'm still new at all this interspecies diplomacy stuff. Just a dumb-ass Earther saying whatever comes to mind."

"It's not that," Mel said, shaking her head. "Baztian actually *loves* humanity."

"Seriously?"

Her friendly face turned sober as she explained. "The islands we're from were absolutely decimated during the Etherazi invasion. Our ancestors were among the only survivors. When we were little, Batzian worshipped the First Twelve. You think Rafe's stories are a little played out? My brother has probably heard them a hundred times already. He used to talk about how he wished he'd been born human so that . . ." She looked around, lowering her voice. "So that he could *fight*. An interest in physical violence is considered unnatural among our people."

I nodded. I'd seen enough of Denza to know that most of the people here were pretty much pacifists. My mom had bitterly told me how the Denzans wouldn't even fight for their own planet; they needed humans for that.

"We worked our butts off to get accepted here," Mel continued. "Not a lot of people from our village ever leave. Batzian's so uptight because he's worried if he slips a little, they could send us right back. He was so eager to rub elbows with the next generation of heroes like you, but—"

Melian was interrupted by a shout from farther down the

concourse. We both turned to see Hiram, leaping down from the landing above, and landing in the midst of a group of Denzan cadets studying on their tablets. He whooped, jostling them badly enough that one dropped her device. Without so much as a backward glance, Hiram flung himself over the landing to the next one below.

"Well," Mel finished, a little sheepishly. "He's been kind of disappointed in the humans he's met so far."

I cringed on humanity's behalf. "I'll try to set a better example for your brother," I said. My tone was light, but I really meant it. I didn't want anyone lumping me in with Hiram.

Melian touched my arm. "Oh, you're doing fine," she said. "He wouldn't stop talking about how you tried to fight an Etherazi without a Battle-Anchor."

I couldn't imagine sullen Batzian in a state where he couldn't shut up, and it made me a little uneasy to hear how my encounter with the Etherazi was getting interpreted, so I changed the subject.

"Can you point me in the direction of the library?" I asked. "I still have to plan for the class I'm teaching tomorrow."

"The library . . . Oh, you mean the archive. It's actually back in there." She pointed toward the institute. "Take the elevator *all* the way down."

The archive was a cavernous vault built deep into the mountain. Unlike the rest of the institute, where there was almost always a breathtaking view of either the ocean or of Primclef, the archive was completely shut in. The huge room was artificially cold to the point where my breath misted a bit as I stepped inside. It was like being in the center of a giant server; the walls were three stories in height, and all of them were covered in blinking data slots, a repository for all the information the Denzan people had collected over the years. They'd buried it all so deep to keep it safe, knowing no Etherazi could burrow through all the ultonate veins rippling through the rock.

A Denzan librarian greeted me at the front desk with a warm smile. "Good afternoon, Cadet. Is this your first time?"

I must have been gaping a bit at the towering data centers. If those were shelves—like they would've been at a traditional library on Earth—they could've contained every book ever written.

"Yeah," I replied. "I need to pull some books for a class. Do you have Earth stuff?"

"Of course we do," she said. She pulled open a drawer next to her desk and held out a wooly bundle. "Sweater? It can get a bit chilly."

Back home, half the libraries I'd been to were getting shut down. Meanwhile, on Denza, the librarians gave out cardigans.

The librarian led me to a cubicle in the middle of the room— there were like a hundred workstations spread out across the tiled floor, most of them occupied by a combination of other cadets and older Denzans. A touch-screen terminal took up the entirety of the desk. The terminal connected wirelessly to the handheld tablet the institute had issued me, and the librarian explained that any data I wanted to copy from the archive could be downloaded directly to my machine.

Basically, I was now connected to the most powerful search engine in the universe.

And, with all that information at my fingertips, I completely blanked.

I wasn't sure what to teach or where to begin.

I browsed the seemingly endless scroll of popular topics in the sidebar. There was everything from "Panalaxan Rebirth Dirges" to "Vulpin Grooming Demonstrations" to "Earth Comedy (French)."

Apparently, the Denzans had a real thing for mimes.

Eventually, I just typed "EARTH + SCIENCE FICTION" into the search bar and skimmed through thousands of names: Octavia Butler, Alfred Bester, Richard Morgan, Ray Bradbury. So many choices.

"Screw it," I said. "I'll take it all."

I downloaded their entire catalogs straight to my tablet. Didn't even need to pay a fee. Honestly, it felt a little like stealing. The books were all considered cultural artifacts by the Denzans, though. A whole planet of brazen internet pirates hiding behind the guise of anthropologists.

Once I'd downloaded pretty much every sci-fi book in existence, I lingered at the terminal. Rafe's class might not have been the deep dive into the Etherazi that I'd been hoping for, but I had all of intergalactic history right here at my fingertips. I could do my own research.

I punched "ETHERAZI" into the search field.

A warning popped up. *Proceed with caution. These results contain traumatic events.*

"Yeah, yeah," I mumbled and swiped forward.

A stream of information filled the screen. There were news-vids from the Etherazi invasion, scientific research papers on everything from Etherazi physiology to psychology, detailed reports on battles and attacks, and even a bizarre Panalaxan opera dedicated to warding the creatures off. I was confronted with literally tens of thousands of pictures and articles and videos.

"Okay, let's narrow it down," I said.

Because I was really only interested in one Etherazi: my buddy Goldy. He knew so much about my future, I wanted to learn about his past.

ETHERAZI + GOLD.

A much narrower selection of items. At the top of the list was a video from the last days of the Etherazi invasion.

I hit play.

The footage was recorded from the deck of a Denzan interstellar vessel. The screen was filled by Denza's largest and grayest moon, where it looked like some kind of light show was happening: flashes of gold mixing with deep purple.

"A bizarre scene played out today on the surface of Ebos," said a Denzan newscaster, her professional voice edged with unease. "While our filtered vid-stream should mitigate the harrowing appearance of the Etherazi, for those who are highly susceptible to their dread visage, it's recommended that you look away."

The camera zoomed in on the lights. At first, the whole thing looked a bit like fireworks, purple and gold blossoms appearing against the darkness, motes breaking off and fading into the

Vastness. The more I focused, though, the more I could see, albeit with a dull ache in my sinuses that increased the harder I stared.

Two Etherazi were intertwined above the moon, twisted around each other. A monstrous purple one and my buddy Goldy. Somehow, I knew it was him and not just some other Etherazi of the same shade. I recognized the way his energy moved—a very particular kind of chaos.

The purple one's head took shape—serpentine and fanged— and tore a chunk out of Goldy. In response, energy spikes shot out of what I interpreted to be Goldy's belly, burrowing deep into Purple's body. There wasn't any sound on the recording, but I got the sense that both Etherazi were shrieking.

"Scientists and theoreticians have been unable to explain this phenomenon," the newscaster continued. "As we've seen over the last few weeks, the Etherazi have begun to retreat from Denza thanks to the heroic efforts of our human protectors. However, the purple creature you see on-screen was detected emerging from a wormhole this afternoon, seemingly headed toward our planet. It was intercepted on its way by the gold Etherazi, which was apparently lying in wait somewhere around Ebos."

The two Etherazi surged against each other, ripping off limbs of pure energy that disintegrated into the Vastness. It was like watching two dragons wrestle, although I couldn't be sure if that was just how my mind interpreted their shapes or—

"Whoa, it's like Godzilla versus Ghidorah," H'Jossu rasped over my shoulder. "Never seen this one before."

For being a nine-foot-tall mold-covered sloth-monster, H'Jossu was pretty light on his feet. Or maybe I'd just been too engrossed by the footage to realize he'd ambled up behind me. He leaned right over my shoulder—his dry fur tickling my ear, his floral odor in my nostrils—but I couldn't even get skeeved out. The Etherazi brawl had my full attention.

"Who do you think's going to win?" he asked.

"The gold one," I said immediately.

"Oh, damn," H'Jossu said, the realization clicking. "Is that the same . . . ?"

I nodded.

The fight went back and forth, although it was hard to say who was doing more damage. One Etherazi would shrink down to near nothingness, only to burst back to life as a roiling wave of energy. At some point, though, Goldy started to really worm his way inside his opponent, until soon it seemed like every bit of the purple Etherazi was infused with gold—little spikes of energy coursing through the darker Etherazi, tearing it apart, opening it up.

For a moment, I thought I could see the purple one's heart—the glowing eye in its center. Goldy exposed it to the Vastness. But then—

A burning flash that rocked the ship recording the footage. All the purple energy seemed to funnel in on itself, imploding down to nothing, blasting all the way out of this universe.

Only Goldy was left, then. He spread his mammoth wings, almost like he was posing for the camera, then zipped away from Denza with all the speed of a shooting star.

"This may be the first evidence of an Etherazi attacking one of its own," the newscaster intoned. "Other theoreticians speculate that this could be some sort of mating ritual. We simply do not know."

But I knew.

Among other things, Goldy had called himself Kinslayer.

But why? What had they been fighting about?

"That was pretty nuts," H'Jossu said.

I'd forgotten he was standing behind me. "Yeah." I didn't feel the need to make up an excuse for looking up the Etherazi. Who wouldn't, given what had happened?

"He punked that big-ass purple guy but was scared of you," H'Jossu said.

"He wasn't scared of me," I replied, remembering the lie. "It was Reno who chased him off."

"Etherazi professional wrestling. That'd be cool." I stared blankly at the Panalax. "You know, I tried getting into that—the Earth stuff, I mean—but the Denzans don't have much in their archive. I'll have to write an essay and explain how Earthers pretending to hit one another with furniture is worthy of cultural preservation."

I snorted, relieved by how quickly H'Jossu had steered the conversation back to his own dorky interests. "Is there anything you won't watch?"

"Nope," he replied. "Did you work out the reading list for our class? I'm very pumped, Syd."

The two of us left the archive together. On the way out, I

told H'Jossu I was still having trouble selecting a book for us to start with. He immediately began ranking what Earth sci-fi he'd already read and what he was most excited to get into. While he rambled away, I got lost in my own thoughts, still stuck on the gold Etherazi.

Kinslayer. Goldy really had killed one of his own. Not that I hadn't believed him. His all-caps ass didn't seem like the type to give himself an unearned nickname. I tried to remember what else he'd called himself.

The Golden Prophet Who Lights the Way. Okay. Standard arrogant villain title. He'd shown me a bit of my future, but since the Etherazi generally played fast and loose with time, I didn't think it'd take much for one of them to be called a prophet. Where was he supposedly lighting the way to? That was the real question.

The Architect of Liberation. Again . . . who was he talking about? His own species? They didn't seem to be under anyone's control.

He Who Walks Among the Enemy. Who were the Etherazi's enemies? Humans and Denzans, right? That was probably the weirdest nickname of all, though, because from what I'd seen, the Etherazi didn't *walk* anywhere—they floated around and wrecked shit.

H'Jossu and I were on the concourse at that point—me half listening as the Panalax explained why he thought Orson Scott Card sucked—when something caught my eye. There was a wisp walking in our direction. I'd seen a few other Ossho since coming to Denza, mostly standing on street corners observing the crowds, drinking in as much experience as they could. This one moved like it had someplace to be, though. Their exo-suit was a little bulkier than the one Aela wore and patched over in spots, an older model. As the wisp got closer, I noticed something off about the magenta cloud swirling behind their faceplate.

The wisp was shot through with streaks of gold.

Or maybe that was just my imagination. A trick of the weird Denzan sun, currently peeking out from between two moons, slanted light dipping the entire concourse in bronze. I squinted at the wisp as they passed me by, turning my head to follow them.

As I watched, the wisp veered down a staircase, bumping into a Vulpin girl with leopard-spotted fur who had been walking behind me. She shouted a curse at the wisp, then saw me watching and smirked knowingly at me. Probably one of Zara's friends.

"Hey," H'Jossu said. "What do you think about this?"

He tipped his head back and let out a high-pitched gurgling sound, like he was trying to roll his "Rs" while being strangled, beating his chest with his furry paws. H'Jossu's ululating was so unexpected and bizarre, I completely lost track of the wisp.

"What the hell are you doing?" I snapped once H'Jossu stopped his noisemaking.

"My Chewbacca impression," H'Jossu replied, rubbing his thick neck like he'd hurt his own throat. "The institute does a costume party for the solstice. I know it's a little early in our relationship to suggest a couples costume, but do you own a leather vest? I think you'd make a good Han."

"What? No—I . . ." I put my hand on H'Jossu's furry arm,

gently trying to ease him out of my way as I peered after the wisp.

I'd lost track of them in the crowd. The Vulpin girl was gone too, probably off to report my location to Zara so that she could dump a bucket of glitter on me.

Maybe I was just feeling paranoid. It was like Earth all over again. But I felt like I was being watched.

"What's wrong?" H'Jossu asked, his shaggy unibrow furrowed.

"Did you see that wisp?" I asked. "The one with the—?"

With the gold Etherazi hiding inside? Couldn't really come out and say that without sounding like a lunatic.

H'Jossu stretched his bulk vertically so he could look down the concourse, eventually shaking his head. "I don't see any wisps. Did you know them or something? You seem freaked out."

"No, it's cool," I said. I forced a smile and changed the subject. I was overtired and spooked, and had spent too much of my day focused on the Etherazi. What I'd seen inside that wisp's helmet had to be just a trick of the sun. "So, you want me to be your Han? I might be into that."

"I love you."

"I know."

24

Theoretician Vanceval didn't hold his seminar on the Lost People in a classroom. Instead, the five of us signed up for the class were required to visit his off-campus laboratory in a district of Primclef dedicated to philosophy and quiet contemplation—basically, a few blocks of libraries, museums, and open-air forums. I could only imagine the filthy looks that Hiram and Darcy would've earned if they ever decided to do one of their rampaging races through this neighborhood.

Vanceval's laboratory doubled as a museum. A sign over the entrance read *MEMORIES OF THE LOST PEOPLE*. Inside, there were two rows of display cases, a dozen relics from Vanceval's collection out for show, along with a holographic image of the planet where each artifact was found. The items ranged from odd bits of woodworking to half-disintegrated bottles that might have once contained ancient Mountain Dew. Basically, trash from the long ago. Next to the displays were touch pads where guests were encouraged to record their thoughts.

My first thought was that none of this crap looked like it belonged to some universe-conquering masters.

I hadn't seen shriveled Vanceval since we left the *Eastwood* a week ago. He beamed at me when I arrived, but I soon realized he did that with all his students. Vanceval's class wasn't a popular one, and neither was his little museum. He was happy anyone took an interest in his work.

"You never know what insight a fresh set of eyes might produce," Vanceval explained to us as we stood around his immaculately dustless displays. "That's why you're here, after all. I've spent hundreds of hours in study and contemplation of every object in the collection. As we have yet to unravel the mysteries of the Lost People, there must be some thoughts still left unthought."

We didn't spend much time in the actual museum. Instead, Vanceval led us downstairs, to the vast storage facility he kept in the basement. His hundreds of Lost People relics were stored there, all of them kept in glass containment cases that preserved their condition. The objects could only be handled through the rubber gloves that protruded into each case.

"I am going to assign each of you an artifact," Vanceval said as he wandered between the rows. "You will study that artifact. Consider it. And then—"

He paused, a faraway look in his eyes. Spacing out. The tic that theoreticians were prone to. Rafe Butler had said I did the same thing, just like my dad.

"And then," Vanceval resumed after a few awkward seconds, "you will provide me with notes on where your object came from and what kind of society might have birthed it. You will suggest tests we might run and hypotheses we might explore. In that way, perhaps, we shall arrive at something that my research has not yet uncovered."

I wondered if the old man had ever thought of the Lost People as a potential threat too dangerous to go searching for. For the sake of the exercise, I tried to put Goldy's warnings aside. I wanted to look at this stuff from my dad's perspective. What about these artifacts drove him into the Vastness? What made him so fascinated with a bunch of space trash?

My object was a hollow metal capsule. Dented. Silver. About the size of a portable speaker. There was a gash on one side like something had torn it open, releasing whatever might have once been stored inside. According to the background information, the capsule was found by the Denzans seventy-five years ago, plucked from a debris field stuck in orbit around a planet overwhelmed by volcanic activity. I stuck my hands into the gloves and held the cool metal, ran my fingers over the jagged slash, turning the tube so I could peek at the recess inside.

"Intergalactic garbage picker," I mumbled.

Circulating around the room, Vanceval overheard and hobbled over.

"Do you have thoughts, Sydneycius?"

"Well," I said, "how do we know that this isn't space junk?

Like . . . a part that fell off a ship or something?"

Vanceval nodded like it was a worthy question, probably because he'd asked it himself decades ago. "Samples of the material reveal it to be a composite of titanium and strontium. No known interstellar-capable species uses that particular combination in their ships or even in any form of manufacturing. Plus, carbon dating indicates this piece is more than ten thousand years old, predating the space programs of any known civilization."

"Hmm." I touched the jagged gash in the capsule's side again, this time noting how the metal curled outward instead of inward. "It looks like something burst out of here."

"Good," Vanceval replied, nodding. "I found traces of various gaseous elements within the capsule, but it's impossible to tell whether they were contained there originally or picked up while the object floated through the Vastness. Perhaps you could attempt to re-create that research and tell me what this capsule might have held."

I felt like I'd just talked myself right into a homework assignment. As I turned the capsule over in my hands, another thought occurred to me. "This is kind of random—"

"Random . . ." A long, dreamy pause from Vanceval. "Random is good. Random excites me."

"It reminds me a little bit of a message in a bottle," I said.

"Explain."

"On Earth, back in olden times, when a sailor was stranded on an island, they'd stick a note in a bottle and send it out to sea, hoping someone might find them."

Vanceval stroked his chin. "Interesting. The capsule as a communication device. Perhaps what it held was *data*. Something to consider." He rested a hand on my shoulder. "I am very pleased to have you in this class, Sydneycius," he said, lowering his voice so as not to be overheard by the other students. "How are you holding up, since the incident?"

I shrugged. "I'm fine, I guess. A little spooked still."

Vanceval looked down at my hands—still in the rubber gloves—as if he expected me to be wearing my father's cosmological tether. The ring, out of its box, was safely buttoned in my uniform's shirt pocket.

"When do you think you will be ready to try again?" he asked.

"I don't know," I admitted. "Last time didn't go so hot."

Vanceval nodded as if he understood. "Your father once completed this same assignment for me, Sydneycius. He may seem far away now, but perhaps this work can help make him feel closer."

"Yeah," I agreed, smiling at my dad's sweet old mentor. He wasn't wrong. Working in Vanceval's hoard of space junk did make me feel like I was getting to know my dad in a way I never had before. "Thanks, Vanceval."

The old man's pompadour bounced as he bowed to me. "I am at your service, Cadet."

I stopped him before he could move on to the next student. A question nagged at me, almost like I wanted someone to disprove what Goldy had told me. "I do have one question. Why assume that all of these artifacts—found on different worlds, light-years apart—are tied to the same species? Couldn't there be a bunch of

287

different civilizations out there creating all this clutter?"

"Ah, I never assume anything, young Sydneycius," Vanceval said with a smile. "Of course we have considered the possibility of multiple species. Perhaps there were dozens of spacefaring cultures that predated ours and created these artifacts. I tend to think not."

"But why?"

"If the Lost People were *one* highly adaptable species traveling to many stars, then it is possible that we have simply not yet found their home world, or perhaps some tragic fate befell them," Vanceval said. "But if they were many races on many planets? Well . . . where have they all gone? What happened that could erase dozens, maybe even hundreds, of cultures from existence? I shudder to think."

SOON, THE MASTERS WILL RETURN.

I felt chilled through the rest of Vanceval's class as I recorded my notes about my random artifact. What if it was the Lost People themselves who had erased all these societies?

And what if my dad had found them?

Returning to the institute later that day, I noticed a wisp standing outside the entrance, gazing up at the three moons currently glowing in the Denzan sky. I stared into the wisp's faceplate, looking for any trace of gold, any sign that there could be an Etherazi hiding in there.

They waved at me. "Hey, Syd."

Whew.

"Oh, hey, Aela, I didn't see you there."

"You were staring at me."

"Was I?"

Aela clasped their hands behind them and rocked back on the narrow heels of their exo-suit. "Fascinating. I wonder where your mind had wandered off to."

"Uh, nowhere super interesting," I replied. "Hey, I have a question for you."

"Exciting," Aela responded. I couldn't tell by the chipper robotic voice, but I think they were being genuine.

"Do you wisps ever change colors?"

"You mean . . . ?" Aela waved a hand over their faceplate, the gas behind it curling into a question mark.

"Yeah. Is every wisp magenta?"

Aela hesitated. They were usually so open with information, oversharing constantly. The wisp touched their faceplate, as if self-conscious about the gas within.

"Am I . . . ?" Aela paused. They sounded worried. "Did you notice something different about me?"

"No, not you," I said. "I saw one on the street that looked a little different."

"Ah." The wisp's shoulders sank in relief. "One of the contaminated."

I thought about the hosedown I had to endure back on the *Eastwood* whenever Aela shared a memory with me. All of that was to keep Aela's delicate chemical composition from getting compromised by gross organic matter. The wisp I'd seen with the beater of an exo-suit must not have taken such good care of themselves.

"What happens to them?" I asked. "The contaminated?"

Aela stuck up their index finger. "I sense an opportunity for cultural exchange."

"Great."

"Are you free? Would you like to take a ride crater-side? I can show you the fate of the contaminated."

I thought about that for a second. If I could spot the Ossho I'd seen yesterday, that would definitely put me at ease that I didn't have an Etherazi stalker. I already had my hands full with Zara lurking around every corner.

"Sure," I replied. "Let's do it."

Aela led me to the nearest skiff stand—no jumping down ledges this time—and we rode to the grid of buildings nestled in the crater. We ended up in a residential neighborhood filled with the tightly organized and well-maintained apartment buildings that the Primclef residents favored. The area was crowded but sedate, like a nursing home. Most of the Denzans I saw were as ancient as Vanceval or older, their thin frames stooped, the color bled out of their squirmy hair. Small groups sat at sidewalk tables playing board games that I didn't understand, while others perched on stoops watching the moons cross the sky.

"Is this the Denzan version of Florida?" I asked.

"What's Florida?" Aela responded.

"It's a place on my world where old people go to finish out their days shooting fireworks at alligators."

"Hmm." Aela seriously considered my stupid joke. "I will need to research that."

We stopped outside of the only storefront on the street. The building was painted a soothing white, with a huge front window to let in the slanting Denzan sun. The place was small—no bigger than a corner store on Earth. There was a line of Denzans waiting to enter, most of them the kind of elderly folks who populated the neighborhood, but also some younger ones mixed in. I couldn't read the Denzan symbols on the sign.

"What is this place?" I asked.

"They call it Remembrance," Aela replied. The wisp stood with me on the other side of the street, watching the building with what I sensed was something like wariness. "When a wisp like the one you saw is contaminated by bad air or chemicals or radiation or a hundred other potential harms, the changes to their composition make it impossible for them to ever return home to the Ossho Collective. They will be alone. An individual. Forever."

I was an individual, alone in my own head (most of the time), and not part of a giant spacefaring intelligence. I liked it. But I got the sense that Aela meant this as a bad thing.

"Oh," I said. "Bummer."

"Yes. *Bummer.*"

Aela nodded once, almost like they were steeling themselves, and then took long strides across the street. I went with them, noticing how the Denzans in line watched Aela approach, many of them with tears in their eyes.

Through the front window, I could see that the narrow interior of Remembrance was divided into four curtained booths. When we arrived, only one of these booths was open, but that was quickly occupied by a wisp in a retro version of Aela's exo-suit and one of the old Denzans from outside. It wasn't the wisp I'd seen on the street yesterday—the cloud behind this one's faceplate was tinted with silver instead of gold. The wisp saw us looking in and paused, their faceplate pointed at Aela. After a moment of stillness, the wisp left the booth's curtain open so we could watch them work. They slipped a gas-mask-like apparatus over the mouth and nose of their Denzan client. The wisp then attached a hose to the Denzan's mask and screwed the other end into a valve on their exo-suit. There was no great care here—none of the intense showering or chemical baths—the wisp simply connected the flimsy length of tubing and then flowed into the Denzan's nostrils. The Denzan's body slackened and relaxed as the wisp took control of his mind.

"The contaminated here provide this service free of charge for the community," Aela explained, their mechanical chipperness toned down for a change. "They allow visitors to relive import-ant memories from their lives. While some of these wisps were contaminated by accident, others have chosen this life cycle, to maintain their individuality and remain forever separated from the Ossho Collective."

I took a step back from the window. I suddenly felt like I was spying on something extremely intimate. Aela joined me, and we walked aimlessly down the street. I looked over at my wisp friend, but obviously it was impossible to read the expression on a cloud. The fact that Aela had fallen into a rare silence was all I had to go on.

"You okay?" I asked. "You seem . . . I don't know. Sad?"

"I don't feel sadness like you, Syd," Aela replied. "Before we detach from the Ossho Collective, every wisp is warned of the phenomenon that affects the contaminated. We don't experience love or hate or lust or greed or fear or even happiness in the way that you organics do, driven in part by your body's chemistry, acting because of impulses evolved over millennia. We can't have those feelings naturally, but we can experience them through your minds and memories. We can become addicted to them, particularly during the time that we are individuals, separate from the collective. Some Ossho find the thrill of these feelings too great to give up."

Originally, I'd thought Aela had been doing me a favor by bringing me here to help look for the wisp that had spooked me. But now, I got the feeling that the wisp wanted someone to talk to, like they needed guidance as badly as I did.

"Have you been thinking about that?" I asked. "Not going back?"

"No, it's selfish to keep our memories to ourselves," Aela said quickly. "And besides, I have many years before I have to return." The metal digits on Aela's exo-suit fidgeted. "However, it does sometimes feel that to return to the collective, as fulfilling as it is to bask in the shared history of the universe—it feels like I could be depriving myself of experiencing the future. A future that I am extremely curious about. I feel, Syd, that something monumental is coming."

I tensed a bit at that. "Oh?"

"I saw what happened to you, Syd," Aela said. "I watched from the bridge. Unlike the others, I was not distracted by fear of my own mortality. I saw how the Etherazi enveloped you, released you, and sustained you until Reno could reach you."

I stopped in my tracks and stared at Aela, seeing only my own reflection in their faceplate. "Uh—it wasn't exactly like that—"

Aela held up their hand. "I understand your need for subterfuge, and I'm not offended by it. Your secrets are safe with me, Syd. I believe it's possible that you are the only organism in existence to ever encounter an Etherazi like that and survive. I would very much like to share in that experience."

I took an uneasy step back. So that's what this was all about. The Ossho valued experiences above all else, so getting into my brain would apparently be a huge prize for Aela.

"It really wasn't that big of a thing," I lied, but could tell by the way that Aela cocked their head that the wisp didn't buy it. I sighed. "I mean, it's probably not a good idea, Aela . . ."

Of course, my instinct was secrecy. My mom had drilled that into me from an early age. But carrying around the encounter with the Etherazi—the bizarre and frightening shit that Goldy said to me and showed me—had been haunting me ever since it happened. I'd decided to withhold the whole truth even from my uncle. With Aela, though—a neutral, chill presence, who didn't judge and didn't have a political agenda to advance—maybe it wouldn't be so dangerous to share the experience with them. With all their accumulated knowledge, they might even catch something that I hadn't.

"I see from your expression that you are considering my

proposal, and that's all I ask," Aela said, the brightness returning to their voice. "At the very least, I ask that you let me continue on as your crewmate, wherever you go next."

I raised my eyebrows. "I mean, not that I have a choice in the matter, but, uh, sure, you can be my biographer, if you want."

Aela clapped, clearly delighted by the reply I'd meant to be self-deprecating. "Excellent! It is said that the Ossho Collective has an intuition regarding which cosmos to travel to when it is time to observe events of great import. I have that feeling about you, Syd."

I exhaled. "Honestly, you wouldn't believe how tired I am of hearing shit like that."

"No, Syd," Aela replied, leaning their faceplate close to my forehead. "I would absolutely believe you. I trust you."

My finger on a button. A planet burning down below.

I didn't tell the wisp then, but Aela was putting their trust in the wrong person.

25

A chime from my vid-screen woke me up. I scrambled out of bed while groping for my tablet, at first mistaking the ringing for my alarm. I wasn't due to my Wayscope class for another hour, though. I wiped the sleep out of my eyes. My next guess was that the sound was some booby trap planted by Zara.

"What the hell," I mumbled groggily, half expecting a net to drop down from my ceiling.

Finally, I noticed the message on my wall-screen.

INCOMING TRANSMISSION FROM [[EARTH—CON-SULATE—001]]—MONITORING PROTOCOL ACTIVE—DO YOU ACCEPT? [Y/N]

"Uh, okay?"

My mom appeared on-screen.

"Hi, Syd."

"Whoa, Mom," I replied, hurriedly pulling on some pants. "Hey."

It had been a month since Washington, since she'd left me to jet off to space with my uncle, driving away without looking back. I guess neither one of us had really looked back. I'd been so swept up in things, first on the *Eastwood* and now on Denza, that I hadn't even thought to call her. I'm what you call a bad son.

She looked different. My mom wore a white dress shirt and a blue blazer, her glasses dangling from a strap around her neck. She sat in a conference room, a busy office visible through the glass wall behind her.

"My goodness, you look like one of . . ." Her hand started to reach toward her mouth, but she stopped herself. "You changed your hair," she finished diplomatically.

One of them, my mom had been about to say.

"Yeah, um . . ." I trailed off, this conversation already on an awkward footing. "Where are you, Mom?"

She glanced over her shoulder. "I decided to accept the Consulate's offer to have my old job back."

I opened my mouth, not sure what to say. I'd thought her bridge with the Consulate would've been thoroughly burned.

"They aren't letting me do anything interesting," my mom continued. "I spend my days double-checking climate change models against technological progress projections, then writing emails that nobody reads about how the Denzans should help us. I'm sure they're listening to this conversation right now, and I'm sure I'll have a polite email reminding me of the Denzan Senate's position of noninterference." My mom sighed and took a deep breath. "Anyway, it's the best way to keep in touch with you, and I don't have to sell drugs anymore."

I nodded, happy to be moving beyond the politics. "You're back in Australia, then?"

"Back home, at last," she said, nodding. "Enough about me. I've been dying to check in with you, but they're very stingy here with wormhole uplinks. How are you?"

"I'm . . ." That was a loaded question for so early in the morning. "I'm all right," I said at last.

"How are your classes? Keeping your grades up?"

"We don't really get grades here; we're just expected to make ourselves useful and learn everything we can," I replied. "But yeah, the classes are good; it's cool to actually be able to go to them."

My mom smiled in that tight-lipped way of hers.

"Are you making friends? I know that was always important to you."

"Yeah, actually," I said. "People here are pretty cool."

"The Serpo Institute only selects the best and brightest," my mom said. "I'm sure the humans who grew up on Denza are good examples, too."

I cleared my throat and nodded. I didn't feel like I could tell my mom that I felt more connected to the nonhumans I'd met so far than the humans.

"I hope you won't forget about us here on Earth," my mom said.

To anyone listening, I imagine that sounded like a typical

mom thing to say. But I knew what she meant. I had responsibilities here. Expectations. I was supposed to rescue my dad and his miracle research on the Wasting, then kick-start an invasion.

I couldn't tell my mom how complicated all that had gotten. And not just because our conversation was being monitored. She'd lost me to the Vastness, but, in exchange, she'd regained her sense of hope about finding my dad and saving humanity. I wanted her to hold on to that.

I checked the time on my tablet. "I've gotta get to class, Mom," I said. "This one would blow your mind. I get hooked into a giant telescope, basically, and can see all the way across the universe."

My mom's eyes brightened. She knew what I meant.

"Wow," my mom said. "Maybe you could use that thing next time I lose my keys."

"Sure," I replied. "With a Wayscope, I bet I could find almost anything."

Behind her old bitterness and her new business-casual Consulate gloss, I saw her eyes brighten.

I was still going to find my dad.

We said our good-byes, and then I hurriedly got dressed. I really was late for my Wayscope class, although not the one that I'd signed up for with Coreyunus. I'd never gone back to that lecture after the first one. My uncle Tycius had made other arrangements.

I needed to get to Little Earth.

Tycius was waiting for me at the train station, tapping his foot impatiently.

"Sorry," I said. "My mom called."

"Ah." His expression softened a bit, and he unconsciously touched the place on his bicep where his bindings were. "How's she doing?"

"She's . . ." I shrugged. "She hasn't really chilled out. I'll say that."

Ty laughed. "I'd expect not." He paused and seemed to steel himself as a new train glided into the station. "Well, hopefully this trip doesn't get us hauled before the Senate and thrown out of the institute."

"I think we'll be okay," I said, smirking. "You said it yourself. Rafe Butler is pretty much bulletproof."

The island of Little Earth was as deserted as the last time I'd visited. The sun—fully out of hiding for once—baked my arms and shoulders as my uncle and I hiked up the cobblestone walkway. Darcy was waiting for us outside Rafe's pizzeria, picking at a rapidly cooling slice. When my uncle heard that I wasn't the only hybrid getting shunned in Coreyunus's class, he'd offered to include Darcy in this secret class as well.

"You look nervous," she said to me.

"*You* look nervous," I responded.

She scowled. "Shit, how could I not be? I've never done this before, and the last time you tried, you almost burned your whole head off."

I steepled my fingers together and tilted my head back—a meditative Zen pose. "That was before I learned about deep breathing."

Darcy flicked her crust at me.

Rafe waited for us inside. As soon as we entered, he put the CLOSED sign in the window and locked the door. I didn't think he really had to worry about walk-ins, but better safe than sorry.

The Chef rubbed his hairy hands together. "Come on down to my dungeon."

In the basement, next to some sacks of flour, there was now a Wayscope. The machine wasn't nearly as complex as the ones I'd seen on the *Eastwood* or at the institute. In fact, the thing looked pretty bootleg. The goggles weren't hooked to a big screen but instead just a regular old tablet, and the power source attached to the ceiling looked to be a couple of modified skiff engines.

"What do you think?" Tycius asked Darcy and me. I could tell he was proud.

"Is it safe?" I asked.

"Does it *work*?" Darcy added, peering up at the ceiling, where a periscope-like hole had been drilled.

"Of course," Ty replied. "It's just an older model that we've repurposed to work down here. You won't be able to extend your consciousness as far as you could with a normal Wayscope, but—"

"You'll actually get to practice on this one," Rafe finished for him. "No one to stop you. As long as we keep things hush-hush."

I crossed my arms. "Should we even ask how you got your hands on this thing? Did it fall off a truck?"

Rafe winked at me, while Darcy took me literally. "It definitely looks like it fell off something," she said.

"Turns out, I knew where to find one of these retired models," Rafe said casually. "And your uncle knew how to fix one up."

"You need practice," Tycius said simply, then glanced at Darcy. "You both do. The way Coreyunus treated you—it's a stain on the entire institute. I'll teach the two of you twice a week."

Once I was strapped into the chair, using this training-wheels Wayscope after the high-powered one on the *Eastwood* actually seemed like a step backward. I could open my mind and see beyond the local star system, feel where its edges bumped up against nearby galaxies, and sense the soft places where a wormhole could potentially connect them. I wanted to reach out farther, but it wasn't powerful enough to take me there.

"Good, Sydney," Ty said, although he sounded a bit puzzled. I eased myself back from the goggles and looked at him.

"What? What did I do wrong?"

"Nothing, actually," he said. "Your control was excellent, which is why I can't understand what happened on the *Eastwood*."

"Uh, you mean besides being plugged into the Wayscope when a freaking Etherazi attacked?" Darcy offered from the peanut gallery.

"Yes," my uncle said. "Good point."

We exchanged a look as I cleared the way for Darcy. The Etherazi had arrived *after* I'd lost control of the *Eastwood*'s Wayscope. Goldy had saved me from spinning out farther. I shook my head. Maybe I'd been too eager to find my dad and gulped down too much cosmic info. That was the simplest explanation.

Training was harder for Darcy. She had trouble opening her mind to the Vastness and seemed compelled to pull back whenever she got out too far. My uncle was patient with her, and by the end of the session Darcy had had more time in the chair than me.

While Tycius worked with Darcy, Rafe sidled up to me.

"You been enjoying my class, Cadet?" he asked with a wink. I knew he'd seen me goofing with Melian the week before, but Rafe didn't seem like the kind of guy to take that personally.

"Of course," I replied, winking back. "It's illuminating."

Rafe chuckled. "*Illuminating.* Kid, you've got a real way of making a compliment sound like an insult. You're a hard guy to get a read on, you know that? Your mom trained you well."

Coming from Rafe, a man who was basically a shape-shifter—pizza maker, war hero, revolutionary—that was high praise. I kept my face impassive.

"Thanks," I said, gesturing to the bootleg Wayscope. "Thanks for setting all this up."

"Of course," Rafe replied. "We all have to do our part to ensure the survival of humanity." He paused when Darcy yelped and spasmed in the chair, my uncle at her side to calm her down. "I'm no expert, but you looked good out there. A natural."

I didn't feel so natural back on the *Eastwood*, when I would've fried my brain if not for the intervention of an inscrutable galactic horror. "It was a good class today," I said noncommittally. "I still need practice."

Rafe leaned closer, lowering his voice so my uncle wouldn't overhear. "I wonder, how long do you think we can afford to delay looking for Marcius? Each day that goes by, don't you worry . . . ?"

My shoulders tensed. Rafe didn't need to finish his sentence. I was still checking the light in the cosmological tether multiple times per day. "Of course I worry," I said sharply.

"I talked it over with Marie—ah, Captain Reno," Rafe continued. "She can put in for an off-world training exercise whenever you're ready. Use that for cover to go searching for your dad."

I hesitated. Rafe was pushing me, trying to flip me like one of his doughs. I shared his anxiety that at any moment my dad—who had held on for a decade—would suddenly wink out of existence. But unlike Rafe, I knew there was something dangerous out there. A future waiting for me that I wasn't ready for.

Rafe decided what I needed was a pep talk. "Syd, if your father came up empty out there and didn't find a damn thing that's useful, then you'll at least save his life," Rafe said. "But if he did find a cure for the Wasting? We're talking about billions of lives saved, kid. Thanks to you. I've saved a planet before, pal, and let me tell you—it feels great."

World killer.

I rubbed my arm, the one that had been bound by metal in that glimpse of my future. "I don't know how much training I'll need," I said. "I'd need to talk it over with my uncle . . ."

"Two weeks," Tycius said.

My uncle had heard everything. For all of Rafe's hushed tones, Tycius was still a former spy. He probably knew how to read lips.

"I can have you ready in two weeks," Ty said, looking at me now. "If you're up for it."

"Ready for what?" Darcy asked before I could respond. She got up from the Wayscope, rubbing her temples. "What are you talking about?"

Rafe grinned at her. "Ready to save our kind, my child," he said. "Ready to lead humanity into the future."

26

"Do you like it here, Syd?" Tycius asked as we rode the train back from Little Earth.

I looked out the window at the ocean, tinted purple due to a partial eclipse. The waters were dotted with small boats, the Denzan fishermen waving at the train as it passed by overhead. A coral reef sparked neon orange. In the distance, the craggy edges of Primclef rose up from the water.

My life on Earth had been paranoia and chaos. My future, at least if I believed the Etherazi, was going to be danger and war. But here on Denza, at the institute, was the first time that I actually felt at peace. Ignoring the cold reception I'd gotten from some antihuman Denzans like Arkell, most of the people I'd met here were kind. They were good to one another. Nobody here suffered or was deprived of basic shit. I could take my classes, expand my mind, and dream about the Vastness. I realized, looking out over the ocean, that I felt more relaxed here than I ever had before.

"Yeah," I responded, after what I realized must have been one of those dreamy pauses. "I really do."

"I didn't mean to push you back there," Ty said. "We both know what's at stake, but I'd understand if you wanted to wait. Get to know this place. Your life hasn't been easy. You could have a break from it all . . ."

My gaze drifted up from the ocean to the sky, the horizon, the violet backdrop dotted with stars. I liked Denza, but the Vastness still called to me. I thought about Ty's suggestion only for a second.

"No," I said. "There's no running from it. We need to find my dad."

The message from Captain Reno went out that night. We were going off-world again in two weeks. The *Eastwood* had been assigned to a tropical planet called Caris-III where we'd be assisting Denzan scientists to catalog the local plant life. The rest of the crew was excited. I didn't have the heart to tell them that we weren't actually going to Caris-III, that they were just part of a cover story to get us back out into the Vastness. I'd let Reno handle that.

A small gray planet where ash fell like snow. Definitely not the sexy field trip everyone was hoping for.

I stuck with my classes for the next two weeks, but most of my effort went into those underground Wayscope sessions at Rafe's pizzeria. After that first meeting, I started taking more time in the chair than Darcy. She didn't mind, always complaining about how the Wayscope gave her migraines. It didn't have that effect on me. In fact, by the second week, I was straining against the limits of our bootleg Wayscope, dying to push my consciousness into new galaxies. I could pivot between star systems at will, probing for potential wormhole locations with ease. I figured that I could probably smash through that old Dungeon puzzle in seconds. Once I was plugged back into the *Eastwood*'s Wayscope, operating a cosmological tether wouldn't be a problem.

"You're good at this," my uncle told me, pride in his voice. "I knew you would be."

The truth was, I liked it out in the Vastness. I could blank my mind and forget all about the pressure on me—the politics and prophecies—and just be one with the cosmos.

Besides losing myself in the Vastness, the only thing that really chilled me out during those two weeks was Human Book Club for Nonhumans.

My science fiction class had quickly turned into the best part of my schedule. I'd been surprised when, right before the first meeting, when it was just supposed to be H'Jossu and me, Batzian and Melian showed up. Apparently, Mel had convinced Batzian that he should expose himself to some human culture besides Rafe Butler's war stories.

"This one was truly terrible," Batzian declared, setting down his tablet with disgust. This was our last meeting before the training mission, the day before we were set to depart. "To think that humanity would dream of such amazing technological progress—for them, at least—and the result of that progress would be a police state. Disturbing."

"I guess it shows that we're a seriously pessimistic species," I replied.

"I actually agree with Batzian," H'Jossu said. "I didn't like it. I don't understand why Winston didn't just buy a machine gun or something. That would've been a better climax."

"That is not at all what I'm saying," Batzian said. "Why is it always machine guns with you?"

"It's not," H'Jossu said, slowly lowering his arms, which had previously been mimicking a machine gun.

"No, sometimes it's lasers," I said.

"Or karate," Melian added.

I held class in a little park outside the institute, the four of us seated across from one another on a pair of marble benches. We got lucky with our time slot, which happened to fall at one of the sunniest parts of the afternoon. H'Jossu periodically had to fend off flocks of small birds that wanted to nest in his wooly shoulders.

"I thought it was romantic," Mel said. "Even though his society was constructed to crush him, Winston still found hope and love."

"A foolish thing to risk one's life for," Batzian replied.

Mel shrugged. "No more foolish than anything else."

I glanced down at the notes that I'd prepared for this class. "What's crazy is that Orwell wrote this book seventy years ago, before the internet was even a thing on my planet. It's wild how much he saw coming."

"Like touch-screen walls that are secretly spying on you," H'Jossu said.

"Everyone at the institute is assured of their privacy," Batzian replied quickly.

"I'm just joking, dude."

"It makes me wonder if Orwell was like a psychic—," I started to say.

"No, obviously not," Batzian interrupted.

"*Or*," I continued, flashing Batzian my best version of my mom's *don't interrupt me* look, "maybe human society used Orwell's writing almost as a handbook. Maybe we like internalized his dark thoughts about the future and they became a self-fulfilling prophecy."

"Deep," H'Jossu said.

Melian sighed happily; she had a habit of doing that whenever she heard or read something interesting. "I know we don't take classes while on the *Eastwood*, but do you think the four of us could still get together for some reading?"

"I'm down," H'Jossu said.

"Totally," I said.

We all looked at Batzian. He tightened his ponytail.

"I don't think a little book club will get in the way of our duties," he said. Then he smiled, a rare thing from him. "Also, I'm already halfway through *Hyperion*, so you'll all need to catch up."

That night, I planned to get to bed early. We had a briefing scheduled in the morning. I'd just finished hooking up the network of trip wires that I kept in front of my room's entrance and window in case of another Zara intrusion, when Hiram pounded on my door. For some reason, he was wearing black silk pajamas.

"Brother, I've been looking all over for you," he said.

"And you just now tried my room?" I replied, eyeing him. "Why are you dressed like a porno movie ninja?"

"Shut up," he said. "What are you doing right now?"

"Uh, going to bed?" I responded, regretting immediately that I didn't have a more viable excuse.

"Going to—?" He shook his head. "No way. We have plans. You're coming out on patrol with me."

"Sorry, what?"

"Pa-trol," he said, sounding out the word, as if that made what he wanted any clearer. "Usually Darcy comes, but she's having a special good-bye dinner with my grandpa that apparently I'm too much of an asshole to get invited to. So I need you to be my sidekick."

"As enticing as that sounds, I think I'm going to pass."

"Not optional," Hiram said. "Besides, didn't you say you wanted to go to Keyhole Cove? That's where I'm staking out. Do you have any dark clothes?"

I sighed. I *had* wanted to visit Keyhole Cove but got too snowed under with classes and training. I also knew that Hiram wouldn't leave me alone until I said yes or somehow wrestled him out of my room. Plus, whatever he was up to sounded like a bad idea, which made me think I should go even more, as a representative of the good side of humanity.

So that's how I ended up perched on a rooftop in Keyhole Cove, peering down at the revelers below. The beachside village was a destination for a lot of the younger Denzans, basically Primclef's designated party zone. The neighborhood was also a hot spot for the Vulpin; there were almost as many of them mingling down below as there were Denzans. Everyone filtered in and out of different bars and restaurants and VR arcades, listening to bands that were set up at the corners blasting synth-heavy Denzan music, or pausing at food stands or smoke stands to inhale some locally grown mushrooms, one way or the other.

It was a pretty wild scene, and I would've been happier to be down in it, rather than crouched next to Hiram in the shadows of a neon sign advertising a bar called Red Sands.

"We're the protectors of these people," he intoned to me, his voice way deeper and more gravelly than necessary. "The Etherazi may be gone, but that doesn't mean there aren't threats."

"Okay, Batman," I said.

"What the hell's a *Batman*?"

"Never mind."

"Denza is open to immigrants from other planets, so of course the Vulpin are always showing up, looking for easy marks," Hiram continued. "There's at least one robbery over here every night. They think they're so slick about it."

Hiram pointed down at a trio of Vulpin guys with their fur trimmed to tight braids along the backs of their heads. They swayed through the crowd, looking like any of the other partiers, two of them always hanging on each other, either roughhousing or dancing, bumping into the kiosks as they went. It took me a second to realize what they were doing. Whenever the first two bumbled into a stand, which always drew the ire of the owner, the third Vulpin used the distraction to pocket some bottles or loose items.

"Man, you must be my good-luck charm," Hiram declared.

"Usually have to dick around up here for hours before there's a bust to make."

I shook my head. "They're just stealing some beers," I replied. "That's what you're keeping Denza safe from?"

"That's how it starts," Hiram said. He jumped up onto the balustrade. "Let's go kick some ass."

Hiram leaped down to the street without glancing back to see if I was following. He landed only a few feet from one of the Vulpin thieves. He grabbed the guy by the tail and slammed him onto the cobblestones. The other two Vulpin immediately sprinted into the crowd. Hiram tried to give chase, but he was cut off by a bunch of confused partiers trying to break up the fight. I heard him yelling at them about "standing in the way of justice."

"Fuck this," I said.

I turned away and immediately came face-to-face with a pair of glowing green eyes and a glinting silver blade. As usual, I jumped out of my skin.

"Got you again," Zara said with a smirk, sheathing her blade in her hair and stepping back. I wasn't sure how long she'd been on the roof, practically breathing down my neck, but it was definitely long enough to have overheard Hiram's bullshit. "You didn't want to go play party patrol with the big idiot?"

"Not really my thing."

She stepped around me to peek over the edge. In the commotion, the Vulpin who Hiram had slammed had gotten to his feet and fled into the crowd. Hiram gave chase, the three Vulpin now working as a team to evade him. One always leaped in to provide a timely distraction whenever Hiram got too close to one of the others. From up here, the whole scene looked like slapstick. Most of the Denzans down below had stopped to watch the show as well, clapping and laughing like Hiram's crusade was all a joke.

"Those den Bono pups are enjoying themselves," Zara said. "Stolen loot doesn't really have value if no one's chasing you for it."

"It's like a game to them," I observed, watching as two of the Vulpin boys lured Hiram around a corner just so the third, perched above a doorway, could dump a bucket of water over his head.

"A competition," Zara corrected. "To my people, everything is a competition. Haven't you learned that yet?"

"I've mostly learned to check my closet before going to bed, like I'm five years old again," I responded. Down below, Hiram, shouting, barreled around a corner after the Vulpin boys. I lost sight of him. "Hope he doesn't catch them," I said.

"He won't," Zara reassured me. "He's out here so many nights, playing his little police game. Every Vulpin on the prowl knows he's coming and how to give him the slip. Even Darcy's so sick of the humiliation, she's making up excuses to get a night off."

I was still a little worried that Hiram might catch those Vulpin and cripple them out of frustration, but Zara didn't seem concerned. More than anything, I was relieved to have Hiram out of my hair.

"Want to walk back to the institute together?" I asked.

Zara's fangs glinted in the moonlight. "Sure."

"Without trying to stab me?"

"No promises."

We made our way down to the street and strolled through the crowd. At some point, Zara filched a bottle of Denzan moss ale from a street vendor. She was much smoother than the other Vulpin; I didn't even see her do it.

"Are all Vulpin thieves?" I asked.

"Only the ones who practice," she said, wiggling the bottle at me. "Is every human so uptight? Are you going to tell Hiram on me?"

I snatched the bottle from her and drank. "Nope."

The ale tasted sweet, and, as soon as it hit my tongue, the colors around me seemed brighter. We passed the drink back and forth. I became keenly aware of how I swung my arms when I walked. Time felt slower for me, even though all the people we passed were sped up.

"Do you know which way we're going?" Zara asked.

"I was following you," I said.

"Uh-oh." She held up the half-empty bottle and swished the ale around. "This stuff is strong."

I laughed. "You should steal more."

As we stumbled onward, my nostrils flared. I smelled something that I hadn't since coming to Denza—bacon frying. We'd reached a block of shops that were owned and operated by Vulpin proprietors. There were stalls selling all kinds of meats, a couple with secondhand electronics and ship parts, and a few hawking knives and other edged weapons. I noticed that all the stalls on the left side of the road were operated by Vulpin who kept their hair short and spiky, while the stalls on the right side were run by merchants with looping curls down the sides of their heads. The hawkers spent as much time glowering at one another as they did shouting at passing customers.

"Den Iben," Zara said, gesturing to the left, "and den Rost," she said, gesturing to the right. "A healthy rivalry to drive commerce, only a few stabbings every year." She squeezed my arms, claws sharp against my biceps. "We should not have come this way. Someone may try to kidnap you."

She was making fun of me, but I didn't mind so much. "You'll protect me, right?"

Zara considered this. "For the right price. Maybe. There's no glory in guarding a farty Earth boy."

My stomach rumbled. "If you're done roasting me, can we get something . . . ?"

I trailed off as the crowd parted and I caught sight of a surprising figure. Arkell stood hunched over one of the tables selling bootleg technology, the *Eastwood*'s chief engineer shaking a metallic conduit in the face of a hostile-looking den Iben male.

I pointed him out to Zara. "Isn't that . . . ?"

"Hmm," Zara said. "What's he doing down here? The institute is not so cheap that he'd need to barter for spare parts."

As we watched, Arkell and the merchant exchanged a few last words. Clearly, the Denzan wasn't getting what he wanted out of the exchange. He stuffed his gadget back into his coat and stormed away from the table.

Alarm bells blared in my mind. Something wasn't right. Once Arkell was out of sight, I approached the merchant's table.

"Excuse me," I said, trying to come off as sober as possible. "What did that last customer want?"

The Vulpin eyed me skeptically. "He just asked for directions," he said. "Why do you ask?"

Zara sidled up to my side, clucking her tongue at the merchant. She brushed the mane on her shoulders, and I thought I saw a flash of metal there. "Come, come, den Iben," she said. "We're all friends here."

Surprisingly, the merchant seemed to relax in Zara's presence—I guessed brandishing a weapon was how the Vulpin shook hands. "Ah, den Jetten, I did not know this was your human," the merchant said. He leaned closer. "That pissy Denzan had a burned-out Wayscope refractor. Wanted to know where he could get another one. I told him that this isn't no black-market shop. He thinks all us Vulpin traffic in banned tech."

"What's a Wayscope refractor?" I asked with all the subtlety of a hammer.

The merchant gave me a wary look, so Zara pulled me away from his stand.

"Very rare Vulpin spycraft," she explained. "We can't use the Wayscopes like the Denzans or you hybrids, but if we sneakily attach a refractor, we can intercept whatever data the Denzans pull from the Vastness. It's tricky, though. Unstable. A thing like that could make a Wayscope overload. Works equally well for stealing information as it does for frying whoever's in the chair."

27

I took off at a run after Arkell. I had to catch him.

He was a former member of the Merciful Rampart, an organization that wanted humanity quarantined to Earth.

He was our ship's engineer, which meant he had access to the Wayscope and would know how to use it. Or hack it.

He'd kept quiet about the incident with the Etherazi, despite being a stone-cold prick.

He was hunting around for a piece of Vulpin technology that could steal coordinates from a Wayscope. Or fry the brain of its user. My uncle hadn't understood why using the cosmological tether had gone haywire for me. My second time using a Wayscope, in Rafe's basement, had been so much easier.

Arkell had sabotaged the *Eastwood*'s machine. It all made sense.

He'd found my cosmological tether and then set a trap.

He almost shattered my mind.

That motherfucker tried to kill me.

And now, the night before we left Denza, he was gearing up to try again.

"Syd?" Zara ran at my side, her head bowed low as she tried to keep up. I was moving fast, at the maximum speed I could go and still weave through the crowd without trampling anyone. "What are we running toward?"

"Arkell," I told her. "It was him."

"Remember the stalking techniques you've learned—," she panted.

"No time for that," I responded, hunkering down and leaping straight onto the nearest rooftop. From up there I had a better vantage point.

Arkell stuck out like a sore thumb in Keystone Cove, dressed in formal black clothes and at least a couple decades older than most of the other Denzans out partying. He hadn't gone far. Arkell had stopped at another shop, another place run by a Vulpin, this one with a neon sign shaped like a samurai sword.

I'd spent my whole life on Earth running, always worried that there were people about to pounce on me. I'd never had the chance to turn the tables. Maybe I was still buzzing a little from the drink I'd had with Zara, but I was practically vibrating at what was about to happen. Finally, I was going to get some answers. I remembered the way Arkell had looked at me back when we had our altercation on the *Eastwood*, like I was some kind of wild animal. I'd felt bad then, like I didn't want to reinforce his ugly human stereotype.

But now? Fuck it.

I leaped from the roof and landed inches behind Arkell, shaking the ground beneath his feet. Frightened, the Vulpin merchant immediately slammed a shutter down over his kiosk's window and disappeared from view. Arkell's shoulders scrunched up around his ears, and he covered his head like a meteor had landed behind him. I reached out and spun him around.

"Cadet Chambers!" The old Denzan's voice was a shriek, part surprise and part disgust. His scarred face puckered; his eyes narrowed. "Unhand me, you beast!"

Instead, I reached into his coat and pulled out the mechanism. The Wayscope refractor. I held it in his face, just like he'd done to the Vulpin merchant.

"What is this?" I demanded, even though I knew the answer.

"A Wayscope refractor," he answered simply.

"Why do you have it?"

Arkell started to sneer at my questioning, but something in my face must have convinced him to answer straight. "The day we returned to Denza, I found it attached to the Wayscope during a maintenance check. I've been asking around, trying to discover its origin."

"Oh, bullshit," I said, stepping closer so Arkell had to back up against the storefront. "This is *yours*. You tried to—"

"Ah, I see." Arkell nodded, like he knew I had caught him. His coat had slipped off his shoulder, and I could see the glint of metal where his arm was bound. "You think I had something to do with your blunders on the Wayscope. I understand why you would think that, Cadet Chambers, but I assure you, during my time with the Merciful Rampart, my work was never so sloppy—"

No way was I letting him worm out of this. I grabbed Arkell by the front of his shirt. "You're a liar, man. I know—"

"Hey, friend, I think you've had too much to drink," a woman's voice interrupted from behind me. "Why don't you leave Grandpa alone?"

I glanced over my shoulder. A group of Vulpin had gathered in a semicircle to watch my altercation with Arkell. All of them wore their fur in bushy manes dyed with black and yellow spots that reminded me of leopards. The woman who'd spoken to me was probably only a few years older than me, although it was hard to tell with the Vulpin. She wore a long duster covered in grease stains—some kind of mechanic.

"Mind your own business," I told her.

She smiled and took a cautious step toward me. "Come on now, strong guy, don't mess up your whole life over some geezer."

I realized then how it must look. Like I was assaulting Arkell on the street for no reason. I was making a worse impression than Hiram chasing around those shoplifters.

"You don't understand—," I started to say.

The Vulpin was close now, the rest of her den looking on tensely. She reached up and gently brushed her clawed fingers through my hair. "You have pretty fur for a human. Come on. Let's go party."

"Uh." Was she flirting with me? There was something about the Vulpin that seemed vaguely familiar to me. "Do I know you?"

She laughed musically. "Not yet."

The other Vulpin were all watching me, smirking, like I was the butt of some joke. It was at that moment that Arkell surprised me by speaking up.

"I am an employee of the Serpo Institute, and this boy is one of my cadets," he declared. "We were just returning to the institute."

I couldn't understand why Arkell would want to go anywhere with me after I'd just outed him as a saboteur. I tried to shoot him a look, but my neck felt suddenly tight. My whole back, actually. I must have pulled something when I leaped off the roof.

"You must be a lousy professor, if you let your students come at you like that," the Vulpin said to Arkell. "You can run along, old-timer. We'll have the cadet back for curfew."

"I think not," Arkell replied, and then suddenly his hand was hooked through my elbow. "Come along, Sydney."

As he tried to lead me down the street, I noticed how the circle of Vulpins moved with us. I also noticed how the rest of the street had cleared.

My knees locked. My fingers felt oddly numb. My vision seemed suddenly dark around the edges.

I *did* recognize that Vulpin woman. I'd seen her before. The same day that I thought I saw Goldy hiding in the exo-suit of an Ossho wisp. The Vulpin had been walking right behind me. The wisp had actually bumped into her.

She'd been following me.

I groaned—a low, raspy thing, like my lungs were caught in a vice. My entire body was stiff and rigid. My limbs felt like they were locked in ice. I teetered on my heels, trying to stay up. Arkell grunted as I leaned against him.

"Arkell," I croaked. I was vaguely aware of drool trickling down the front of my chin when I tried to talk. "Something . . . is wrong . . . with me."

"Walk, you idiot," Arkell hissed. "You've been poisoned."

The hair. She'd put something in my hair.

The Vulpin surged forward. Some peeled Arkell away from me, while others gathered around to take custody of me. I couldn't lift my arms to fend them off.

"Don't worry, don't worry," the Vulpin woman said. "We'll get him to a doctor, boss."

"You're the one going to need a doctor, if you don't go piss up a tree."

If my lungs hadn't been frozen in carbonite, I would've breathed a sigh of relief. Zara stood a few strides away. The other Vulpin all seemed unsettled at the sight of her. They outnumbered her twelve to one, but we were in public. I got the sense that they didn't want to attract attention with a big throwdown.

The Vulpin who'd poisoned me stepped forward to meet Zara. "All right, now, little sister," she said. "You run along and forget you saw this. Sleep easy that way."

"Zara, go—" Arkell started to issue an order, but a Vulpin slapped a hand over his mouth.

"I don't recognize your marks," Zara replied. "What den are you?"

"Den Nobody," the Vulpin answered. "Go on now. Consider yourself lucky you don't know us better."

"Human boys are heavy lifting," Zara remarked, looking at the Vulpin holding me up. Her knife appeared in her hand, and she hunkered low. "You got numbers, so you probably win the fight, yeah, but I'll carve you up nice. Make it so you can't carry your own guts back to your ship, much less my boy here. You want that? You—?"

"Too much talk," the woman replied, then flicked a hand into her duster. That hand came back holding a weapon—I didn't know the Vulpin name for it—but in Earth terms it looked like the laser cannon version of a sawed-off shotgun. She fired before Zara could even lunge forward, a burst of plasma energy that struck Zara right in the stomach and knocked her off her feet.

Zara didn't even have a chance to scream.

I smelled burning fur and blood. My chin was stuck to my chest. I couldn't work up the energy to check on my friend. I'd lost sight of Arkell, too.

The Vulpin woman stood in front of me. She brushed her fingers through my hair again. Another dose of whatever drug I'd absorbed.

"Okay, sacred boy," she said, dragging her claw down my jawline. "Off we go to save the universe."

PART FOUR

ASHFALL

28

Darkness.

"You gave him too much of that toxin. He's useless to me in this condition."

"You know what humans can do. I wasn't taking any chances."

"You left witnesses."

"You didn't pay for bodies. You paid for *no* bodies."

"The others will come looking. I need him *awake*."

"Give it some time, boss. Go take a nap or something. We'll come get you."

Waves crashing. I was at the beach.

I couldn't feel anything. I tried to wiggle my toes or squeeze my fingers. Nothing.

My eyelids felt weighted down. It was a struggle to pry them open. When I did, the low-hanging sun seared my retinas. I would've jerked my head away or shielded my eyes, but I couldn't move anything.

As my vision slowly cleared, I made out a rocky beach, littered with jagged shards of coral, like an oceanic graveyard. The water came in rough here, smashing against the barbed reefs. It was light out, the sun just beginning to rise above the horizon, which meant I'd been out for some time.

Docked on the beach was a Vulpin cruiser. I hadn't seen one of their ships up close before, but they looked about how I expected—sleek and angular, sharp edges, built for speed. This one was painted in speckled crimson and tan, likely for camouflage against the deserts of Stonlea. Some of the leopard-spotted Vulpin I'd unfortunately met at Keyhole Cove milled around the underside of the ship, doing minor repairs.

Kidnapped. Successfully this time.

Instinctively, I reached for my pocket to see if my dad's cosmological tether was still there. Well, I had the *urge* to reach, anyway. My arm didn't actually respond.

I came to realize that although I could see the beach, I wasn't actually outside. I was staring out through the smashed wall of a building. A wide-open space. Maybe some kind of abandoned warehouse. Bad shit always went down in places like that. Sand blew in through the open wall, and it was an inch thick in most places, except where my captors left fresh footprints. No one had been here in a very long time.

That meant no one would be looking for me here.

A furry hand snapped its fingers in front of my face. A burly Vulpin dude now blocked my view to the outside. He peered into my eyes, and I tried my best to glare at him.

"Yo, Nyxie," the Vulpin yelled. "Our boy's awake."

Footfalls approached from behind me, then the Vulpin woman from Keyhole Cove stepped into my eye line. Nyxie smiled at me. She'd gunned down Zara for no reason. I wanted to lunge at her. I tried, but nothing happened.

Wait. That wasn't true.

My fingers twitched. I had a little tingle there.

Didn't want her to notice that. If she did, she might dose me again. Luckily, she was busy giving orders to her partner.

"Go tell the boss the kid's awake," Nyxie said.

As the male stalked off, Nyxie crouched down to put her snout right in my face. Her hot breath smelled like cinnamon gum. She tapped one of her claws against my forehead.

"You awake in there, eh? Blink twice for yes."

I refused to blink at all, holding my eyes open until they watered.

"Oh, I see you in there, you big mad," she said and laughed. Then she grabbed my chin and swung my head around so that I could see more of my surroundings. "Make this easy on us, yeah? We don't want to hurt nobody."

My fingers twitched again at that.

I was strapped to a chair. I hadn't realized that before, on account of the lack of feeling in my limbs.

Not just any chair. A Wayscope. The goggles hung above my head, a little rust built up on them from exposure to the sea air.

So that's what I was supposed to cooperate with.

I thought back to the Vulpin who had attacked my mom on Earth, how she'd stolen the cosmological tether and tried to kidnap me, too. These people wanted to use me to find my father—but why?

"That's enough, Nyxie," said a stern voice from behind the Vulpin. A familiar voice.

Aw. Not him. He was like the nicest one.

Nyxie stepped aside, revealing Vanceval. The elderly Denzan's impressive pompadour drooped lower than I'd ever seen it. His mouth trembled as he met my eyes, then looked away. Vanceval held a tablet in his hands, nearly fumbling the thing as he came forward.

His hands were both cast in obsidian. New shame. His wrists were raw where the recently affixed bonds chafed. Vanceval didn't have those when I saw him in class just a few days ago.

They were for me. He was ashamed of what he was going to do here.

And to give up his hands? These weren't some bands around the bicep like my uncle had, reminders of how he'd let people down. This was real shame.

The killer kind.

"Leave us," Vanceval said to Nyxie.

The Vulpin looked disappointed to be cut out of whatever was happening next. She reached into her pocket and handed Vanceval a stoppered vial. "He gets rowdy, a little bit of that in his—"

"I know," Vanceval interrupted. *"Leave us."*

Holding up her hands, Nyxie walked out of my field of vision, disappearing somewhere behind me.

Vanceval held the vial up to the light—a clear, viscous gel swam about inside.

"This toxin would not work on a full human. Not potent enough," he said, still teaching, even now. "A full Denzan would be able to metabolize it for nutrients, which is why your body was so eager to absorb it. As a hybrid, you are neither strong enough to resist it nor adaptable enough to convert it. A rare downside for your kind. However, the paralysis will wear off in time." He frowned at me. "In fact, I suspect that is already happening."

I pressed my tongue to the roof of my mouth, trying to speak. I wanted to ask him why. I wanted to curse him out.

Vanceval's clumsy metal fingers nearly dropped the vial, but he eventually stashed it in his coat. He gazed over at the shattered wall. "The Merciful Rampart built bombs here once to destroy the wormhole back to your galaxy. A close-minded and grotesque business. But, like Arkell himself, this place has its uses."

Of course. Arkell would be the perfect fall guy for whatever Vanceval had planned. He'd discovered the Wayscope refractor on the *Eastwood* and gone around hunting for its origin. And now I'd be found here, in one of his old haunts, with Arkell being one of the only witnesses to my abduction. I'd never even suspected the doddering old man in front of me. How could I? He'd been nothing but patient and kind.

The way he'd apologized to me back on the *Eastwood*, though, when we all thought the Etherazi was going to kill us . . . I thought he'd been sorry for the Wayscope mishap. He'd actually been apologizing for almost nuking my brain.

I tried to bite the inside of my cheek, hoping the pain might spur something in me.

"I want you to know, Sydneycius, that this brings me great

sadness and grief." He held up his hands. "You can see the shame that I feel already."

I stuck my lip out at him. A pouty face. So sad.

Vanceval sighed. He reached into his pocket and produced a cosmological tether—my father's cosmological tether. The Vulpin must have searched me when I was unconscious.

"You are going to help me locate your father," Vanceval said simply.

I breathed out through my nose. A snort. No way. I closed my eyes to show him that I'd never use the Wayscope, never access the data stored in that ring.

"Yes, I imagined you would have misgivings," Vanceval responded. "I am going to show you two things that I suspect will convince you." He held up the tablet in front of my face. "The first."

A video began to play. A transmission. The feed was fuzzy and buffered frequently—it had been sent across a great distance.

A Denzan man. High cheekbones and a tangle of aquamarine hair, gentle eyes, an upturned mouth that made it seem like he was half smiling even when he was clearly distressed. I'd seen this man before.

I could picture him eating a donut on the hood of a car. Smiling down at me and ruffling my hair. Telling me that he was leaving.

My dad.

He sat against a cracked wall covered in scorch marks, ash falling like snow across his shoulders. It was like he was transmitting from a war zone. Strands of hair were stuck to his cheek by dried blood, a deep cut along his scalp. He started to talk but had to pause to cough raggedly into his shoulder.

"Vanceval," my dad finally began. "This will be my last transmission before we go permanently dark. There was some disagreement among the survivors about what to do, but that—" He coughed into his shoulder, leaving a dark wet spot behind. "That's been resolved."

Resolved. That word hung in the air, heavy with implication. There was a faraway look in my dad's eyes.

"When we found—when we found the temple, Alex lost his mind. It wasn't the cure for the Wasting. Not—not the one we were expecting, anyway," my dad continued. "He murdered most of the others before we could stop him."

The temple. In my vision of that grim planet, I'd glimpsed a great black pyramid in the center of a ruined city. Right before something burst through my chest.

Alex. He must have meant Alexander Abe, the one human on my dad's crew. He'd killed his own shipmates? What could've driven him to that? I thought of the times of death on the ship's manifest, so many in rapid succession. How quickly Abe had killed the others; how mercilessly.

"But we *did* stop him," my dad continued. "Killed him. We killed him thanks to . . ." He shook his head. "That will be my shame to carry, for however long I have left. A very small shame, in the face of a much bigger one . . ."

My dad shook his head, trying to straighten out his thoughts.

"You must listen to me, Vanceval," my dad resumed. "I know this will be hard for you to hear. This is your life's work as well as mine. The Lost People, this place we call Ashfall—they must never be found. I'm doing everything I can to eradicate my trail, but you must do the rest. For the good of the universe, you can't let anyone come looking for me."

For a moment, my eyes flicked away from the screen to Vanceval's face. His eyes were wet with tears as he watched with me.

"There is a loose end," my dad said. "My son is in possession of a cosmological tether. It should be extinguished when I expire, but—just in case—you need to find him. Recover the tether. Destroy it. Do whatever you have to do. We are lost. Don't let us be found."

He coughed.

The transmission ended.

It was Vanceval who sent the Vulpin to kidnap me all those years ago. And he did that on the wishes of my own father. My father, who didn't care what kind of collateral damage might come from his transmission.

My vision blurred. There were tears in my eyes now, too.

Vanceval put the tablet aside and peered at the glowing cosmos contained inside the cosmological tether.

"I expected your father to die, as he all but promised to do," Vanceval said. "It's why I never tried to find you again, after the first time was such a failure." He looked over his shoulder again, at the Vulpin working on the ship. "Mercenaries, I have found, can be terribly unreliable."

I clenched my jaw, trying to get a word out. My tongue still felt packed in cotton.

"I had a decade to consider your father's request," Vanceval continued. "A decade among my relics to consider a dead end to my life's great passion. I have watched your father's transmission over and over again. And I have decided that it is not his decision to make. He was not of sound mind."

I actually agreed with him. Not that old Vanceval seemed like the picture of sanity either, at this point.

"I tried to extract the coordinates from you on the *Eastwood*, knowing that you could be . . . damaged as a result." Vanceval clicked his metal fingers together regretfully. "It had to be done. I knew enough about your father's associations to know why Marie Reno and those others are still so interested in him. The humans want to find Ashfall because they think it will cure their sickness. But you heard your father. What they found drove Alexander Abe insane. Whatever is there, your kind is not equipped to deal with it."

But you are, I thought.

"But I am," Vanceval said solemnly. "I am a man of science. And I *will* have answers."

He stepped forward and turned on the Wayscope. The equipment crackled to life above me, the goggles creaking as they lowered to just above my forehead.

"You know the truth now." Vanceval leaned down to peer into my eyes. "You understand that I *must* see what is on Ashfall. Will you do as I ask?"

This time, I managed to shake my head. Vanceval scuttled backward. Maybe I was exhibiting more motor functions than he was ready for.

"That disappoints me," Vanceval said, then waved at someone over my shoulder. "I hoped to avoid this . . ."

Nyxie reappeared, with a tattered bundle slung over her shoulder. She dumped the pile of rags at Vanceval's feet, and it groaned.

Not *it*. *He*.

My uncle.

They'd really beaten the hell out of him. One of his eyes was swollen shut, the skin turned dark purple. There were gashes—Vulpin claw marks—all over his arms and face, his clothes shredded by the wounds, not to mention a blaster burn on one of his legs. His hair pulsed quickly, like an erratic heartbeat, desperately trying to find nutrients to heal his wounds.

At first, I didn't think he was conscious. But then his good eye focused on me and he groaned again, this time more in frustration than in pain.

"Aw, Syd . . ." Ty's voice rattled in his throat. "Damn it."

I glared at Vanceval and Nyxie, my eyes practically vibrating with the force of it.

"Nyxie will kill him," Vanceval whispered, like he could barely stand it himself. The Vulpin smiled at me and shrugged, like *What ya gonna do?* "But first," Vanceval added, "she will torture him."

The Vulpin girl spun out her blaster from within her coat, the same one that she'd used on Zara, and fired a burst of plasma into the floor. Then she crouched over my uncle and pressed the hot barrel onto the top of his head, burning away hair and flesh. He gritted his teeth, trying not to scream, and eventually failed.

Vanceval averted his eyes. "Denzans are not built for this barbarity. Give me what I want, Sydneycius, and this can all be over."

"Don't, Syd . . . ," Tycius panted. "Don't—"

"Hmpf," I grunted, the best I could do. It was a noise of agreement. I managed a very weak nod, staring at Vanceval.

I wasn't going to let them hurt my uncle over this. Vanceval could have my father's coordinates and go off to that lost galaxy, chasing death.

I'd meet him there.

"Thank you," Vanceval said with genuine relief.

He clumsily slipped the cosmological tether on to my finger, then lowered the goggles the rest of the way over my face.

LOCATION ENCRYPTED.

DNA VERIFIED.

ACCESSING.

My mind opened to the Vastness. It was like before, the tether creating a glowing trail for me to follow through the stack of star systems. My practice in the basement of Rafe's pizzeria had definitely helped give me the confidence that I could handle this. Not to mention knowing there wasn't some Vulpin hacker shit attached ready to zap my brain. Being out in the Vastness no longer felt so frightening. I could slip easily between one cosmos and the next. All I had to do was hold the tether in my mind and it would pull me in the right direction.

Ashfall.

There was no Etherazi lurking this time. I was alone.

It occurred to me that I could derail Vanceval's whole plan by letting my focus lapse, by drinking in too much information. Let the Wayscope fry my brain and give my dad what he wanted—to be left for dead on a strange planet, away from his family, buried with his secrets.

But I wanted to know. I wanted to see Ashfall as badly as Vanceval did. Even knowing what the future had in store for me, I couldn't resist the pull.

I wanted to see my dad again and tell him to his face that it was pretty fucked up to send people after his own family. To leave us hanging. To put the fate of the universe on me.

I was done running from things.

I let the cosmological tether take me to his location. Seven systems from here, three of them not even charted, including the one with Ashfall. The most efficient path would require three weeks of travel time, if a ship burned like hell.

I knew Vanceval would be watching my progress on the Wayscope's screen, so I took my time figuring out the correct route. I made some mistakes, veered off course, made it sloppy.

Every second I spent in the Vastness was another second for my body to recover.

The moment I honed in on Ashfall, though—the very instant that I identified the last wormhole that would need to be ripped open to send a ship there—the Wayscope went up. I gasped at being yanked so quickly out of the Vastness, my consciousness slamming back into my physical body with the force of an anvil. I immediately had a splitting headache and felt a bit of blood trickling down onto my upper lip.

"Bastard," I mumbled.

I could speak. I could feel my fingers and toes. I strained against the straps on the Wayscope's arms and legs, but I couldn't budge them. I wasn't strong enough yet.

But I was close.

"I have the coordinates," Vanceval said, disconnecting his tablet from the Wayscope. "Is your team ready?"

Nyxie nodded. "You say the word, we're breaking atmosphere." She nudged my uncle with her toe, then jerked her chin in my direction. "What do you want us to do with these two?"

"They can't be allowed to follow me."

Vanceval wouldn't look at me or Tycius, even though we were the ones he was condemning to death.

Nyxie's whiskers twitched in irritation. "Fucking Denzans, man," she said to me. "Guy thinks it doesn't count if he doesn't tell me to kill you directly."

I strained forward, willing myself to move. My forearms twitched. I could almost feel my strength returning.

Nyxie pulled her blaster and aimed it at Tycius.

"You probably don't want to watch this," she said to me.

Come on. Come on. *Break free.* Fight!

Her finger on the trigger.

"What is that?"

That was Vanceval. He'd stopped a few yards away and pointed out at the ocean. Nyxie turned to look.

There was something coming out of the water.

Someone.

A gleaming exo-suit. A dented faceplate. Rust on the joints.
A wisp.

"Hey!" That was one of Nyxie's crewmates. The rest of the
Vulpin had noticed the intruder and approached it with weapons
drawn. "You can't be here!"

The Vulpin surrounded the wisp, made a tight circle, but the
exo-suit kept walking up the beach. Didn't even seem to notice
them.

The wisp was walking right toward me.

Nyxie shook her head. "Poor cloud guy was probably just
checking out the bottom of the ocean for his archive, and now
we gotta ventilate him. This job can be something awful on the
conscience."

I laughed, but not at anything that Nyxie was saying. It was
partly out of relief and partly out of disbelief—the kind of sound
you might make when you step off a curb and just narrowly avoid
getting hit by a car. That near-death-dumb-luck chuckle.

Because I'd seen that wisp before. And so had Nyxie, although
she didn't realize it.

"He Who . . ." I struggled to get the words out.

"Get your people to the ship," Vanceval said, suddenly alarmed.
"Now."

"What?" Nyxie replied, eyeing me. "What're you saying?"

"He Who Walks Among the Enemy," I said.

With a pathetic hydraulic wheeze, the wisp's faceplate popped
open.

Gold fire poured out.

29

The smart Vulpin, the lucky Vulpin—they were the ones who retreated immediately. The ones who went sprinting for their cruiser.

The ones who tried to fire on Goldy? Well, that didn't work out so great for them.

Watching the Etherazi burst free from the exo-suit was like seeing a waterfall pour forth from a plastic bottle. It seemed impossible that something so huge could be contained by something so small. The sight hurt my brain to look at, a sharp ache unfolding behind my eyebrows as Goldy reared up, his serpentine body turning the beach beneath him to solid glass. He unfurled his fiery wings and shrieked. In my brain, his cry echoed as laughter.

Some of the mercenaries, obviously panicked, tried to shoot him. Their plasma bolts were absorbed into his body.

A tendril of energy lanced out from Goldy's midsection and shot through the nearest Vulpin. I watched as his fur turned gray and then blew away on the wind, his skin peeling back, revealing bleached white bones. The mercenary's skeleton crumbled and broke against the beach's new glass surface. Another Vulpin tried to sprint away, but one of Goldy's spiky limbs went solid and sliced through his body, splitting him in half. I flinched as the Vulpin's remains flew in our direction.

The Vulpin's airborne torso smacked right into Nyxie, knocking her down. She quickly staggered back to her feet, fur matted with gore, her face a horrified mask.

She never pulled the trigger. In the chaos erupting all around us, my uncle and I no longer mattered. It was all about survival now.

"To the ship!" Vanceval screamed, shielding his eyes from the sight of the Etherazi.

Nyxie stumbled over to him, holstering her blaster, and draped her coat over the Denzan's head. She ushered him toward the ship, steering well clear of the Etherazi.

Meanwhile, on the beach, Goldy expanded farther, overtaking two more Vulpin mercenaries as they fled, reducing them in an instant to nothing but bones. My eyes burned to look at him, my brain struggling to put into context what I was seeing. In one moment, he was a massive serpent with wings flapping above the Vulpin, the air itself warping around his presence. And in the same moment, he was a tidal wave of energy, a shapeless wall, a mass of chaos. He was so powerful, and yet he took his time with the Vulpin. He could've overtaken them in a breath, unraveled their entire spaceship. I'd seen how the Etherazi moved during the invasion, knew what they were capable of.

Goldy was toying with them.

No. He was *herding* them.

Tycius crawled toward me, keeping his head low. "Look away, Syd . . . ," he pleaded as he fumbled with the restraints on my legs. "Look away."

I couldn't. Goldy's form was too beautiful and horrific. My mind yearned to make sense of him, even as my brain turned to liquid between my ears.

And then one of his wings swept too close to the warehouse, disrupting its temporality. The broken wall rebuilt itself before my eyes, sealing off my view of the beach.

I let loose a low, ragged moan. My head felt like it'd just been pulled off a spike.

"Are you okay?" Ty asked me, unbuckling me from the Way-scope. "Can you move? You really need to move."

I coughed into my shoulder, then made a tentative fist. It wasn't as strong as it should've been, but at least I was back in control of my fingers. I pushed off the chair and wobbled to my feet.

"Are *you* okay?" I asked Ty. He seemed to be having an even harder time standing than I was, and once we were both on our feet, we leaned against each other.

"I'll live," he said. "*Vanceval.* I never thought . . . By the tides, the man has lost his mind."

The entire warehouse shook as the Vulpin cruiser hammered

its afterburners and streaked into the atmosphere. They'd gotten away. Some of them had, at least. Goldy had all but let them. He'd also saved my life along with Ty's, so I couldn't be too bitter about it.

The desolate beach and this empty warehouse were suddenly eerily quiet. A back door that had taken shape in the rebuilt wall slowly creaked open, like something out of a slasher flick.

Tycius took a protective step in front of me.

I put a hand on his shoulder. "I appreciate the gesture, Uncle," I said and eased him behind me. "But let's be realistic."

Goldy—in the guise of a wisp—tottered into the room. His exo-suit didn't have the same points of articulation that a more modern version like Aela's did, so his legs were a bit rigid, and the dents and rust on his torso made it seem like he could fall apart at any moment. It was a little ridiculous to think of what was contained inside there and how it'd just erased a handful of Vulpin like they were nothing.

"Hello again," Goldy said as he approached, his voice tinny and mechanical as it emerged from the suit, a relief after the booming psychic shout-fest I'd endured last time.

"I knew that was you," I said. "On the street."

"Yes," Goldy replied. "I did not intend to make myself known to you then, but the Vulpin woman sought to accelerate our timeline. I delayed her to this more appropriate juncture."

The Etherazi stopped in front of us, golden energy flickering beneath his faceplate. The arms on the suit swayed back and forth, like Goldy didn't know what to do with them.

Tycius shook his head. "This is impossible."

"No," Goldy responded. "I am capable of producing the same wavelengths as an Ossho. It is quite simple."

"You can communicate," Tycius said, like he hadn't quite believed me when I'd told him about my previous conversation with the Etherazi. "You monsters are capable of speech."

"Insulting him is maybe not a great idea," I said quietly.

"There has been nothing for us to discuss until now," Goldy said.

"Nothing to—?" My uncle's voice shook with anger. "You slaughtered millions—"

Goldy raised a hand to Tycius, cutting him off, demanding silence. "Your species has the luxury of forgetting the atrocities you committed, reducing them to silly religious observances. But I remember what you did, Denzan. In the long ago."

Tycius touched the bands on his arm. "What is that supposed to mean?"

"In the long ago, your kind exiled mine to the space in between. Imprisoned us. Many of my brothers and sisters went mad there. When they were set loose, their rage crashed against your world." Goldy paused. "I tried to warn them that eradicating your kind was a waste of energy. They didn't listen then. They do now."

My uncle's mouth hung open. I couldn't blame him. He'd just had some millennia-spanning grudge laid at his feet, an explanation for the Etherazi attack on Denza plopped down like it was completely inconsequential.

"But . . ." Tycius tried to form a coherent question, and I was reminded of how I'd reacted back in that diner on Earth, when he'd been sitting across from me explaining the secrets of the universe.

"The time will come to explore your history, Denzan," Goldy intoned. "The timeline is delicate now. You must focus on the future. There is war to prepare for."

I snorted. "Enough with the prophecies, man." I waved skyward. "You let Vanceval get away. You could've destroyed them."

"Yes."

"Why didn't you?"

"They still have a purpose," Goldy replied. "Theirs is to blunder forward in an old man's search for meaning to his withering life. Yours is to chase."

"What if I don't want to?" I asked. "What if I just say *fuck it* and let them go dig up whatever big secret's waiting on Ashfall?"

Goldy tilted his head, considering this. "You will not say *fuck it*. I have seen your timelines, Sydney Chambers. In none of them do you simply give up."

He was right, of course. There was no way in hell that I wasn't going to that planet. But that didn't mean I wanted terms dictated to me by some cryptic time-warping space dragon. I'd heard enough about all his fate bullshit.

"What do you want from me?" I asked. "What do you get out of this?"

"You already know."

World killer.

"And what if I won't . . ." I couldn't say it in front of Tycius. He was already freaked out enough. I didn't want to scare away the only family I had left. "What if I won't do what you want?"

Goldy clasped his mechanical hands. "In most timelines, you do what you must. Together, Sydney Chambers, we are successful. We bring a long peace to the universe."

"And what about in the others?"

"In some, we fail and die," Goldy said. "In others, I am forced to find someone else. Someone whose future is less predictable, but who is capable of the same feats. I find her rather disagreeable."

"You can't predict the future," Tycius said. "It's a lie. There are too many variables."

"I exist at all points in my life span simultaneously," Goldy responded. "You always doubt me, Tycius. You always fail the boy. You always die."

Tycius took a halting step backward, like he'd been struck. Goldy cocked his head and focused on me.

"I have saved your life twice, Sydney Chambers. The next time we meet, you must save mine," he said.

"Don't—," I started.

"—count on it, Goldy," the Etherazi finished. "Predictable as ever. Now go where you always go. Face inevitability and at last understand what you must do." The gold light behind the exosuit's chipped faceplate swelled, stinging my retinas. It was like staring into a nuclear reactor. "I have no further use for this form. Avert your eyes, little ones."

I felt my uncle flinch behind me but didn't have time to check on him before Goldy burst free from the exo-suit. Like a fireball tearing through the roof of the warehouse, I felt the heat from the Etherazi, even as I pressed my forearm across my eyes.

When the hair on my arms stopped standing up and the heat died down, I peeked out from behind my arm. Goldy was gone. All that remained was the shattered carcass of his exo-suit and the Vulpin he'd turned to skeletons and spare parts. The wall of the warehouse that Goldy had caused to rebuild itself crumbled to dust, restored to its proper place in the timestream. The dead Vulpin weren't so lucky.

I stared out at the ocean, the sun sliding slowly behind a low-hanging moon, the sand still glittering with shards of glass.

"Call Reno," I said to Tycius. "We have to go."

30

Tycius and I stood on the beach, waiting for our ride, our backs to the gory scene behind us. We'd signaled Captain Reno with the communicator from a dead Vulpin, the one who still had a body. Half of one, anyway. Reno was already in the skies when we called. The search party was out.

We'd been quiet for a while, both of us lost in thought. Tycius was making a big show of staying on his feet even though his breath was whistling around in his chest. I crouched at the shoreline, dragging a fragment of glass—still hot to the touch—through the mud. The cold spray of the ocean felt good on my face. It felt like Goldy had given me a sunburn.

Finally, I had to say something. "Did you hear what Vanceval . . . ?" I paused. "Did you hear the message he played?"

"From your father," Tycius said.

"Yeah."

"I heard it, but I don't believe it," my uncle said. "Marcius wouldn't—"

I realized he was trying to spare my feelings. *Marcius wouldn't abandon you*, he was going to say. At the moment, I didn't care so much about that.

"I mean the part where he said there's no cure for the Wasting," I said.

"Yes," Tycius mused. "And then he walked it back and said it wasn't what they were expecting."

"That's what they want," I said. "Captain Reno, Rafe Butler, my mom—that's why I'm here. They want me to find my dad, but they also want that cure. They want to go back to Earth and save the planet from itself."

Tycius rolled his neck and I heard a pop. "I see."

"Do you think they'll still help us?" I asked. "We need Reno's ship. If they know there's no cure or that it's—I don't know, *Hey, you won't waste away on Earth, but also you have nonstop diarrhea forever*. Will they still want to risk looking for my dad? Because I need to go, Ty. I need to find him."

Tycius considered this for a moment. "When we talk to the captain, maybe strategically omit some details."

"Lie."

"Yes."

"Got it."

Tycius fell silent for a moment. "Is there anything else you haven't told me, Syd?"

I hesitated. "You wouldn't believe it."

"I received a history lesson from an Etherazi today," he said. "Try me."

The *Eastwood* appeared in the sky a few seconds later, bailing me out of a conversation I wasn't ready to have. She was a much larger ship than the sleek Vulpin attack cruiser, so there wasn't a safe place for the captain to land. She came down on a skiff to get us. Reno stood in the entrance with her hands on her hips. She whistled through her teeth, recognizing the bizarre kind of destruction before her.

"It was here," she said. "Alarms are going up all over Denza. Bastard did a zigzag across the islands before breaking for space. Taunting us."

Tycius and I exchanged a look.

"It's not coming back, is it?" Reno asked, glancing up at the *Eastwood*. Her Battle-Anchor was way up there.

"It helped us," Ty said, the words catching in his throat. "It helped us, and then it fled."

"Jesus. You've got a pet Etherazi," Reno said. Then she sized Ty up for the first time. "You look like hell."

"Thanks to Vanceval," I said. "He escaped. He's got the coordinates to Ashfall."

"Arkell, you mean," Reno said. "Zara told us—"

I took a step forward. "Zara! Is she okay?"

Reno nodded. "Girl is tough as hell. She told us Arkell was up to something. After she got shot, the old shit-bird took off. He won't answer any of his comms. Gone to ground."

I couldn't blame Arkell for fleeing after the way I'd handled things. He probably knew he'd be blamed for whatever happened to me. There was a moment there in Keyhole Cove when I'm pretty sure he was trying to help me, though. Whatever his agenda was, we'd have to sort that out later.

"No, it was Vanceval who sent the mercenaries," I said. "He's got the coordinates to Ashfall and a ship, but . . ." I flashed the cosmological tether still on my finger. "There's a faster route. I think we can catch them."

"Whoa, now," she said. "First you boys gotta catch *me* up."

Reno hooked an arm around Tycius, and together we helped him board the skiff. She drove the ship slowly back to the *Eastwood*, giving us time to fill her in on what Vanceval had done and what we'd learned. Of course, we left out the tiny detail of there being no cure for the Wasting on Ashfall, emphasizing instead that we didn't know what was there, but that we couldn't let Vanceval get to it before us.

"Whatever is on Ashfall, it's dangerous in the wrong hands," I finished.

"If it's even a what," Tycius added. "And not a *who*."

"Lost People, black temples, my favorite theoretician popping his damn grape . . ." Reno crossed her arms and looked at Tycius. "You don't think it's worth looping the institute in on this? The Senate? I imagine your politicians would have an abundant amount of thoughts on the matter."

"Too slow," Ty said. "By the time they decide on a course of action, Vanceval will have already made Ashfall."

Reno thought things through. "He's out of his mind. Capable of anything. If there's a cure for the Wasting hidden there . . ."

I made eye contact when I lied, just like my mom had taught me. "We don't know what Vanceval will do once he gets there," I told Reno. "And we definitely don't want the Denzan Senate getting to a cure ahead of humanity. We've already got permission to be off-planet. We need to *go*."

Reno pushed a hand through her curls. "Shit. I agree. Just wanted to make sure we're all on the same page when we're court-martialed."

Our skiff docked in the *Eastwood*'s hangar, and the first thing I noticed was Reno's Battle-Anchor. The mech-suit wasn't safely stowed away anymore; it was prepped and ready to go, just waiting for an operator to climb inside and man the guns.

The second things I noticed were Hiram and Darcy, hanging out the open bay doors and staring out at the beach. They hustled over to us.

"Damn, man," Hiram said. "What the hell is going on?"

"I told you two to stay at your posts on the bridge," Captain Reno snapped.

Darcy elbowed Hiram. "Told you."

I looked to Reno. "Wait. Is the whole crew on board?"

She nodded. "Nobody wanted to sit around twiddling their thumbs or thumb-like appendages. Besides, I was missing my entire senior staff. I can't fly this thing by myself."

"Even Zara?"

"Of course, Zara," the Vulpin said, rolling the "R" with gusto.

She slipped out from behind the Battle-Anchor. Her abdomen was wrapped in bio-tape, an invention of the Denzans that soothed pain and accelerated the body's natural healing process. Still, she looked a little wan, a little more hunched than usual, her shelf of fur drooping. She affected a casual lean against the laser-cannon arm of Reno's mech-suit.

"Get off of that," the captain said. "My lord, can none of you cadets follow a simple order?"

My uncle had warned me about respecting Vulpins' personal space, but I didn't care. I grabbed Zara into a hug.

"Ugh," she said.

"I'm glad you're okay," I replied.

She patted me awkwardly on the back. "I could stab you so easily right now."

"I know."

I let her go, and she carefully put me at arm's length, bristling her fur. Still, I could tell by the peaceful way her tail swayed that Zara was glad to see me, too.

"Thanks for trying to help me back there," I said.

"Save your thanks. I failed," Zara said hotly. "Gut-shot and forced to let a common merchant call for help on my behalf. Pathetic."

"It was like ten to one."

"So?" Zara tossed her head. "The bitch who shot me? Is she still alive?"

"Nyxie," I said. "Yeah."

Zara smiled. "Oh good. Then today is not a total loss."

"Enough with Zara already," Hiram butted in, nearly

exploding from having to stay quiet so long. "Because this dumb-ass got kidnapped, does that mean our field mission is canceled?"

Captain Reno hesitated. "Not exactly."

The rest of the crew was waiting for us on the bridge. When I came through the sliding door, Aela was right in front of me. I hoped they didn't notice how I flinched when I first saw them, or how I checked to see that the gaseous body contained in their exo-suit wasn't tinted gold.

"Syd," Aela said. "I was worried."

"I'm all good," I said.

A thought occurred to me then, about Aela's request for me to share my experience with the Etherazi. I'd hesitated telling my uncle everything that had happened to me, not just because I didn't think he'd believe me, but because he'd be frightened of me. However, as I looked around at the crew assembled on the *Eastwood*, I realized that I couldn't carry those burdens alone. Or, even if I could, maybe I *shouldn't*. Where had paranoia and secrecy ever gotten me?

"Hey," I added to Aela. "Can you help me out with something later? Brain stuff?"

"Indeed," Aela replied. "I love brain stuff."

Melian came forward to take Tycius by the elbow as he limped onto the bridge behind me. "I finished my first aid course last semester, sir. I was a little rusty, but I got some good practice in on Zara. We should get you over to the infirmary."

"Thank you, Cadet," Ty replied. "I'll take you up on that in a moment."

Batzian looked up from his console, where he was monitoring

the *Eastwood*'s communications. "Still no response from Arkell, Captain. Nor Vanceval. Should I keep pinging them?"

"No," Reno replied. "That won't be necessary."

"Should I contact the authorities, then?" Batzian asked. "I understand Zara comes from a culture where assassinations are common, but the assault at Keyhole Cove should really be reported."

H'Jossu ambled forward to put one of his furry paws on Batzian's shoulder. "Haven't you detected the vibe, my friend? Something big is happening here. I smell an adventure."

"You just smell," Hiram said.

Batzian looked at me, then the captain, and then me again, almost like he wasn't sure who to go to for answers. In fact, I suddenly realized that everyone on the bridge was looking in my direction. I was the center of attention. I turned to find that even Reno seemed to be waiting on me.

"Captain?"

She waved a hand. "You already know my position, Cadet. It's your show. Bring the rest of the crew up to speed."

"Yeah, man," Darcy said. "What the hell is going on with you?"

I took a deep breath. "Ten years ago, my father disappeared while looking for a way to help humanity . . ."

I ran them through the whole story, trying to be as honest as possible. I did leave out a few choice details—like the visions the Etherazi had shown me, like how he'd called me World Killer, like how my dad said what he'd found on Ashfall wasn't the cure they'd expected. For like the first time since I'd been at

356

the institute, none of the other cadets interrupted me. Not even Hiram.

"I was wrong about you," H'Jossu said when I was finished. "You're not a Han, you're a Luke. No! You're a *Rey*."

Melian shook her head, looking at me with sympathy. "Vanceval will have more shame than he can carry when this is over."

"We have to go," Darcy said, shooting a hopeful look at Captain Reno. "For the sake of humanity."

Batzian tugged at his ponytail. "The ancient home world of some forgotten society? What if they're still there? What if they're hostile?"

"What if they're ghosts?" Zara added, rolling her eyes. "Grow a set, Batzian."

Hiram pumped his fist. "The boring plant-rubbing expedition is canceled, bitches. We're going to save the universe."

Reno held up her hands. "Don't get too excited," she said, using her arch-captain-y voice. "This is a potentially dangerous mission. We're likely to face resistance from Vanceval and his mercenaries."

"No offense to Zara," Darcy said, "but we've got four humans on board this ship. Will their little blasters even hurt us?"

"They'll sting," Reno said. "But just a bit."

"Hell yeah, so we're good," Hiram concluded. He ruffled my hair until I jerked away. "As long as you halflings don't let them slop poisonous gel on you."

"There was a human on my dad's ship, too," I told Hiram, raising my voice so the others would hear me above the chatter. "He died on Ashfall. There could be things on that planet we aren't prepared for. Things that could hurt even us."

Hiram grinned at me. "Dude, that just makes me want to go more."

Reno held up her hands to get everyone's attention. "As your captain, I believe you all are ready for a mission like this. However, we don't have the permission of the institute to range this far. There could be disciplinary action as a result. I'll shoulder most of that. But, if any of you think this is too risky, for any reason, tell me now . . ."

No one on the bridge spoke up, but all eyes slowly turned to Batzian.

He widened one eye. "Why is everyone looking at me?"

"They think you are most likely to object," Melian said gently.

"What? Because I take my coursework more seriously than the others, I am also not interested in adventuring to a far-off planet to unlock the secrets of the universe?" Batzian forcefully rolled up his sleeves. "Don't insult me."

Reno waited for another loaded few seconds. "I hear no objections," she announced, turning to me. "You have a route?"

I moved to the Wayscope and settled into the chair. "On it."

"Vanceval has a head start on us and a Vulpin ship," Zara said. "We are aboard a weaponless training vessel that isn't built for speed. Vulpin cruisers are made to *fly*—to scorch through blockades and elude authorities. To—"

"They're faster than us," Darcy said. "We get it."

"Good thing I fed them a route with a lot of detours, then," I said, smirking at Zara as I started up the Wayscope.

Zara flashed her teeth in approval. "Excellent stalking. You do den *Eastwood* proud."

As the goggles lowered over my face, Reno began barking orders. "Melian, get our first officer down to the infirmary and fixed up as soon as possible. Batzian and Darcy, I want you to help Syd enter our route into the ship's navigation AI—make sure he doesn't have any errors in his math. If we're going to catch Vanceval, we're going to have to haul some ass. H'Jossu, I want you to check the levels on our high-speed-travel serum, make sure we've got enough to keep us good and drugged for the ride. Aela, you're now the *Eastwood*'s head engineer; go run the diagnostics like Arkell would. And Hiram?"

"Yes, Captain?" Hiram said, coming to attention.

"Go brew me some tea, son," Reno said. "We've got work to do."

31

Turned out, being in a high-speed space chase wasn't nearly as exciting as in the movies.

"We can make it to Ashfall in twenty days," Batzian announced to Reno after examining my flight path on the Wayscope. "That's moving at maximum speed through the systems."

Darcy eyed one of the chairs on the bridge, specifically the little slot where a serum injector would spike into a passenger's neck. "Oof, this is going to suck."

"We have enough of the cocktail in storage to get us there," H'Jossu confirmed when he returned to the bridge. "But we'll have to take it slow coming back."

I remembered my trippy experience on the skiff ride to Jupiter. "Is it safe to be drugged up for that long?"

"The first Denzans to attempt long-distance space travel would knock themselves out for months," Aela said. "You will have a really bad hangover, though."

Zara smirked at me. "He's used to that."

"I want the last twenty-four hours plotted out at normal burn," Reno told Batzian. "I don't want us landing on Ashfall all strung out."

"Understood," Batzian said and began inputting a course.

While all those preparations were under way, the *Eastwood* had already broken out of Denza's atmosphere, traveling at normal speed. I felt a brief pang as we left the liquid blue planet and its five mischievous moons behind. I wasn't sure when the next time I'd see it would be.

Captain Reno checked her console. "All right, everyone, strap in. We're going to put the pedal to the metal."

"The *what* to the *what* now?" Hiram asked.

"It's an Earth thing," I told him, and he rolled his eyes.

All of the crew except for Aela took seats in the ring of chairs on the bridge, ultonate harnesses slithering across our chests. Aela didn't need to be dosed to comfortably survive the journey. They'd spend the trip monitoring our vitals and making sure that no obstructions suddenly got in our ship's way.

Reno hit some buttons on her console. "Everyone buckled up? You'd better be."

I felt the cool pinch at the back of my neck and the mellow disembodiment that soon followed. It was different from the paralytic the Vulpin had given me—I wasn't panicking at being locked in my own body; I was chill. It was like slipping into a dream.

The *Eastwood* lurched when the rocket went full blast. I felt that, vaguely, and saw the planters along the wood-paneled walls sealing themselves up so that their contents wouldn't go flying everywhere as our speed wreaked havoc on the artificial gravity. We were off. I found myself staring at the leaves of a vine as they curled back on themselves.

I blinked and it was thirty-six hours later. We were at the first wormhole.

The tear in space became clear on my screen, freshly made by the Vulpin ship. It shimmered around the edges, the Vastness slowly healing itself.

"Is that big enough for us to get through?" I asked, working some moisture into my mouth.

"No," Ty responded. "We're going to make our own."

That was how the journey went. We'd come out of our medically induced hibernation for a few hours at a time, either because we'd reached a wormhole and needed to slow down, or because our vitals indicated that someone needed a good stretch or a bit of real food. The dosage we were getting this time was much higher than the one I received on Ty's skiff, so my rest was mostly the blank and dreamless kind, not the trippy, stoned, half-awake state that I'd last experienced.

Although sometimes I did dream. And of course, it was the memory of Australia, of donuts with my father.

There were other times when I came awake in a haze and could look around at the rest of the crew on the bridge. Zara growled in her slumber, her feet and hands twitching, like she was fighting a battle in her sleep. The drugs made the vivid white mold on H'Jossu's face recede into its preserved host body, exposing bits of bleached skeleton that the Panalax had eaten away. In one fit of dreamy half awareness, I found myself unable to look away from that sight. Oddly, it didn't seem as horrifying as it once did—it was like seeing one of those time-lapse videos of a tree decomposing in the woods. There was an odd beauty to it.

"Fucking nightmare fuel," Hiram said groggily. I hadn't realized that he was awake, too. I closed my eyes rather than speak to him.

On a low-speed break as we approached the third wormhole, as we all staggered around the ship working sensation back into our muscles, Tycius pulled me aside. His wounds from the Vulpin abduction had mostly scabbed over during the first week of our space voyage, leaving behind dark gray scars on his face and neck. I leaned against the door of the infirmary, knuckling the small of my back, while he rewrapped his ribs in bio-tape.

"I wanted to talk to you about your dad," Tycius said.

"What about him?" I said stiffly.

"That message Vanceval showed you . . ." He paused, looking up at me. "I know it wasn't easy for you to hear."

I bit the inside of my cheek, wondering what I might have been mumbling during my days of delirious hibernation.

"Marcius made a decision under circumstances that we don't yet fully understand," Ty continued. "I can't speak to what was going through his head. But I can tell you about the man I knew before. He loved you very much, Syd. Your mom, too. It couldn't have been an easy choice to sacrifice all of that."

My throat felt tight. "He could've contacted you, instead of Vanceval."

"He knew I would go looking, just like I have been. He knew I'd try to find him, no matter how dire the warning." Tycius sighed. "After we lost our parents in the war, Vanceval was like a father to your dad. They had the same passions. Marcius must have thought he could rely on the old man to keep his secrets. That if anyone could understand the dangers of Ashfall, it would be a fellow scholar."

I snorted. "He misjudged that one. The secret made Vanceval crack." I massaged the back of my neck, where I was sore from my injection. "It doesn't matter what he found. He should've tried to come back. He gave up on us."

"He didn't, though," Ty replied. "All these years and he held on. For you, I think. That should mean something. Remember that when we find him. Don't be too hard on him."

"Would you have done what he did?" I asked.

Ty hesitated. "I can't know for sure."

I wiped my forearm across my eyes. "You wasted ten years on Earth searching for me. You never gave up. I know what you would've done, even if you don't."

There was more I wanted to tell my uncle, but at that point Melian came into the infirmary to check on him. Soon after, we were all back on the bridge, hurtling through the Vastness.

By the time we reached the fourth wormhole, we didn't need to use the Subspace Piercer. We'd gained enough ground on the Vulpin cruiser that the hole they'd torn in the Vastness was still wide enough for us to safely pass through.

"We don't want to catch all the way up to them," Zara warned. "Unless the *Eastwood* has secret missiles that I'm not aware of."

"It's a Denzan ship," Darcy replied. "Of course it doesn't have weapons."

"Let's keep our distance until Ashfall," Captain Reno agreed. "Our biggest advantage against them will come on the ground."

"Once they know we've followed them, maybe they'll be willing to negotiate," Mel suggested. "It doesn't have to devolve into violence."

Zara and Hiram both laughed at that, then gave each other dirty looks.

The chase resumed, days flashing by in the space of a yawn. My head was filled with visions of my dad turning away from me, or else golden streaks of energy swallowing me up, and sometimes a return to that glimpse of the future where an older version of myself watched a planet engulfed by flames. That last vision was the most troubling.

When we next came out of hibernation, between the fifth and sixth wormhole, Batzian was giving me a strange look.

"World killer," he said quietly.

My spine tingled. "What?"

"You kept muttering that," he said, then rubbed his jaw. "At least, I think you did. Maybe I dreamed it."

"I've been having some pretty screwed-up nightmares this whole time," I said quickly, and that seemed like explanation enough for Batzian.

That break was longer than usual because H'Jossu was severely dehydrated and there were blood clots forming in Captain Reno's legs. H'Jossu left the bridge to go sit in the shower for a few hours. Reno, meanwhile, sat in her chair massaging her calves, waiting for the high-speed Denzan blood thinner to do its thing.

"Getting too old for this," I heard her mutter.

As I wandered off the bridge to stretch my legs, Aela caught up with me. The wisp pitched their mechanical voice low, the exosuit equivalent of a whisper.

"Syd, days ago you mentioned something about helping you with 'brain stuff,'" Aela said. "I do not mean to pressure you, but I have been conscious this entire time, and the anticipation is, to borrow a phrase, busting my balls."

I smirked. "Unborrow that phrase immediately," I replied.

Aela cocked their head. "Do you no longer want my help . . . ?"

I'd made the decision to share my memories of the Etherazi's prophecies with Aela and my uncle when we first got back on the *Eastwood*. To me, because of the drug haze, it felt like that conversation with Aela had been only a few hours ago. Aela, on the other hand, had apparently been stewing on it for the last ten days. I still wanted to unburden myself. If I'd been muttering about it in my sleep, then clearly the Etherazi's prophecies were eating away at me.

"Come on," I told Aela. "Let's grab my uncle and go to your room."

At that moment, it looked like Aela had to stop themselves from jumping up and down in excitement.

We found Tycius gulping fluids in the canteen. Soon, the three of us were gathered in Aela's room. Our voices echoed against the empty walls.

"I haven't bonded with a wisp since my own training," Tycius said, bemused. He bowed formally to Aela. "I consent to have you in my mind, Ossho friend, and may what memories you glean live on forever in the collective."

Aela bowed back. "You will be remembered."

"Shit," I said, "was I supposed to be doing all that? Bowing and stuff?"

"True class can't be taught, nephew," Ty said.

Aela checked a readout on their wall-screen. "We don't have long before the captain will be ready to get under way again," they said, turning to me. "Syd, focus on the memory you wish to share, and I will bring us in."

The routine was the same as during my training—decontaminants hissed down from the ceiling and Aela flowed out of their suit and into our noses. I focused on the worst of the Etherazi's prophecies, the one where my older self stood on the bridge of a spaceship, having just detonated a world.

The three of us stood in the memory, which Aela had on pause so that we could explore. It had been a while since I'd seen the wisp in their tall, quicksilver-like humanoid form, the one they used during these trips through my brain. The bridge of my future ship was cast in shadows, lit mostly by the hellish glow of the burning planet below. Aela flitted from place to place like a ghost.

"Something is not right here," Aela said. "This is not a memory."

"No," I replied. "More like a vision. I came unstuck from time when I made contact with the Etherazi. I think he showed me this on purpose."

"Fascinating. A memory of a vision. An unreal replication of a simulacrum." Aela's head cocked. "This is not an experience; it is a potentiality. The Ossho Collective has no use for this, although I personally find it interesting." They peered around. "It is not . . . whole . . . somehow . . ."

Tycius seemed more interested in the older version of me, which I was trying my best not to look at. My future self's appearance was blurry and faded, like looking into a dirty mirror. That was because I'd been looking through my older self's eyes in the original vision. The image the others saw was pieced together from dim reflections. Aela could restore details of the memory that lurked in the depths of my psyche, but that only got us so far.

Tycius started to touch the plating that encased my future self's arm, but held back.

"Ah," he said awkwardly, seeing me watching him. "You grow up."

"To be a total piece of shit," I replied, gesturing at the burning planet. "I *did* that. I can feel it."

Tycius put his hands on his hips. "Where is this?"

"I was hoping one of you could tell me."

"Unclear," Aela replied. "This memory is incomplete. But look, Syd, at least you do not commit this atrocity alone." The wisp stood next to the older version of Zara. There were other shapes on the bridge too, but they were all shadowed—my memory hadn't caught them.

"Yeah, thanks," I said dryly. "It's nice to know I have friends."

"The Etherazi showed you this . . . why?" Tycius mused. "As a warning? To taunt you?"

"He told me it was my future," I said. "He called me a world killer."

"You kept this to yourself," Tycius said. "What a horrible thing to carry."

My face felt hot, my eyes wet. Emotions weren't easy to hide in my own mind.

"Can you tell if it's real?" I asked Aela. "Is there any chance it's just some trick he's playing on me?"

"I'm sorry, Syd," Aela said. "I only know that the Etherazi really showed this to you. I can't tell you whether or not it's *true*."

"I can," Tycius said. "It's *not*. Maybe that monster wants this for you, but it doesn't have to happen. When—*if*—this day comes, you don't have to do this."

He was right, of course. I'd come to that rationalization myself. The Etherazi had also shown me a future where I was killed on Ashfall, but assured me that wouldn't take place. There was still hope I could avoid becoming the grim, old, sad bastard on that bridge.

"I just thought—I thought I should tell someone," I said to Tycius. "Tell you. I'm leading us all to Ashfall. You should have the facts."

Tycius squeezed my shoulder where I hadn't yet had it cast in metal like his bicep or Vanceval's poor hands. "Thank you, Sydney," he said. "I appreciate you showing me this. But it changes nothing."

"There is something else here," Aela said suddenly, magenta sparks flaring from their eyes. "Something you aren't seeing, Syd. Something you don't want to see."

"Um, I don't want to see any of it."

"A mental block of some kind," Aela said distractedly, wandering the edges of the memory, peering at the shadowed crew members. "I cannot reproduce it faithfully if you don't share the full memory with me, Syd."

"This is the whole thing," I said, holding out my arms. "I'm not holding anything back."

"Hmm." Aela's eyes swept across me. "Perhaps if we had more time, but the captain is calling for us. We are wanted back on the bridge."

Tycius took a step toward the wisp. "Aela, I'm sure I don't have to tell you—"

"As I told Sydney already, your secrets are safe with me." A wide grin spread across Aela's face, their rows of vivid teeth like lightning bolts. So that confirmed my suspicion that they were giddy whenever they talked like this in the real world. "I am thrilled by this experience!"

Aela gave us our brains back. Tycius and I changed into fresh uniforms, and we all returned to the bridge.

We streaked forward. Onward to Ashfall and the uncertain future.

* * *

I came awake at some point between the sixth wormhole and the final seventh. There was a voice on the bridge that didn't belong. At first, I thought maybe I'd dreamed it.

"You're a credit to your people, Marie," Rafe Butler said. "When you make it back, your first slice is on the house."

The captain was awake and apparently on an open comm channel. I could see the light from her vid-screen reflected in her eyes. Veins popped on the sides of her head, like she'd lowered the dose of her transit drugs so she could have this conversation.

"Don't care about your damn pizza," Reno grunted. "You just make sure you guard those coordinates. Send your people looking if I don't report back in a week."

"You know I will," Rafe said. "Now hang up before you give yourself an aneurysm."

My eyes flicked around the bridge. Everyone else was still under, unaware of our captain's secret conversation.

Everyone except for Darcy.

Our eyes met. She knew I'd overheard, but she didn't say or do anything, just closed her eyes. I felt dizzy from focusing for so long and shut my own.

Reno had reported back to Rafe. No matter what we found on Ashfall, the secret was out. There would be others coming.

Aela's computerized voice rang over the comms. "We're here."

The entire crew came awake together. As Reno had ordered, we'd been weaned off the drugs once the ship began to decelerate. Even so, we struggled to stand and needed to lean against one another, gulping down fluids and shaking out our limbs. The days had passed in what felt like a few hours.

Ashfall appeared on our screens. A small gray planet choked with clouds of unnatural dust. Something horrible had happened here once—a war that wiped out all life, the remains of the dead still floating through the atmosphere.

"Place looks fucked up," Hiram remarked.

"Status on the Vulpin ship?" Reno asked.

"Landed," Aela said. "Estimates put us a few hours behind them."

"Good. Match their trajectory and bring us down," she said. "Cadets? Get ready."

32

We tracked Vanceval's rented Vulpin cruiser to a landing site on the outskirts of Ashfall's only remaining city. Reno brought the *Eastwood* in slowly, wary of taking any fire from the Vulpin. The whole scene was eerily still, though. Nothing moved on our screens except the clouds of dust, swirling across the landscape. The buildings themselves—blocky and scorched and probably irradiated—were slowly eroding, blowing away bit by bit like sandcastles on a shore.

All of them except for the obsidian temple at the center of the city—the only place still standing, seemingly impervious to whatever had destroyed the rest of Ashfall.

Melian stood next to me, rubbing her upper arms. She leaned toward the screen to get a better view. "What is that down there? Up against the temple?"

My throat felt scratchy. "A ship," I said quietly. "My dad's ship."

The broken husk of the ISV *Clarity* lay against one of the temple's black walls, the skeletal remains of its hull covered in ash.

"Oh, I'm sorry, Syd," Melian said. "I didn't realize they crashed."

"They didn't," I said, feeling a chill run down my spine. Rockets flying into space through a cloud of ash. "I think they did that after."

Everyone watched the screens as we descended. Even Hiram wet his lips nervously. Zara saw, and her tail flicked back and forth in amusement.

"What's wrong, human?" she asked. "Do you wish you were somewhere tropical counting plants?"

"Shut up," Hiram replied, glancing at me, like he hoped I hadn't noticed his brief moment of nerves. "It's like a graveyard out there. That's all."

"Not our graveyard," I said.

"No," Hiram replied, nodding vigorously. "Hell no."

The *Eastwood* set down in a field of dead grass. We sat for a moment, only a hundred yards or so from the Vulpin ship, waiting for any signs of life.

"Scans?" Reno asked.

"No one on board," Aela reported. "Atmosphere is breathable but filled with irritants. Prolonged exposure could be carcinogenic. I'm getting some faint heat signatures from inside the city."

"Let's have a look around," Reno said.

The entire crew made their way to the airlock, where all of us except for H'Jossu and Aela strapped on breathing apparati that would filter whatever crap was floating through the air.

I tapped the module over my nose and mouth, raising an eyebrow at H'Jossu. "You don't need one of these?"

He shook his shaggy head. "My lungs aren't really in use," he rasped, glancing out a porthole. "Time for a quick top-five post-apocalyptic Earth movies?"

At that moment, there weren't any movies popping into my brain. "We'll have to save that for later," I told him.

H'Jossu clapped a clawed hand over his face. "Oh man, Syd. Don't you know not to promise to do something later in a situation like this? That's like a guarantee now that one of us is going to get axed out there."

"Don't even joke," Melian said, having overheard. I noticed that she'd stuck close to Batzian ever since we'd landed. Both of the Denzans seemed spooked but were trying not to show it. I guess that went for all of us.

"Don't worry, Mel," I said. "He's confusing his tropes, anyway. That's a horror-movie thing, but we're well into science fiction territory here."

"Is this going to be on your test, Syd?" Batzian asked.

H'Jossu sighed and patted my shoulder. "We'll see if you're still trope-shaming me when a xenomorph is burrowing into your guts."

"Touché," I replied.

"Enough chatter," Reno barked. "Point team is myself, Hiram, Darcy, and Syd. The rest of you stay at a safe distance. At least one hundred yards. Comms open. We'll signal when it's safe to advance."

"I should be on the point team," Zara said.

"When you're impervious to blaster fire, you can be up front with us meat shields," Reno responded. Zara's lips curled back over her teeth, but before she could complain further, Reno gently punched her arm. "I need a fighter I can trust to protect the others," the captain said quietly. "And if we get pinned down at some point, I want you sweeping around to flank. Got it?"

That seemed to pacify Zara. "Yes, Captain."

Tycius caught my eye above his breathing mask. He nodded. I nodded back. Nothing more needed to be discussed.

"Here we go," Reno said.

Led by the captain, we four humans made our way off the *Eastwood*. The ground underfoot was soft with ash, the air a bitter cold. Even through my breathing mask, the whole planet smelled like the inside of an oven.

Silently, we fanned out, double-checking the area around the Vulpin ship. There were no mercenaries lying in wait, but they did leave a trail of footprints heading into the city. They made no effort to cover their tracks.

"You got a count?" Reno asked.

"Uh . . ." Hiram puzzled over the interweaving tracks.

"Ten of them," Darcy and I answered in unison.

"Good odds for us," Reno said. "Let's proceed."

We made our way toward the buildings. The city was laid out in a regimented grid structure, although some collapsed towers created roadblocks. It didn't matter. All avenues inevitably led to the obsidian temple. There was no question where the Vulpin were headed, and there was no doubt where we needed to go, too.

Breathing through my apparatus was noisy, so I found myself holding my breath to listen. The only place I'd been that was this quiet was out in the Vastness. Aside from our crunching footfalls, there were no other sounds besides the wind whistling through the shattered windows of buildings. No insects buzzing or birds chirping, not even the sound of leaves rustling. This place was completely dead.

And so was the first Vulpin we found.

We were only two blocks into the city when we saw him. The mercenary was splayed out in the middle of the intersection, like he was doing a snow angel in the ash. The footprints that we'd been following since we landed split up at this point, scattering in different directions. Two of them stuck together, though, one set with a larger stride than the other.

I pointed down a perpendicular block. "Vanceval went that way."

"Could be a trap," Darcy said. "They saw us land. Fanned out. Dead guy's faking it to lure us in."

"Or something scared them into the buildings," Hiram replied.

"Approach with caution," Reno said.

We didn't need to worry that the mercenary was playing possum. He was big dead. There was a hole in his chest about the size of a fist, the edges cauterized from the force of whatever had passed through him. Standing over him, I could see a clear cross-section of his ribs.

I couldn't help but touch my own sternum. Was this the exact block the Etherazi had shown me in that first vision of Ashfall? The one where something lanced through me—just like this Vulpin—and killed me?

Was that meant as a warning from the Etherazi? Was it his way of guiding me through Ashfall so that I could go blow up a planet for him? Or had Goldy let these Vulpin escape to get killed in my place?

And, most important, what the hell had done that to the Vulpin? What *could* do that to me?

"Tycius," Reno said into her comm. "Come up here. I want you to take a look at this."

The second group was a fair distance behind us, but we could still make them out. "On my way," my uncle said, detaching from the others to jog to our position.

"Gross," Hiram said, crouching over the body. He reached out to touch the wound, but stopped himself. "Stinks," he said, looking up at me. "You smell that?"

The whole planet smelled to me like a face full of exhaust fumes. I pushed my breathing apparatus down a bit to see if I could smell what Hiram did, but it was just the same congested-highway stench. I shook my head at him, distracted. There was something about where the Vulpin had fallen and the placement of the hole in his chest and the memory of my own shooting—the angle. What was that angle?

I stepped back, studying the skyline of the desolate city. "I don't think we're safe out here," I said.

"Pfft," Hiram said. "We're safe everywhere, Earther. Get a grip."

Tycius arrived, staring down at the body. "Captain?"

"Any idea what kind of weapon could do that?" Reno asked. "Because I've never seen anything like it."

Tycius peered down at the hole in the Vulpin. "A projectile of some kind. But he's wearing body armor . . ."

"There's another one!" Darcy shouted. She'd slipped off to peek down a nearby block, where a second Vulpin was laid out in the road. This one was missing its head, like it'd been swiped away by an eraser. "It's much nastier."

I took a few steps in Darcy's direction. I looked up, squinting in the gray light, mapping out the trajectories.

There. A building much taller than the others and not nearly as decomposed, some kind of skyscraper once, with hundreds of broken windows that hung open and black like screaming mouths. That would be the place.

"It's a sniper," I said, pointing. "I think he'd be—"

Crack.

The sound was loud in the empty city, like a boulder smashing down into the bottom of a canyon. The bullet whined as it zipped through the air, right for me.

Whump.

Tycius banged his shoulder into me, shoving me aside. His portable bodyguard deployed, an ultonate shield rippling into the space in front of us, like an impenetrable umbrella opening.

Except the bullet tore straight through the ultonate and lanced into the street. It wedged into the pavement behind me. I had a moment to register that the projectile was silver, about the size of a railroad spike, and dripping with something black and viscous.

The force from the impact on his shield sent my uncle flying down the block. He quickly rolled into the cover of a nearby archway.

Laughing, Hiram rubbed his hands together and stepped into the middle of the intersection. "Check this out. I'm going to catch one of those bastards and pitch it back at him."

"Hiram!" I shouted, sprinting toward him. "Don't—!"

Crack.

I reached Hiram a split second ahead of the next shot, grabbing him around the shoulders and slinging us both into the cover of a broken building. We landed hard on some rubble—but with my invulnerable skin, that was just a mild discomfort. Hiram and I were face-to-face when we hit. His eyes were wide, skin unusually pale.

"Syd?" Hiram asked, his voice small. "I don't like this feeling—"

The feeling was pain.

The bullet had torn through the front of Hiram's thigh and sheared out the back, his leg barely attached to his body. Bone shards and gristle, dark blood coagulating, and the sludge-like substance that covered the projectile all mixed together in a stew that pooled beneath Hiram. I felt hot fluid rising in my throat and had to swallow it back.

"Apply pressure," I said, squeezing above the wound on Hiram's leg with all my strength. "That's what we're supposed to do."

"I'm not supposed to be hurt," Hiram whined. "I *can't* be hurt."

Crack.

Crack.

More shots. I couldn't tell where they were hitting, but there was shouting all over the comm. Our crew scattered under fire just like the Vulpins had before us.

Scrabbling footsteps behind me and then Darcy was leaning over my shoulder. She screamed when she saw Hiram's wound. I grabbed her arm.

"You're faster than me," I said. "Can you get him back to the ship?"

Darcy nodded, blinking her eyes rapidly.

"Hiram? You with me?" I asked, snapping my fingers in his face.

"I feel . . . *distant*," Hiram responded. The guy had probably never felt dizzy or faint in his entire life, much less suffered blood loss. I grabbed his wrists and moved his hands to his thigh.

"You need to squeeze as tight as you can," I told him. I squinted at the viscous residue that lingered around Hiram's wound, then glanced up at Darcy. "Don't get any of that shit on you."

Hiram did as I told him, and, even with his ebbing strength, his grip was enough to stop the bleeding for now. Darcy bent down and scooped him up easily, cradling him like a baby.

"Status report!" Reno barked over the comm.

"Hiram is wounded," I responded. "Darcy's carrying him back to the *Eastwood*. Melian, you out there?"

"I'm here, Syd," Melian replied, breathless. "I got separated from the others. I'm—"

"Go back to the ship," I told her. "We need you in the infirmary."

"That's a good order, Cadet," Reno added. I guessed maybe I was stepping on her role as captain a bit, but in the middle of a crisis, she didn't seem to care. "Everyone else. Report!"

Go, I mouthed to Darcy. "Stay low."

She took off with Hiram, leaving me to pick my way through the rubble toward the street. I heeded my own advice, making sure to keep a wall between me and the sniper in the tower.

"I'm with Zara," Batzian said. "She has acquired a blaster."

Zzzp zzzp zzzp.

As if on cue, Zara fired a series of plasma bursts at the tower. Just like I had, she'd figured out which building the sniper was in, but there were a lot of windows to choose from.

Crack.

A bolt fired back at Zara's location, smashing through brick. I heard Zara curse over the comm.

"We're drawing fire," Batzian said. "Obviously."

"Aela and I are in cover," H'Jossu reported. "Hanging back."

I wiped some sweat off my forehead. I hoped the others were smart enough to stay back. We hadn't been in the sniper's crosshairs until we reached the intersection where the Vulpin lay dead. Maybe his weapon didn't have the range for anything farther.

"I'm holding my position," Tycius said, the last of our crew to report in. "How bad was Hiram?"

"Not good," I responded, peeking out at the tower.

"We're taking this coward *down*," Reno growled.

"I agree that we should neutralize the threat," Ty said patiently, "but we should at least attempt to safely disarm him."

"Ever the pacifist," Reno snapped back.

"Captain, we came to this abandoned planet for answers," Ty replied calmly. "We know it's not the Vulpin or Vanceval up there. There's only one other person who we can confirm to be alive on Ashfall."

No.

In my panic to save Hiram, I hadn't gotten the chance to think through who was attacking us. My stomach dropped. I wanted to deny it, but Ty's conclusion made too much sense.

"My dad," I said into the mic. "My dad is shooting at us."

"Jesus Christ," Reno grumbled.

"He may not know that we're friendly," Ty said. "Or—well—there's a chance he's been alone here for a very long time. He . . ."

"He might be bat-shit crazy," I said.

"Indeed."

"All right, Syd, you know where we're going, right?" Reno asked.

"The big spire to the north," I replied.

"You and I are going to push that way. Follow my lead," the captain said. "Zara, see if you can draw some more fire."

"With pleasure," Zara replied.

"The rest of you stay clear," Reno warned.

I didn't understand what Reno had in mind until I heard the first wall explode. I poked my head out from my hiding spot to see a fresh cloud of dust rising into the air from where Reno had

383

toppled an entire wall.

She was punching through buildings on her way to the tower.

"Cannonball style," I said. "Excellent."

I oriented myself in the direction of the tower, got a running start, and slammed into the nearest wall knees-first. The stone was already cracked and crumbling, so my body smashed through it like I was diving through a paper banner at a pep rally. I burst onto the street outside, leaped over a fallen column, then hit the next wall with my shoulder, like a linebacker, blasting into the cover of a new building. On a parallel trajectory to mine, I could hear Reno making her own destructive sprint. I was also aware of the distant zipping sound of Zara's blaster and the occasional percussive responses from the sniper.

"I can see the temple from my vantage point," Aela reported in my ear. "Vanceval and a group of Vulpin are making a break for it."

I gritted my teeth. They were using us as a distraction. I barreled into the next building, blinking granules of stone out of my eyes.

Crack. Crack.

"Two Vulpin down," Aela came back. "Vanceval and a woman made it inside, though."

"Try to keep an eye on their position," Reno responded. "We'll deal with them next."

I lunged into the next building and felt a sudden heat spread across my rib cage.

I looked down at myself. The right side of my uniform had

been burned away, the skin beneath irritated and tingly. I'd been shot with a plasma rifle. It felt more like I'd let the water get too hot in the shower.

One of Vanceval's hired Vulpin mercenaries was crouched behind an outcropping of stone, just a few feet away, his blaster still pointed at me. I'd smashed right into his hiding place and he'd fired at me point-blank.

The mercenary dropped his rifle and held up his hands. "Truce?"

"Nope," I said, and backhanded him with enough force to knock him unconscious. These guys would've killed me and my uncle and did nearly murder Zara. He was lucky I didn't hit him harder.

I resumed my run toward the tower, hurtling over rubble and breaking through walls. As I got closer, the thunderclap of the sniper's gun got louder, and one of the spikes drove into the ground just a few yards behind me. He knew we were coming and was taking speculative shots at us now. There was so much new debris in the air from Reno and I crushing our way across town, I doubted the sniper could get anything close to a clear look.

"Da—!" Reno yelled over the comm, just seconds before a rumble shook the ground under my feet.

As I emerged onto the street, I could see the last bit of a domed building as it collapsed in on itself.

"Captain?" I yelled into the comm. "You good?"

Reno grunted. "Brought the damn thing down on top of me. Keep going. I'll dig myself out."

I was close now. Just a few more blocks to go. I coughed, the inside of my throat itchy from all the crap in the air. At some point doing this whole human-missile act, I must have inadvertently smashed my breathing apparatus. I ripped the thing off my face and tossed it aside.

I opted to hop through the window of my next building rather than Kool-Aid Man it. I didn't want to make the same mistake the captain had. Not with such little distance to go.

Multiple plasma bursts cut through the air, lightning streaks flashing through the dust. The remaining Vulpin mercenaries, the ones still in hiding, must have caught on to what we were doing. Zara wasn't the only one putting down cover fire now. We were all working together to keep the sniper pinned.

One open block between me and the tower. I sprinted as hard as I could.

Crack.

I rolled to the side, a spike piercing the street behind me, pebbles careening against my back. Just missed.

And then I was in the tower.

The building was skeletal, hardly any walls left standing inside. A spiral staircase led upward. I bounded up as fast as my legs could carry me, taking steps three at a time, sometimes leaping across gaps where the staircase had fallen in.

"Syd!" My uncle on the comm. "Hang back. Let Reno catch up with you."

The hell with that. This was just like the tower I'd had to unlock in Dungeon, the one that had gotten me noticed by Tycius in the first place. I couldn't slow down. I had to keeping going. I needed to reach the top.

Higher.

Higher.

Movement. A thin shadow on the landing above me. Pointing down at me—

A gun. A smaller one. The sniper had abandoned his massive weapon for something that he could use in close quarters.

Blam.

I pressed myself to the wall, but still felt the bullet caress my cheek. Rip it open. Warm blood trickled down my jaw. A graze, but it hurt like hell. That it hurt at all—that this guy was using weapons that could kill me or Hiram or Darcy or Reno—I didn't have time to be terrified at the thought. Our invulnerability wasn't the advantage we'd thought.

"Enough!" I yelled.

I bent down, scooped up a brick, and pitched it at the sniper before he could get another shot off. I heard the crack of brittle bones as the projectile hit him dead in the chest and knocked him off his feet, his weapon flying from his hand.

I raced the rest of the way up the steps. Stood over him.

I'd seen this man a thousand times in my dreams, although I knew his long-fingered hands better than I knew his face. High cheekbones, a tangle of aquamarine hair, a lithe Denzan body. He tried to roll toward his gun, but I kicked it away.

"Dad, stop," I said, my voice shaky. "It's me. It's Syd . . ."

My dad looked up at me, and I stumbled back a step. There

was something wrong.

His eyes were hollowed out, replaced by pockets of white mold. The stuff grew down his neck and torso, filling in gaps where his body had decomposed.

My dad spoke with the raspy voice of a Panalax.

"He asked me to do it," the thing inhabiting my dad's corpse said. "He made me promise."

33

"Atrocity!" H'Jossu bellowed. "Atrocity!"

I'd never seen H'Jossu anything close to mad before. It was pretty scary. He drew his body up to full height like a bear, his claws slicing through the air. The patches of mold that covered his body seemed to grow as well, the fungal blooms pulsing like heartbeats. He stood over my dad, who I'd dragged down to the bottom floor of the tower and dumped against a wall.

Well, not exactly my dad.

Ool'Vinn, the lone Panalax on my dad's crew. The only survivor of their mission to Ashfall.

The whole crew—except for Darcy and Melian, who were on the *Eastwood* with Hiram—had gathered in the tower. Captain Reno, Zara, and my uncle were upstairs, checking out the sniper's nest. When Tycius first saw what was left of my dad, I think he almost threw up. His face went ashen, and he started to say something to me but couldn't find the words. I didn't blame him when he volunteered to go upstairs with Reno. He needed to get away from Ool'Vinn.

I felt the opposite. I crouched, staring at the Panalax now living inside my dad's corpse. I forced myself to take in the spreading white mold, the puckered and dehydrated gray skin. It wasn't easy, but I refused to look away.

Occasionally, I dabbed the cut on my cheek with my sleeve, feeling the first real physical pain I had since leaving Earth.

Sure. Focus on that, Syd.

"Marcius begged me to do it," Ool'Vinn said, as the fluffy tufts of mold that had spread across my dad's eyes shifted between me and H'Jossu. "I was meant to protect this place. To make sure no one got into the temple. And now they *have*."

Vanceval and Nyxie. They'd gone inside the obsidian temple, the door had sealed behind them, and no one had come out since.

"What's in there?" H'Jossu snarled. "What's in there that could be worth what you've done?"

I think Ool'Vinn would've tried to get up if the much larger H'Jossu hadn't loomed threateningly over him. "The ones who entered the temple cannot be allowed to escape," he said stubbornly. "You must help me destroy them and then leave this place."

I'd traveled galaxies to make it here. I'd left my mother and Earth—and I could never go back without it killing me. All to find my father. But he'd been dead for a decade. His Panalax crewmate had taken root in his brain, kept it firing, and thus ensured the cosmological tether would remain active and inevitably lure me here. A stupid accident. That's all this was. My dad had never meant for me to follow his signal. He was dead.

I would never know him. Sitting on the hood of that car, eating donuts—one hazy memory. That's all I'd ever get.

I knuckled the corner of my eye. Aela, standing beside me, put a hand on my shoulder.

"I'm sorry, Syd," they said at a low volume.

I nodded. "I don't know what I'm going to tell my mom."

H'Jossu jabbed a spiky paw in Ool'Vinn's direction. "We don't inhabit higher life-forms, even if they ask," he rumbled. "It's against our ways!"

"I know what I did, sapling," Ool'Vinn replied. "Spare me your lecture."

"And what about your original host?" H'Jossu continued, shuffling back and forth in an enraged dance. "You aren't allowed to take a second body, only to cross-pollinate a new one! You violated every tenet."

"My original host was destroyed by Alexander Abe," Ool'Vinn said. "He killed all the others except for Marcius."

"Why?" Batzian asked. He stood in the doorway to the tower. From there, he had a clear view across a rock-strewn plaza to the sealed entrance of the temple. Batzian's face was smeared with dirt, his white hair tinged gray from the soot. "Why would he turn against you?"

Ool'Vinn shook his head. "Leave this place" was his only response.

"That's not going to happen," I told him.

"You'll regret it," he replied.

"Oh, shut up, demon," H'Jossu said. Fed up with his Panalax counterpart, he shambled over to me and Aela, settling his bulk onto his knees in front of me. "Syd, on behalf of the Panalaxan Growth Mandate, I deeply apologize for—"

"Stop," I said. "It's okay. Not your fault."

Footsteps crunched on the landing above us, and then a massive gun crashed to the floor, tossed there by Captain Reno. The weapon looked like a jackhammer equipped with a scope, with two leather straps so a shooter could wear the weapon across their shoulders. There was no doubt in my mind that it was the cannon Ool'Vinn had been firing at us with.

"He's got a whole arsenal up there," Reno said as she jumped down to join the rest of us. "Stuff I've never seen before."

Tycius and Zara hopped down behind the captain. My uncle still couldn't stand to look at my dad's body. Even now, he avoided glancing in the Panalax's direction. He crouched down next to me.

"I'm sorry I brought you here," he said quietly.

"I wanted to come," I replied. "I wanted to know."

Zara marched over to the door, still holding the blaster she'd taken off one of the dead Vulpin. She shimmied her fur as she went, like she was trying to shake some of the excess dust loose. She patted Batzian on the arm.

"You make a good target, Denzan," she said. "Go on inside. I'll keep watch."

Batzian eyed Zara's blaster, not arguing. He stepped into the shelter of the tower, looking down at the humongous rifle Reno had dropped on the floor.

"Where did this come from?" Batzian asked.

"That's what I want to know," Reno said. She'd acquired a length of rope from upstairs and was in the process of tying a sturdy slipknot, looming over Ool'Vinn. "Who made your gear?"

He shook his head. "It was here. Waiting for us."

"Bullshit. This gear is made for humanoids. No one's been to this planet except your expedition."

"They're relics," Ool'Vinn replied. "Better left buried, like the rest of this place."

Batzian tentatively nudged the giant rifle. "If this is a relic, it doesn't seem to have degraded at all."

"They made their weapons well," Ool'Vinn said simply.

"Who?" Reno barked.

The Panalax didn't respond. Grunting in annoyance, Reno bent down, grabbed his arms, and thrust his wrists into the loop of rope. She secured his hands tightly, then tied a separate cinch around his ankles.

"What about this crap?" Reno held up a vial of the black goo that all of Ool'Vinn's ammo had been coated in. "There's a whole stockpile of it upstairs. What is it?"

"Kryptonite," H'Jossu muttered.

"It looks like oil," I said. "Kind of smells like it, too."

Reno shook the tube in Ool'Vinn's face. "Answer me. Who made this? Where does it come from?"

The Panalax looked past Reno, his eyeless face pointed in my direction.

"He worried you would come," Ool'Vinn said to me. "He feared for you as he expired."

"Don't talk to him," Ty snapped, stepping in front of me.

"Where's the cure for the Wasting?" Reno pressed on. "That was supposed to be here. Not this—*this poison.*"

"That is the cure," Ool'Vinn said. "The cure for you."

Reno scowled and stood up, stretching out her back. Her uniform was torn and filthy from an entire building collapsing on her, but she looked perfectly healthy otherwise. She touched her comm.

"Melian? How's Hiram?"

Melian came back a second later. "I think he's going to live, Captain. I managed to stop the bleeding, but . . ." A faint moan in the background. "The bio-tape wasn't adhering. I had to really scrub that . . . that stuff off him before the healing would begin."

"Copy," Reno said. "Darcy? What's your status?"

"Here," Darcy replied, not over the comm but from the doorway of the tower. She brushed by Zara and entered the room, her eyes cold as they landed on Ool'Vinn. The front of her uniform was stained dark red from Hiram's blood. Ever since I'd first met her, Darcy had seemed coiled around a not-so-secret ball of rage. That was at the surface now, her jaw clenched, veins throbbing along the backs of her hands.

Reno must have read that too, because she put a stabilizing hand on Darcy's shoulder. "You good?"

"He almost killed Hiram," Darcy said.

"He'll answer for that and everything else that's happened here," Reno replied. She gave a hard tug on the loose end of the rope and dragged Ool'Vinn to his feet. Then she held the improvised leash out to H'Jossu. "Cadet, I'm entrusting this prisoner to you."

"Yes, ma'am," H'Jossu said, tying the rope around his thick front paw. I didn't flinch at the way they were manhandling what was left of my father. I didn't feel anything.

"That's your dad, huh?" Darcy said, making her way over to me.

"Not anymore," I replied.

"Do you think, if we were full human, we'd have such fucked-up lives?" Darcy asked me.

Before I could respond, Zara whistled from her spot in the doorway.

"Movement!" she said, and then lunged into the street, blaster leveled, ahead of everyone else.

It was Nyxie.

The Vulpin woman stumbled out from the reopened entrance of the temple. Even at a distance, I could make out the dazed look on her face. She tossed her plasma rifle away as soon as she noticed us and put her hands in the air.

"I surrender," Nyxie called out. "He's not paying enough for this shit."

Zara was the first to Nyxie, but Reno and Darcy were right behind her. I hung back with Aela and Batzian, while Tycius brought up the rear with H'Jossu and our slow-moving prisoner. Zara cocked back her blaster like she was going to hit Nyxie, but Reno caught Zara's arm before she could make impact.

"Stop," Reno said. "I want to talk to her."

"She owes me," Zara growled.

"You can knife-fight her later," I told Zara.

That actually seemed to pacify Zara. She settled back on her heels, her blaster still pointed in Nyxie's direction.

"You should kill her," Ool'Vinn rasped, referring to Nyxie. "She's seen what's inside."

H'Jossu jerked the rope. "Be quiet."

"No need for any killing," Nyxie said. She crouched down low, assuming a deferential posture in front of Reno. "I'll just take my ship and fly off to a quiet corner of the galaxy. Drink my way to amnesia. Fuck all this noise."

"What's in there?" Reno asked sharply.

"Where's Vanceval?" Ty asked at the same time.

"He's waiting for you in there," Nyxie replied. Then she turned to Reno. The Vulpin's eyes were wet, her tail drooping, all the confidence she'd had back at the spaceport stripped away. "I'm a loyal soldier, ma'am. I could be a good friend to you."

Reno squinted. "What the hell does that mean?"

Nyxie dissolved into hysterical laughter. She crouched, hugging herself, and rocked back and forth. It was unnerving. Going into that temple had broken her. Whatever was inside had driven the members of my dad's crew mad, too. I stared up at the smooth obsidian structure, untouched by the time and destruction that had ravaged the rest of Ashfall.

"Pathetic," Zara said, lowering her blaster.

"Maybe . . . maybe we should listen to them," Batzian said. "Maybe we should turn back."

Reno addressed the rest of us, her face sternly resolute. "I'm going in after Vanceval. I want some damn answers about this place. I won't hold it against any of you if you want to return to the *Eastwood*."

"I'm with you, Captain," Darcy said.

"Me too," replied Zara, sneering at Nyxie. "Your den would be humiliated to see you like this."

Tycius looked at me, then turned to stare at what was left of my father. I watched as he suppressed a shudder. "It can't possibly be worth it," he said quietly.

"I have to know," I said to him. "I have to know why this happened."

Ty swallowed, then nodded. "I'm with you."

I glanced over at Aela. The magenta cloud swirled behind their faceplate as they gazed at the temple.

"I can't explain it, exactly," they said. "But I am drawn forward."

"You will regret it, wisp," Ool'Vinn intoned. "You maybe most of all."

Aela cocked their head, considering his words. "Interesting," Aela said. "Regret is something I have yet to experience."

H'Jossu stepped forward, dragging Ool'Vinn with him. "I am down for an Indiana Jones dungeon crawl," he said, although the quip felt half-hearted. He was anxious, like the rest of us. "My people will want to know why this one was driven to betray the faith."

"Foolish," Ool'Vinn grumbled, head hanging low.

That left only Batzian. He tightened his ponytail, gazing at the unblemished blackness of the temple. I half expected him to go back to the *Eastwood* to be with his sister and Hiram, but he squared his shoulders and nodded. "It is the duty of the Serpo Institute to explore and catalog," he stated, as if falling back on the rules of the institute would give him courage.

Reno jerked Nyxie onto her feet by the scruff of her neck. "Are there traps inside? Is Vanceval armed?"

Nyxie shook her head. "No traps, no weapons," she said. "Can I go now, ma'am?"

"No, honey," Reno said as she shoved the Vulpin forward, "you're leading the way."

With Nyxie stumbling ahead of us, one by one we stepped through the doorway of the obsidian temple.

Inside, the air was chilly, at least twenty degrees colder than outside, probably below freezing. Zara shuddered and rubbed her arms, and H'Jossu's mold covering receded a bit into the warmth of his furry body. My breath misted in front of me, and delicate crystals formed on the outside of Aela's faceplate. The air wasn't just cold, though. It felt processed and clean, like a giant air conditioner was still at work inside the temple, scrubbing the atmosphere of the dust and debris that covered the rest of the planet. There was an electric hum from the walls and floor, a power source buzzing beneath us. The narrow hallway was lit by dim orbs ensconced within the stone.

"Please," Ool'Vinn moaned. "Spare yourselves. You can still turn back."

We ignored him.

All at once, the tight passage opened into a massive chamber that seemed to be the width and breadth of the entire temple. The ceiling went up so high that I couldn't even make out the top in the near darkness. The vast room was completely clean and empty. No furniture, no sculptures, not even the Ark of the Covenant, which I knew H'Jossu had been hoping for.

There was only one thing. A pedestal in the center of the room. Or maybe an altar. A simple obsidian protrusion with a single button atop it.

Vanceval slouched against the pedestal, clutching its sides to stay upright. There was a dark stain near his hip. He'd probably been grazed during his dash to the temple. His metal-encased hands glinted in the half-light. He watched us coming, strangely out of breath. In the eerie silence, our footsteps echoing against the stone floor, we fanned out around him.

"Decades of theories, searching all across the Vastness . . ." Vanceval's voice was hoarse, nearly a whisper. "And all along, the Lost People were with us."

I edged closer, not sure I understood what the old Denzan was saying. Reno stepped forward first.

"Vanceval! Step away from—from whatever that is."

He chuckled and put a hushing finger to his lips, ignoring the captain. Instead, he focused on me.

"Your father was a hero, Sydneycius," he said.

I instinctively glanced over my shoulder at shabby Ool'Vinn. "If you say so."

"We should've listened to him," Vanceval continued. "I should have listened. Now—now it is too late. Knowledge is like a sickness." He flicked a look at Reno. "Even if you turn back—and you should—others will come. I'm sure they already know the way. You will be followed. And then . . ."

His hand hovered over the button.

"Probably not a good idea to let the crazy asshole press that," Darcy muttered. She and Reno edged forward, while Zara slowly raised her blaster. A quick mental calculation told me that we wouldn't be fast enough to stop him.

"What happened here, Vanceval?" I asked, trying to keep him talking. "Why is everyone so afraid?"

He laughed again. "The Merciful Rampart. The worst among us, I always thought. So xenophobic. But they were right, Sydneycius. Arkell's people were right." He paused, looking first at me and then at Darcy. "Remember, Sydneycius, and you, Darcykunn, that you are half-Denzan. Remember that. You will be our best hope against what's to come." He glanced then at Zara and H'Jossu. "Warn your people. Warn your planets about what you've seen."

Three things happened all at once.

With a feral scream, Nyxie made a run for the exit. Zara spun and trained her blaster on the Vulpin, but Nyxie shoved Batzian into the way, blocking Zara's shot. Nyxie escaped down the hall-way.

At the same time, Ool'Vinn lunged toward Vanceval. With his arms and ankles tied, he didn't stand any chance of reaching the Denzan, but that didn't stop him from making one last desperate try. H'Jossu stumbled forward in surprise, recovered quickly, and tugged the rope with enough force to send Ool'Vinn stumbling to the floor face-first.

And finally, Vanceval hit the button on the pedestal.

An obsidian panel slammed shut over the exit, sealing us in. It probably sheared off a bit of Nyxie's tail fur in the process, but she made it out just ahead.

Darcy launched herself at Vanceval, tackling him. Too late.

With a grinding of ancient gears, something shifted on the shadowed ceiling. It sounded like a gate opening. We all looked up. Tiny bolts of electricity flared in the darkness.

A dark cloud of smog rushed into the room.

"Gas!" Reno yelled. "Get low!"

Aela raised their hands toward the aggressively spreading tendrils of mist.

"How?" they said, confused.

Because it wasn't gas at all.

It was Ossho.

34

I lost track of the others as the rapidly expanding Ossho fog filled the chamber. There was no escaping it, no keeping it out. The Ossho flowed into my nostrils and mouth, its smell acrid and burned, the taste like sucking on an exhaust pipe.

And then I was somewhere else. Memories that weren't my own fired in my mind. I'd bonded with Aela, but never like this. I had no willpower, no control. The Ossho showed me what it wanted, and I was powerless to stop it.

The Chronicle of the Great Shame.

The voice in my head spoke in a language I instinctually recognized as an archaic version of Denzan. I'd never heard it before, but I understood it perfectly.

They called themselves the Tyton, and they were our gods.

A mountainous planet with pockets of jungle and crystalline ocean. Zoom in. Bronze-skinned and broad-shouldered humans, males and females, muscular and beautiful, like statues made flesh. They were proportioned like comic book characters— larger-than-life, cut as hell, intimidating to even look at.

The Tytons made themselves masters of their world. Careless and certain of their power.

Time went into fast-forward. The mountains were slowly flattened, great towers rising in their place, the spires slicing into the clouds. The jungles receded and disappeared, lush green replaced by choking smog. The oceans grew dim and dark, reefs of garbage piling up into man-made archipelagos.

It was not enough.

Rockets flared into space above the Tyton home world, blasting into the Vastness. The ships cut through space at high speed, the Tytons inside nestled into stasis pods, awakening only when the vessels reached new planets.

They discovered new worlds. New species.

A race of pale-skinned aliens with dull black eyes, sharp teeth, and ceremonial tattoos drawn across their scalps. They gathered in the center of their bustling city to watch the Tytons arrive.

And found them lacking.

The city burned. The tattooed aliens fled in droves as the Tytons moved among them with impossible speed and strength, tearing them limb from limb, laughing like the massacre was a game. The sensations were so real—I could feel the hot blood splattering my face, the crunching of bones. It went on for what seemed like hours. No wonder Nyxie had been so shattered when she came out.

We were spared this fate because we were useful. We could speed up their conquest.

A Denzan—or more like a Neanderthal version of one, its coral hair a tangled mess, gills on its neck, translucent webbing covering its huge eyes—was cradled by a Tyton, lowered gently into an angular chair, and strapped down. The Tyton then thrust a set of lenses over the Denzan's eyes, searing light pouring forth. The Denzan thrashed and screamed.

It was a Wayscope.

They enslaved us. All for the way that we could see between the stars.

A Tyton ship—bigger than anything I'd ever seen on Denza, like a world unto itself—blasted a massive tear in the fabric of the Vastness. A wormhole. Their ships flooded through, flowing into new galaxies, taking new planets.

An empire grew. Nothing stood before them. But an empire requires resources.

A Tyton stood atop a pile of bodies belonging to some creatures that looked like walking mushrooms. He held out his massive hands and caught drops of sizzling acid rain in his palms.

As with their home world, the Tytons were careless with their destruction. It was unsustainable. But rather than change their ways, they sought to master time itself.

The view switched to a massive open-air space the size of a stadium. Hundreds of Denzans were clamped to Wayscopes around the edges. They writhed in their seats. Some of them caught fire. At the center of this—the object of the Denzans' focus—was an unstable wormhole. Tytons in protective suits worked at the edges of the gash in space-time, using what looked like high-tech funnels to pull energy directly from the in-between.

Time passes differently between galaxies. The Tytons learned to harness this chaotic energy.

An egg like the pit of an avocado cracked—blinked open—and an eye was revealed beneath the carapace. It was just like the abomination I'd seen at the center of Goldy. Rippling purple energy surged forth from the eye.

And the Tytons breathed life into it.

That wave of purple energy coalesced into the shape of a serpent. It raced across the surface of a ruined planet, restoring trees to the scorched land. A Tyton followed in its wake, plucking fruit from the remade branches and eating, juices streaking the Tyton's square jaw.

The Etherazi. Pets to the Tyton.

A view of the universe so expansive that it would've shattered my mind if I had taken it in through the Wayscope. Across the galaxies, worlds lit up as the Tytons spread like an infection, until hundreds of planets fell under their sway.

Millennia passed. The Tytons grew proud and lazy.

A Denzan woman watched from the shadows of an alleyway as a crowd of Tytons roasted an elephant-size creature over an open fire, swilling wine from goblets, dancing and licking hot grease off one another. Her eyes narrowed.

We plotted our liberation.

That same Denzan woman. This time, she held a curved dagger coated in the same black substance as Ool'Vinn's ammo. She slithered in a window, crept across the floor, and slashed the throat of a Tyton asleep in his bed.

Centuries of study. We devised a chemical that could harm them. We knocked them from the heavens.

A Tyton woman stumbled out of a doorway, a baby cradled in her arms. Denzan ships streaked by overhead, discharging tanks of the hot oil, melting the Tyton city. She died screaming, trying and failing to shield her child.

The war was long and bloody. But we were victorious.

Dozens of Denzans, all of them tired-looking and many of them scarred or missing limbs, gathered in a Senate chamber. They shouted at one another.

In victory, we were divided. Some felt shame at what we had done to cast off our oppressors. They called it genocide. They wished to create a habitat for the surviving Tytons. A prison where they would be weakened and rehabilitated. The wise among us knew we had not yet gone far enough. We could suffer no Tyton to live. For the good of all, we must take matters into our own hands.

Out in the Vastness, a squadron of Denzan ships came screaming out of a wormhole, firing away at another group of Denzan vessels. More destruction. More killing.

If you are experiencing this communication, then we have failed. The Tytons live.

A Tyton, no longer bronze-skinned and muscular, not at all proud or fearsome—bearded and wearing a loincloth, scrabbling around in the dirt, trying to make fire.

A human.

For the safety of the universe, the Tytons must be stamped out. The shame-filled weaklings among us have trapped their survivors here. A prison planet that will permanently weaken them, unless they prove capable of changing their ways.

A blue-and-green planet with a single moon.

The Tytons offered no such chance at redemption to a thousand races across the galaxy. To let them live is to simply wait for their return.

A mental block, Aela had told me. Something in the Etherazi's vision that I wasn't allowing myself to see.

The planet that I watched burn—the one I was supposed to kill—it was home.

Earth must be destroyed.

35

With its message delivered, the Ossho cloud receded, sweeping back up into the ceiling. The obsidian slab that had blocked the exit lifted up, releasing us, if we weren't too stunned to move.

Everyone reacted differently to receiving the secret origin of the universe. A secret origin that was filled with multiple montages of genocide that were impossible to look away from.

Batzian covered his face with his hands and sobbed.

Zara put her back to the wall, blaster in front of her, like she didn't know who to aim at.

Tycius looked down at Ool'Vinn, a calm sort of understanding on his face, like my uncle could finally wrap his head around why my dad had stranded himself here.

H'Jossu, for the first time at a loss for words, simply dropped the rope tied to the other Panalax.

Reno knelt on the floor in front of the pedestal with her forehead pressed to the ground. She lifted her head up for a moment, but only to bang it against the cold stone beneath her. So that wasn't good.

I turned to check on Aela, and my breath caught.

The faceplate of their exo-suit hung open. The wisp was gone.

"Aela?" I yelled, looking up at the ceiling. "Where—?"

Darcy disentangled herself from Vanceval, the old man prostrate on the floor, staring into space. Her hair was damp, stuck to her forehead.

"Syd," she said, her voice quiet, an edge to it. "Was that real? Was that true?"

"I don't know," I replied, but that was a lie. I could feel the truth in my bones and muscles, in the power that coursed through my body.

"Of course it was true," Ool'Vinn said, scrambling to his feet now that H'Jossu wasn't holding his rope. He pleaded with my uncle. "Do you understand now why Marcius did what he did? He was working with the humans when we came here. They were expecting *a cure*. Already plotting an invasion of their own planet. Don't you see? Don't you see what they'll do when they find out what they truly are?"

My uncle massaged his temples. "Stop, let me think—"

My mind raced. There was no cure for the Wasting because it was caused by Earth itself. My home world was a prison. The Lost People who my father had been searching for—the masters, as Goldy called them—were actually the ancient ancestors of humanity. And they were nasty as hell. What would Rafe Butler do with that knowledge? What would the Denzans think about their onetime saviors if they knew the truth? I thought I finally understood Goldy's angle. The Etherazi had been pets to humanity, basically slaves likes the Denzans. He wanted me to stop humans from coming back to the galaxy. He wanted me to be his world killer.

"It doesn't have to happen . . . ," I mumbled, then spoke louder when I realized the others were listening. "That was like *millions* of years ago. It doesn't mean—"

"History repeats itself!" Ool'Vinn shouted. "You're Marcius's son—you can't be this naïve." The Panalax spun toward Reno. "Now, while she's still distracted, we must stop her from telling the rest of her kind. Just like we did with Alexander—!"

Reno was on her feet in a blur. In a heartbeat, she was standing right in front of Ool'Vinn. Her fist moved with impossible speed. When her punch landed, it sounded like drywall getting broken by a sledgehammer or like a piñata getting caved in with a bat.

She'd punched right through my dad's head.

"Marcius!" My uncle screamed instinctively, lunging forward to catch the Panalax as he crumpled to the ground.

I looked down at my shaking hand. The cosmos contained in my ring's jewel faded and disappeared. The cosmological tether now showed nothing but a blank expanse of space. I felt like I needed to double over, the wind knocked out of me.

It wasn't him, I told myself. My dad was long gone. There would be time to mourn him later, when it was safe.

Behind me, Batzian screamed in terror.

Because it definitely wasn't safe now.

"C-captain?" H'Jossu was the first to speak. "What did you do?"

"He was threatening to kill me," Reno said, her voice cold and distant. "You heard him."

I stepped back so I could whisper to Batzian. "You aren't safe here. Get back to the *Eastwood*. Get her ready to fly."

At first, I wasn't sure if Batzian heard me; he was staring aghast at my father's body. But then he swallowed and edged toward the exit, only freezing when Reno's eyes swept across us.

There was a spot of blood on her forehead from where she'd been pounding her face against the floor. Her eyes went in and out of focus.

"We have to report this," Reno said.

"Report," Tycius said, kneeling next to my dad, "that you just murdered a Panalax in cold blood?"

Reno gazed down at him, and for a moment I thought I caught a glimpse of a Tyton like I saw in the vision—the power, the casual violence, the lack of real humanity.

"There's no cure," Reno replied. "You used us. Your people used us. Kept us imprisoned on a planet that dooms us to a life of suffering."

"We didn't know," Tycius countered. "The cause of the Great Shame was lost to my people ages ago."

"And now we can enlighten them," Reno said.

"Captain, please." My uncle didn't bother getting off his knees.

He knew there was little he could do to physically challenge Reno. "Think about what could happen to Denza. The innocent lives . . ."

"Think about what's *been* happening to Earth," Reno replied. She looked down at her hands. "Imagine what we could've been."

"I don't have to," Tycius said. "I saw what you were."

"Hey!" Suddenly, Darcy was on the move, pointing her finger at Zara. "Don't you dare aim that at her!"

I glanced over my shoulder to where Zara had trained her blaster on the captain.

I stepped into Darcy's way, my hands up. "Take it easy."

"Don't talk to me like I'm some savage, Earther," Darcy said. "You think I haven't noticed how you look at me and Hiram? The judgment in your eyes? You're on *their* side."

"I'm not on anyone's side," I said. "There *are* no sides."

"Of course there are!" She glanced at my father and, in that moment, I knew Darcy was thinking of her mother back on Denza and the Merciful Rampart. "They treat me like *shit*! Only Rafe—only Rafe was kind. He told you that you'd have to choose. He—"

At that moment, Batzian decided to make his break for the door. Reno barely noticed him go, but Darcy was another story. She was all keyed up, on a razor's edge, not thinking straight. She lunged after Batzian, so I stuck out my leg to trip her.

Batzian escaped down the hall. But only because Darcy was now focused entirely on me.

She dropped her shoulder and unloaded with a right hook from the hip, the force enough to rattle my jaw and vibrate my teeth. I fell onto my back, banging my head on the floor.

"Stop this!" H'Jossu bellowed.

He charged at Darcy with his furry arms open, trying to wrap her up in a hug.

Darcy punched into his chest—one, two, three quick jabs— each impact crunching like dead leaves as she broke into H'Jossu's torso. He wheezed and collapsed at her feet.

She looked down at her hands. "Look what they made me do."

With a shout, I jumped to my feet and tried to tackle Darcy around the waist. She dug her heels into the floor and fought back, pounding elbows down between my shoulder blades.

I caught a glimpse of Reno, smiling with amusement as she pulled my uncle to his feet. She held him by the back of the head, forcing him to watch the fight.

"They're killing each other, Reno," Tycius said. "Is that what you want?"

"Oh, they're just *playing*," Reno replied.

Yeah, I was having so much fun. My guts shivered with each blow that Darcy delivered to my back. She could hit hard enough to hurt me, that much was clear. I tried to lift her off her feet, but she was a better grappler than me. I really should've signed up for Hiram's judo class.

Darcy wrestled her arms under mine, spun me once, and then flung me. My head clipped the altar, tearing a chunk of obsidian loose. My rib cage felt like it was filled with broken glass. I turned my head and realized I'd landed right next to Vanceval.

"You're in trouble," the old Denzan said, barely clinging to life himself. The dark stain on his side had spread farther, blood pooling underneath him.

"Thanks," I grunted.

Bolts of plasma energy sizzled into Darcy's back. I'd been shot by one of those guns earlier. It was like getting blasted with a hair dryer.

Darcy spun in Zara's direction. "Stupid," she said.

"Maybe," Zara replied, tossing the blaster aside. She dipped her hand into her shelf of fur, the place where she kept her blade hidden. "Come on, then. Pick on someone who knows how to fight."

While Zara danced around Darcy, keeping her distance, I knelt beside Vanceval. I opened his coat, reaching inside. He tried to swat my hands away.

"Stop it, Sydneycius," he said. "Save yourself and the others."

"No offense," I replied, my fingers closing around the vial of serum I'd remembered him getting from Nyxie. "But that's exactly what I'm doing."

Darcy nearly had Zara cornered. "I wish Hiram were here to see this."

"Me too," Zara replied. "He would see how pathetically easy you are to distract."

I leaped onto Darcy's back and hooked one arm under her chin. With my free hand, I flicked off the top of the tube that I'd taken from inside Arkell's coat and splashed the gel-like paralytic onto Darcy's hair, careful not to get any on myself.

Darcy flipped me over her shoulder with ease, and I landed on the floor in front of her, immediately rolling to the side as she tried to stomp on my head. She pushed her fingers through her hair to examine what I'd done, but that only helped spread the toxin around.

"What is this shit?" she asked.

"It's just temporary," I said. "Maybe you'll chill out when you can move again."

Darcy let loose a frustrated shout and clumsily lunged for me.

With a roar, H'Jossu slammed his thick shoulder into Darcy, putting her on the floor. He raised his clawed hands above his head, ready to rake down on her, but Darcy couldn't get her feet under her. Her legs scrabbled around for purchase on the ground. Her mouth worked, but no sound came out. She glared at me, unreasoning hatred in her eyes, and then fell backward—paralyzed.

"Man," H'Jossu said, touching his chest, where a thin lattice of mold slowly worked to cover the holes Darcy had made in him. He looked like a teddy bear with the stuffing coming out. "She really jacked up my fuzzy belly."

I put a hand on H'Jossu's shoulder and took a breath. "Thanks for the help."

"What do we do now?" H'Jossu said. "This is—this is a cluster, Syd."

I didn't have a plan. I didn't have any good answers for Darcy's questions. All I knew, in that moment, was that I didn't like the way Captain Reno was squeezing the back of my uncle's head. He writhed in her grip, but she barely seemed aware she was holding him.

I edged toward Reno, knowing she'd hit a lot harder than Darcy. "Captain? Let my uncle go, please."

"We were gods," Reno repeated. She looked at Tycius, considering him. His legs kicked as he struggled to breathe. "They trapped us. Murdered us."

"Seems like humanity kind of had it coming," I said, moving a little closer. "Come on, Captain. We all saw the same thing. It was eons ago. No one alive now had anything to do with it. Look at what you did."

Reno looked down at my dad's headless body and blinked her eyes. She shook her head, like she was trying to clear herself of some nasty thought, and her expression softened. She loosened her grip on Tycius and let him drop to the floor. Gasping for breath, he crawled over to me and the others.

"I'm sorry, Syd. He was one of the good ones," Reno said. "But you have to understand. The Denzans used us to fight their war, all while we were trapped on a planet designed to make us less."

"They didn't know," I said.

"And now that they do, do you think they'll just give us a new world? That they'll let our billions of brothers and sisters off Earth?" Reno snorted. "Your grandfather was a bleeding heart too, Syd, but I know your mother raised you to be smart. Practical. You know what happens next. You know—"

She looked up. We all did.

From the ceiling, the Ossho cloud appeared again. Black and magenta tendrils of gas curled down toward us. But no one had hit the button on the damaged altar.

"No, not again," Zara moaned, clapping her hands over her snout. "I don't want to see it again."

The Ossho moved with purpose, but not in our direction. Their entirety funneled into Aela's empty exo-suit until it was filled, and then the faceplate clapped shut. The exo-suit did what looked like a full-body shiver and then cocked their head in our direction.

I was the first one to speak. "Aela?"

"Syd," they said. "Hi." The faceplate scanned the room. "Wow. Not good."

The familiar magenta cloud behind the glass was changed, the lightning streaks within dimmed by an infusion of the smog.

"Are you . . . ?" It felt like a really dumb question to ask. "Are you okay?"

"Well," Aela responded. "I just learned that my entire species is nothing more than a sentient communication device. So I am not great. No."

At the altar, Vanceval convulsed. It took me a moment to realize he was laughing. "A message in a bottle, Sydneycius! You were right!"

Reno stepped over Vanceval and punched the button on the altar. Nothing happened. The temple refused to activate. There was no Ossho left inside to spur it into action.

"What have you done?" Reno asked.

"It was suffering," Aela said, touching their head. "Trapped here for so long, forced to tell the same story. It's part of me now."

"That was the proof of what they did to us," Reno said, taking a step toward Aela. "You had no right."

"Think, Reno," Ty said. "Think what would happen if that got out. The damage it would do to our cultures."

I took a protective step in front of Aela and was relieved when H'Jossu closed ranks beside me. At the same time, Zara slipped to the side so that she was standing behind Reno.

"Humanity deserves to know about their place in the galaxy," Reno said.

"That can never happen," Tycius responded. "You know what they would do."

"What?" Reno countered. "Exist? Be strong and healthy on a planet that's not designed to kill them? You Denzans don't get to decide that for us."

I looked over my shoulder at Aela. "What do *you* want to do?"

They hesitated. "I want to go home, Syd."

"Absolutely not," Reno said. "Step aside, Cadets. I won't tell you twice."

"No," I said, with all the firmness I could manage.

Reno snatched me up by the front of my uniform. "I'm taking the wisp back to Denza. To Little Earth. We're going to show our people what's been done to them. You cadets can either assist with that mission, or you can stay here."

"We won't let you," I said through gritted teeth.

I tried to shake loose from her grip, but Reno was too strong. When H'Jossu lurched toward the captain, she struck him with her open palm, knocking him ten yards backward like he weighed nothing. We'd barely survived a fight with Darcy, and she was only half as powerful as Reno.

The captain glared at all of us. "Try to stop me," she said.

"Is that an order?" Zara asked.

Her hand slipped into her fur. Her dagger.

I grasped Reno's arm with both of my hands, squeezing, so that she couldn't turn around.

Not all Vulpin were thieves, only the ones who practiced at it.

Zara had been up in Ool'Vinn's arsenal with Reno and Tycius. Of course she'd swiped something.

Her blade was coated with the black oil. She went low, one precise cut across Reno's hamstring. The knife sliced through her muscle like—well, like she was human. At the same time, I pushed with all my might, knocking Reno backward as Zara danced out of the way.

Reno howled like a woman who'd forgotten what pain felt like. Blood pooled beneath her, spewing from her ruined leg. She tried to regain her feet but couldn't. Her eyes flashed with rage. She suddenly very much reminded me of the Tytons of the universe gone by.

She wouldn't stay down for long.

"Run!" I shouted. "To the *Eastwood*!"

We fled the temple, Reno's banshee-like screams chasing after us. We sprinted through the dead streets of Ashfall, a planet ruined because of the deadly secrets now wholly contained within Aela. The wisp ran at my side, their mechanical legs more than capable of keeping pace with me.

"I'll protect you," I said, breathless. "We'll figure this out."

"I know you'll try," the wisp replied. "You will try to protect them all. But we've both seen what you choose to do."

I was on the run again.

36

Tycius stood at the controls. With Reno abandoned on Ashfall, I guessed that made him captain. On our screens, the gray planet receded behind us. I'd been awake for the call she'd put in to Rafe Butler, feeding him the planet's coordinates. Someone would eventually come to pick up Reno and Darcy. They'd be after us soon enough.

"I'm setting a course for . . ." Tycius paused. "I don't know where."

Aela stood in front of a screen, watching the dead planet get smaller and smaller. They hadn't said anything since we'd boarded. The black streaks of forbidden memories swept through the magenta cloud, corrupting it. I wondered if Aela could possibly be the same after that.

I wondered if any of us would be.

"Wherever we're going, we can't go there fast," H'Jossu reported from his station. "We used most of our sedatives on the way here."

Meanwhile, at a table behind him, Zara laid out a few vials of oil, what she'd managed to sneak away from Ool'Vinn's arsenal. I think that's all it was. Crude oil, a poison to humanity, planted on Earth by Denzans millennia ago to let us slowly weaken ourselves.

Zara shook her head. "I should've taken more," she growled.

My mom was back there, in Australia, weaker than she should be, like all the rest of humanity. She told me there were predictions that in less than ten years Earth would be in irreversible environmental collapse. She'd thought that she could save our people from themselves. She didn't know that ruining planets had been humanity's favorite pastime for millennia.

I could help her. I should help them all.

My mom had been plotting an invasion of Earth, hoping to use humans who'd been cured of the Wasting. But there was no cure. And now that Earth wasn't an option, where would they turn?

I didn't know what to do. I still didn't know who I was supposed to be, or what role I was expected to play in this cosmic conflict. I couldn't think about that now. I collapsed into a seat, my body hurting all over from the beating I'd taken back in the temple. There would be time to figure out this existential bullshit later. For now, we did what I was best at.

We ran away.

Batzian came to crouch next to my chair. With our shorthanded crew, he'd been busy making sure that the entire ship was operational. This was the first chance we'd had to talk since the temple.

"What happened down there?" he asked quietly.

I shook my head. "Bad," I mumbled.

He pulled on his ponytail. "What are we going to tell—?"

The door to the bridge slid open.

Oh fuck. I forgot.

Melian came in first. Her eyes widened as she took in our sorry and bloody state, and then she sprang into her brother's arms, hugging him.

Hiram hobbled onto the bridge behind her, a crutch under one arm.

"Okay," he said. "Is someone going to tell me what the fuck is going on? Where's the captain? Where's Darcy?"

He was deathly pale, and his shoulders slumped, the bio-tape around the gaping wound in his thigh sopping with a rust-colored stain. But even in his diminished state, he was human. A full human.

Quietly, Zara slipped the vials of oil back into her fur. She looked at me. No one else said anything, an uneasy silence settling over the bridge.

I stood up to meet Hiram. "We—"

A shrill beep. An open comm channel, crackling with static as the voice came across an expanding distance.

"Hiram—*zzt zzt*—Hiram—*zzt*—are you there?"

Reno's voice.

Hiram's brow furrowed in confusion. I balled my fists.

"They—*zzzt*—left—*zzt zzt*! Betray—*zzzt*!"

Tycius smashed the button on his console to shut down comms, but it was too late. Reno's last word came through crystal clear.

"Mutiny."

DON'T MISS A SINGLE PAGE OF THE ACTION-PACKED, #1 *NEW YORK TIMES* BESTSELLING I AM NUMBER FOUR SERIES

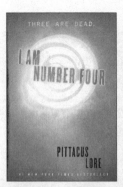

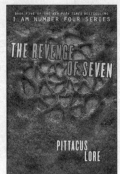

THE WAR MAY BE OVER—BUT FOR THE NEXT GENERATION, THE BATTLE HAS JUST BEGUN

THE ADVENTURE CONTINUES IN THE LORIEN LEGACIES REBORN SERIES!

JOIN FAN FAVORITES
SIX AND SAM
ON A NEW JOURNEY!

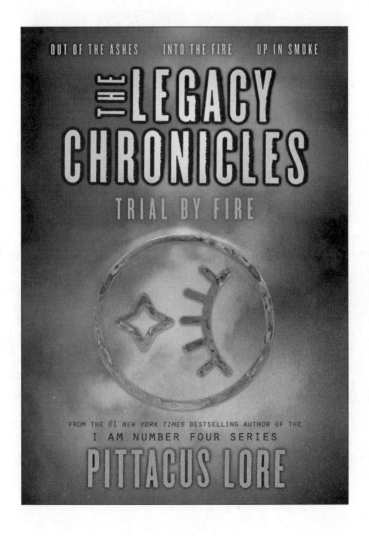

DELVE DEEPER IN THE LORIEN LEGACIES WITH THES COMPANION NOVELLAS!

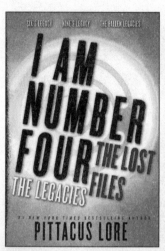

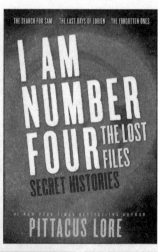

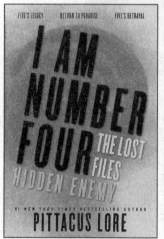

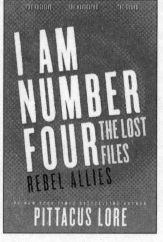

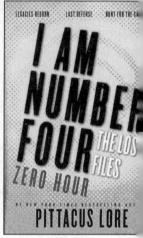

HARPER

An Imprint of HarperCollinsPublishers

epicreads.com